ISBN

Cop,

The author has asserted their moral rights under the Copyright, Designs and Patents Act 1988, to be identified as the author of this work.

All rights reserved. No part of this publication may be reproduced, copied, stored in a retrieval system, or transmitted, in any form or by any means, without the prior written consent of the copyright holder, nor be otherwise circulated in any form of binding or cover other than that in which it is published and without a similar condition being imposed on the subsequent purchaser.

This is a work of fiction. Any resemblance to any real persons living or dead is entirely coincidental.

For my mother

When trials heavy and sudden fall upon us; when adversity takes the place of prosperity; when friends desert us, still will she cling to us.

(Washington Irving)

Ben Blake is on Facebook, at
https://www.facebook.com/benblakeauthor.

Follow Ben's blog at http://benblake.blogspot.co.uk/

Or email him at ben.blake@hotmail.co.uk

Also by Ben Blake

The Risen King

Cover art by Mark Watts

Blood and Gold

Songs of Sorrow Volume One

*This is the book of thy descent:
Here begin the terrors;
Here begin the marvels.*

The Lancelot Grail (author unknown)

Book One

The Little Foxes

Catch the foxes, the little foxes, that ruin our vineyard in bloom.

Solomon 2: 15

One

Safe Harbour

He would remember, much later, thinking that so many new things were about to begin. A lifetime's worth of them.

He'd been restless for days. The ship made its slow way through a sea barely stirred by wind, the red-striped sails hanging limp from their masts, and home never seemed any closer. Calesh would rest in his cabin for an hour, chat to one of the soldiers or a bare-footed sailor, but always he would be drawn back to the rail at the ship's prow to search the skyline for a glimpse of land. In the end he smelled it first, a faint aroma of vineyards and rich earth that brought memories tumbling into his mind all at once.

Playing among the orange trees behind the house with his little brother. Burying that brother not long after when the plague came. A remembered scent of freshly-turned soil then, black and moist in the rain. His father handing him a wooden sword, showing him how to hold it, with dirt ingrained in the lines of his hands, when Calesh was eleven. The first woman he'd known, older than he was, as they pulled at each other's clothes in old man Charn's olive grove. She'd taught him to be patient; it was a strange thing for him to recall now, he reflected wryly. And on top of that came a new thought, the one he would remember: *so many new things are about to begin*.

Luthien would tell him he was wrong, no doubt. Nothing was ever so simple that a man could point and say, "It began there"; God's creation was too complex, too layered, for that to be true. Origins always lay far back in time. The beginning of Calesh's homecoming might have been his departure, eleven years before, when he was a half-trained young fighting man being rushed into battle before he was truly ready. Perhaps it was when his grandfather had made the same voyage in answer to the All-Church's first call for warriors to fight against the infidel. Or it could be further back, so far distant that the skein of events tangled and faded into a half-forgotten past, more myth than history. Before anyone had even heard of Tura d'Madai, or argued over the indivisibility of God, and the Hidden House was only stones in a quarry.

Luthien might be right. He usually was.

But new beginnings could happen, or could be made to happen. It had to be so, if men were not condemned to spend their days in grief for the sorrows of the past. There were places in a life when one could choose, as Calesh had chosen, which was why he was on a ship nearing home, with his years in foreign fields behind him and an uncertain future ahead, which might – who knew? – include his children playing carelessly among the orange trees.

He liked that future, and a man was permitted to dream. Even if it was unlikely the dream would ever come true. He smiled a little, and that was when he heard a footfall on the deck behind him, as soft as the breath of sleep.

*

She rested her arms on the rail beside him. Her skin was the colour of almonds or dark molasses, glowing in the sun. She was the same height as Calesh, though he was a tall man. The thousand braids of her hair fell in a curtain past her face, concealing it.

"So the journey ends," she said in her warm-honey voice. "It will be good to have firm ground under me again."

Calesh nodded agreement. He hadn't been seasick, either on this trip or the one that had taken him to the desert more than a decade before, but he still didn't really like sailing. He felt exposed on a ship, vulnerable to storms and whatever creatures might lurk in the deeps, waiting for unwary sailors to happen by. Heaven knew, enough ships went missing between one port and the next, either through bad weather or pirates, or something even worse. And if a man was left drifting in the water, his chances of survival weren't good. A shipwreck wasn't like falling off a horse. There was nothing solid to land on.

"How's your knee?" she asked.

"Fine," he said. "I could ride through the day and still manage a dance in the evening."

Her black braids swung as she shook her head. "It's still sore, then."

"Hurts a bit," he agreed. "By my heart and eyes, Farajalla, it's not polite to tell a man you know he's lying."

"Forgive me," she murmured. "I know so little of your customs. I am most contrite."

He couldn't help laughing. She knew his customs perfectly well, having been raised in a court where they were observed, and of course she wasn't contrite at all. Farajalla and contrition did not coexist. Pride, yes, and certainly fierce possessiveness: she was more lion than lamb, and just as likely to show claws. He'd seen them unsheathed, once or twice. It was Farajalla who had killed the assassin in the yard of her father's castle, while Calesh sprawled helplessly on the ground with a barbed arrow embedded in the muscle above his knee.

"So, I'm not sorry," she said when his laughter faded. "But you should be. A husband should not lie to his wife."

He snorted. "If I didn't, I'd have no secrets from you at all."

"You mean you do?" She turned her head slightly towards him, so he could see the quick flash of her smile. "I will have to amend that."

"I expect you will," he said, amused again. "I must say, I never expected having a wife to be such hard work."

"Ah," she said. "Now I am distraught. My lord is disappointed in me."

"Hardly," he said.

She turned to face him, one arm still on the rail. Calesh had thought her beautiful the first time he saw her, across a courtyard in the summer sun, and every time since he thought her more lovely still. She regarded him from under a fringe of short braids, her eyes unreadable. Without thinking Calesh reached out to touch her brown-skinned hand: not to hold it, but simply to touch, to assure himself she was real and she was here. Luthien said that certain philosophers from the east claimed the world was merely illusion, a trick of the mind. When he touched his wife, however faintly, Calesh knew it was not so.

"I'm glad," she said. "That... matters to me."

He smiled. "And to me."

"Perhaps this home of yours," she began, and checked herself. "Perhaps this home of *ours* will be a good place for a child."

"It's a *wonderful* place for a child," he said.

Behind them, the captain shouted orders. A moment later the ship wallowed as topsails came down amid the rasping of hemp ropes. Sailors in calf-length trousers and stained linen shirts scrambled to furl them, barefoot on the dry deck. Calesh glanced forward again. The blur of land had drawn closer now, allowing him to pick out details: a patch of forest on the shoulder of a steep cliff running down to the sea, and the square shapes of fields. Houses clustered in a ramshackle sprawl, dotted here and there with the square tower of a Church or the slimmer, tulip-shaped spire of a Madai temple. In front of it all lay the harbour, three long breakwaters thrusting out to enclose a pair of artificial bays in which ships rode at rest. Tiny moving specks of colour were longshoremen at work, loading one vessel or emptying another, while the owners looked on and shouted at them to move faster.

"Will he be there?" Farajalla asked.

He looked at her, hearing the new note in her voice that meant she was no longer being playful. "I think so."

"And if he isn't?"

"Then he isn't," Calesh said. He hesitated. "Perhaps I should put on my armour. Just in case."

"I'll help you."

"No, you stay here. I can manage."

"I'm sure you can," she murmured. "But with your knee still sore, husband, it will take you some time, and sap your strength. And if your friend Raigal *is* in that town, you might need your energy for dancing this evening."

"Not likely," he grinned. "Raigal isn't one for dancing."

"I am," she said, all wide-eyed innocence. "Does my lord not wish to dance with his wife?"

"Of course I do," he said. "But the sort of dancing I have in mind shouldn't be done in public. Or standing up."

"Oh, my," she said. She looked up at him through her eyelashes. "Then it seems we'll have a child to raise here in no time at all."

He pulled her close and kissed her, tangling the fingers of one hand in her braided hair. Farajalla slipped her fingers inside the back of his belt, yanking his hips into hers. One of the sailors whistled, and Calesh made a rude gesture in his direction with his free hand even as the captain bellowed furiously for the man to pay attention to his work.

They parted. Farajalla ran a hand up his back.

"No time at all, indeed," she said.

Calesh chuckled. "I'll armour up. Let me do it," he said when she started to turn from the rail. "You stay here. Have a look at your new home."

"I'm already home," she said softly. "You're with me."

He looked at her for a moment, with no clear idea what to say to that, and then went to the hatch. A moment later he was in the shadows below decks, away from the sunlight and the sight of home, and from his wife. He rubbed his knee surreptitiously. If he had to dance tonight, his leg was going to be pure murder in the morning.

*

It was astonishing, really. Love was not usually a part of marriage, whatever the poets and bards might claim in their songs. Daughters of noble houses married to secure alliances and treaties, while poor women married to find a measure of security in a harsh world. Love was a matter of chance.

That she had found it, and in such a man, made Farajalla feel like the heroine of one of those bards' tales. Her heart went on thumping for a full minute after Calesh had slid down the ladder, and that after nearly three years of marriage, when she should surely be used to being near him. She turned back to the bow and the land ahead, to hide her face from the crew. She was sure her feelings must be written in her eyes in letters of fire.

It was three years ago now, when he had ridden through the open gates of the fortress at Harenc. Madai warriors had been roaming the countryside for days, testing the Duke's defences, which were weaker that spring than ever. There were simply not enough men, not enough warm bodies and willing hearts to hold the lands the All-Church had taken. Farajalla, half Madai and half conquering Gallene, wasn't sure how to feel about that.

Calesh had brought two hundred soldiers, all of them clad in the distinctive black and white livery of the Hand of the Lord. Piebalds, the other Orders called them, usually with a sneer. Attracted by the hubbub of their arrival, Farajalla came to the top of the steps just as Calesh swung down from his horse, a big raw-boned animal that stood calm and serene in the dust. The rider was big too, at least as tall as she was, and wearing armour of silver mail, dusty and stained from long travelling. The armour of a fighting man, made for hard use and not for show. His head was bare, and he was barely on the ground before he turned and his eyes met hers, and everything changed forever.

She had thought her father would have to acknowledge her publicly as his, before she could hope to find a noble-born husband. And that had never been likely. He might tumble the servants when the whim took him, but he would not admit the consequences. Few nobles would. That meant Farajalla would have to find a Madai man, assuming there was one on the earth who would not mind the pollution of foreign blood in her veins. She had been resigned to it: women faced worse, after all. Her mother had, not least when the lord of Harenc had laid his roving eye on her, and then his hands. Women in the castle called Sevrey *the grunter*, and from the whispers, grunting was the least of it.

Yet now here Farajalla was, standing at the prow of the *Promise of Plenty*, a ship of the Tyrian Sea-Fish guild about whom so many stories were told. Here she was, five hundred miles from her old home and less than a mile, now, from the new one she had never seen. She had come here with her husband, who was not a noble but had proven himself so much more. What she had told him was true: home was wherever he was. This ship was home, while he was on it. A roofless crofter's hut would be home if he was there.

The harbour was closer now, three curved fingers of stone jutting out into the waves, filled with masts. Beyond them the town spread out, a mass of narrow streets and alleys between houses roofed with reddish slates. Not much different from home, really, except that in Tura d'Madai the roofs were yellow, or grey. Further away she could see the indistinct shapes of rocky hills, marked with ribbons of road which led to the places Calesh had told her about: the Margrave's seat at Mayence, and the Hidden House, and the Academy Farajalla had heard of even in Tura d'Madai. To her ears they sounded like names out of myth, fantastical places she would never see, but now she was going to. If they were still there.

She turned and looked to her right, along the line of ships. They had started to straggle as sails came down, some managing the shift better than others, but they were still quite close. More were strung out to the other side, making nearly a hundred of them put together, and all within sight. The captain said that was a result of good weather throughout the journey, and very unusual. Normally the fleet would be scattered like waterholes in the desert, and would limp into Parrien in twos and threes over a week or more.

Farajalla thought that perhaps it was fate. Whatever the situation was in Sarténe – and it might all be over by now – the little army would face it together. She was thinking that, and studying the town ahead for any hint of danger, when boots rattled on the deck behind her.

"Lady," Captain Seba greeted. He stopped a yard from her, his feet planted wide on the deck. The sea was calm today, but that stance would keep him secure in all but the most savage wind. It was habit to him, and just as horsemen walked with a bow-legged gait, so sailors moved with their feet splayed outward when they were on land, like crippled ducks. "We'll make land in a few moments."

"I see that," she said. "It's been a good voyage, captain." Farajalla had never set foot on a ship before leaving Tura d'Madai, so she didn't really know how good the voyage had been, but there wasn't anything to complain about. Nothing except the shifting deck and the unsettling creak of timbers in wind, anyway, and there was no way to avoid that. At least there had been none of the sea monsters the crew all swore lived in the deeps. "Thank you."

"My pleasure," Seba said. He squinted at the harbour. "It looks pretty full. We might have to put you off on the outer quays."

"That will be fine," she said, thinking again of the stories told about the Sea-Fish. They knew how to reach harbours no one else could find, it was said. They possessed charms to ward off the sea monsters that preyed on other ships, and knew where sirens waited with their come-hither songs to lure unlucky sailors onto rocks. The best of them could sail to where the sun sank into the waves every evening, and trade for shells and corals with merpeople. Seba had said nothing to suggest such claims were true, of course. If the Sea-Fish captains chattered, their secrets would not be secret very long.

The captain scratched ruminatively at the three-day stubble on his chin. "I can still hardly believe it, you know. It doesn't seem possible, whatever your young lord says."

"It's possible," she said. "I saw the letter myself, when it reached us in Elorium."

She had seen Calesh open it, come to that, slicing through the envelope with a slender silver knife. They had been laughing over some joke or other across the remains of breakfast, a few forgotten figs and olives and the last of the fresh-pressed lemon juice. She was wearing a loose robe, not yet dressed for the day, while Calesh lounged in a wicker chair with crumbs on his shirt. Another ordinary morning, on a terrace in the rising sun.

He had gone pale, the paper crumpling in his white-knuckled hands and laughter dying on his lips. Less than an hour later he sent riders galloping out of the city to all the Hand of the Lord garrisons, ordering every man in Tura d'Madai to pack their gear in preparation for departure. They were leaving the holy city they had fought and bled for these past fifty years. Some of them were married, as Calesh was; some had fled problems at home, and others had invested money here in Tura d'Madai. It didn't matter. They were leaving.

Nobody could countermand the order; the Hand answered to the Margrave of Mayence, sometimes, and to the Hierarch in Coristos, but they were both hundreds of miles away. So was the Lord Marshal, the only officer senior to Calesh. Not even the King in Elorium could order the Hand to stay. Farajalla had sat alone for a long time, watching the sun climb over the crowded buildings and streets of Elorium, before she picked the letter off the floor and read.

Someone murdered a priest of the All-Church on the Ferry Road by the river Rielle ten days ago. The Hierocracy will use it as a pretext for war.
Come if you can.

The paper was expensive but the script was an angular scrawl, as clumsy as the writing of a child just learning to join his letters. Or as the work of a man determined not to be identified. There was no signature, nothing to say who had written it, save a strange glyph at the bottom that she thought must be some kind of a code. The envelope, when Farajalla checked it, contained only her husband's name and position in the Hand, in the same awkward letters. But the letterhead was an ornate cross flanked by lions, and even Farajalla knew what that meant. Every woman and child in Tura d'Madai knew.

Come if you can.

"I have to go," Calesh said from the doorway. She hadn't heard him return. "We've been hearing rumours of trouble at home. I don't have a choice."

"Of course *we* don't," she said, with emphasis.

He looked at her. "Sarténe isn't much like your home."

"I am your wife," she said, "and Sarténe will be my home, as long as you're there."

That was two months ago now. It had taken over a week for the five thousand men of the Hand to pack up and ride out of Elorium, following the winding road that led through rocks and dust to a coast bedecked with lavender. Half the city came out to see them go, Madai and Crusaders alike. They watched in total silence. Not even the Justified called out, though usually they took every chance they could to toss insults at the Hand of the Lord. Another fortnight for the journey itself, and then ten days waiting for enough ships to carry them all to be hired and gathered in the busy harbour at Jedat. The rest of the time was spent sailing, crossing the sea from east to west, with the desert of her home further behind every day.

The mainsail came rustling down, and the *Promise* slowed. Several sailors hurried below decks to work the long sweeps that would guide the ship to harbour, vaulting through the hatches with the ease of long years aboard ship. A cluster of fifteen soldiers watched them go, but made no move to help. Captain Seba had made it clear that his crew needed no assistance from men who didn't know what they were doing. Farajalla supposed that was fair. The Hand of the Lord would not appreciate the aid in battle of a gang of sailors with marlinspikes and no clue how to stay alive.

"There are stories," Seba said after a long silence, "of a group of people long ago who sailed away from the world we know. Away from Gallene, and Alinaur, and Tura d'Madai. Sometimes I think we should do the same ourselves." He scratched his chin again. "Find a place to start over, without anyone to tell us what to do and what to believe."

"That's a dream," Farajalla told him. She thought it was strange, that the Tyrian Sea-Fish told the same tales of others that landsmen did of them. "I've heard the story, but I can't imagine there's any truth to it. After all, if they went, why wouldn't they have sent a ship back?"

"Well, now. There's two things I'd say to that." Seba rested rope-callused hands on the rail. "First is that if I'd run from someone, I'd think long and hard before I let them know where I was. Second, oceans aren't like deserts, Lady, as easy to cross from west to east as from east to west. You might be on a lee shore, with the wind always against you, or the currents might not be right, or maybe something I've not thought of. Anyhow, it might be easy enough to sail to a place, but damn near impossible to sail away from it."

Soldiers began to pass baggage out from the hold to their colleagues on deck, shifting it from hand to hand to be piled close by the port rail. Farajalla watched, trying to seem only idly interested. She relaxed when a brass-bound chest of black wood was hauled out, with much grunting from the sailors, and lifted safely onto the deck. The rest could be replaced. That chest could not.

Calesh clambered out of the hatch right after the chest, favouring his right leg a little. He wore a coat of age-green copper armour, plated like the scales of a lizard, which her father had given him for a wedding gift three years before. Expert smiths in some deep, long-ago cavern had treated the metal to make it harder even than iron, something modern metalsmiths couldn't replicate. Giving it away was as close as Sevrey could come to acknowledging her as his daughter, she knew, but as Calesh buckled the sword belt around his waist she hardly thought of her father. In the evening sunshine Calesh looked so much like the man she'd first seen in her father's courtyard that her breath caught. For an instant she could smell the hot sand of the desert, and hear camels snorting in their pens within the walls.

"The inn must be somewhere in that row of buildings behind the harbour," Calesh said as he joined her. He brushed her hand with his fingers, the way he often did. "*Kissing the Moon.* Fool name for a tavern." He was grinning as he spoke. "Raigal never did have any taste."

"And of course my husband does," she murmured.

He chuckled. "Of course I do. I picked you, didn't I?"

"I thought it was me who picked you."

"Was it?" he said. "I had to all but tie you down before you'd talk to me."

"Oh, you liar," she said, and fisted him under the ribs. He'd put on his armour though, so all she did was skin her knuckles, but she wouldn't give him the satisfaction of seeing her wince. "If you tell these friends of yours that, you'll be sleeping on the couch, I swear."

"Cruel, love," he laughed. "When we're about to sleep in a bed for the first time in weeks. I crave a proper bed, the same way I crave a good mug of ale." His eyes became dreamy. "I haven't had a decent tankard of ale since I left here."

"Then you should indulge yourself," she said. She didn't bother to add *but not too much:* Calesh knew that anyway. His grin widened though, and she tried not to sigh.

Two

Kissing the Moon

One of the other vessels reached the harbour before the *Promise of Plenty*, steering neatly on a course that brought her alongside the nearer breakwater. Calesh was unsurprised to note that it was the *Quiet Return* , recognisable even at distance by the irregular patch of crimson canvas that had been used to mend a split brown sail. Time, he had decided, turned all sails brown in the end. Perhaps it was the sea air, or the salt that flew in sprays in even the lightest winds. It didn't matter.

He was home, and what matter if Amand had got there first?

Promise cruised in just astern of *Quiet Return*. The name augured well, Calesh supposed, but he rather doubted their homecoming would ever be described as quiet. Already work had come to a halt across the harbour, as bare-chested men stopped to shade their eyes and peer at the incoming fleet. Even for a port as busy as Parrien, the sight of so many ships arriving all at once was unusual. It spoke of the peace that had lasted here for so long that nobody panicked, or ran shrieking for the Watch to come. Nobody sounded the rusty iron bell that hung above the harbourmaster's office. Instead people pushed forward for a better view, crowding to the edge of the wharves and onto the jetties themselves. Not all of them were longshoremen or sailors, Calesh saw. Many looked like ordinary townsfolk, to judge by their clothes, and some were women. He even saw a few children.

"If the attack comes, these people will be torn apart before they know it," Farajalla said.

He nodded. It was true. "The attack will come. But it hasn't yet. They wouldn't be so relaxed if it had."

None of them had known, sailing west, if they would be in time. They might sail into the burned-out harbour of a ravaged town, to find nothing there to save but memories. Light winds had pushed them along the whole way; it made the journey comfortable, and was better than a dead calm, but still Calesh had paced up and down with frustration at the delay. Now, one brief glimpse of the waterfront of Parrien made him sure that the All-Church had not attacked. His relief must have shown: Farajalla reached across to put her hand over his on the rail, and he smiled gratefully.

The captain of *Quiet Return* shouted a leather-lunged command, and the last of his sails came down in a flutter of canvas. The ship slowed abruptly. She drifted towards the outthrust quay, and Calesh was sure for a moment that she would stop before she came alongside. Then a wave pushed her sideways, just hard enough to nudge her into the jetty with a soft bump. Calesh glanced back to see Seba scowling furiously.

"No need to try to match that skill," he called back to the aft deck. Relief had begun to give way to a rising joy. *I'm home.* "I wouldn't expect it of you, captain."

"Mind your manners, landsman!" Seba growled. He lifted an arm. "Sails down on my order!"

"Now you've done it," Farajalla said. He grinned at her.

Seba shouted, and the sails on each mast came down as though cut. Sailors scrambled to furl them, or seized ropes ready to throw to men waiting on the quays. *Promise of Plenty* slowed with the curious lurching motion Calesh had come to associate with changes of speed, either faster or slower. He didn't really understand why that should be, but he wasn't Luthien: some answers he didn't need to know.

Longshoremen shouted warnings and sprang back from the edge of the breakwater, just before *Promise of Plenty* struck with a crack. The port bow scraped along the stone with a sound like glass dragged across teeth. Two sailors fell over, to the accompaniment of ironic cheers and catcalls from their fellows. Several more stayed upright and flung ropes to the men ashore, those who had stayed close enough, who snatched them from the air and wrapped them around great stone posts set into the quay. Labourers leaned in to take the strain, muscles bulging. The *Promise* lurched like a straining horse, then settled back. Water gurgled around her stern.

"Well," Calesh said. "The journey was excellent, captain, and thank you. But you need to work on your landings."

The reply blistered the air, but Calesh only chuckled. He was home. Already seamen had run out the gangplank, and he nodded to the soldiers on deck to give permission for them to cross. He wanted to himself, quite badly. He wanted to find some of Sarténe's rich black earth and dig his fingers into it, bury his nose in it, and absorb the scents of oranges and olives and all the long generations of love.

But the eagerness on the faces of his men told him they felt the same, and the joy that bubbled inside had put him in a generous mood. With what he knew was about to descend on Sarténe he shouldn't be happy, but he couldn't deny what was in him.

Some of the crowd peered curiously at Farajalla, but probably more for her fine clothes than the colour of her skin, or her uncovered, braided hair. Parrien had always had its share of outlanders. The entrepot city drew traders throughout the year, many of them from the Jaidi people in the south. To an untutored eye, the Jaidi were almost indistinguishable from the Madai. Certainly they fought just as hard.

Well, that part of his life was over. Strange, that he had left this land to fight the Madai, in the name of religion, far across the world. Now he returned, married to a Madai, to fight former comrades in the name of religion, if he had to. He supposed the Lord Marshal of the Hand of the Lord might have something to say about that, but whatever he said, Calesh would not stand by while this land was burned.

"Do you mean to wait there all day?" Farajalla asked.

He came to himself, suddenly aware again of the sunshine on his face, and the people now crowding onto the breakwater itself. Most of the ship's soldiers were ashore now, forty men in armour with their surcoats on top, one half black and the other snowy white. In the centre was a circle in which the colours were reversed. It was the symbol of the Duality, the worship of God and fear of the Adversary, a struggle fought in the soul of every living man and woman. For more than a hundred years the All-Church had never understood what that emblem meant.

Now it did, and they would kill over it.

"No," he said, and smiled. Even that thought wasn't enough to dent his good mood. "Shall we go?"

Further along the quay, soldiers from the *Quiet Return* had formed a line, to stop townsfolk pushing in while their comrades began to unload cargo. Most important were the horses, which had been kept below decks without a break for weeks now. Simply feeding them and mucking out the stalls had kept the men busy, but Calesh didn't envy them the task of bringing the irate animals ashore. Three sailors were already swinging the big winch into place, with the sling hanging below. Others worked to lift sections of the deck aside.

All that made the *Promise of Plenty* rock, and Calesh went down a gangplank that creaked alarmingly as it shifted.

"Oh," he said when he stood on the solid quay. It seemed to be moving under his feet. His injured knee grumbled as he tried to find his balance. "I think I need to sit down."

"Not here, husband," Farajalla murmured.

He looked at her, then at the crowd, and understood. The Hand of the Lord had come home, and if war had not invaded Sarténe yet, the rumour of it would certainly have done. It wouldn't do for the Commander of the returning heroes to sit down with his head between his knees, right where everyone could see. Calesh wanted to, though. What made it worse was the sight of Amand, striding up the breakwater with the confident steps of a man who could keep his feet in the middle of a landslide. Calesh sometimes thought that when the Hand was gone and forgotten, Amand would still be there, as reliable as stone and harder than baked cactus.

"Commander," the older man said as he came up to Calesh. His hair was shot with grey, and his face so cadaverous that it seemed he must not have had a sip of water for days, but his salute was perfect, right fist to left shoulder. He had managed to iron his uniform too, somehow. On a ship under sail, and every crease was perfect. Calesh didn't know how he managed that.

"Captain," Calesh acknowledged. "Good to see you."

"And you, sir." Behind Amand his men had raised a standard, of the same design as the men's surcoats and kite-shaped shields. It would tell the other companies where the rally point was, wherever they found berths. Already ships were nosing up to the other breakwaters, slowing as they approached. "I trust you are well?"

"Well enough," Calesh said briefly. "Here's what I want, captain. As I remember it the Hand has two estates just outside Parrien. Pick out two groups of men and have them ride to those estates at once. Hire horses; don't wait for our own animals to be unloaded. They'll be disorientated for a while anyway. Tell whoever is in charge of those farms that the Marshal Commander of the East requires that all their supplies and facilities are turned over to him. Send each Chapter to its billet as soon as you find one. Make it clear that I will be happy with their treatment or I will know the reason why."

"Understood, sir." Amand didn't make notes. He never needed them. "Sir, there is a boy in the crowd who says he knows where *Kissing the Moon* is. Shall I send him through?"

That made Calesh blink. Amand was always efficient, but he'd truly outdone himself this time. "No need. I'll go to him myself." He gripped the other man's arm as he walked by. "Well done, Captain."

"How must it be," Farajalla said softly as they moved away, "to so easily win the hearts of men, I wonder?"

He frowned at her. "What do you mean?"

"Perhaps that's the answer," his wife said in musing tones. "Perhaps it only works for those who genuinely don't know."

"I look after the men, and in return they go where I say." He was finding his balance now, as his legs grew used to solid ground beneath them again. His knee ached horribly though. "That's really all there is to it. I'll leave it to Luthien to come up with some bafflingly complicated explanation. Which I don't doubt he will."

"You're being disingenuous."

"Ah," he said, and let a smile widen. "Now I am distraught. My lady is disappointed in me."

Amusement glimmered deep in the pools of her eyes. "Hardly."

Then they reached the double line of soldiers across the quay, and a ragged-trousered youth of fourteen or fifteen who waited just inside the cordon. That made him almost old enough to join the Hand, and hardly the boy Amand had called him. Beyond the soldiers townsfolk clustered, all trying to peer around one another's shoulders to see what was happening. There was a panicky snorting from the deck of *Quiet Return*, out of sight above them, as the first horse was coaxed into the sling.

"Is it true?" someone called as Calesh and Farajalla came up, and suddenly everyone was shouting.

"Is there going to be war?"

"Have you come to fight for us?"

Calesh raised his hands for quiet, but he still had to shout over a restless stirring. "There's no war today, at least. The Hand of the Lord will stand with you if one comes. Beyond that, I need to talk to the Lord Marshal before I know what will happen. Now, I suggest you go about your business. A lot of horses and men are going to be using this jetty for the rest of today."

There was a renewed burst of muttering, but Calesh turned to the youth. "What's your name?"

"Japh." His dark hair was cut in an untidy line. "I work in the stables next to *Kissing the Moon.*"

That was a stroke of luck, though perhaps finding a lad shirking work to gawk at ships and soldiers could pass for normal. "Does Raigal Tai still own the inn, then?"

Japh blinked. "You know him?"

"I do." He tossed a coin to the youth, glinting silver as it spun. Japh snagged it out of the air and goggled: it was a full sester, probably more money than he'd earn in a month. "Take me to him."

"For this I'd take you to the Margrave himself," Japh said.

Calesh chuckled. "No need for that, lad. Just take me there. Though if all this ruckus hasn't been enough to pull his beard out of his own beer and move his bloated arse, I'm not sure anything will be."

"He doesn't have a beard any more."

"Found a razor, did he?" The inner joy was back, lighting him from within. Raigal was here, and close. "Never mind. Take me there."

*

An escort of twenty soldiers went with them, pushing through the crowd so Calesh and Farajalla could walk along unmolested. That still felt strange to her, as alien as having a servant to wait on her at table or fold her clothes. She had *been* a servant most of her life, with nothing but dreams of acknowledgement by her father to take her mind from the dourness of her life to come, and as she grew older not even that. Now she felt like an impostor. Sometimes she still half expected someone to jump out and tell her it had all been a mistake, or a joke, and send her back to the kitchens and the laundry in the basement rooms of the castle at Harenc.

Except there was Calesh, and of him, she never had a moment's doubt. His men were the same, following him with eagerness and something very close to devotion, whatever he might say about *all there is to it.* When new recruits came out to Tura d'Madai they didn't know him at all, but within weeks they almost fell over in their haste to help Calesh with the least little thing. And he hardly seemed to do anything to earn it. He made sure they were paid on time, and that their armour was mended and the horses cared for, and he usually remembered the soldiers' names. That was all, and it didn't make sense. She had asked Amand about it once.

"One of the men took a blade in the chest at Kiderun," the captain had answered after a moment. "A fellow called Malian, new to Tura d'Madai. Baruch Caraman killed the man who dealt that blow."

"One of Calesh's friends," Farajalla said. "One of the four."

Amand nodded. "The sword point snapped off inside the wound. Every breath Muret took worked the sliver deeper, and if it reached the lung, he would die if he was moved. So Calesh cut it out. Men were fighting all around him, but he just knelt down and cut it out, and his hands never trembled. Malian fainted halfway through, but he survived."

She could imagine that, in fact. Amand didn't say, but Farajalla thought her husband's three friends might have stood around him while he cut: Baruch, Raigal with his great axe, and Luthien Bourrel dancing like quicksilver amid the carnage. They were always together, back in the days when there were still victories. Before the others had come back home.

"Malian was killed later, at Iskellar," Amand said matter-of-factly. The captain had a memory like a taxman's ledger, and every page was crammed. "Some men just don't have the luck, I suppose."

Farajalla thought that might be part of it. Calesh had the luck, whatever gift it was that kept some men alive while others died, and his soldiers stayed close in the hope that it would rub off on them. Also, of course, he was simply a fine man, this tall outland husband of hers. Others could recognise that as well as she could. One of the keys for the brass-bound chest she had seen unloaded hung around her neck; the other was with Amand, and not Calesh. He could be trusted with it. Many of the soldiers could, but Amand knew Calesh well, and for him the captain would keep the keys of Heaven itself.

They let Japh lead them along the breakwater to where it joined the main wall of the harbour, then turned left along the quay. Merchant ships were tied up in a forest of masts, though few of the labourers were doing any work. Several men in well-cut wool clothing glowered at Calesh as he went by, traders irritated that their loading had been interrupted, but none of them had the nerve to say anything. On the other side of the wharf was a line of low wooden warehouses, most of them with open doors and a clerk sitting on a stool just inside, a large ledger at each hand. One for stock brought in and one for that taken out, Farajalla supposed.

More townsfolk were still coming through the double arches that led out of the Port Quarter and into Parrien, and the soldiers slowed in the throng. The citizens saw the escort and realised Calesh must be important, so sometimes questions were shouted to him, but less often than might have been thought. He didn't look much like a Commander of the Hand, after all, in his peculiar green armour and with a Madai woman at his side. She grinned to herself. He had been Sarténi when he came to Tura d'Madai, and now when he came back to Sarténe he was, perhaps, part Madai in his heart.

"I'll fetch Master Tai," Japh said abruptly. The escort had all but halted in the crush of people now. Japh dived between two of them and wriggled away into the crowd, his progress marked by a wake of suddenly irate townsfolk cursing and clutching at bits of themselves. He was heading for a gap between warehouses, and peering up the slight incline Farajalla saw a brown-timbered building on the left of an alley, with a smoke-dulled sign swinging above the porch.

That would be *Kissing the Moon,* then. She glanced at her husband, only to find him looking up the alley with eagerness in his eyes, and almost dancing from foot to foot. He seemed about ready to burst through the ring of soldiers and rush away on his own.

He'd spoken of Raigal Tai a great deal, of course, along with his other two friends. There was a close bond there, something men might share but which women could never be a part of. Even wives: that was a different tie, with the tangles of love or without them. The friendships of fighting men were forged in taverns as well as battles, and tempered with ale as often as blood. Men were strange. Even the best of them.

She was going to have to share him now, at least in part, and she didn't much care for that. She watched him from the corner of her eye, and then the door of the inn was flung open with a bang and the biggest man she'd ever seen rushed out into the evening sunlight with Japh at his heels.

"*Bullfrog!*" the giant bellowed, and began to race down the street.

Calesh started to laugh. There was no need for him to tell her that this was Raigal Tai; he was just as Calesh had described him, a vast mountain of a man with a shock of tousled blond hair. The only change was the loss of his beard. But that took nothing from his bulk, and the good folk of Parrien began to clear hurriedly out of his way. It was either that, or be trampled where they stood. The soldiers half turned to Calesh, but he had no time to respond.

Raigal burst through them with hardly a pause. He was so huge that the sunlight seemed to lessen when he loomed close. When he reached Calesh he picked him up, completely ignoring the soldiers, and folded him into that great chest like a child cuddling a favourite doll.

"Hey," Calesh managed, pounding his friend on the back. "Hey, that hurts! Put me down, you fat oaf!"

"Fat? Fat?" Raigal set him on his feet hard enough to rattle Calesh's teeth. "I'm not fat. But by the blood of the god, it's good to see you! What have you been doing? Idling in the sun while the rest of us work for a living?"

"Never had the chance to idle," Calesh said dryly. He probed his ribs with one hand as though he thought one might be cracked, even through his armour. "I was busy with a few things. One of which," he added as she came up behind him, "was getting married. This is my wife, Farajalla."

"Wife?" Raigal repeated. He looked at her. "Blood of the god. How did you catch this beauty?"

"In part," Farajalla said pointedly, "by not speaking about me as though I wasn't here."

The giant man stared at her, then roared with laughter and clouted Calesh on the shoulder. "Quite right! My apologies, lady. I'm not normally so rude."

"Yes, you are," Calesh said. He rubbed his shoulder. "To make it up, you can help us with our things." A second knot of soldiers was coming through the crowd, laden with bags. A canvas sack half-hid the wooden chest. "And a decent meal wouldn't go amiss, either. We've had nothing but ship's rations for nearly a month."

"Of course," Raigal said. "And then you can meet *my* wife. And my boy," he added. Before Calesh could answer the big man seemed to notice the soldiers for the first time. "I don't know that there's enough food in the town for all these men, mind. How many are there?"

"More than five thousand," Calesh said.

"All the men in the East?" Raigal Tai began incredulously, and then shut his mouth with a click. Farajalla had caught the quick dart of her husband's eyes to the listening townsfolk, which evidently the huge man had too, and understood the message. *Don't ask me here.* Raigal covered his comment by whirling on the crowd.

"What are you lot doing?" he demanded. "Waiting for the tide to go out? You don't need to worry about Bullfrog here. He's a friend."

"I think we gathered that," someone said.

"From the East," another voice shouted. "From the desert!"

"From Tura d'Madai," Raigal agreed. He punched Calesh playfully on the arm, making him stagger. "He saved my life, oh, about nine times. Saved a lot of other men too. Best man I ever met."

"Maybe not," Calesh said quietly. "There are two others who might have a claim to that."

"And if they were here I'd say the same about them," Raigal said, not at all abashed. "Oh, go home, everyone. Calesh and I have things to talk about. Where are those bags?"

Kissing the Moon turned out to be a typical harbour side inn, the flagstone floor scuffed and every worn wooden surface scarred by the rings of tankards. The cloying scent of old beer hung heavily around the walls. But it was clean, as was the bedroom Raigal showed them to, staggering under the weight of the brass-bound chest and three bags piled on top of it in his thick arms. Someone had turned the bed linen down already.

Once the bags were stored away, and the chests with them, Raigal led his guests to the back parlour of the inn. It was smaller than the front bar, with simple green upholstery on the high-backed chairs and a faint smell of fresh-cut pine in the air. Polish gleamed on the tables. The far wall bulged slightly outward, and was mostly occupied by a long window that looked out over the warehouses and across the harbour, and the sea beyond. The quays were a mass of activity now, soldiers unloading and merchants filling their holds as fast as they could, eager now to make for the open sea. The appearance of an army made a lot of men decide to be somewhere else before the fighting began.

Farajalla's eyes went to the fireplace though, and the huge double-headed axe that hung there, its grip slightly worn and a notch on one curving blade. Above it hung a surcoat marked with the emblem of the Hand of the Lord, halved black and white with a circle in the centre where the colours reversed.

"It can be useful for guests to remember I used to be a soldier," Raigal said, noticing her gaze. "And there's not much risk, because only trusted friends and customers are allowed in here. Anyway, by the time a man's drunk enough to try to attack someone with that axe, he's too drunk to lift it."

Farajalla didn't think she would be able to lift it at all, drunk or sober. She didn't think many men would be able to wield it either. Raigal Tai was truly massive, and by the way he moved, most of his weight was muscle. Calesh had described him often enough, but his words hadn't done justice to the man. In Raigal's hands that axe would look like a doll's toy. The thought of what its blades could do to human flesh made her shudder.

"I can hardly believe you let anyone forget you used to be a soldier," Calesh said. "Not even for a minute."

Raigal pretended to scowl at him. "Sit down while I fetch some ale and a bottle of wine, and then you can tell me everything, Calesh. I want to know where you've been, what you've been doing, and why by the god's blood you took so long getting home. Don't you know we've missed you?"

He squeezed himself through another door, from beyond which Farajalla heard the clink of tankards as their host busied himself behind the bar. She took a pace towards the chairs, but then stopped and turned to her husband, alerted by the sense of him she carried with her wherever she went, whatever she did, to find his eyes resting on her.

He valued her opinions, something not true of many husbands. Another thing she had been lucky in with the man she loved. And she knew that weighing look he wore. She went back to him and took his hands in hers, rubbing her thumbs over his fingers.

"What is it?" she asked, but Calesh had no chance to answer.

"He wanted four copper sesters for a pair of herring, can you believe that? We might as well catch our own fish at that price." A woman pushed through the door from the front corridor, a bag in each hand and a gurgling baby carried in a sling across her chest. She might have been an inch or two over five feet tall, but no more than that, and she was as slender as a twig. "I'll tell you, that's the last time I serve him when he hasn't got the coins to –"

She stopped moving and broke off, staring at the two of them. Her eyes widened at the sight of Farajalla's almond skin. "Who are you?"

Farajalla stared at her. "Who are *you?*"

"My dear," Raigal said as he edged back into the room, "it's possible that we might enjoy more custom if we don't make our guests feel unwelcome." He put tankards and glasses down on a table, pulling bottles from under his arms to join them, and then turned to the little woman. "My wife, Kendra," he explained over his shoulder. He reached down to take the baby from the papoose, and his voice swelled. "And this little thing is my son, Segarn. He's nearly six months old now. He's already got my hair, see?"

"And your father's name," Calesh said, smiling slightly.

Raigal nodded. "A little piece of my home here with me. Yes. I still miss the northlands, you know."

"You've missed the northlands since the day we left for the east," Calesh sighed, "but I notice you've never gone back."

"And he'd better not now," Kendra said sharply. Raigal had his mouth open to speak, but he looked at her and closed it without a word. Farajalla hid a smile; evidently the big man knew when to keep quiet, for all his size. His wife studied the guests with shrewd eyes. "You're Calesh Saissan, aren't you?"

He nodded. "Yes. Home at last."

"I owe you a debt," she said. "You saved my husband's life, many times."

"He saved mine just as often," Calesh told her. "That's what you do in the Hand. You owe me nothing, lady."

She smiled. "Perhaps a good supper?"

"That, then," Calesh laughed, "and we'll call it settled. Kendra, this is Farajalla, my wife."

Farajalla smiled a greeting at the other woman. A flash of surprise crossed Kendra's expression before she could hide it, which Farajalla pretended not to notice. No doubt it was because Calesh had taken a brown-skinned woman for his wife, something as unusual in this western land as the reverse was in the desert. Raigal was cradling his son in one arm and crooning nonsense words at him, while the child chortled and waved his hands in the air.

"I haven't seen the inside of a kitchen for a long time," Farajalla said. "Would you mind if I helped you cook? We can leave the men to exchange lies while we get to know each other."

"I can't remember the last time I had help cooking supper," Kendra said. "But no, you sit down and relax, Farajalla. I'll have a fish stew on the plates in an hour, if you can wait that long."

"And a damn good stew it is too," Raigal put in.

"It had better be good," Kendra shot back. "If I couldn't cook well enough to fill that bulging belly of yours, you'd be gone inside a week." Raigal grinned and rubbed his stomach.

"An hour will be fine," Calesh said. "Thank you, lady."

Kendra leaned over to pull a face at her son, then vanished through the door to the bar while Segarn chuckled sleepily. Her husband fetched a woven basket and laid the boy inside, on the stone rim that fronted the fireplace. That done he lowered himself to a wide bench beside it, close enough to reach out and touch his son's face. He pushed a hand through his tangled blond curls, and looked at Calesh. For a moment neither man spoke.

"Well, then," Raigal said at last. "Now you can tell me what you've been doing all this time."

"Fighting to defend the Kingdom of Heaven against heathens," Calesh said dryly. He took one of the chairs and swung it to face Raigal, grunting a little at the weight, then went back for a second as Farajalla sat down gratefully. "Remember? That was why we went."

"Don't be clever," Raigal chuckled. He reached for a tankard of ale. "Luthien always has enough cleverness for five men, and I don't need you trying to outdo him, thanks all the same."

"You still see Luthien?"

"Of course I do," the big northerner said. "And Baruch too, when he can find time away from his duties. He's still in the Hand, you know. A Commander, like you."

"And Luthien?"

"Luthien took the Consolation," Raigal said.

Farajalla blinked. Luthien had been the finest warrior among the four friends, so good that she had heard his name in Harenc, even before Calesh rode through the gates and into her life. The word among Madai servants had been that he was a drinker, a voracious reader of books, and had eyesight so poor that one of the glassmakers in Elorium had crafted wire-rimmed glasses especially for him. Hardly a typical warrior, yet no weapon could harm the man, they said. He walked under the protection of the One God, or even perhaps of the desert gods. Or all of them. He could not be made to bleed, and when his sword sang lives ended, and widows wept for the dead.

She glanced at her husband, to find him staring at the big man with his mouth open.

"I'm serious," Raigal Tai said when Calesh didn't speak. "It's obvious something important has happened, to make you bring all the Hand home, but you'll never persuade Luthien to help you with it. Not if it means breaking his oath. He took the Consolation three summers ago. He's an Elite, teaching the true word of God at the Academy outside town. He's forbidden to touch meat or alcohol now, or weapons. Or women," he added with a snort of disdain. "I don't know why he did it. No women or meat? No ale? Madness."

"That doesn't seem possible," Calesh said. He still looked like a poleaxed steer. "Luthien was the best of us."

"In battle he was," Raigal said with a grin. "It always used to make me easier in my mind, just knowing he was there. Do you remember what the Madai used to say about us?"

"They said men feared you for your size," Farajalla murmured, "and for that axe, spinning in your hand like a split twig. They trembled when Baruch Caraman strode forward, and shook when Calesh Saissan sounded the charge. But it was Luthien Bourrel they fled from, crying out to their gods for protection and succour as they went."

Raigal looked at her, surprise on his own face now, and she shrugged. "I'm from Harenc, not the far side of the world. We heard stories."

"I see you did," he chuckled. Raigal had an easy laugh, she decided. She couldn't help smiling back.

"You know," Calesh said slowly, "this actually makes sense. All I need to do is stop thinking of Luthien as he was in battle, and remember instead the man who always had his nose in a scroll, or who wouldn't read the *Unfurling of Spirit* unless he washed his hands first. I should have seen this. Luthien was the best of us in battle; fair enough. But he was the noblest of us too."

"I might disagree with that last," Raigal Tai said quietly.

The two men exchanged steady looks. For the first time since her marriage Farajalla felt excluded, witness to something personal of which she could never be a part. She bit her lip and glanced down at her lap.

"Let it be," Calesh said. His voice was slightly strained. "I don't want to be made into more than I am."

"I wasn't doing so," the big man said.

Calesh blew exasperated air. "Let it be, Raigal." His voice firmed: Farajalla knew what an effort that would have cost him. "Well, whatever Luthien has sworn, I need a message sent to him, and to Baruch as well. I want them to come with us to the Hidden House. We're going to see the Lady."

Raigal shifted his weight, leaning forward with large forearms resting on his thighs. "You turn up here with all the Hand from Tura d'Madai, and now you want us all to go to the Hidden House?"

"I'll tell you why," Calesh said. "But I'm not going to say anything at all until I know who's listening outside the door, I'm afraid."

Three

Orders

Calesh had heard the giveaway creak of floorboards from beyond the door twice now, and he knew Farajalla would normally have been aware of it too. Hardly anything escaped her at the best of times. But she didn't know what to expect here, cast adrift in a strange land with him as her only guide, while his own senses seemed heightened, sharper than cuts to the soul.

Raigal stared for a moment, and then twisted around in his chair. The door opened as he did so and a man stepped gracefully through. He didn't look in the least put out by his discovery. Fair hair curled around his ears and flopped over the nape of his neck. He was ridiculously handsome, if in a slightly soft way that spoke of a life spent on couches and in baths, rather than outdoors. He nodded to Raigal and then turned towards Calesh.

"Ando!" Raigal burst out angrily. "Blood of the god, what do you think you're doing? I don't expect guests in my inn to creep around listening at doors, whoever their friends might be."

"And of course I apologise," the newcomer said, his voice smooth. "But still, you can hardly expect me to avoid this charming parlour all evening, now can you? Especially with Calesh Saissan here." His eyes were brilliant green, and rested on Calesh unblinkingly. "I've wanted to meet you for a long time."

"I can't imagine why," Calesh said. He kept his voice calm, hiding his irritation inside. "Unless it's on behalf of those friends Raigal mentioned."

"Only one friend, really," Ando said self-deprecatingly. "The Margrave, as it happens. And as for why…"

He moved to the chairs and reached behind them to draw out a lute, on which he played soft notes with practised fingers and chanted;

> *The green banner trodden underfoot,*
> *Where Cammar lay, his life's blood*
> *Spilled in the pale and thirsty sand.*
>
> *A day of courage, glory bright*

As the sun. Ride now, ride!
The battle gained, but not the war
On to triumph, and the god's voice singing!

"I was going to tell you," Raigal Tai said apologetically. "You're a hero, Calesh. Everyone knows about you killing Cammar ah Amalik."

"Nobody knows about it," he growled. "And I already told you I don't want to be made into more than I am."

"It's too late for that," the big innkeeper told him. "Half a dozen songs have been written about that battle. And the palace in Mayence has a mural of you killing Amalik. It covers nearly one whole wall of the reception hall."

"You've got to be joking," Calesh said.

Raigal shook his head. "Afraid not."

He was starting to be angry. "Nobody knows what it was like, Raigal. Not unless they were there. And certainly the idiot who wrote those lyrics doesn't know. You could improve them with your axe."

Ando stiffened, offended. "Those are my lyrics, in actual fact. From *The Lay of Gidren Field.* It's been sung all over Sartene for three years now, and I'm rather proud of it."

"Ando Gliss," Raigal said, "is the favoured singer and composer of Riyand, the Margrave of Mayence."

"Good for him," Calesh said. "That doesn't explain why he feels the need to listen at doors, though he's no better at snooping than he is at writing. And what's he doing here, anyway?" He glared at the troubadour. "Shouldn't you be in Mayence, writing silly quatrains and couplets for the Margrave?"

Ando drew himself up even further. "I'll have you know –"

"He would rather be in Mayence," Farajalla broke in. "Wouldn't you, Master Gliss? Such a famous balladeer has no need to while away days in a harbour side inn. He stays in the cities, and the houses of the great, doesn't he? But you weren't given a choice. Tell me, singer, how long ago did you know the Hand of the Lord was coming home?"

Calesh stood up abruptly. He hadn't seen that, hadn't realised what the troubadour's presence meant, but he did now. So much for Farajalla not being her usual perceptive self. He should have known better. "Of course. You knew. What else should I be aware of?"

"You're aware of it already," Ando Gliss said. Raigal had risen to his feet as well, a much more imposing sight than Calesh, but the musician faced them both with outward calm. "The All-Church has an army gathering on the far bank of the river Rielle, about seventy miles from here. It was intended to go to Tura d'Madai, but it won't now. The Basilica plans to divert it to Sarténe."

"*What?*" Raigal Tai exploded. "That silly rumour is *true?*"

"It's true," Calesh said. "Why else would I bring the Hand home, Raigal? What other reason would do?"

"But this will leave Elorium almost defenceless," Raigal said. "The men there *need* those reinforcements. Otherwise the holy city will be overrun before the end of the year. Next spring at the latest."

"I know that. You know that, and I'm certain the All-Church knows it too." Ando smiled bleakly. "It seems they would prefer to destroy the heresy here, among their own vineyards and orange groves, than save the holy city itself from heathens."

"The Dualism is not heresy."

"I know *that*, as well," Ando said. "But the army will receive new orders any day now. Why are you preaching to me?"

Calesh controlled himself with an effort. He didn't like this vain, self-regarding man, but it would do him no good to lose his temper. "But why are you here, in Parrien? How did you know where to come?"

"I guessed," Ando said. "It was that simple. I knew from my days as a wandering musician that Raigal owned an inn here. Before I became a famous balladeer," he added with an ironic bow to Farajalla. "I knew he was your friend. And when the Margrave learned of the Basilica's plans, it didn't seem hard to guess that you'd sail for home with as many of the Hand as could follow. How many did you bring, by the way?"

"All of them," Calesh said absently. He was thinking hard. "When did you learn about the army?"

"Two months ago, and from the same source as you. Riyand was told a message had been sent to you in Elorium." Ando's lips quirked. "Did you really think you could slip in unseen? That one and a half thousand men of the Hand, and the hero of Gidren Field, would not be looked for?"

Calesh wanted to hit this man quite badly, but something came together in his mind at those words. It was the way Ando said the Margrave's name that did it; *Riyand*, spoken almost like a caress. That explained why an itinerant musician was trusted with a journey to Parrien on a secret mission. Ando Gliss was more than just a troubadour to Riyand: he was a confidante, and probably a lover. Well, that was their business. The All-Church might say it was a sin, and an obscenity against God, but it had never bothered Calesh very much.

"Wait a moment," Raigal Tai broke in. His voice was thick with anger. "If Riyand knew this was coming two months ago, then why hasn't he started to make preparations? The army hasn't even been called up. Blood of the god!" he burst out suddenly. "We could have been digging fortifications and shoring up city walls, and instead he didn't even tell us what was about to happen. What does Riyand think he's doing?"

Ando, who had faced two fighting men without blinking a moment before, turned slightly pale at those words. *A lover,* Calesh thought again. "He's negotiating. Until that army crosses the Rielle, there's a chance we can get the orders changed. Offer some concessions, or something."

"Maybe we could have done," Calesh said, "if some god-blasted idiot hadn't murdered that priest by the river."

"And mentioned the Margrave," Raigal added, "and then left a witness alive to tell of it. That killer was a fool, whoever he was." He fixed his eyes on Calesh. "That finishes things, doesn't it?"

"I think so," Calesh admitted. "The Basilica won't let the murder of a priest go for the sake of a few concessions."

"So you came back. To fight beside us."

"I came back," Calesh said.

"You're a hero of the wars against the heathens," Raigal Tai said. "You could have stayed in Tura d'Madai. Joined one of the other military Orders. The All-Church would have feted you for it."

Calesh smiled slightly. "Can you see me serving with the Glorified? Or worse, the Justified? They hate me, after what I did at Gidren Field. The Justified would have broken like untrained farmers if Amalik and his infantry had hit them, and they knew it."

"They should have got down on their knees and thanked you," Raigal Tai grumped.

"It doesn't work that way. The Justified can't forgive me for pulling their coals off the fire. What the Hand did that day embarrassed them, and they resent us for it, Raigal. You know they do."

"You could still have stayed away. There are a hundred petty kings and lordlings looking to hire mercenaries, from the Mennos Islands all the way out to the steppe, and Temujin."

"That, I could have done," Calesh conceded. "But it would have meant leaving you to face it alone. You, and Baruch, and Luthien. Not to mention everyone else in Sarténe. When that army comes it will come to burn the ground, Raigal, and it will leave nothing behind it but ashes."

"And this is the man," Farajalla said softly, still in her high-backed chair, "who says he does not want to be made into more than he is. I think," she added, gazing up at him, "that it would be a very, very hard thing to do."

"I think so too," Raigal said. He was grinning. Faced with the shock of this danger, a threat to everything he knew, he was actually grinning. "It looks as though we'll draw weapons together again, eh?"

Calesh looked at them both, the friend of his heart and the wife who had taken it. Both of them were smiling. His chest felt queer inside. No man, he thought, had the right to be so blessed, in this world of matter and sin, as to have two such people love him as these. And neither Baruch nor Luthien was with him yet. They would be; he was sure of that, however the future was shaped. He would see them again before the end, whatever that might be.

"I doubt," Ando Gliss said, his quiet voice intruding, "that five thousand men will make a difference, when the All-Church has more than fifteen thousand across the river. Probably more than twenty thousand, with others to come. Riyand had hoped for more men, Commander Saissan."

"Blood of the god!" Raigal growled from beside the fireplace. "Doesn't he know us at all? The Hand of the Lord trains its soldiers only to fight. We have no assassins, as the Justified do, and no sailors like the Glorified. Certainly no tax-gatherers, like the Order of the Basilica." His lips curled disdainfully. "No distractions, in other words. We're fighting men and nothing else, and we train for that alone. And we have the finest steel and horses money can buy. That's why we're the best. Always have been."

"Still are," Calesh said.

"Good enough to defeat twenty thousand men alone?" Ando asked sardonically.

Calesh looked at him. "Alone? There are some three hundred men of the Hand here in Sarténe already, besides those I brought. Recruiters, mostly. In addition the Hand's estates are worked by retired soldiers and half-trained youths. So the Hand might be able to field seven and a half, perhaps eight thousand men. Then the Margrave employs about three or four thousand – or he did when I was here before. Please tell me he still does."

"He still does," Raigal said.

"That makes eleven thousand men," Calesh said, "near as damn it. It's a decent start. And we'll find more." He turned to Ando Gliss. "You go and tell him what you heard here. And let him know I'll come to Mayence in a few days. I have some business to attend to there."

"Very well," Ando said. "I know Riyand will be delighted."

"I'm sure," Calesh said. He didn't think the Margrave would be quite so pleased when he learned Calesh had no intention of accepting his command, but that was for another day. First he had to ensure he *had* command of the Hand, and that might not be easy. "One other thing, singer."

"Yes?"

"The next time you want to hear what I have to say, come to me and ask," Calesh said. He made sure to keep his voice pleasant. "I don't take kindly to snooping, especially in times of war. If you do it again, I will break all the fingers of the hand you use to play that lute. Understood?"

Ando's lips tightened. "Perfectly."

"Off you go," Calesh said.

"It might not be wise to antagonise him," Raigal said when the musician had left the room. "He has Riyand's ear, and he's destroyed the careers of scribes and advisors with a word."

Calesh listened to Ando's steps recede along the corridor before he spoke. "I find it's usually best to start as I mean to go on. It saves trouble later. Though I think Master Gliss has more of Riyand than his ear."

"You noticed that too?" Farajalla asked. "Yes, our friend the singer is sleeping with Riyand, I think. It's hard to trust the judgment of a man in love." She tilted her head and smiled. "Except you, of course, husband."

He raised an eyebrow. "I don't recall saying I was in love."

"Ah. I'm desolate," she said. "Should I have stayed on the ship, and sailed away from here without you?"

"And leave me desolate?" he asked.

She merely looked at him, saying nothing in reply to that, and Calesh felt his throat tighten. She could still do that to him, years after he had ridden into the courtyard in Harenc for the first time. Three years since they were married in a small chapel in the same city. Sometimes, when her almond eyes were on him, it was hard to think of anything else.

He made an effort, clearing his throat, and saw his wife give a sudden secretive smile. "I do need to speak with Riyand, though. For one thing, I want to know if those negotiations Ando mentioned are likely to succeed."

"Shouldn't think so," Raigal Tai grunted. "What's keeping Kendra? I'm starving away to a shadow here."

"Yes, one more hour and you'll vanish if you turn sideways," Calesh told the huge man. "I also have to know how many men Riyand can raise, and what he plans to do if the negotiations fail. Information on the army by the river wouldn't hurt, either." He thought about that for a moment. "I wonder who's in command? It might be someone we know from Tura d'Madai."

"Baruch will know," Raigal said.

Of course he would. Baruch was a Commander, the same as Calesh, and a very good one too. He would have made it his business to learn all he could about the army poised across the river Rielle. "Then we'll go to Mayence as soon as we can. The end of the week, perhaps."

"Why not now?"

"Ailiss," Calesh said, and saw his friend understand at once. "The first thing I have to do, even if that All-Church army is knocking at the door, is go to the Hidden House, and see the Lady."

*

It wasn't that simple, of course.

Supper was a fish stew every bit as good as Kendra had promised, thick with fresh vegetables and washed down with wine from last summer's vines. Raigal Tai had two mounded helpings, both of which he dispatched at speed while chattering about the old times in Tura d'Madai. Half an hour later Calesh was back down at the harbour, where torches had been set in every available bracket, and more wedged into cracks in walls or driven into the quayside. It was full dark now, but soldiers bustled all around, unloading armour and weapons, food crates and tight-bundled packs, then loading them onto carts to be taken through the town. More men swung the last of the horses off the ships in large slings, the animals snorting through their nostrils. Once ashore they whickered and pawed unhappily at the ground, vexed to find it still and steady for the first time in weeks. Calesh had taken a mount from the stables next to Raigal's inn, picked out for him by Japh. It was too small for a warhorse, and he thought its best days were long behind it, but at least its hooves knew where the floor was.

A fair number of the dockside labourers worked alongside the Hand, eager to put in more hours at the end of the day in return for good coin. No doubt that was where the carts had come from. The Hand of the Lord always paid fair prices, unlike some of the other Orders, and because people knew it they were usually willing to help. Vendors were still out as well, and a few soldiers were sitting on the edge of one cart eating cold meat pies, while others passed baggage along a line of hands and into the back.

"At the estate north of the town, sir," a soldier said when Calesh asked where he could find Amand. "Through the arch and up the main street a ways, then turn right just after the apothecary's and follow the track."

"Thank you," Calesh said. He swung into the saddle.

"Sir?" The soldier's face looked very young in the torchlight. "Is there really going to be a war?"

"There usually is," Calesh said, "somewhere or other. As for here, we'll just have to see, won't we?"

There was no need for Calesh to find his own way to the camp. All he had to do was locate the apothecary's, and then follow the tracks left by hundreds of horses and scores of wagons. He wasn't entirely surprised when an escort of six mounted men fell into a loose half circle behind him, kite shields angled over their left legs and their faces concealed by helmets. There was danger here, just as much as there was in Tura d'Madai, and the men would know it. More importantly, Amand would know it, and that man never missed anything. Calesh was almost sure it was his aide who had told men off to escort him.

Parrien normally had a lively nightlife, mostly due to students who slipped out of the Academy for an ale or two in the taverns, but now the streets were quiet. A few people were out, but less than half the numbers Calesh would have expected. Citizens had a knack for scenting trouble, and the arrival of an army usually meant that. Folk caught sight of armour and hid their valuables and their daughters; usually, he thought with a wry chuckle, in that order.

The riders caught up to a pair of wagons jouncing up the track, and slowed to keep pace with them.

A sack fell off the wagon as it hit a rut, and split open to spill flour over his horse's hooves before Calesh could move away. He controlled the animal with a muttered curse, then inhaled a lungful of flour and started to cough. His eyes teared. He had not expected his return to be like this.

But still, he knew he was home. It was a feeling as much as anything else, a sense of something inevitable that had been too long delayed. That was strange, because in eleven years in Tura d'Madai he'd never *wanted* to come home. There was nothing here for him. But now he was aware of tangible things, some of which he had almost forgotten about until now. He could smell the land, dark earth heavy with burgeoning crops, and hear the faint rustle of olive groves and trees on the hillsides. Tura d'Madai was almost wholly treeless, and those which did grow were mostly poor, scraggly things, dotted in ones and twos wherever a crack in the rock allowed a trickle of water to seep to the surface. There was the scent of water, too: only someone who had travelled the great arid wastes of the east was likely to know that water *could* be smelled. But it was there, wet earth and leaves slick with moisture, damp mulch huddled beneath a fallen tree, and the long, slow seepage beneath the surface. Calesh felt a sudden glad surge within him: he was home. He was *home*.

A squad of soldiers stood in the light of half a dozen lanterns, flanking the gateway to a meadow. They waved the cart through after only a cursory inspection, then caught sight of Calesh behind it and snapped off rapid salutes. He nodded impassively in return. Tonight a little laxness was understandable, and nobody was likely to attack them for a few days yet. He'd have to make sure it didn't become a habit though. Even a small amount of sloppiness had a way of taking a heavy toll when it came time to fight again.

He left his horse with the guards and entered the camp, neat rows of tents made shadows by the night, and studded with the flickers of cook fires. Here the scents were of frying bacon and sausage, and the sounds of murmured conversation. Beyond the meadow Calesh could make out the blocky shape of a farmhouse, with a long dormitory running away to the right and a row of tall barns behind. Lights glowed in the windows. The officer here was awake then. Probably Amand had set him to work, and the other man was cursing him for it.

Soft chanting came from another pool of lantern light, and by squinting Calesh could make out a robed figure surrounded by the kneeling forms of men. Someone had found an Elite already, then, to guide them in their prayers. He started towards it without thinking, suddenly certain the Elite would turn out to be Luthien, holding his last ceremony before he belted on his sword once more.

It wasn't Luthien, of course. This Elite was a woman, golden-haired and pretty, and Calesh had never seen her before. He ought to have expected that. He felt a moment of disappointment, but then he went forward and knelt among his men. The fellow on his left shifted along in the grass to make room for him. Calesh waited until he was sure he knew the place in the chant and then joined in, keeping his voice almost too soft to hear. Soldiers had an uncanny knack for knowing when an officer was among them, even in the dark, and just for a moment he didn't want to be an officer. Just a man trying to catch a fleeting sense of his God, like the brush of a finger on his ravelled soul. The same as everyone else, he supposed.

The chanting ended. Afterwards the night seemed very quiet. A handful of cicadas chirruped in the grass, too foolish or too excited to realise the light had gone out of the day.

"I will not keep you," the Elite said into the near silence. The darkness made her green robe seem almost black. "You men have fought the infidel in the name of God, and it's not for me to tell you what to do, or how to be. You know Belial the Adversary made this world of matter, as he made your bodies of flesh, but it was God who made your souls. God knows all your names, my friends. Just remember, in the days to come, that the kingdom of God is not in Tura d'Madai, or even in Heaven beyond the Gate of Angels. It is in you, in your hearts, and there you may hear God speak. If you bring that forth, if you nourish your souls and spirits, they will save you."

She lifted her hands, palms upward, and finished with the ritual words. "You have suffered me to speak, and this shall be your consolation. Go in love."

The men rose, already beginning to talk among themselves before some of the nearer of them noticed Calesh. The murmur of their voices rose in pitch. Calesh affected not to notice; word that he had been there would spread soon enough, and to good cause. Soldiers liked to know their commander shared their lot, whether it be risk in battle or cold, unsatisfying rations after a hard day. Or communion with God. Not that their approval was why he had prayed.

Amand joined him by the first of the tents, his cadaverous figure taking on form as he stepped from the gloom.

"Seems she was in the farmhouse," Amand said, inclining his head towards the Elite. "Coincidence, I'm sure, but a happy one. The men haven't had a proper service since we left Tura d'Madai."

Calesh nodded. "And a soldier takes solace when he can, since it may always be his last. Any news for me?"

"We have a number of requests from townsfolk who want to join the Hand," Amand said as they began to walk. "Seventeen, at the last count. Most of them are youngsters, of course, but several are older men. They heard why we've come home, and they want to help defend their land."

"Naturally," Calesh murmured.

"I can't see any reason to turn them down," Amand said in neutral tones.

Calesh could. The coming war was not likely to be long, unless something unexpected happened, but it would be bloody and brutal, and almost all the pain would be on the side of the Sarténi. Eleven thousand men, however well trained, couldn't hope to stand against two or three times as many, despite what he'd said to Ando Gliss. Anyone who joined the Hand of the Lord now, or enlisted with the Margrave's Guardsmen, would be placing himself at enormous risk with very little chance that it would count for anything.

Still, he had to admit that it *might* count. Half of soldiering was watching and waiting for events to turn in your favour, and there was never any telling when they would, or how. You just had to be ready when they did. Besides, every extra sword made that slim possibility of success a fraction larger. If the men who carried them knew more or less what they were doing, anyway, at least enough not to get in the way of the serious soldiers. Calesh hesitated.

"You can't control everything," Luthien had told him once, as they snatched a cold supper on a dusty roadside with soldiers pitching tents all around them. "You certainly can't control the choices men make. Save your energy for the things you *can* control, Calesh, or you will gnaw yourself away with remorse and be no use to anyone at all."

"Let them join," Calesh said in the damp meadow, "as long as they look capable of holding a sword without stabbing themselves in the foot. Detail someone to find them weapons and gear, and someone to train them too."

"At your orders," Amand agreed, this time sounding pleased. His presence was much of the reason why Calesh had managed not to gnaw himself away, in fact; the gaunt man had a boundless supply of energy, never seemed to need sleep, and took care of endless minor details before Calesh could even think of them. His judgement was impeccable. Having him as second-in-command was like Calesh owning four pairs of arms.

"You wanted a message sent to Baruch Caraman in Mayence," Amand went on. "With your agreement, I suggest we send one of the new men, and keep the experienced soldiers together."

"Makes sense," Calesh said. "Pick someone and tell him to be at *Kissing the Moon* an hour before dawn tomorrow. There'll be a letter for him."

"So early?"

"I want to outrun the news," Calesh said. "Word will spread soon enough that all the Hand has come back from the East. There's only a little time before that, and I want to use it."

"Very good." Amand frowned as a youthful soldier hurried across the grassy aisle between tents with a brimming bowl in his hands. The young man caught his glare and blanched, spilling water on the ground. "I've also picked out a squad to make the run south you wanted, across the mountains into Alinaur. Might I ask why it's necessary?"

"Mercenaries," Calesh told him. "Alinaur is thick with companies of soldiers for hire, from the ragged and unwashed to some more capable groups. If we can hire a few, it will even the odds a little."

"Not much," Amand muttered.

"We do what we can," Calesh said with a shrug.

"And how will this be paid for?"

"Promissory notes from Tura d'Madai," Calesh answered, "though I'd rather you didn't bruit that about. They're in the chest. Trust me."

Amand's gaze was sharp. "There are some companies of the Hand down in Alinaur as well."

He sighed in mock dismay. "I can't hide anything from you, can I? All right. Yes, the squad will also carry notes from me calling the Hand home. It's only around two hundred men, but –"

"We do what we can," Amand finished for him. "And you didn't mention this because you don't want the men to pin their hopes on aid from the south?"

"Right," Calesh said.

"They'll hear nothing from me."

"Then I'm for bed," Calesh said. "Wake me two hours after midnight to take over. You know where I'll be."

"I can manage," Amand said.

A smile tugged at the corners of his mouth. "Don't be stubborn. You can't control everything, Amand, and if you try you'll only gnaw yourself away to nothing. Just when I most need to rely on you, too. Wake me."

"At your orders," Amand acknowledged.

Calesh clasped hands with his aide and turned back towards the town, and the winding road back down to the harbour and *Kissing the Moon*. He didn't feel like riding back, though in truth he was surprised at how weary he felt. He'd done little or nothing for weeks, really, ever since boarding the ship back at Jedat. Prowling up and down the ship for day after day hardly counted as work.

The real work was about to begin. Funny that it should come here, back in Sartene, where he had never thought to set his feet again. Calesh had joined the Hand of the Lord when his father died, six years after Calesh's younger brother; his mother had been dead so long he could not remember her face. Just a recollection of auburn hair above him in the darkness, and the crooning of a lullaby, though now he had forgotten the words and only the tune remained. There had been nothing to keep him here, nowhere he wanted to live, now the ramshackle farmhouse was filled with nothing but memories and long-ago voices, ricocheting around the walls like trapped flies. So he had gone to the desert, crusading for a church in which he had no belief, perhaps seeking death and perhaps a new life. Luthien might know, or think he did, but Calesh did not.

He hadn't found death, though Calesh knew how lucky he was to have survived those first terrible months. He had been a boy, callow and half-trained at best, thrown into the desperate struggle to beat off the Madai who prowled around the rocky hills, their footprints concealed almost at once by wind that swirled endlessly through the dust. Then more soldiers came to help, disembarking in their thousands at Jedat and the half-built harbour of Pilgrim Castle, and everything was all right. For a time.

It was ironic, Calesh thought, that he had once been so glad to see the banners of the Justified and the Glorified, the two great military Orders which fought in Tura d'Madai. Within a month he had lost his liking for them. Within a year he loathed them more, by far, than he did the Madai. The Servants of the Justification of God, who justified nothing they ever did, however cruel or mean-spirited, except by the words *in the name of God*. The Knights of the Glory of Heaven, who polished their armour and washed their grey cloaks and curried their horses, but were always the last to ride out to face the enemy and the first to ride away. *Afraid to get blood on their cloaks* was what the Hand said of them, and the Glorified knew it. Just as the Justified knew the Hand said they skulked forever in shadows, afraid to come out into the light.

The Hand of the Lord had not been making friends, Calesh thought, even before Gidren Field.

He had truly thought death was there for him that day; for all of them, in fact, all the men of God who stood on the side of the valley and watched the far bank of the river teem with warriors. There were so many that they kept marching into one another, banners bobbing and tangling as their bearers tried to find space to deploy. Sometimes a good general could take advantage of that confusion, but not today, and not against such numbers.

By then Calesh had been a captain, and had seen enough blood to last him. He knew what the size of that army meant. In a head-on clash of armies, the outcome nearly always depended on numbers, unless one side was significantly better than the other. The All-Church soldiers were better than the Madai, in general, but probably not by enough. The army swarming beyond the river Gidren would annihilate them where they stood.

And among that mass, Calesh could see one banner of rich green, with a palm tree flowering in the centre. The banner of the Nazir infantry, the best in the whole Madai army, and their captain Cammar a Amalik, whose name alone struck fear into the hearts of the God-fearing. It was said he walked on water, and could not be killed by the weapons of mortal men. He sharpened his sword on the rays of the rising sun, and no armour could withstand it. Watching the banner move towards the centre of the Madai line, untroubled by the jostling and the arguments all around, Calesh had almost believed it himself.

Well, he had survived, and even become a hero of sorts. He hadn't realised his name was known in Sarténe, though. It was one thing to be admired by your own men, and grudgingly by at least some of the men of the other Orders, but it was quite another to discover that troubadours composed songs in your honour and the Margrave himself had a painting of your deeds on the wall of his reception chamber. Calesh found that unsettling, if he was honest, and there were practical concerns too. It had always been likely that the priests in the Basilica would quickly learn that the Hand had left Tura d'Madai, and come home. If Calesh's fame was so great then he thought they must have been watching, and probably knew already. He wondered if it would affect what they did.

He walked down the cobbled street through Parrien, glad now of the lantern light that spilled from windows to illuminate his way. It was late, and there were fewer people in the streets than ever, but those who were stopped to point him out and murmured behind their hands. Hooves clopped on cobbles as the soldiers riding a discreet distance behind Calesh moved a little closer, alert to the possibility of danger, however remote it might be. But it didn't stop the pointing, or the whispers. He wished Ando had never written that ridiculous song, or that it had been someone else who killed Cammar a Amalik, there in the wreck of Gidren Field.

The harbour was still torchlit when he reached *Kissing the Moon*. Figures moved to and fro in the darkness, little more than silhouettes thrown into relief by yellow glows. Wagons waited in a line for their turn to be loaded with supplies, their drivers leaning idly against the boards. Calesh nodded to them and turned towards the inn.

From inside the hum of conversation was loud, and suddenly Calesh didn't want to face the soldiers who had lodged there with him, to take turns as his escort. There had been no refuge on the ship, and he deserved quiet for once, before events crowded in on him. He slipped around the rear of the building, by the sea wall, and went inside through the back door that draymen and labourers used. A pair of soldiers on guard there hesitated in mid-salute when he held a finger to his lips. He pulled off his boots, standing on one foot at a time: Kendra wouldn't thank him for tracking meadow mud through her house, and if she didn't mind, he certainly did. He left the boots just inside the porch. Maybe he could wash them off when Amand woke him.

He slipped inside, wincing as the door gave a loud groan even while he moved it with slow care so nobody in the common room would hear. An old memory made him want to laugh; he had crept home once after sharing a jug of apple brandy with his friends, aged about thirteen, and had made absolutely certain to slink into the farmhouse in total silence. He was sure he would have got away with it, except that he woke up next morning on the flagstones of the kitchen floor. Presumably he hadn't made it as far as his bedroom. His father had already risen and gone out to work, but he'd tossed a blanket over his son. And left the pig bucket by Calesh's head, and the shovel beside it.

Muffling his chuckles, he padded to the stairs and started up in the darkness. He remembered which door was his, and needed no candle to see his way. The first few stairs creaked outrageously under his weight, and abandoning stealth for speed he hurried up the rest and along the corridor. Perhaps the chatter in the common room would hide the noise, but he wanted to take no chances. He opened his door, went inside and closed it, all in one movement.

"Now you're mine," Farajalla said, "for a few hours."

She rose from her seat at the table, where a lamp stood by a sheaf of papers. The curtains were drawn, shrouding the room in darkness except for that spill of light. She was wearing a simple robe of pale blue, cinched with a belt of filigreed silver in a pattern of interlocking crosses, and then she drew the linen down over her shoulders and it was hard to breathe. Her hair was damp and he could smell her scent, the rose water she used for bathing, and a faint hint of cinnamon. The world had changed in one step, or else was not the same world as the one outside this bedroom door.

He was home.

"I'm always yours," he said.

She draped her arms around his neck. "On the ship this morning, you said this was a wonderful place to raise a child." Her lips touched his, very gently. "Let's try, my love."

Four

Mayence

Five hundred years before, it had been one of countless little villages scattered through the rocky hills north of the mountains, the area known by locals as the Aiguille, in air heavy with lavender and olives and rosemary. Then the king of Gallene chose it for the site of a border fort, to guard against the outlaw bands hidden in their mountain fastnesses, and Mayence began to grow.

It was a sizeable town two centuries later, when the Tei-jo warriors of Jaidi swarmed out of the desert with their curved, jewelled blades to begin the conquest of Alinaur, south of the Raima Mountains. It wasn't long, a generation perhaps, before they had taken almost everything up to the peaks, and seemed poised to cross them and fall on Sarténe. It was said they never lost. Only a few outposts remained of Alinaur, soldiers penned in mountain fortresses even the Jaidi couldn't capture, or felt they could safely ignore. Refugees fleeing the war came to Mayence along the new road that wound out of the peaks, bringing new skills in metalwork and masonry and tanning, and a thousand other things besides. Artisans in the burgeoning city began to learn techniques never known before, or else forgotten for so long that nobody remembered them at all.

Men came the other way too, soldiers from Gallene and beyond, every land between the sea and the steppe. Some came from Rheven in the far north, big bearded men with heavy axes and round shields, who prayed to strange pagan gods as often as they went to a true chapel. But they were ready to protect the devout from the heathens pressing against the mountains, which was all that mattered in those days. Even the All-Church gathered fighting men, and sent them to guard against the new threat from the south.

There were fewer than a thousand of those, captured mercenaries and criminals as often as not, given a chance at respectability if they wore the white and gold tabard of the Church and risked their lives to defend it. Some promptly fled into the mountains to join the outlaw bands, and died there: the Jaidi were not tolerant of brigands. Those who remained became the first soldiers sworn to the All-Church itself, owing loyalty to no land or king, but only to the Hierarch. It was that seed which would one day give rise to the flowering of the Crusades to Tura d'Madai. Those first Church-sworn men became the Order of the Basilica. Others, sneeringly, called them the Shavelings.

But the Jaidi did not come. People gathered in the streets to wonder why, as one summer passed and then another, with no sign of the expected assault. Perhaps the Jaidi were exhausted by their efforts in Alinaur, or perhaps they had simply taken enough territory and desired no more. It was only later that Mayence learned of a schism among the Jaidi, an argument over some obscure point of religious dogma concerning the treatment of people in the conquered lands who did not share their faith. The invincible warriors had stopped their advance and fallen to killing each other instead. It was all rather peculiar, the chatterers agreed, but what could one expect from heathens?

For whatever reason, the Jaidi who came across the mountains were merchants, rather than the Tei-jo who had taken Alinaur. Mayence found itself the centre of a new, bustling trade, sending pepper, spices and silk north, bringing furs, amber and wheat to sell in the south. Figs and dates appeared in the markets, and nets of gutted herring from faraway seas. The town became a city, one in which different cultures mixed, if not always easily. For every chapel there was a Jaidi temple, topped with a brightly-painted onion dome. Minarets carved with date trees and palm fronds sprang up alongside older, square-cut towers, and pointed church steeples. The new Hall of Voices, where the city fathers met in debate, topped its stylishly traditional Galleni portico with a Jaidi dome.

Then the All-Church summoned warriors in the name of Heaven, to retake Alinaur for the glory of God.

Soldiers poured into Mayence, in military Orders formed in their homelands. The Servants of the Justification of God, commonly called Justified, wearing a white cross set against red. The Knights of the Glory of Heaven, or Glorified, with a red cross against a winter skyline. From the All-Church came the Order of the Basilica, the Shavelings, still clothed in white with a cross of gold. Sarténe formed its own order, based in Mayence, called simply the Hand of the Lord. They carried shields divided into halves of black and white, with a circle in the centre in which the colours were reversed. Good and evil, at war in the world.

There was no cross.

Most of Alinaur fell to the Orders, in the forty years that followed. The Jaidi had grown plump on the fruits of their conquest, as victors so often do, and after their years of bickering could no longer unite. Supplies and fresh troops came through Mayence on their way south, while wounded soldiers and booty passed the other way. Denied safe passage across Alinaur, Jaidi merchants from the distant deserts began to sail north instead, and the port of Parrien grew to accommodate them. The Margrave used some of his wealth to found an Academy in the town, in imitation of the universities common in ancient times; the All-Church had ordered them closed, centuries before, for fear they would produce heretics and unbelievers. After that the traders brought scrolls and books to sell alongside their spices. Jaidi scholars took posts among the staff. There were philosophers from Caileve in the east, mathematicians from Temujin on the distant steppes, theologians from Gallene and Boromil. The library was extended, then extended again.

Scholars were invited to banquets in noble houses, serenaded by musicians and poets who travelled from court to court. After a time the musicians began to be invited in their own right. Nobles elsewhere professed disdain for such mingling with commoners, but that hardly mattered, for as time passed Sarténe owed ever less fealty to Gallene. Instead she grew ever more tightly linked to the new, unofficial capital: Mayence. And gradually, in the midst of so much change, a new kind of cleric began to appear, teaching that God had created men's souls but Belial, the shadowy Adversary, was responsible for physical matter, including men's bodies. The forces of light and darkness were matched, and the balance was fought in men's hearts. To be truly devout, one must abandon certain worldly things – meat, alcohol, physical love – and accept the Consolation of spirit in their place, becoming Elite. Material things could not be holy in themselves, not even so-called sacred ground, however consecrated. Only the soul could be divine.

And if this was so then Adjai, the Saviour at the heart of the All-Church's faith, being clothed in tainted matter, in flesh, could not have been divine. Much less the son of God.

All-Church priests in Sarténe saw what was happening, but did nothing about it. They took their bribes and sold services to those with money to pay, and hoped the Basilica would not look too closely in their direction. Only a few sent messages to the Bishops, warning of this new cult that stole their worshippers and refused to accept the salvation of the God-Son. Too few to be taken seriously. Congregations fell; pews were empty even during the main services. Finally, with Church income falling across the province and a trickle of rumour becoming a flood, someone took the evidence to the Hierarch himself. The war in Tura d'Madai still absorbed most of the Basilica's time and attention, but an emissary was spared to go to Sarténe and find out more. Six months later he was on his way back to the Basilica with his findings when he was murdered on the banks of the river Rielle, by a man in a broad-brimmed hat and cracked, heel-worn boots.

*

Word of that was all over the city. Baruch heard the story twenty times a day in the streets, in shop doorways and outside taverns, from youths sitting on the edge of the fountains and grey-haired women clucking their tongues by the grocers' stalls. The killing was more than two months old, but so far the gossips hadn't lost their taste for the tale.

"The Rielle is only seventy miles away," they said. "And there's an All-Church army there. It could be here in a week."

He and the soldiers with him pointed out that it couldn't, even if it was ready to set out at once. Ten miles was a decent day's march for an army, if provided with good roads across level fields, and friends along the way. In hostile territory, or hills and valleys like the Aiguille, six or seven miles would be about the best that could be managed. Besides, that Crusade army would have to cross the Rielle first, and on barges that would take a long time. If it set out for Mayence today, it might possibly arrive in a fortnight. It couldn't be much sooner.

"Anyway," he told a man with stained forearms outside a dye shop, "the army was raised to go to Tura d'Madai. The Crusade there is in trouble, I hear. Too much fighting and not enough men. There's word that the Madai might try to retake Jedat this year."

"There are never enough men," Leutar said as they strolled away. "It was just the same when I was there."

"I wouldn't mind if the Justified got a bloody nose though," Athar put in. "I don't mean I want to see them beaten," he added hastily when Baruch cocked an eyebrow at him. "Just… knocked about a bit."

"You tend not to get 'knocked about' on a battlefield," Baruch said dryly. Athar hadn't yet been sent away from Sarténe to fight, but that didn't really excuse the romantic view he had of war. The lad's tutors and arms masters ought to have taught him better than that, out on the farms and estates. "It's not like a drunken scuffle outside a wine shop. In battle you get dead, or crippled for the rest of your life. Or the other man does."

"We shouldn't be dealing with drunken scuffles anyway," Leutar grumped. "That's the Watch's job."

Baruch nodded. It was true, but that made no difference. "Too much trouble and not enough men."

Leutar nodded reluctant agreement. A vivid, puckered scar ran down the side of his neck and vanished under his leather vest; Baruch knew it extended all the way down to his ribcage. A pair of good healers among the Faithful in Tura d'Madai – the Faithful of the All-Church, that is – had saved Leutar's life, when it seemed the Adversary must surely claim him for his own. Beside him, Athar seemed even more fresh-faced and naïve than ever.

The trouble was that the Hand of the Lord had men here, those who had gone on Crusade to Tura d'Madai and returned, and others who were not yet fully trained. That meant they found themselves being corralled into doing whatever work there was to do, when the Margrave found he needed warm bodies for one thing or another. The Lord Marshal shouldn't let it happen. The Hand of the Lord was meant to dedicate itself only to fighting: that single-mindedness had made it the most feared of the Orders, among the Madai. Its soldiers should not be reduced to breaking up brawls in the streets.

The Hand did still fight, of course. Over five thousand men were still in the East, fighting the endless, draining struggle against the Madai. Some three hundred men were down in the south of Alinaur, trying without much success to clear out the remnants of the Jaidi from the mountains. Some of those craggy fastnesses were the same ones from which the last free men of Alinaur had defied the Jaidi, two centuries before. The men of the Hand probably didn't appreciate the irony in that. They only fought at all to keep the Basilica happy, and stop anyone looking too closely at the state of religion in Sarténe. For generations they had been risking their lives, and losing them, in the name of a religion and a Saviour in which they had no faith, and now one man in the broad-brimmed hat might have ruined all that careful work with a single ill-judged blow, because now the All-Church *was* looking closely. It wouldn't like what it saw.

And young fellows like Athar knew more about patrolling city streets like Watchmen than they did about battles. None of them could be relied on in combat until they had lived through it.

Perhaps he would benefit from a tour of Alinaur. Rumour said the Jaidi had chosen a khalif for themselves, somewhere in those bony mountains, and if that was so they were likely to be more unified than they had been for a long time. At any rate, Tei-jo warriors knew their trade, and when cornered they fought like ferrets in a sack. After a dance or two with their curved swords, Athar would come back wiser and less prone to romance, and with a scar or two to show off to the ladies. If he came back at all.

Well, it was several years since Baruch had seen a battlefield. The wound that had removed the top of his left ear had long since ceased aching even in cold weather. He only remembered it now when he noticed the white flash in his hair the injury had left him. It wasn't right, that a man should have a witch's streak when he was thirty. It made him look old.

Baruch wiped his brow. None of the three soldiers wore armour, but summer had come on strong in the past couple of days, and the street air was heavy with heat. "I think we deserve a break. What do you fellows say to quarter of an hour in a taproom with a cup of wine?"

"I know a good place," Leutar said. "The *Languorous Nymph*. It's on Old Palm Street, next to the pie shop. The one with the Temujini panelling on the windows at night."

"You always want to go there," Baruch grinned. "But you're a soldier, all right. Always thinking about the next meal, aren't you?"

Leutar shrugged. "They're good pies. Especially the beef."

"Fresh?"

"Listen close and you'll hear them moo."

"Good, then," Baruch said. "The *Languorous Nymph* it is, and a quick bite of lunch after. And don't tell the Lord Marshal. Right, Athar?"

The young man put on an innocent look. "Tell him what? We're not going to do anything."

There was hope for the lad yet.

The three men made their way down the avenue, staying under the shade of the palm trees when they could. People thronged the street, most of them shoppers hurrying to or from the market, though some gathered in doorways or by fountains to mutter about the army that still waited beyond the river Rielle. The ships of the Glorified should be assembling now to take those men to Tura d'Madai and put an end to all this nervousness, but there was no sign of them and unease fed on itself and grew. The only people who seemed calm were the outlanders, easy to spot in the crowds: here a Jaidi's dark face, or there the paler skin of a Cailevi. Maybe they knew they could pack their goods on a ship and leave if war really did come, or maybe they were just more sensible.

The three men crossed Musicians' Square, a wide plaza with a round pool in the middle, in the middle of which stood a statue. Not the usual effigy of a mounted warrior with sword raised, or one of the All-Church's multitude of saints: this was simply a man with a lute in his hands, fingers plucking at the strings. On the plinth beneath it was an inscription, written in plain letters;

For every song of joy, there must be a song of sorrow.

"We Sarténi," Luthien had said, the first time he saw that, "have melancholy souls, don't you think?"

Singers and harpists lined the edges, a careful ten paces apart, each with an upturned cap or a tin on the ground in front of him. A musician could play in the square without a license, which gave newcomers to Mayence a chance to make their name before they paid the guild fees. After that they gained entry to the inns and banquets which saw so much of the city's life, and where they could establish themselves. If they were any good. A couple of men lounged at the edges of the square, their fine clothes identifying them as agents looking for the next great talent to enter the city. They eyed the musicians without much interest. Apparently the next great talent was still on the road. Baruch winced as they passed a flautist who missed a third of the notes, and kept stopping to frown at his instrument.

"It ain't the flute's fault," Leutar told the man pleasantly. Baruch managed to stifle his guffaws until they were past.

Every second-rate village fiddler wanted to make a career in Mayence. Every piper or warbler in homespun clothes with pig shit on his shoes, the crack-fingered gittern players and tone deaf piano-thumpers; all of them came here to seek their fortunes. A musician who gained a reputation in this city could name his fee all across

Sarténe, and these days beyond it. The temptation was enormous. Unfortunately it blinded many people to the truth, which was that they'd lose a musical contest with a wooden plank.

It was the same with poets, and playwrights, and god only knew what else. Some of the writers could barely string two words together, and stammered when they tried to declaim. Baruch had heard the Academy had a similar problem with its students. Noble fathers who wanted their sons to be properly educated sent them to Parrien, where half of them eyed the quills as though afraid they would bite. Luthien taught there now and didn't seem to mind; he smiled when Baruch mentioned it, and said that every youth had the right to an education. Even so, the faculty was talking about bringing in an entrance exam, so the terminally thick-witted wouldn't hamper the students who really could learn.

Still, among all the dross that clogged the squares and the classrooms, there was some genuine talent. Quite a lot of it, in fact. A surprising number of mud-footed farmers really *could* write, or sing, or solve fiendishly difficult equations without creasing their brows. Baruch remembered one man who had been able to tell you what day of the week it was on a given date fifteen years ago, or fifty, or five hundred for that matter. Those nobles whose sons failed so miserably were often irritated to find that a bumpkin from some forest clearing sailed through problems as though born to it.

"I wonder," Luthien had said, "if we could send people out to the villages and test children somehow. Find the more gifted among them and bring them here younger, say when they're twelve. It's a shame that so much talent goes to waste. I hate to think of a youth with the mind of a philosopher living his whole life in a muddy shack, and never learning to write."

That was Luthien all over. Sometimes it was hard to remember him as he'd been in Tura d'Madai, still stained with blood – never his own – as he wolfed a haunch of meat and chased it down with wine drunk straight from the bottle. Once he'd stained the pages of a book – and been horrified at himself for it – by absently propping it open with a slice of pork, so he could use both hands to eat. These days he lived on nuts and chickpeas and drank fruit juice, while musing over the theological implications of the indivisibility of God. And Luthien himself was one of those village children; without the Crusade to Tura d'Madai, he would likely still be knee-deep in the mud of his father's fields, and watching for herons flying south so he knew when to plant the barley.

The three men moved down Waggoner's Way, keeping to the raised walk at the side of the street. Carts rumbled past to their left, mostly empty and leaving the city at this time of day, though a few came the other way loaded with sacks of grain and clay jars filled with olive oil. Just after sunrise it was the other way around, the street choked with incoming wagons, their drivers shouting curses as they tried to manoeuvre their way past one another in the crush. There was a collision almost every day. This morning a cart carrying peaches had overturned, spilling ripe fruit across the street, where it was quickly pocketed by passing citizens who were more readily opportunistic than helpful. The driver had been all but weeping with impotent rage as he saw his profits scattered and lost, and the men in the carts trapped behind hardly less angry.

Halfway down the Way, a stray tendril of incense tickled Baruch's nose, and he looked up at the church on his right. An All-Church priest stood at the top of the steps, swinging his brass censer from side to side as his voice rose and fell in sonorous rhythm. His white robe was bordered with vivid red, like blood. The doors stood open to reveal a shadowy space within, and the rearmost wooden pews. The priest's gaze fell on the soldiers and his voice faltered, just for a moment, then resumed a little louder than before.

"He doesn't like us much," Leutar observed.

Baruch grunted. "Not many of them do."

They never had, but it had been worse since Rabast was murdered by the banks of the Rielle. Baruch had been on guard at the gates of the Margrave's mansion when the priest arrived, and had taken a dislike to him from the first glance. It wasn't really anything Rabast had said, just the man's general attitude – two parts arrogance, one part stupidity, mix well and serve. Sometimes you met men like that. A lot of them seemed to be priests.

But the clergy of the All-Church did not like it when one of their number was killed, and they were looking for someone to blame. Priests were supposed to be inviolate, protected by God, so they could walk the highways and byways of the world without fear. Take that away and there would be places the priests could not go and that, to them, was unacceptable.

The three men turned left at a crossroads, watched over by a fifteen-foot bronze horseman in full armour, the mark of the cross on his shield and a torch held in an upraised hand. This time it was a classic All-Church image, a devout soldier bringing the light of God to heathen lands, and the pose was ridiculously noble. At least, it was until a pigeon perched on the statue's helmet shifted and deposited droppings on his shoulder. Baruch grinned to himself. Mayence kept a few All-Church symbols on show in the streets, intended – like the soldiers of the Hand fighting in Alinaur and Tura d'Madai – to keep the Basilica from asking too many suspicious questions. The statue would be cleaned before morning, but it was amusing to see the Church's sculpture befouled.

Baruch wasn't sure that token gestures such as the statue were very important any more. The Dualists worshipped out of doors whenever they could, in the full glory of creation rather than shut inside a drab stone hall, but they needed somewhere to go when the weather was bad. Their round temples outnumbered All-Church chapels by two to one now, and all of them were packed every day while the chapels struggled to fill two rows of pews. Someone in the Basilica was sure to notice that in the end, however myopic the All-Church might be. Maybe someone already had, and the snooping presence of Rabast was the result of it. Baruch lost his smile. If that was true, the murder of the hapless fool was more likely than ever to bring serious trouble, and soon.

A hundred yards along Old Palm Street they reached the *Languorous Nymph*. Tables lined the street outside, at which men sat enjoying the sunshine with their cups of wine and ale. An Elite sat in his green robe with a cup of fruit juice on the table before him, talking with two men built like blacksmiths but who wore light silk shirts, the sort favoured by nobles and the wealthier merchants. Over the taproom's door was a carving of two overlapping circles, the arc of each one passing through the centre of the other: the mark of the Duality. Two forces of equal strength, forever locked together. The same symbol adorned the walls of every circular temple, though nobody told the All-Church priests what it meant. It was the basis for the reversed circle on the shields of the Hand of the Lord, and in all the years Baruch had spent in the Order, he'd never met a single All-Church believer who seemed to realise what the design really was.

"Wine or ale?" he asked the others as he reached the bar. Out of the sun the air was noticeably cooler, a sure sign that summer hadn't elbowed spring aside quite yet. "I'm buying."

"Heaven preserve us!" Leutar exclaimed. "Is the world coming to an end?" Athar burst out laughing.

Baruch scowled at them.

The barman finished serving a quartet of labourers and came over, pausing to snag three cups from beneath the counter. Baruch ordered wine for all of them and dug in his pocket for coins.

"Excuse me," someone said behind him, and he turned.

The speaker was a youth of about sixteen, his brown hair and farmer's clothes heavy with dust. Obviously he'd been travelling, and either had not had time to wash or else was plain lazy. He wore a short sword at one hip, hardly more than a long knife, and something in the way he stood made Baruch think the lad wasn't used to carrying it. Still, it was unusual for anyone to wear a sword inside the walls. Baruch frowned at him. "Yes?"

"I noticed your hair," the youth said. "Your white streak. Is your name Baruch Caraman?"

The frown deepened. "Who's asking?"

"My name's Japh. I have a message for you, if you're Baruch."

"I'm Baruch," he said. "Give me the message."

The lad shifted his feet. "Uh, I was told to ask you something first. To make sure you're really Baruch."

"Of course he's Baruch," Leutar said irritably. "What game are you playing, boy? Give him the message."

Baruch stared at the youth. This was very strange, both in that the lad had a message for him, and that he was so secretive about it. Maybe Japh was one of the young idiots who thought warfare was all honour and secret codes. Or maybe the Lord Marshal knew Baruch's habit of taking a quick unofficial break after all, and had sent a message to him at the taproom. Not that old Darien had any right to complain about another man's drinking, with the warm smell of brandy always heavy in the air of his office. Probably that was why he allowed his men to work as constables when they ought to be preparing for war.

"Then ask," he said at length.

Relief flooded the lad's face. "Uh, thank you. I was told to ask you this: what did the Madai call the pig farmer?"

His first thought was *what on earth?* Baruch had no idea what the lad was talking about. He stared at Japh in bafflement. And then all at once he knew, the memory bursting on him like sand and grit flung in his face. He could smell the desert, here in the common room of a tavern in Mayence in the spring, air heavy with heat and burning rock, and see the knot of Madai youths huddling in a far corner to point fingers as the man they so feared walked by.

"*That's him,*" the remembered voice said in his mind. Baruch could see the speaker's face now, thin and drawn, and grimy with dust through which large eyes stared at the soldiers. A boy with too much to fear and not enough to eat. "*The man who slaughtered Cammar ah Amalik at Gidren Field. They say he can't be killed, and they call him –*"

"The sand scorpion," Baruch said. His voice was hoarse. "They called him the sand scorpion."

Japh nodded and reached into his shirt. "That's right. This is from him." He withdrew a folded paper and handed it to Baruch. A thick, shapeless blob of wax held the letter closed. "He's back."

"Back?" Baruch repeated. He felt as though he'd been hit between the eyes. "Are you telling me Ca –"

"He said," Japh broke in, "that it would be best if nobody knew, for the moment. The letter explains, I think."

"Explains?" He made an effort to calm himself. His hands were trembling, and he held the letter carefully in both of them. "I see. Er, how did Ca – how did you know to find me here?"

Japh shrugged. "I asked your commander. He said you usually spend a few minutes at a tavern during your duty, and this one was on your route for the day. So I waited. I was almost certain it was you as soon as you walked in. A man with half an ear and a white streak in his hair above it, I was told." He stopped suddenly. "Uh, sorry. I don't mean to be rude."

So old Darien knew about the illicit cups of wine after all, then. Suddenly that didn't seem to matter very much. Baruch took a deep breath and broke the wax seal. His hands were still shaking. He unfolded the paper and saw the familiar, slanting script, and knew before he read a word that the boy was right, and Calesh was back in Sarténe at last.

Baruch,

Your friend the sand scorpion has returned, and is with our comrade from the north. Forgive the secrecy; it's necessary, though I can't explain in a letter. Something is happening and I need your help. You'll remember the windmill on the ridge above my

father's old farm. Meet us there as soon as you can. Tell nobody. I would not ask, my friend, if it were not of vast importance. I think you know that. We shared a great deal in the east. Believe me when I say this is a greater thing than all we have done before.
  I also want you to meet my wife.
  You have always held my trust. I hope I hold yours.

  There was no signature. Baruch didn't need one: the style was right, as well as the handwriting, both exactly as he remembered them. The writer was Calesh, beyond doubt. He was home, six long years later than his friends, time spent in the endless sand and stone of Tura d'Madai. There had never been anything to draw Calesh back; no family, no home, no memories softened into nostalgia by the passing seasons. For him the Order was a haven, and a reason to make a new beginning in another land. Calesh had not gone to Tura d'Madai in the name of God, either the Duality's or the Basilica's. He'd gone in the name of forgetfulness, and if he found rebirth along the way, so much the better.

  For Baruch the Hand was wife, mother and sons, all the life he needed or wanted. He often said *I am married to the Hand,* a coarse soldier's joke that even he didn't find very funny any more. But it was true. He had never needed anything else to make him happy.

  Yet now Calesh was back, and with a wife at his side as well. Baruch had always thought his friend was even less likely to marry than he was himself. His fingers tightened, making the parchment crackle, and his knuckles began to turn white.

  You have always held my trust. I hope I hold yours.
  There was never any doubt what he would do.

*

  He sent a message to Darien, telling the Lord Marshal he was taking a few days off. Baruch had it coming; the Hand really was his life, and he rarely took the time to go fishing, or plant cabbages in his garden. He went to the stables, his mind whirling as he gathered tack and a saddle and went back to the stalls.

  Calesh was back. That was something Baruch had never thought to see, though it wasn't the first time he'd been wrong. After three years, he still couldn't quite grow accustomed to the sight of

Luthien in the green robe of an Elite. When they met up they still went to taverns, and it felt strange to drink wine while Luthien stuck to tisanes and fruit juice, and dined on salad and nuts. But Baruch was certain that no threat, however severe, would be enough to make Luthien abandon his vows and take up arms again. From what Japh had said, it seemed that Calesh wasn't convinced of that yet.

"I was told to take the same message to him," the boy had said, when Baruch tried to save him a wasted trip to Parrien. "So I will. Whether he comes or not, I'll do as I promised I would."

The boy might make a decent soldier one day. The short sword at his hip was still so new to him that his movements with it were awkward; once he'd tripped on the scabbard and fallen against a wall. But he had the right spirit, and in the end survival in a battle was as much due to courage and heart as it was to ability. You couldn't teach those. The Hand spent years training its recruits, building up their strength and skill, yet even so a few of them froze when they first found themselves on a battlefield. It was the smell of slaughter that did it, Baruch believed. Up until that stink hit the nose it was just a game, played with swords and armour but still a game, and somehow not real. When you smelled the spilled insides of shrieking men, it was suddenly real all at once.

That was when you found out who might be able to survive. It was those men who, leaden-armed and soul weary after three hours of constant fighting, found a fire still burning in them and managed to keep going. Those without it, however gifted, ended in the dirt with the dead men.

After Gidren Field, Calesh had told the company to just lay down and rest, right in the middle of a valley thick with dead and dying men. And they had done it, sleeping through the pitiful pleas and screams of the wounded. Battle did that to men. Something in them grew hard. It was learning how to live with death, and yet still remember how to live, that broke so many of them.

One thing young men never realised, or believed if they were told, was that battle wasn't about heroism and glory. It was about staying alive no matter what came; sieges inside the walls and out, standing with spears levelled as heavy cavalry charged in, or trying to hold a company together in the middle of a swirling storm of steel. A good soldier was simply someone who could stay alive through all that, and find the courage in himself to face it again.

Baruch had only ever known two men he would call heroes. One was Cammar a Amalik, captain of the Nazir infantry of the Madai. His men claimed he walked across water and sharpened his blade on the rays of the rising sun. They would follow him into the desert with no water, or into battle against an endless sea of foes. In the battle of Azerun they had shattered twice their number of Justified, strewing the dry ground with dead men. At Gidren Field, shortly afterwards, three regiments of Justified had shifted and begun to shrink back at the mere sight of the Nazir starting forward, threatening to leave a wide hole in the centre of the All-Church army. Amalik had swung his men straight towards the gap. The rest of the Crusaders hesitated, on the point of flight.

Then the second hero, unasked, raised a cry and charged.

Baruch remembered plunging forward as well, the rest of the Hand's soldiers behind and alongside him, barely keeping something like order as they raced across the broken ground. Shields went up as bowstrings sang, somewhere to the left of them. A heartbeat passed, then two, before arrows rattled off metal. Baruch heard one pass close by, whining like metal on glass. The Nazir turned to meet the threat in perfect ranks, unruffled, frighteningly competent. Amalik was in the centre, just ahead of his green banner marked with a flowering palm. And Calesh, who had given that shout and charged, was aiming right for him, three paces ahead of anyone else in the company.

Around them the battle seemed to stand still, everyone in both armies turning to see. Then the last few yards between the companies were gone, and men crashed together with a volley of shouts and ringing steel.

That was the day when Baruch lost half his ear. A Madai sword struck his helmet before he could duck and cracked it, driving torn steel into the side of Baruch's head. His vision blurred and he stumbled back, cursing, blinded on one side by blood. He was too stunned to feel much pain, but he was afraid the eye might be gone. The Nazir warrior came after him and then the huge shape of Raigal Tai was there, bounding forward with his axe coming down. The Nazir collapsed, cut almost in half despite his armour, and Raigal's backswing sent another man flying. The big man grinned ferociously through a beard soaked in blood – his own helmet was gone, somewhere – but Baruch wasn't looking at him.

He was looking past, towards the green banner, and Calesh. The tall man delivered a short, chopping stroke, reversed his sword, chopped again. And Cammar a Amalik went down amidst his men, immortal or no, sunlight-sharpened sword dropping from his fingers as he fell. Baruch could see the splash of blood on his surcoat. The Madai nearby screamed in horror and disbelief, and all at once they were running, as though their spirit had been lost along with their captain. They even abandoned the green banner, something no Madai ever did. Luthien pulled it out of the dust and snapped the staff across his knee, a gesture of utter contempt, but one hardly spoken of, afterwards.

    Soldiers on both sides remembered those two quick, hacking blows, and the fall of a champion. And they remembered Calesh, raising his bloodied sword to point at the fleeing Nazir. The emergence of a new champion, standing astride the body of the old, while a hot wind off the mountains whipped dust devils along the space between the two armies.

    Baruch shook his head. He had a hundred memories of Tura d'Madai, some pleasant and others less so, but none more vivid than that. There had been talk among the army's leaders of commissioning a painting of the scene, an idea that foundered on Calesh's indifference and the opposition of the Justified. It was their men who had been humiliated at Azerun, after all, and who had shrunk back like dying flowers when the Nazir approached them at Gidren Field. They were not eager to be reminded of it.

    A bard here in Sarténe had written a ballad around the scene, though. Ando something or other, if Baruch's memory didn't fail him. He hadn't heard the song, which was likely the usual sort of romanticised mush written by fools who'd never breathed the carrion stench of a battlefield, but if word spread that Calesh was back home it would be impossible to avoid. Second-rate bards would sing it three times a night at every hostel and tavern in Mayence. It was enough to make Baruch glad he was leaving the city.

    With his mount saddled he appropriated a pack horse and loaded it with his armour, carefully wrapped in muslin and then oiled leather to keep out the rain. He couldn't remember having used the breastplate once since he came back from Tura d'Madai, six years before. After a quick trip to the larders he'd added enough dried food to keep him going for a few days. There were benefits, he decided as he rode out of the barracks, to being a soldier in the city rather than a Watchman, who would have had to pay for a pack animal and supplies. As it was the purse behind his belt was nearly full, and he had some coins registered with the Notaries in case of emergency. He'd didn't need to go to them yet. The money he had would keep his belly full for a while.

On impulse, he reined the horses into a narrow side street near the racing track, and hitching them to a rail he went into a circular temple to pray. It wasn't something he usually did: he preferred to leave the god-bothering to Luthien. The small man prayed enough for half an army, after all, and surely even God didn't have time to listen to *every* plea mortals made. God knew what you did anyway, and no amount of begging would make an iota of difference to His plans, so if God was in your heart then why bother to pray?

But this time it was different. Maybe it was just his imagination, but Baruch thought he could feel a quickening in his blood, or perhaps in the air around him.

Calesh was back. They were four again.

Passing through the gate in the north wall, he began to whistle.

Five

The Orange Groves

Calesh assured her they could trust Raigal Tai. Very well, then; she would trust him. Farajalla knew how deep her husband's bond with his old comrades ran in him. It was a thing never to be questioned, never doubted, as much a part of him as his soul, or his bones, and she could not be part of it.

She held his heart, though. She couldn't doubt that. Calesh's love was a shining truth in her life, bright rainbow colours reaching into every part of her, everything she did and thought and felt. So he was part of a close fellowship of men; well, he was allowed that. A wife could not be everything to her husband. He needed some things she couldn't give.

In honesty, she found that… difficult. It had been easier in Tura d'Madai, when she was the sole focus of his love, and his friends no more than cherished memories. Farajalla didn't speak of that though. Her husband needed to know she trusted him still, and loved him as much as ever. And she did love him, fiercely and with all the heart she had. She would not let him be harmed, whether the All-Church sent an army or not. For him she would stand against the world with a dagger in her hand, and never complain.

So Raigal had stayed in the ruined windmill, up on the ridge overlooking a narrow, deep valley, with five thousand soldiers around him and a quarter of a million gold sesters in promissory notes stacked against a wall in the upstairs room. And she was trusting him with that.

It was strange, the things love could lead you to do.

The hillside was a quilt of fields, mostly olive groves at this height, gnarled knots of root driving into the soil to anchor them to the steep slopes. Orange orchards stood further down and then ploughed fields at the bottom, either ready to be planted or already fresh-sown. It reminded her of home a little, though it was certainly more fertile, and the scents were different. She inhaled deeply, tasting rosemary and tarragon, swift and sharp on her tongue.

In the valley houses clustered to form a half-hearted village, with farmhouses scattered apparently at random among fields that climbed the lower slopes of the ridge. On the far side, facing north, the hill had been left in its natural state, a ragged spill of loose stones and hardy bushes. It gave the vale a lopsided look, like an unfinished sculpture.

"There," Calesh said, when they were a little lower down. He pointed to his right. "That was my father's farm. The house with the yellow gate."

Farajalla stopped to shade her eyes against the afternoon sunlight. She picked out the gate at once, though what had once been a splash of canary yellow was now a pale peach, desultory against the green of trees and vineyards. Behind it stood a ramshackle house, roofed with reddish slates, its walls seeming made entirely of ivy. It was tiny. She wondered if there was only one room, or two very small ones.

"It looks very peaceful," she said tactfully.

"It looks like a shack," Calesh said. He wasn't wearing his armour, though his sword still hung at his waist. He'd stopped to stare at the house, frowning slightly. "A rundown little shack. Isn't that peculiar? Even in my memories, I never saw it that way before."

"Sometimes memories play tricks. You're seeing with fresh eyes now."

He nodded slowly. "I'm not the same man. Not the youth who left here eleven years ago."

"Who owns the farm now?"

"After my father died it passed to me." He shrugged. "I sold it to buy my first set of mail, a sword, and a horse. Not much to show for my father's life, was it?" He shook his head. "And at that, I needn't have done it. The Hand supplies all recruits with weapons and armour better than anything I could have bought myself. I didn't know that at the time."

"You sound as though it still bothers you," she said carefully. She'd never seen Calesh this way before. He hadn't looked at her since he first spoke.

"I suppose it does," he said, and then he did look at her, sensing her disquiet. "It shouldn't, I know. My life has gone another way since I was last here, and it was a long time ago. No point living in the mud of the past." His lips quirked in the not-quite smile she so loved in him. "I've become a hero, of all things. No doubt it's silk sheets and palaces for me now."

She laughed. "Last night we slept in a derelict windmill, and the night before in a little inn huddled tight against the sea. I haven't seen a silk sheet since we left Harenc. Have you been hoarding them for yourself?"

"Of course I have," he said, with a proper smile now.

"Then you owe me a forfeit." She grinned back, glad to see him more like his usual self. "What will it be? Maybe I'll ask you to sing me to sleep every night for a month."

"Better not," he said. "There's a reason Raigal calls me Bullfrog. And knowing you, the forfeit will be to make love to you all night with a rose clenched in my teeth, and make you purr like a cat."

"You don't need the rose," she said, "and as for the rest, you already do that. Didn't you know?"

He turned to face her. Not a muscle moved in his face, but she saw something flash in his eyes. Everything fell away from her. The hillside, the valley, might not have existed. There was only him.

"By my heart and eyes," he said, his voice thick, "I could take you now, right here on the hillside."

Warmth rushed into her, flushing her throat and stomach and thighs. *Damn* him for being able to do that to her, with just a few words, or a glance across a crowded room. It was suddenly hard to breathe. She pushed all that away and made herself smile at him, as cool and calm as a lady of the court, bewitching without being bewitched.

"I'm not sure that would be wise," she said. "We're trying not to attract attention, after all, and the way you yelp and gasp would bring every yokel for miles around."

Startled, Calesh broke into laughter, which gave Farajalla the chance to draw a steadying breath without being noticed. Her mother had once told her that real love was like this, sharp daggers in the heart and hot enough to burn, but that it faded after a year or two. She'd been half right. It was all daggers and heat, but it hadn't faded in the least.

"Tonight," she said when his mirth faded. "If you can wait that long, and be extremely quiet. That windmill isn't large enough for privacy."

"I can wait that long," he said. "Barely. The sweetest water is the glass that ends a long thirst."

She raised an eyebrow. "So you say. As though you've been thirsty once since we were married."

"I'm terribly weak," he conceded. His gaze slipped away from her, down into the valley. A hint of his earlier distance came back. "Come on. We need to move if we're to be back at the windmill by sundown."

They went on down the hillside. Soon they reached a field of apples trees and entered the shade beneath, hidden from prying eyes. Even after all these years away, Calesh obviously knew where he was going. He led her through the orchard, close enough to a farmhouse that Farajalla could see it through a thin screen of branches, and then into an orange grove whose trees were barely taller than she was. A pig with brown stripes on brown looked up from snuffling at roots to give them a glance, then went back to more interesting things.

"There," Calesh said again.

Ahead of them a low wall cut across their path, built of dry stones fitted more or less together. When Farajalla stepped atop it the slab moved under her foot, almost tipping her over. She jumped hastily down on the far side and looked around, still in the shade of the orange trees.

The curved wall of a building stood ten yards in front of her, white plaster shining in the sun. It was plainly made, and devoid of even the simplest decoration. Only grass grew in the space enclosed by the wall. Here and there it covered a mound, each one marked at the eastern end with a slate, carved into an oval and engraved.

Calesh stepped down beside her. His face was very pale. When he moved on Farajalla hung back a pace, letting him go first, if not quite alone. He walked up to the rounded wall of the temple and knelt beside a grassy mound with an aged wooden board at one end. After a moment his fingers reached out to touch the grass, a bare kiss of his skin.

"Hello, brother," he said softly. "There's someone I want you to meet."

*

"He was eight," he said. "We used to play in the orange groves behind our house. Father wouldn't let us swim unless he was with us. A girl drowned in the river around the time I was born, apparently. I grew up with tales of Jinny Greenteeth, a spirit that lurked in the water and waited for the chance to seize small children and pull them in."

They were sitting with their backs against the dry stone wall, facing the temple and the graves. To their right the sun sank towards the horizon. Everywhere was the buzz of cicadas, though none were in sight. Farajalla pushed braids away from her face and let him talk.

"So we played in the grove. Warriors and kings, mostly. I suppose little boys everywhere do that. We'd stalk each other through the trees, pretending to be heroes on a quest to rescue a princess. Tavi used to hate being the evil guard, so a lot of the time I let him be the hero. The good warrior always had to win, of course." He looked away, up at the orange groves and back into memory. "I can't remember how many times I pretended to die here."

Make-believe heroes, rescuing a make-believe princess. Not guessing that one day, in the distant unimaginable time of adulthood, one of them would grow up to be a real hero, marry a beautiful lady in a distant land, and discover how different reality was from games.

And the other one...

"The plague came when I was ten," Calesh said. "It wasn't much of a plague, really. Father said he'd seen a lot worse. The three of us went to the funeral of an old man from the village, and later our neighbour Charn's mother. That's her grave," he added, pointing. "A couple of other people died as well. All of them were better than sixty, and most were frail."

He leaned against her, resting his head on her shoulder. Farajalla stroked his hair, waiting for him to speak again, but for a long time he said nothing. The cicadas sang on. Voices drifted up from the village, together with one man's heavy laughter, and behind them the pig snuffled happily. The shadows of the trees were nearly at the temple wall.

"Tavi got sick the week after his birthday," Calesh said at last. Her hand went on stroking his hair. "At first Father thought it was just a cold. For a week Tavi sneezed and coughed, and nobody thought anything of it until he complained that his arms were aching. Father made him take off his shirt, and saw his armpits were black with plague sores."

"He sent me to stay with Charn. I wasn't allowed near the house at all, even in the garden. Every evening I'd creep through the orange grove until I could see the window of the room Tavi and I shared, and I'd sit there until it grew dark, listening. If I heard him moan or cry out it meant he was still alive." Calesh stopped, swallowed. "Then one day it was Father who cried out. It sounded as though his throat was torn in half."

He closed his eyes. Nothing had shown in his voice, but a tear ran down his cheek. Most westerners let their emotions rage, but Calesh might have been born Madai, he controlled himself so well.

"We buried my brother that evening," Calesh said. "Father wept so hard he could barely stand. I remember I kept looking around for Tavi, expecting him to spring out of the trees and say it had all been a joke. When they put him in the ground I screamed, I think. I know I did." He paused to draw an unsteady breath. "Afterwards I ran into the orange grove and smashed every branch I could reach. Father never even lectured me for that."

She kissed the top of his head and put her other arm around him. After a moment she felt his arms come up and encircle her waist.

They had sat the same way once before, in the mountains south of Harenc, only then it was she who wept for her lost family as Madai combed the burned ruins where the castle had once stood. Losing her father had been hard enough, but parents were expected to die before their children, so a part of the heart was always prepared for it. The loss of a sibling was different, sharper somehow. Farajalla still thought of her half-brothers, tall and young and proud, but fated never to watch their own children grow. They had used to give her sweets, when she was small. When the army came they stood on the walls and were lost.

She'd never known what happened to her mother.

She wondered if the pain would fade, when she and Calesh had a child of their own. Perhaps new life would make the deaths more bearable. In truth, Farajalla had expected to have a baby by now, after three years of marriage: her father's wives and mistresses had spawned children like plums dropping from a tree. Women in Tura d'Madai never had to worry about fertility. Farajalla had begun to wonder about her own though, a worm of unease gnawing at her mind. What would Calesh do, if she couldn't give him the children he longed for so desperately?

"I know my brother isn't here," Calesh said softly, breaking into her thoughts. "Even though I spoke as though he is. He's gone to the next world, by God's grace. I always thought I knew where I would go after my own death. But then I went to the East, and I realised that the All-Church's god is the same as ours, and the Madai's. They just worship him differently. And kill each other over details." He shook his head. "Now I don't know where souls go, and I want to cling to this world while I can, for as long as I can."

He straightened, pulling away from her, and looking across the graveyard he said, "Hello, Charn."

Farajalla gave a start of surprise. An old man was standing by the wall of the temple, staring as though shocked to find them there. In the last of the sunlight the creases in his face were plain. He looked like an ancient walnut. The blue eyes that stared from those wrinkles were bright and clear though, and after a moment they narrowed in recognition.

"Calesh," he said in a voice like rasping sand. "By my heart and eyes, you're Calesh Saissan, aren't you?"

"Your eyes are still good." Calesh climbed to his feet. "And you look as well as ever, Charn."

"Liar. I've one foot in the next world already, and I look like it." He studied the younger man for a moment. "Your face isn't any worse than it was, though. It's good to see you made it back alive."

"And with a wife," Calesh said as she stood up. "Farajalla."

"Pleased to meet you," she said.

Charn glanced at her, then back to Calesh. "A Madai? I bet the All-Church just loves you for that."

"They don't need other reasons not to love me," Calesh said. "We're not staying, Charn. I just wanted to stop by and speak to my brother."

The old man nodded. "He'll be glad of that, I reckon. But I'm surprised you're here, Calesh. I thought you'd never come back from the desert. Did you leave the Hand, then?"

"No," he said. "I brought it with me, Every man. We're needed more here, I think." Farajalla shot him a sharp look, but he ignored her. "Do you know anything about that, Charn?"

The old man's frown deepened. "The All-Church? I heard a man from the Basilica was murdered a couple of months ago, by the Rielle."

"That's why," Calesh said. "They're coming for us, Charn. Almost certainly. They want the Dualism gone."

Charn chewed on that for a moment. "Then it's good you're here, I'd say. But still, you broke your oath to defend the holy city, didn't you? There are some who'll say you should have done differently."

"Some oaths matter more than others," he said. "Would you have me sit in the desert and fight for the All-Church, even while it burned my home?"

He couldn't have done, of course, oath or no oath. The All-Church wouldn't have stood for it, unless Calesh abandoned the Hand and joined one of the other Orders instead. Otherwise they would have had him killed, probably using a Justified highbinder to assassinate him. That Order had tried once already, she was sure: the man who had fired that arrow at Calesh in the courtyard of Harenc was almost certainly a highbinder, though dressed in the hooded robe of a Madai holy man. Calesh hadn't seen the crossbow appear from under the robes. He ought to have died. The Madai had bitter reason, learned over years and in grief, to know how efficient the Justified assassins were.

It was said when the highbinders were alone they wore gloves backed with human bones, and once they had accepted a contract they never stopped until the target was dead.

But they weren't perfect. The westerner hadn't seen the woman with Calesh as a threat, as he ought to have done. Farajalla *had* seen the crossbow. She pushed Calesh aside, so the arrow struck him in the knee instead of the heart as the assassin tried to follow his sudden movement. Then she killed the man, her thrown dagger flashing into his throat while he still gaped at her, unable quite to believe that a woman could be dangerous. He must have been new to Tura d'Madai. Anyone who'd been there long would have known.

While Calesh had played games with his brother among the orange groves, Farajalla had learned to fight with her half-brothers, and that had not been a game. Not in Tura d'Madai.

"No," Charn said at length. "No, I wouldn't have you do that, Calesh. But you ought to go now. There's a new All-Church priest in the village, and he's keener than a sharp sickle. Likes to stick his nose in everyone's business." He sniffed. "The way most of them do."

"We're going," Calesh said. He hesitated. "Don't think too badly of me, Charn. Broken oath or no."

The old man smiled. "I never thought badly of you before, lad, and I don't see reason to start now. You always did try to do the right thing. I reckon your father knows that, even now."

"Thank you," Calesh said quietly. He glanced aside, towards his brother's grassy grave, and then shrugged his shoulders as though shaking off a weight. "It will be good to think so, at least."

He took her hand and they went away through the orange trees, climbing back the way they had come. Calesh didn't talk, and she let him have his silence. He would come back to her, when he had shaken off the sombre mood that filled him now, close to his brother's grave. She didn't usually like to wait, but for him, she would.

At the edge of the valley she looked back, down at the tiny shack where he had been born. At this distance it was a vague shape among the fields, marked out only by that faded yellow gate. It would have been easy for Calesh to become like Charn, growing old in a village that might as well have been all the world, for all he knew or cared. Instead he had crossed the sea to the desert, and to her, and by the time he swung down from his horse in Harenc's courtyard he had been nothing like Charn at all.

Raigal was still at the windmill when they got back, dozing with his back propped against the brass-bound chest and a half-eaten turkey leg in one hand. Soldiers stood at the building's door, or what remained of it. The camp lay all around, stretching from the olive groves to the wood that crept up to the ridge line, and across the road between them.

"Let him rest," Calesh said. He gestured at the sky, where gloomy clouds had begun to drift in from the west. "We're going to have a blow tonight. I think sleep will be hard to come by."

She looked at the trees that dotted the hillside, standing silent in the still air, and then at the clouds. Rain was rare in Tura d'Madai, but the occasional winter storms came from clouds that looked rather like these. She couldn't see that this would be much of a storm.

She was wrong.

*

"Blood of the god!" Raigal whooped, several hours later. He ducked half out of the doorway to peer at the black sky, heedless of the rain. "Did you see that? Hoo, it can't have been half a mile away!"

Farajalla kept her eyes closed, waiting for her vision to come back. She'd been looking out of the door when the lightning came to earth, and now purple lines danced across her eyelids. Rain hammered on the windmill's broken roof and dripped through the hole on the far side of the room, to one side of the door. She could barely hear it over the wind.

Sleep will be hard to come by, Calesh had said. He was wrong, though: sleep was impossible in this storm. An autumn blow, Raigal called it. Nothing out of the ordinary for Sarténe at the start of May, when the last storms of fading spring swept in from the ocean.

He grinned at her from the doorway, rain dripping from his blond curls.

"This is nothing!" he shouted over the noise. "Back in my homeland we have gales that tear boulders from the cliffs, and the rain slashes at you sideways. Blood of the God, I miss that!"

Farajalla had no doubt he was serious.

Lightning flashed again, illuminating the triangular shapes of tents in the valley below, where the soldiers had moved their camp to be out of the worst of the wind. In the glare silhouettes of trees seemed to leap out of the night as though to attack. They had barely faded back into the night when thunder boomed right overhead and rattled the old planks of the upper floor, or what was left of them. Something high in the derelict windmill groaned under the assault. A gust of wind blew rain through the canvas sheet they had hung across the doorway, spattering across aged bales of hay and a few forgotten ears of corn. The small fire in the hearth guttered like a failing candle. In the back room one of the horses snorted unhappily, though without panic. Probably they were used to it. Raigal only laughed again, waving his arms.

"Lets you know you're alive, doesn't it?" he bellowed. "I hope the soldiers hammered those tent pegs home hard!"

The man was insane. Nobody could really enjoy this. Farajalla wondered if Raigal was afraid of the storm, deep down, and hid that behind laughter and boisterous delight. She wasn't going to suggest that aloud. As for her, she was terrified, which was no shame. Everyone felt fear, sometimes over irrational things, and that was all right. Especially when you'd never seen anything like it before. But if you had pride you never, ever let your fear show.

"Back home we say storms are when the old gods fight to come back to the world," she yelled across the room. She was sitting with her back against the chest, just as Raigal had done earlier. "The thunder is the roar of their anger, and lightning is Anu driving them back."

"We say that back in Rheven!" Raigal shouted. "About the gods fighting, anyway. We don't believe in Anu."

"Yes you do," Calesh said. He was leaning against the wall, arms folded across his chest. "You just call him God, that's all. It's the same deity. All across the world, from the desert to your rain-soaked northern forests, Raigal, it's the same god. Different prophets and different doctrine, but underneath all the chants and incense and catechism, it's the same god. People just like to dress him up with frills and silly incantations, that's all."

Raigal frowned for a moment, then shrugged his massive shoulders. "I suppose it would be, at that. So much of the rest is the same, from one land to another. I should have thought of it before."

Farajalla studied her husband with some concern, though she didn't let him see it, or realise she was watching. Tension was in every line of him, from the crossed arms to his rigid stance, and his face was pale. She understood that, especially since she'd seen the house where he grew up. Calesh was a farmer's son, raised by war and then love to be something much more, with all the responsibilities that came with it. From his choices men lived or died. Sometimes she knew he felt the weight of that, as though he could sense the ghosts of long-dead soldiers watching him with judgement in their eyes.

He glanced back at her then, feeling her gaze on him after all. Suddenly he smiled, a bright flash in the gloom, and the tiny lines in his forehead smoothed over. "Lucky there's enough roof left to keep us dry, isn't it?"

"It will be luckier if there's any roof left at all by morning," she answered. "Does this sort of storm happen often here?"

"Only in spring and autumn," he said. "Summers are dry and calm, and winters are wet and calm. The weather hoards its malice in Sarténe."

"This is nothing," Raigal said again. "You've never seen a storm until you've been to Rheven."

Calesh rolled his eyes. "Oh, of course. And the summers are always balmy there, and the grass grows lush and green, and the women are all pleasingly plump with smiles like the breaking dawn. You know, I'd forgotten just how much you adore your homeland."

"You can laugh," Raigal said, "but I'm going to go back one day. I want to be buried on the bluffs over the cove where I grew up, so I can look west towards the Distant Isles, where the last sunlight falls at the end of every day. That's where my father's buried, up where the Wild Hunt never goes. I think I'd like to rest a while with him."

"The villagers had better start digging now then. The size you are, they'll have to hollow out half the bluff to fit you under it."

"Most of the folks are as big as I am," Raigal laughed. "They could dig out a hole for me between supper and sundown, and still have time for a dance." He poked his head out of the door again. "Hey, I think it's letting up. I can see stars away west now, anyway."

Farajalla managed not to sigh in relief. The conversation had eased some of the tightness in her husband, she could see that, and as a bonus the weather's malice had begun to fade. Thunder rolled once more, but this time further away, and there was no brilliant flash of lightning. Still, she needed something to distract her. "What's the Wild Hunt?"

"Old pagan belief," Calesh said. He craned his neck to see out of the door, his lips pursed.

Raigal shot him a scowl. "Mock if you must, Bullfrog. The Wild Hunt rides on winter nights," he said to Farajalla, "with the Queen of the Waste Lands at its head, and all her elves and dogs straggling out behind her. They hunt the winter god, and some night when snow is thick on the ground and trees crack in the cold they catch him and drag him down, and spatter his blood across the snow before they nail him to a tree to die."

"Who's the Queen of the Waste Lands?"

"The ruler of the elves," he said with a shudder. "She hates humans, you see. Once elves ruled the whole world, but then humans came with their buildings and roads, and drove the elves back into the shadows of the forests. We're too strong for her to destroy now, but she can kill our god and bring the winter, even if she can't hold back spring, and the god's rebirth. Some day we'll find ourselves facing the Hoar Rime, a time of ice and snow with no spring to follow, and cold so bitter that the breath freezes in your throat. Then the Queen will have won."

Farajalla stared at him.

"The All-Church adapted its teachings to popular traditions," Calesh said from the wall. He gave her a crooked smile. "Now you know where they got the idea for the death of the Adjai, the God-Son."

"That's a very… pessimistic belief," she said to Raigal Tai. "But I would never have believed that from it, in your cold and rain-swept land, your people might have created something of such poetry."

He shrugged, visibly embarrassed. "Ah, I can't tell it very well. Too long away, and I was never much of a bard in any case. When the real skalds tell their tales around a fire, you can feel the cracking of frost under your feet, and hear the barks and calls of the Wild Hunt in the dark."

"You're wrong," Farajalla said. "You tell it beautifully."

A log broke in the fire, and sparks went crackling into the smoke, where they died. Raigal grinned at her and turned quickly away, but not before she saw the redness creeping up his neck. It was odd to see him embarrassed, a huge man blushing like a child offered a compliment. She had no time to think about that though, because Raigal stiffened as his gaze went back to the doorway, and he reached behind him for his axe.

"Someone's coming up the road," he said. Farajalla had carried that axe into the windmill, struggling under its weight, but Raigal Tai lifted it as though it was a twig. "A soldier, I think. There are two horses, anyway, and one's laden with what looks like armour."

"In this weather?" Farajalla scrambled to her feet. There was a blade in one of her boots and another hidden in her sleeve, but she made no move to draw either. Most warriors here thought women posed no threat, which might be useful. "He must be crazed."

"Or desperate," Calesh said. He unfolded his arms, but didn't move from the wall. "If there's a packhorse it can't be one of the men, but whoever it is must have got past the sentries. I wonder, what fool would brave a storm to come to a nowhere little windmill?"

"Baruch?" Farajalla asked. Calesh smiled and nodded, utterly unconcerned. His earlier tension had blown away with the fading storm, replaced by a preternatural calm. Raigal frowned at him, then looked out into the rain again, and after a moment he burst into laughter.

"You're right!" He cupped hands to his mouth. "Hurry up, slow bones! There's a fire here to dry you!" He pulled out his cloak and began to wrap it around him, pulling the hood over his unruly hair.

"How did you know?" Farajalla asked her husband softly. "You didn't even bother to look."

"The All-Church doesn't know we're here," he answered. "Not yet. Certainly the priests haven't had time to send the Justified's expert killers after us, and even if they had the sentries would have sounded the alarm. They didn't, which leaves the only people who know to come to this windmill: Baruch and Luthien. It had to be one of them."

Raigal Tai plunged out into the rain. Moving across the room, Farajalla saw him seize the approaching man and lift him into the air, just as he'd lifted Calesh back at the harbour. It was too dark to make out details, and she wondered how Raigal had recognised him. Something in his movements, perhaps: his face was too shadowed for it to be anything else.

"God grant I am strong enough for this," Calesh said softly from the wall.

Farajalla studied him again. "For meeting an old friend?"

"Not that," he said. "For all of it. I keep thinking of a line in *The Unfurling of Spirit;* 'What is my strength, that I should hope?'"

She stood for a moment, and then walked over to take his chin in one hand. He made no move to stop her, his brown eyes steady on hers as she spoke. "You are strong enough for anything the God asks of you, Calesh. There's another quote; 'If you bring forth what is within, what you have will save you.' You can do anything you set yourself to do. You were not chosen at random. Do you think it was chance that led you to the fortress at Harenc?"

"I don't know," he said. "But whatever it was, I'm glad of it. It brought me to you. Can I have my chin back now?"

She let him go. "Just believe in yourself. I don't like it when you call yourself weak, even subtly like that. You're not. Remember it."

"As you say, my wife," he murmured.

A horse snorted outside. Farajalla turned to see Raigal leading both animals towards the back room, and then her view was blocked as a stocky man stepped into the windmill. One pace into the room his head turned towards Calesh, and he stopped. Water poured from his oiled cloak, and his boots squelched as he came to a halt. Dark eyes gleamed under heavy brows. There was a flash of white in his hair, above the lopped remains of his left ear.

"Why," Baruch Caraman asked, "did you have to pick such a godforsaken ruin for us to meet in?"

Calesh shrugged. "I'm awkward."

"Oh, I know that," the other man said. He stepped forward again, and suddenly he and Calesh were pounding each other on the back and laughing, hardly able to speak. She had never understood why men behaved like that. When two male friends met up there always seemed to be a great deal of hitting each other on the arm, or hugging one another as Raigal liked to do, often followed by too many glasses of beer and loud, lewd songs.

"You look well enough, anyway," Baruch said at length. He drew back to study Calesh, his eyes slightly narrowed. "I take it you've finally managed to get the sand out of your boots."

"You look well too," Calesh answered. "Life in the Hand still agrees with you, I see. Raigal says you made Commander."

"Someone thought I might be just competent enough to give orders." Baruch unclasped his sodden cloak and threw it over the remains of a hay bale. Underneath he wore travelling clothes of thick wool, stained and patched with wet where water had seeped through. "It's a shame we're not at Raigal's place. This deserves a glass or ten of ale. I'm sorry, was that funny?"

Farajalla swallowed another laugh. "No. I was... thinking about something else."

"My wife, Farajalla," Calesh said. "Fara, this is Baruch. The third of our old band from the east."

"It's a pleasure," she said.

"For me, too." Baruch took her hand and bowed over it. "Though I'm surprised you put up with this untutored yokel. Your voice has the sound of education to me, my lady."

"That's true," she admitted. "But I'm working on his education, and Calesh learned a lot in Harenc."

There was a pause.

"Harenc?" Baruch repeated. "I heard the city had fallen to the Madai, and been burned to ash."

"You heard right," Farajalla said quietly.

"That isn't the half of it," Raigal said as he hurried back inside. His cloak was already soaked. The thunder had passed, at least for now, but rain still fell in sheets. "Calesh has gone and brought all the –"

"Perhaps I might tell this," Calesh broke in. His voice was quiet, but the huge man stopped speaking. Calesh turned to Baruch, to find the stocky man watching him with a tiny smile on his lips.

"There are a lot of tents down in the valley," Baruch said. "You brought all the Hand back from Tura d'Madai, didn't you? This is about the All-Church army on the Rielle. God in Heaven, the rumours were right."

Calesh nodded. "Sit down, my friend, and we'll get you something to eat while you dry off. And then I'll explain."

Six

The Halls of Academe

It was a war waged between two mighty cultures, the strongest in the world in their day, which between them stretched from the Middle Sea to the distant east where the river Irates flows. Yet all the fighting took place in a small area of land controlled by neither. No major cities were sacked, no fields burned or temples looted. It was as if neither side truly wished to destroy the other.

Why, then, did they fight? And not only fight, but do so for twenty-six long years, with a savagery as great as anything in all the annals of warfare? The typical soldier is not a monster. He might go into battle because he has been ordered to do so, but if he shows such brutality as was commonplace in the Isthmus War, it is because his soul is filled to brimming with hatred. What lay behind that? What caused the men of each side to loathe the other with such passion?

The desk was cluttered with the debris of erudition: an inkpot bristling with quills, books open at pages marked with scraps of paper, and crumpled scrolls jostling for whatever space they could find. One rested partly over a bowl in which a few peanuts huddled. A lantern hung on a rafter above, adding its glow to the dreary morning light that slunk in through the window. The walls of the little room were jammed with books and scrolls, all of them copies, which was just as well. Most bore inky fingerprints on their creased pages, a legacy of their own time spent at the crowded desk.

The man seated there wore long green robes, and a round cap of the same colour. He took off his glasses and polished them with a piece of cloth, then pushed them back on his nose again. These days he had to squint to make out all but the largest letters unless he had his glasses. It was strange, because he could see something ten yards away perfectly well. He knew that for some people it was the other way around.

Perplexing. It was the sort of puzzle that had always intrigued him. Perhaps one of the physicians over at the medical school might be able to suggest an answer. Maybe if he went over and asked them to… no. He had to keep his mind on the task in hand.

Luthien read the passage through, frowned, and chewed absently at the end of the quill. He wasn't sure about *Twenty-six long years*; maybe he could drop *long* from that. A year was as long as it was, after all, and this was a history and not a romantic play. In the end he left it there. Otherwise he'd have to rewrite the whole of the second page.

"Before you write something down," he muttered, "make sure you want it in the text."

He dipped his quill, and wrote:

Documents recently found in the libraries of Caileve cast some light on these questions. Perhaps more important was the discovery of an original account of the first eleven years of the war, written by an under-marshal of the Ossanian army in the form of letters sent to his wife. They were found by the author, quite by accident, in the catacombs underneath Elorium, when he himself had cause to experience the brutality of war. It has been the work of four years to translate the letters, and they form the core of –

Someone rapped on the door and Luthien jerked in surprise. The last letter ended up with a squiggly tail where the quill had taken advantage of his twitch to wander across the page. He looked at it in dismay. Obviously he was going to have to rewrite the page anyway. It was enough to test the patience of even the most pious man. He very nearly swore.

At least he could get rid of that awkward *long* now.

"Come in!" he called.

The door opened and a young man poked his head into the room. He wore a fuzzy beard on the point of his chin, just a fluffy patch of dark hair really, in the current fashion among the Academy's students. The hair hanging past his collar was curled and dyed jet black, in the style of the nobles of Tura d'Madai. Another of today's fashions.

Luthien felt a surge of anger. The boy's beard was harmless enough, but not the hair. This youth had never even *seen* the Madai lords he imitated in battle array, and would probably wet himself if he did. Wearing his hair like that was an insult to the men who fought in that desert, and… and that was not, Luthien told himself, a thought worthy of an Elite.

"Yes?" he asked, keeping his voice level.

"Tutor Luthien," the lad said, "the Dean asked me to tell you there's a man at the main office, asking for you."

He frowned. He'd made sure to keep today free of appointments, so he could make the long-awaited start on his history of the Isthmus War. And it was days since Luthien had gone into Parrien; there was no need, when everything was close to his hand here at the Academy. "Who is he?"

"The Dean says he won't give his name," the student replied. "It's very odd. And he looks a bad sort, if you ask me."

"I'm sure Heaven trembles at your perception," Luthien said dryly, which was sarcastic but appropriate enough, under the circumstances. "All right, I'm on my way. You can go about your business."

In truth, Luthien thought as the youth ducked back out, this *was* odd. He couldn't remember the last time anyone had visited him at the Academy, apart from Baruch, and his face was known well enough. Even Raigal Tai didn't come up from the town very often. And the stranger had a disreputable look, if a young student's opinion could be trusted. Very peculiar. It was a long time since anything this curious had happened.

Luthien looked longingly at his book. He hadn't even finished the first page, and already he was called away.

He picked up his cloak and left the office, taking care to place his glasses in a clever little oblong box he'd had made for them. He never left them out, not when the nearest makes of spectacles was five hundred miles away in Tura d'Madai. He locked the door behind him too: there had been a distressing rash of thefts over the summer, and though the culprit had been caught and expelled, all the tutors locked their offices now. It was a pity, but with students now coming from all over the continent, he supposed it was inevitable. Men's spirits might belong to God, but their baser instincts came straight to them from the Adversary.

He walked along a narrow corridor and went down a flight of stairs, then through a side door and out into the May sunshine. Last night's storm had passed, leaving behind it a day cloudy and chill and sopping wet. There were times when Luthien almost wished he could go back to the desert.

Still, it was only a short walk to the main office, along a gravel path between two new, white stone lecture halls. Over a dozen of them had sprung up during the last three years, spreading up the hillside as ever more students came to the Academy from further and further away. Fifteen hundred students now, learning everything from history to philosophy to literature, and taking it all home with them when they passed their final assessments. They took a metal badge too, shaped in the likeness of an owl. The badges were made of tin, and all but worthless, but in Gallene and Alinaur and far-off Rheven men wore them with pride because of what they represented: *I am a scholar of the Parrien Academy.* Luthien had even seen nobles wearing them, pinned to their silk shirts and satin coats, as though the tin badge was worth as much as all their lineage.

A generation from now, one of the students would probably write a book that revolutionised the received wisdom about the Isthmus War, after which the name Luthien Bourrel would be a half-forgotten footnote in some bibliography, known only to the learned. That was all right. Education hadn't been his first calling, after all. If he managed to teach some bright young lad enough that the boy supplanted him, that would satisfy him. And if not, teaching was still better than hacking men to death in the desert. Even if it was sunnier there.

The main office was at the front of the old manor house, donated by the Margrave fifty years ago when the Academy was founded. Built long ago of the same white stone as the lecture halls, the manor had a grey and weary look now, raddled with ivy, and one of the chimneys hung precariously over the eaves. Luthien had meant to climb up there and dismantle it over the summer, before it collapsed on the head of an unfortunate student. He really ought to get around to that. Another storm like last night's might be one storm too many.

He pushed open the main door and went into the office.

It had been the Entrance Hall, when the manor still received noble visitors to masked balls and intimate dinners where plots were hatched and treacheries began. Desks lined the walls now, with a clerk seated at each one to record attendance and deal with enquiries, while benches were lined up in the middle of the room like swallows waiting for autumn. At the top of the sweeping staircase a large metal owl watched over proceedings with round eyes, its claws wrapped securely around the oak rail. The school's motto was carved on the wall over its glinting head: *Always seek the truth.*

The Dean stood near the far end of the hall, almost underneath the owl. He was tall and very thin, with a pinched face that narrowed to a sharp chin, and he looked morosely unhappy. That was usual with Cerain, though in fact he was very rarely glum. Give him two glasses of wine and he was likely to start singing the latest ballads. With him was a young lad, about sixteen years old, in clothes heavy with the dust of travel. Nearby a pair of the Academy's watchmen loitered, watching him from the tails of their eyes while they pretended to talk. It was a shame that such men were needed, but there was inevitably a call for them. Lately Parrien's adolescents had decided it was the height of humour to sneak into Academy grounds and throw rotten fruit at the buildings. It was very hard to teach while tomatoes splattered against the windows.

The young man bore a short sword at his hip. If he knew how to use it and intended to harm Luthien, the two watchmen would be of no use at all. Luthien smiled to himself and started towards them.

"Good afternoon, Dean," he said as he came up. "God has blessed us with a wonderful day."

"Yes, yes," Cerain said. "I'm sorry to drag you away from your history. Have you started writing yet?"

"I've finished almost a whole page," he said. "Hardly a work to make the titans of literature quail in their shoes. And now I understand this young man wishes to see me." He smiled at the youth. Now he saw him closer to, Luthien didn't think he knew how to use that sword at all, or was even used to wearing it. "I begin to think God doesn't desire me to finish my book."

"Japh more than wishes to see you," the Dean grumbled. Apparently he was morose after all. "He insisted. He said he would stand in the courtyard and shout until you spoke with him."

"It's important," the lad put in. "And urgent. I need to speak with you in private, sir, at once."

Luthien's eyebrows climbed. Obviously the boy had given his name after all, but that seemed to be the limit of his candour. "I'm sure you can say it here. Whatever it is."

"In private," Japh repeated. "Please. It truly is important."

"You have a sword," Luthien said mildly. "You might mean to use it, for all I know."

For answer, the boy unbuckled his belt, nearly dropped it, and laid the scabbard on a desk. The clerk behind it scowled and pushed it away from his ledgers with two careful fingers; and Cerain pursed his lips, not bothering to hide his disapproval.

"I don't have any hidden knives," Japh said. "And it wouldn't matter anyway, if half what I've heard about you is true, sir. You could stand me on my head and bounce me off the floor if you wanted to."

"Once I could have done," Luthien agreed. "Not now. I took an oath. I can use force in self defence, but no more than that. Who is the message from?"

"That's private too. I'm sorry." Japh pushed a hand through his matted hair. "Blood of the god, you're awkward. I don't know what to do. Stay here and bicker until we draw attention, or just give you the message and hope the wrong ears don't overhear it."

"Come with me," Luthien said. "We'll talk in private."

Surprise gave way to relief on Japh's face as Luthien led him towards a side door, watched by a scowling Cerain. Whatever the Dean thought, Luthien knew now there was no danger here, for the simplest of reasons.

Blood of the god. There was probably only one man who swore that way in all Sarténe, and he owned a neat little inn by the harbour in Parrien. Japh couldn't have picked up the oath except from Raigal Tai. And that meant he could be trusted. Luthien led him into a room stacked with old entrance papers and reports, closed the door, and turned to him.

"Very well," he said. "What's the message?"

Japh took a parchment from his pocket and handed it over. Luthien pushed his glasses onto his nose again, and as he read, his eyebrows climbed almost into his hair.

The sand scorpion has returned to Sarténe. Need your help. The windmill on the ridge. Vast importance.

Calesh was back. Luthien's heart was beating very fast. He made himself breathe deeply, fighting to stay calm.

You have always held my trust.

They had always held one another's trust, all four of them. Always, and without question, but Calesh most of all. Without him they would merely have been three men, good friends, comrades-in-arms who might meet from time to time and share fond memories as they grew older. With him they were brothers. With him, friendship became love. It had never been the same, since the three of them came home and Calesh did not.

"Is he well?" Luthien asked finally.

"As far as I could tell," Japh said.

"And his… wife?" Saying that felt odd, for some reason. Raigal was the only one of the four to have married before now. Luthien had sworn himself to God, and Baruch was too committed to the Hand of the Lord to have time for a wife, or to want one either. *I'm married to the Hand,* he sometimes said, rather coarsely. Still, for some men that was best. Wives did not always come between the friendships of men, but often they did, and they always changed them. How would this woman, whoever she was, change Calesh?

That brought on a thought, and his eyes narrowed behind his glasses. "His wife is Madai, isn't she?"

Japh nodded. "She's beautiful, too. I mean really gorgeous." He stopped suddenly, blushing. "Er, not that I… I mean… I wouldn't –"

"You'd better not," Luthien said absently. "Calesh really would pick you up and bounce you on your head, and then he'd get nasty." He read the letter again, trying to pick out a hint of its deeper meaning, but found nothing. Calesh was being extremely careful, as well he might be. It sounded to Luthien as though his friend had deserted his duty in the East.

This would not stay secret for long, however careful Calesh was. The Sarténi were proud of him: everyone knew the story of the death of Cammar a Amalik. He was one of the heroes of the war for Elorium, perhaps the best known soldier the Orders had ever produced. Troubadours sang of his deeds – mostly imagined or exaggerated – and artists painted frescoes of his battles, while children playing soldier games argued over whose turn it was to be Calesh Saissan. Luthien had seen that himself, each time with a faint thrill of shock. Whatever had happened, Calesh would have some explaining to do.

"Wait a moment," he said. "Wait just a moment. You know Raigal Tai, by the way you swear. Calesh came ashore in Parrien, then?"

Another nod. "Yes. Four days ago now."

"And he sent a letter to Baruch as well. Baruch Caraman."

"I know who you mean," Japh said. "I delivered that message two days ago, in Mayence."

"And Baruch will have gone," Luthien realised. He didn't need Japh's confirmation. "They're together again."

"Yes," Japh said, smiling now. He looked like a puppy, all wide eyes and wag-tailed eagerness to be off. "We can be well on our way to them before sundown. How soon can you be ready?"

"What?" Luthien came out of his reverie. He had been thinking the same, he realised, falling easily back into the patterns of thought that had become habit during those years in the desert. How quickly he could pack, how long the journey would take, all the necessary details of a life spent on various roads with a sword belted at his side. But that was over. He had sworn as much.

"I'm not going," he said, with some effort. *It has never been the same, since the three of us came home and Calesh did not.* He thrust the letter into Japh's hands. "Take this back. If I read it right, Calesh is tangled up in some sort of trouble, and that part of my life is over."

The youngster blinked. "But he needs you."

"To do what?" Luthien asked. "I could hold a service for him, I suppose, but I prefer to do that here. I'm a writer and teacher now, not a soldier any more. I'm sure Raigal told him that."

"He still needs you," Japh said stubbornly. "It's... look, it's important, Master Luthien. Really important."

"So you said." He peered at the lad over the top of his glasses. "What's he got himself tangled up in, then? It must be something big to bring him home, and in such secrecy, but nothing has happened in Tura d'Madai for –"

He broke off, realising. That wasn't the point, was it? Nothing that could have happened in Tura d'Madai would be enough to send Calesh scurrying for home... but something in Sarténe would. Luthien felt himself go cold. His hands clenched into fists at his sides.

"Oh, sweet God in Heaven," he said. "It's that army by the Rielle, isn't it? The rumours are true. It's coming here."

"We think so," Japh agreed. "Master Saissan is certain of it."

"And Calesh brought the whole army," Luthien said wonderingly. "The Lord Marshal will give him fits about that, and Calesh must realise it. He knows something. He must do."

The boy's lips writhed, as though he wanted to say more but knew he shouldn't. Youthful impulse won out in the end. "Someone inside the Basilica sent him a warning, just after the priest was murdered on the Ferry Road. That's why he came home."

Luthien's mind raced. A killing such as that could easily be used as an excuse for war. And the All-Church had been losing patience with the Dualism for several years, and with the Margrave too, who constantly promised to clamp down on the heretics and never quite did. Probably because he was one himself, though the Basilica didn't know that, and probably also because Riyand was an idiot. If there was a way to antagonise the All-Church Riyand would find it, sure as flowers in spring and rain in autumn.

At any rate, it was nothing unusual these days to go Crusading against unbelievers in other lands, the Jaidi in Alinaur, and Madai in their own desert homeland. People were used to the idea. Perhaps more importantly, the larger military Orders had no love for the Hand of the Lord, and the Justified hated Calesh personally. Given those two things, it might not be difficult for the All-Church to take the extra step of launching a Crusade against someone in more familiar lands, and persuade people to join it.

"There will be war, then," Luthien said at last. "Here in Sarténe."

Japh nodded. "Almost certainly." He shot a nervous glance towards the door. "Word of this can't get out, Master Luthien. Calesh doesn't want the All-Church to know he's back until the last possible moment. You must realise what they will do if they learn of it."

"I know exactly what they'll do." Assassins first of all, almost certainly Justified highbinders with bones sewn into the backs of their gloves. And if they failed a regiment might be ordered to track Calesh's in battle and cut him down, ignoring all other considerations until that was done. The All-Church could be unswervingly single-minded, and terrifying in its determination. Nothing less could have launched army after army across the sea to Tura d'Madai, in a steady stream for well over fifty years.

Well. War, then. Luthien remembered what it was like; the problem, usually, was how to forget. He drew a deep breath.

"Tell Calesh I wish him well," he said.

Japh stared at him in dismay. "You're not coming?"

"No." He needed another steadying breath, it seemed, and then a third. "I won't say I'm not tempted, lad, because I am. But not enough. I lived the life of a soldier, and found friendship and camaraderie there, but the price I paid was too high. It's too high for any man, if they could only realise it. No, Japh, I won't go. I will pray every day for God to smile on my friends, but I will not put on my armour again, for any reason at all."

The youth's head lifted. "You will not put it on? You still have your armour, don't you?"

"I have it," Luthien admitted. "It's yours if you want it, lad. You're about the same size as me."

"I don't want it," Japh said. "I want to know why you kept it, if you never plan to wear it again."

He opened his mouth to reply.

And had no words. There was no answer he could give, except the treacherous voice that sneaked around the back of his mind: *because I might need it again, after all.* He could not say that. He *would* not say that, or accept it as true. His days of dealing death were over: he had sworn so, with one hand on a copy of the Unfurling of Spirit and the other on a reliquary, the glory of God shining in his heart. He had never felt so whole as when he spoke those words, bound himself with that oath, and it was an vow he wouldn't break. He ought to have sold his armour long ago, or had it turned into tools and bracelets. He would not fight again.

"You don't know why," Japh said. The puppyish manner was gone, replaced by something harder and more stern. He seemed a good deal older than sixteen now. "And even not knowing, you'll let your friends face the coming dangers while you turn your face away."

"Don't lecture me on friendship, you little bastard," Luthien snapped, and then stopped in dismay. He hadn't sworn for three years, not once since he took the Consolation as an Elite, and now this lad had pushed him to it. A muscle in his cheek twitched.

"Why not?" Japh asked prosaically. "You seem to have forgotten what it means. Stay here then, and pray to God the All-Church doesn't notice you. I'm a weak reed next to Luthien Bourrel, but I'll stand where you should be and fight the best I can."

He turned and walked out of the room. Luthien stayed where he was, fingers curled into fists and the muscle in his cheek jumping madly. He tried to offer up a prayer, begging for guidance, but couldn't remember the words, or bring them to mind. Rage made his temples throb. How *dare* that young upstart accuse him of abandoning his friends? Japh hadn't been in Tura d'Madai, with arrows raining down on upraised shields and the Nazir screaming battle cries as they advanced across the burning rock. What did he know about standing by your friends when blood ran hot and every breath was a rasp in your throat?

Luthien remembered how it felt to have blood surge in his veins. To feel as though his skin was afire, every sense preternaturally sharp, as his blade fell and rose and fell again, ending lives. No enemy had ever got close enough to Luthien to wound him. They came, and they died, as quickly as he could say it. He had felt immortal, clothed in glory like God himself: until he took the Consolation, he had never felt so vibrantly alive. But it was an illusion. Where God gave life soldiers dealt only death. It was obscene. The thought of it revolted him.

The door opened again. Cerain came in and closed it behind him, looking at Luthien with shrewd eyes.

"The lad has a point," he said.

Luthien glowered at him. "I shouldn't be surprised that you listen at keyholes, Dean, but I am offended. That was a private discussion."

"It won't be for long," Cerain said. "The boy tried to be discreet, but he wasn't very good at it. If he wanted to keep his message quiet he shouldn't have walked straight up to the front desk. Half the students are talking about him already, Luthien. When the All-Church realises Calesh has returned, they'll soon learn that a message came here to you at about the same time." The thin man frowned. "In fact, I suspect they already know he's back. They have agents everywhere."

"I know," Luthien said. The same thought had occurred to him. Either the All-Church already knew Calesh was back, or else a pigeon was flying right now towards the Basilica with a message taped to its leg. Calesh was an idiot if he thought he could stay hidden for long.

"What do you think they'll do?"

"I have no idea," Luthien grated. "I am not a Cardinal."

"No," Cerain said, "but I'm beginning to think you're a fool. And don't dissemble, Luthien. You know exactly what the Basilica will do when they learn of this."

That was true, of course. The priests would call on their assassins, perhaps their own oft-denied corps of killers, perhaps Justified with bone gloves and iron hearts. And Calesh would not be the only target. His friends would be at risk too, and Luthien would have the choice of breaking his oath or dying. Very well then; he would die. He would not break that vow.

"There have been rumours for years that the All-Church would come for us," Cerain said after a moment. "Perhaps this time it will be the same. Lots of rumours, and then nothing happens."

Luthien doubted it. He thought it very unlikely that nothing would happen now, with a priest dead by the river and the Hand of the Lord home from Tura d'Madai. "Rumours are often wrong."

"But usually based on truth," the Dean countered. "Which is why the mere whisper that Calesh Saissan sent you a message will cause the Basilica to act. Do you really want to die here, Luthien?"

"I am ready for what God sends," he said.

Cerain snorted. "We're all ready, but that doesn't mean we go galloping to meet Him before we must."

"What do you want of me?" he demanded.

"I want you to live as the man you are," Cerain said placidly, "and that is not a historian, Luthien."

He turned and left, leaving Luthien to stare at the wall with unseeing eyes.

*

It took two days to reach the meeting place, most of it on the main east-west road up into the Aiguille. Further on the road ran into the Raima Mountains, then turned south into Alinaur where the last Tei-jo warriors held on in their high crags, defying the armies of the church to drive them out. Beyond even that it reached the sea, a narrow channel of turbulent water beyond which lay a sandy waste where the Jaidi still lived, men with curved swords and women in veils and felt slippers. Japh found that a thrilling thought. Perhaps he would go there one day, to lounge idly beside a spring and drink sour wine out of a worn skin, while beautiful desert ladies fed him dates and raisins.

For now, he had duller work to do. He left the road as it climbed into the Aiguille, and was promptly lost in the network of canyons and narrow valleys that tangled about one another between the rocky hills. And he couldn't even ask villagers for directions, since some of them would certainly be loyal to the All-Church, and would report it. So he spent most of the second day riding from one flyspeck village to another, searching for the one with a ruined windmill on the ridge above. Part of the trouble was that half the villages of the Aiguille might have been the one, and Japh couldn't tell for sure until he was very close. He came within fifty yards of three different windmills, in three narrow valleys, before each time he realised he'd gone wrong again.

It was strange, that he saw these hamlets as remote and provincial already. A week ago he wouldn't have thought so. But he had been to Mayence since then, with banners floating from its towers and men from all nations in its wide boulevards. He had watched the Guard change at the Margrave's palace, resplendent in coats of crimson and gold, and gaped at the dome of the Hall of Voices like the small-town lout he was. Such things left a mark. He would never be able to look at Parrien in the same way again.

He knew he'd found the right windmill when he saw that the ground around it had been chewed up by the movements of many men and horses, and found a forgotten tent peg next to the remains of a cook fire. But it was too late by then: the field was empty, the army gone.

Calesh had said it would be, if Japh took too long to return. He looked around in dismay, wondering what he was supposed to do now, and that was when he noticed a note pinned to the inside of the door.

Japh
We are going on. If Luthien is with you he'll know where. If not, go back to the inn and wait. Keep Kendra safe, and we will come to you, or send. Be wary.
C

He stuffed the paper into his pocket. There was no sense leaving it for someone else to find, though the note didn't actually reveal anything, even where the others were going. Japh knew that, actually: the Hidden House. But nobody went there without an invitation or a very good reason. Japh was wise enough not to consider trying.

He went to check the windmill's back room, where the horses had been kept. The spoor he found was a day old at least. For a moment he considered trying to follow the others, but he was a town boy, and what he didn't know about tracking would fill all the halls of the Academy. Besides, the thought of going to the Hidden House was more than slightly unsettling. He had heard stories about it all his life, but actually setting foot there would be a little like sticking a pin in an angel and finding it bled just like anyone else.

Back outside the windmill, he stopped and looked at his horse. Then he took the reins in one hand and began to walk. After five days of riding his tailbone ached; he thought he might have a blister back there. If he rode any more his arse would take on the shape of the saddle before he got back to *Kissing the Moon*. He'd never imagined, in all his dreams of adventure, that much of it would involve weary muscles and skin soaked from a night of rain.

That night he couldn't make a flame catch on wet kindling, and spent the darkness huddled in his cloak against the late spring cold.

Seven

Through the Hills

It was a betrayal. A breach of faith. Across eleven years and two continents, through war and peace, these three men had held true to each other. The fourth had not. Farajalla could see no other way to regard it.

Calesh could.

"Luthien has done what he feels he must," her husband said, when she spoke of it. "As we all have. Friendship is not friendship if one man is compelled. He's followed his soul, my dear."

She shook her head. "He should have come."

"He hasn't seen me for six years," Calesh noted mildly.

"Neither had Baruch or Raigal," she answered in a tart voice, "and they came. What's different for Luthien?"

"An oath." He smiled sadly. "He took the Consolation, and Luthien won't have done so lightly. He was always the most devout of us. And as we know, some oaths are more important than others."

"You don't blame him? You don't feel any anger at all?"

"Anger? No. Regret, perhaps." He fell silent, wearing the inward expression that meant he was thinking. Farajalla waited for him to speak again. When he did his tone was diffident, as he felt for the words he wanted. "You know how there are times when you know something is missing? You might not even know what it is, but you don't feel… right. Complete."

"Like a play," she said, "with one actor missing."

His face cleared. "Yes, exactly. Or a poet with no words to speak. I feel like that now, but it isn't the fault of the actor, or the words."

She understood, in a way, though it still seemed like a betrayal to her. A bond forged in blood and fire ought to be enough to bring any man back to his friends, no matter how much time had gone by since he saw them last. The ties between these four men, which she still didn't really comprehend, should have done so easily. Yet it seemed Luthien had chosen to stand aside and watch his brothers in arms go on alone. He would nurture his own soul while others were put in peril, and Farajalla could only think that if he held on that course, his soul would likely not be worth nurturing any more.

She let the matter drop though. If she saw Luthien in the future she would have hard words for him, but there were other things to occupy her thoughts in the meantime. Such as where they were going.

They rode through the high, rocky country of the Aiguille, halfway between the low hills of Sarténe and the mountains to the south. Farajalla could see them in the distance, touched near their crowns with white and wreathed in clouds that never fully cleared. The horses walked a crooked path between strewn boulders and gullies where hardy plants straggled, spots of green amid the thin, arid soil. The rain of three nights ago had been sucked in by earth parched for too long, leaving hardly a trickle behind.

But there was evidence of the work of water, if you knew what to look for. Those scattered boulders had been moved by floods, rushing down canyons in a frenzy of foam and scoured soil. The few streams meandered through beds of gravel, splitting into braided channels and then joining again, at the bottom of wide gorges with walls of sheer smooth stone. Farajalla had seen the same thing in Tura d'Madai. When rain did come here it came hard, and flowed off the exposed rock into the canyons where it quickly became a flood, strong enough to tear the stone itself. Half a day later it was gone, down into the gentle rivers of the lowlands, and the Aiguille began to thirst once more.

They watered the horses when they could, twice going down into a gully to do so. There was no point trying to hide evidence of their passing. There were only five horses now, the four riders and one animal for gear: the fifty-man escort had been left that morning at a Hand-owned estate near a sizeable village called Verfeil. The rest were scattered across half a dozen larger holdings, whose captains were doubtless all trying to cajole each other into giving them more help. The Hand of the Lord owned estates all over Sarténe, but the sudden presence of five thousand soldiers was straining even those resources.

Still, for once the soldiers could sleep in proper beds, or at least pallets, both of which were better than bed rolls on hard ground. Farms could always find work for idle hands, and besides that, it left hundreds of men to make sure no one trailed after the four riders to the Hidden House.

And besides *that,* not many men were allowed to lay eyes on the Hidden House, even among the Hand of the Lord.

It would be hard for a man to follow here anyway. The horses left little trace on the stony ground, and for long stretches there was nowhere for a stalker to hide when someone looked back, as Baruch especially sometimes did. The stocky man seemed edgy, which in turn began to make Farajalla nervous. Oblivious to it all, Raigal Tai rode with his hands loose on the reins, letting his enormous gelding pick its own path over the ground. Several times he sang in a strong deep voice that echoed off the rock walls, mournful ballads of his homeland, until Baruch told him testily to shut up.

"I already know that mist-wreathed trees are beautiful," he said. "I don't need to hear you wailing about it."

"Wailing?" Raigal grinned at him. "You want to hear wailing? Maybe you should ask Bullfrog to sing, then."

"What Bullfrog does isn't singing," Baruch said. "He makes a noise like a bag of tormented cats."

Calesh only chuckled in amusement. Men were strange. Doubt their honour or courage and they flared up like bonfires, but about minor matters they traded insults with smiles and laughter. Farajalla's back stiffened when they spoke like that to her man. They should not mock Calesh, no matter how trivial the words, or how easily he tolerated it. She would not permit them to. And yet she did, aware still of a bond between these men that she didn't share, and of which she could never be a part, love or no love.

On the morning of the fourth day from the windmill, the wind brought them the faint tang of the sea.

"Nearly there," Baruch said. He sat straighter in the saddle, brushing something from his horse's mane. Farajalla thought he was uneasy, and trying to conceal it.

"Up here?" she asked doubtfully. The wind twisted through the canyons with a low moaning sound. "The Hidden House is up here?"

"Not exactly," Raigal answered. "Blood of the god, it will be good to see trees again."

And that, Farajalla didn't understand at all. She turned to Calesh for answers. He was already looking at her, but he shook his head. "Wait until you see. I don't think I can do it justice with words."

They dismounted to guide the horses down a steep slope, made treacherous by loose rocks that slid and rattled under their feet. Another many-channelled stream ran along the canyon floor, twisting from one wall to the other, so as the party moved on they had to ford it over and again. None of the men got back in the saddle. Farajalla noted that and stayed afoot herself, studying the ground ahead for anything out of the ordinary. She saw nothing.

"Here," Baruch said. He turned his horses towards a gap in the cliff to his left. It was really little more than a crack, and the animals laid their ears back and stamped unhappily until Baruch stopped to stroke their noses and murmur softly into their ears. When they were calmer he went forward again, Raigal right behind him. Calesh touched Farajalla's hand.

"It will be all right," he said.

She smiled. "Of course it will. I am with you."

With that she led her horse into the crack. Two steps in the pale spring sunshine vanished, leaving her in shade so deep it was almost twilight. She glanced back, past Calesh behind her, to the sliver of sun at the entrance.

Then that too was gone, as the passage twisted to the right and narrowed still further. The party moved in single file, edging forward past outcroppings of jagged rock. Above them the cliffs hung towards one another, touching in places to shut out even the dim glimmers of the day. A bird cried somewhere ahead, the screech of a hunting raptor, harsh and bitter. Farajalla felt her heart flutter. They filed beneath a great boulder caught between the narrowing walls of the chasm, so low that Farajalla had to stoop to pass through. The horses ducked under docilely enough, Raigal's big mount almost on its knees. She thought that was odd.

On the far side her nose caught the scent of leaves and damp soil, which was *very* odd. Another turn, and suddenly the gorge opened out into a wide valley, and she stopped dead with her jaw hanging open.

She was standing at the edge of a forest. A track led away in front of her, vanishing into the gloom under trees packed tightly together, their feet lost in a riot of foliage. Low walls ran along both sides of the path, thick with the large blue flowers of hydrangeas, separating the track from the forest. Farajalla turned quickly to her right as movement caught her eye, and was just in time to see a young deer vanish into the undergrowth. Leaves swirled and stilled behind it. Somewhere ahead the bird cried again, and was silent.

"It isn't possible," she said, disbelieving. "I don't… where are we?"

"On the trail that leads to the Hidden House," Calesh said behind her. "It's about a mile from here."

"The Aiguille is full of little enclosed valleys like this," Baruch began, and was interrupted at once.

"Not like this," Raigal said. "The vale of the Hidden House is almost impossible to reach except by this gorge. The slope of these hills," he gestured to either side, "is too steep. Virtually a cliff."

"Even so," Baruch glared at the big man, "even so, it isn't so unusual to step from the dry rock of the Aiguille straight into a lush valley. And it helps the Hidden House stay out of sight."

"It would," Farajalla admitted. "But surely there's always the risk that someone will wander by. Pure chance would seem to say that."

"Why do you think the Hand bought those estates back in Verfeil?" Calesh asked. "If we'd been untrustworthy, we would never have been allowed through. Other farms block the approaches from north and south. We're known," he added when she gave him a quizzical look. "Two of those estates are run by men we served with in Tura d'Madai."

"And it wouldn't matter if they weren't," Raigal said. "We've been here before. The villagers would remember us."

"Let's hope the Lady does," Baruch muttered. He twisted the reins in his hands. "She doesn't like uninvited visitors."

"We weren't invited," she pointed out.

"No," Raigal said, which was not at all reassuring. "But we're friends. The Lady knows that."

"More than friends," Calesh said. "We're the last, best hope of the Duality. All the things Ailiss has dreamed of doing depend on us. Do you really think she'll turn us away?"

"She might not know why you've come back," Baruch said.

Calesh smiled gently. "Of course she knows. She knew where to find the Book of Breathing, didn't she?"

Farajalla looked from the other two men to her husband. "The Book of Breathing?"

"I'll tell you as we ride," Calesh said.

*

The track was narrow to begin with, and drew in even tighter as it wound through the forest. Trees pressed close against the low walls on either side, their branches reaching towards each other overhead, shutting out much of the sunshine. Bit by bit the hydrangeas gave way to gnarled clumps of brambles, and the grass underfoot was replaced by skulking weeds. Above, branches met and tangled, and the path fell into shadow.

"The four of us first met here," Calesh began. He had reined close to her, so his leg brushed hers now and then as they rode. "Luthien, Baruch, Raigal and me. We were half-trained recruits, each of us taking instruction at a different estate. Four youths among many, getting ready to sail away to war and not sure whether to be excited or afraid. And then we were summoned to the Hidden House, suddenly and in total secrecy."

"I was frightened out of my wits," Raigal Tai said quietly.

The hunting bird cried again, somewhere deep within the forest. Farajalla thought it was a hawk of some kind, or a falcon, stooping to pluck its prey from the ground.

"The Lady spoke to us," Calesh said quietly. "She said there was a part of the Dualist holy writings, an introduction to the *Unfurling of Spirit*, that had been lost centuries ago, when the Madai first came out of their deserts and kingdoms fell to them. Among all our holy writings – or anyone's, for that matter – it's the only script left that was written by a man who actually knew Adjai, the All-Church's saviour. And it had been lost for years."

"But she said it was in Elorium," Baruch put in. "In the old tunnels where sewers had once run, a thousand years before the history of our time began."

"How could she know that?" Farajalla asked.

Baruch made a weird coughing sound, almost a laugh. "That's the question, right enough. How could she?"

"Magic," Raigal Tai put in, nodding his great head. "The people of the old world mastered secrets we've forgotten even exist. The Gondoliers sailed across all the seas, but we know almost nothing of them, not even where they lived. And back home in Rheven we say that our forefathers won the land when they drove out a race of men who birthed their children under mounds in the forest, and could call shapes of the night to fight for them in battle."

"Your people aren't so wise," Baruch said. "They still nail horseshoes over the door to keep the luck in."

"Would you both please shut up?" Calesh demanded. "I don't understand how the Lady knew, Fara, but she did. When we reached Elorium we looked in the sewers right where she had said, by the wall to the south of the Valley Gate. They were clogged with refuse, years' worth of it just thrown in there, and we had to do a lot of digging, but we did it. We found the Book of Breathing almost under the wall, wrapped in a dirty cloth that had mostly disintegrated. But the book was intact. As she said it would be."

"Magic," Raigal Tai said again.

There was no sound, save for his voice, but the clopping of the horses' hooves. The hunting bird Farajalla had heard earlier was silent, and any deer nearby stood still and waited for them to pass. She couldn't see any. In fact she couldn't see anything, no animals at all, and that made her skin prickle. Tura d'Madai had few forests, but those she'd seen were rich with life, crawling with it day and night and in any weather. This one was fecund, she could see that by the riot of greenery, but it seemed almost empty apart from the plants.

"You never told me this," Farajalla said at length.

Calesh turned a little to look at her. "I know. It seemed... sacred. Among us all only Luthien even had the nerve to open it and read, let alone talk about it afterwards."

"It was a dilemma for the little man," Baruch said. He sounded amused. "On the one hand his piety, on the other his thirst to learn. He couldn't help himself in the end, but I bet he prayed for forgiveness for *weeks*."

"None of us wanted to think of it too much," Raigal added.

Farajalla nodded, accepting that. "And the Book?"

"Luthien brought it back to Sarténe," he told her. "He wrote me a letter in Tura d'Madai to say he'd delivered it safely. And that was the end of it."

"Was it?" she asked. "I wonder. Why did she choose the four of you, when there were surely older, more capable men? Why you?"

Calesh turned in his saddle again, frowning slightly. She could usually see him following the track of her thought, on the occasions when he didn't get there before her, and took pleasure in it. She liked to be reminded that her husband was a clever man. This time, though, she didn't care for the expression she saw in his face. Calesh was disquieted by the idea she had planted in him. Either he had never considered it before – unlikely, with such a clever man – or else he had simply preferred not to think of it. She had made him do so now. She reached over to touch his hand, but the frown cleared only a little.

The darkness grew heavier. Now the track was barely wide enough for two horses to move side by side, and brambles spilled down from the walls like falling rain. Here and there a ragged blue hydrangea still peeked defiantly. Beyond the wall the trees seemed stumpy and twisted, their bark green and grey with damp moss. Every time Farajalla moved her head she thought she saw something from the tail of her eye, a movement or a shape watching from the forest, but when she looked back there was never anything there. After a while she stopped trying, and kept her gaze fixed firmly ahead.

And then the track turned again, the branches overhead drew away and the brambles slunk back over the wall, and light began to reach the ground. A few yards ahead the path opened up into a meadow. As they rode out of the trees Farajalla turned to look back, hardly able to believe the suddenness of the transformation. From outside the forest looked normal, a huddle of trees with shrubs and nettles swarming around their feet, innocent as a picture. She frowned, not trusting that image at all.

Raigal let out a soft sigh.

The Hidden House sprawled along one whole side of the field, beyond a broad sweep of packed red rose bushes backed by a low, spiny hedge. It looked to have been built in stages, perhaps widely spaced, to judge by the style of different sections.

The centre of the mansion was all square doorways of grey stone, fronted by a pillared portico atop pale steps. To the right it became more baroque, with three small towers and one spire topped with a tulip dome in the Jaidi style. Several moss-covered arches led into what Farajalla thought might be enclosed courtyards, behind walls pierced with high narrow windows set into yellow stone. On the left several low brick structures stretched towards the encircling forest, and beyond them were walls that certainly shut in courtyards. Almost all the house was patched and hung with ivy, even the grey-tiled roofs. The impression was one of great age, and Farajalla wondered suddenly how many of the rooms within were occupied now only by memories, drifting like ghosts while the house waited for new occupants, and new stories to begin.

Well, one was beginning now. She turned to the three men. "Do you plan to sit your saddles and stare at it all day?"

They looked at her, and then at each other.

"Eleven years," Raigal said. "Since we first came here. Did you ever think we'd live so long?"

"I thought we'd live forever," Calesh said. "That's how young I was. How young we all were."

Baruch nodded, a smile flickering about his lips. "Warfare has a way of burning youth away. So does the desert, come to that. We're not the same men we were back then."

"Back then we weren't really men," Calesh said. "Just boys who thought they knew everything. As boys do."

Raigal grinned. "And then Luthien showed us what it's like to know everything, didn't he?"

"What are you all chattering about?" Farajalla demanded.

They looked at her again, and after a moment Calesh smiled. "Just reminiscing," he said. "The way men do. Shall we go?"

She studied him, then nodded her head. There was a thread of tension in his tone that spoke of something more than mere reminiscence, but she knew he would keep no secrets from her, even though he hadn't told her of the book they'd found under the walls of Elorium. He'd had a trust to keep, where that was concerned. She had always put her faith in him, and there was no reason not to now. She turned her horse with her knees and started towards the Hidden House, the others trailing behind her as she went.

There were guards at the doors, she saw as she drew closer. Men of the Hand, one balding and the other running to fat, both of them grizzled with years. Calesh had once told her that such men were dangerous, because anyone who'd stayed alive long enough to grow old in uniform must be as sneaky as a rat in a grain barn. These two men watched the new arrivals with narrow, appraising eyes, and in that moment Farajalla believed it.

An inscription was carved into the stone above the doors, in an elaborate flowing script Farajalla didn't recognise. She had been recognising similarities to her home ever since she stepped off the ship at Parrien, but here too much was strange, and it made her uncomfortable. For the first time this foreign land of her husband's felt alien to her. She was adrift, grasping for something to cling to before the currents swept her away.

She glanced at Calesh, to find him looking at her as though waiting for that. He knew how this made her feel, somehow; knew and understood. It was unusual in a man. Something to be treasured. Farajalla smiled, and in response his whole face seemed to glow.

"Marshal Saissan," the balding soldier said as the party swung out of their saddles. He spoke with a lisp that made his voice very soft. "Be welcome. We have been expecting you."

Farajalla frowned at him. "You knew we were coming? How? And when did you find out?"

"Word reached the Lady some time ago that a message had been sent to the Hand of the Lord in Tura d'Madai," the man said. "She was given the same information, you understand, and from the same source." He gave Calesh a slight bow. "I'm pleased to see you here, sir, though in honesty I never thought you would return to Sarténe."

"Neither did I," Calesh said. "It's good to see you too, soldier. This is my wife, Farajalla, if you don't already know."

The armsman bowed again. "I do know, but that in no way diminishes the honour, my lady." His gaze shifted to the other two men. "Masters Tai and Caraman, be welcome. The Lady was almost certain you would come. I'm very glad to see she was right."

"She usually is," Baruch murmured.

Raigal Tai was leaning forward as though pulled by the nose. "Is that cooking I smell? I could eat a whole boar."

"Some things never change," the plump soldier said with a chuckle. Given his girth, he had no right to mock. "Go on in, all of you. You're expected. Others will tend to your horses."

Farajalla followed her husband under the arched doorway, flanked on either side by fluted pillars, and into a broad tiled hall. A vaulted ceiling curved over their heads. Four doors studded the walls, and to the right a staircase ran up to a balcony that covered the far end. A white-robed figure was walking across the floor with his hands hidden in the broad sleeves, a man of average build, and not especially tall. His dark hair was liberally shot through with grey. Farajalla thought he might be fifty, perhaps a little more.

"Gaudin," Calesh said, sounding surprised. "My blood and bones, you haven't aged a day in ten years."

"I am blessed with good fortune," the robed man replied solemnly. "As you are blessed with a good memory, it seems, to remember my name for so long after one brief meeting." He looked Calesh up and down. "You look the same as well. Despite all the great things you have done."

"Great things?" Baruch repeated. "Stop it before his head starts to swell. I can tell you a few things he'd rather keep secret, if you like."

"Now, look," Calesh began.

"Good idea," Raigal interrupted. "We could start with that time he stabbed himself in the leg when we were training. Do you think that would make an impression?"

"It did on me," Baruch conceded. "I wouldn't go within twenty yards of him for a week in case he chopped my fingers off."

"Thanks a lot," Calesh said. "A fat lot of help you two are."

They were joking in the slightly brittle way men do when they are trying not to think of something, but Farajalla couldn't help chuckling. "Did you really stab your own leg?"

"Unfortunately yes," Calesh said. He tugged at his breeches to reveal one shin. "There's the scar, see?"

"I can't imagine why he never told you before," Baruch said innocently, and Raigal Tai roared laughter and slapped the other man on the back, making him stagger. Farajalla *still* didn't understand why men had to hit each other all the time to show what good friends they were.

"Perhaps he can tell me the details another time," Farajalla said. "But for now, I'd like to be shown to our rooms. I need to bathe quite badly. Gaudin, would you be so kind?"

"Of course," the white-robed man said. "Your baggage will be brought to you. The Lady Ailiss will see you tomorrow, when you have rested."

That stilled the jocularity in the men, all of them at once. They exchanged quick glances, which if Farajalla was any judge contained a hint of unease. By then Gaudin had turned and started towards the broad stairway, and it was Farajalla who was first to set off after him.

He led them up the stairs, while a knot of white-robed servants in one doorway turned like marionettes to watch them pass. Then they turned left along the balcony and into a corridor lined with paintings and tapestries. The passage was too narrow for a viewer to stand back and gain proper perspective, so Farajalla saw them only in glimpses, illuminated by the light that filtered through high windows to one side. Even that was enough to tell her the artwork was exquisite, all of it, from the delicately embroidered hangings to the patient strokes of a brush against canvas. She had seen enough of art in Harenc, backwater thought it was, to recognise real quality when she saw it.

One tapestry brought her memories back more abruptly, a work bordered with interlocking gold palm fronds the size of her finger. It was a detail that had been fashionable in Harenc a century ago. Farajalla felt a sudden ache of homesickness and shook it away. Harenc was gone. She would gain nothing by longing for what she could never have.

Several of the paintings wore faded colours, a legacy of long years exposed to the sun. They must have been brought to the Hidden House from less careful owners elsewhere, rescued from pillage perhaps, or purchased and wrapped for transport by clumsy hands. Here they were treasured, and the corridor was full of the faint scents of ancient paint and worn thread.

The party climbed a short flight of stone steps, walked a little way, and went down another stairway on which Raigal missed his footing. He stumbled, almost fell, and then caught himself by snatching a grip on one of the overhead beams. If he had tumbled he would have landed right on top of Farajalla, and likely suffocated her. He gave her a sheepish grin.

A little further on the corridor walls changed from stone to brick, and then they emerged into an atrium shadowed by an overhanging roof that ran all the way around. Bushes and shrubs grew so thickly that it was impossible to see more than fifteen feet, or to pick out the scattered birds that sang to welcome the visitors. Three gravel paths twisted away into the foliage and were lost from view. Water burbled quietly, out of sight.

"This is beautiful," Farajalla said. Across the atrium she could see the far roof, a good eighty yards away. "The house looked this big, but I never thought it might contain gardens like this."

"The Hidden House is as big as it is," Gaudin replied enigmatically. "Your chambers are here." He indicated doors to their left, along a paved walkway that circled the garden. "If you wish something, pull the bell cord. One of the servants will come to you."

"Tomorrow may be too long to wait to see the Lady," Calesh said. His tone was soft, but there was a firmness to the words which brought Farajalla's head around. "The matter is urgent, Gaudin."

"It nearly always is," the servant replied, unperturbed. "Only urgency brings people to the Hidden House, or earns them licence to enter. The Lady knows you are here, and why. She will send for you when she is ready. You have been here before, Master Saissan. You know this is true."

He nodded. "I do. But still, it *is* urgent."

"I will tell her," Gaudin said. He bowed slightly once more, then turned and vanished back towards the corridor, hidden by a leaning shrub even before he reached the doorway. Farajalla took a half-step towards the garden, tempted to find the source of that murmur of water and dangle her feet in it until the ache went away. Her shoes crunched on gravel as she stopped.

"A bath's what I need," she said, and went to the nearest of the doors along the side of the atrium. She pushed it open and stepped into a small reception room, furnished with two armchairs and a divan set around a low table on which covered dishes and jugs waited. She smelled beef and spiced wine, and her stomach rumbled. Another pair of doors opened to her left and straight ahead, presumably leading to the bedchamber and bathroom. She found herself smiling. This was more comfort than she'd enjoyed since she left home.

She could hear Calesh talking outside, but she ignored him and went to the left hand door. Beyond it was a bathroom with blue and white tiles, and a mosaic of a leaping dolphin across one wall. Someone had already filled the tub and sprinkled rose petals over the steaming water. Four people could easily have shared the tub without touching each other.

"My heart and eyes, but I'm tired," Calesh said behind her. He put his bundles down with a clatter of metal and flopped into one of the chairs, rubbing his face with one hand. "I was all right until we came into the Hall, and now I can hardly make myself breathe."

"You've begun to relax," she said. She went back to him and knelt to pull his boots off, studying him with some concern. Calesh was fading into somnolence almost as she watched. "You haven't had the chance to put down your burdens since we set sail from Jedat, two months ago. But you can't sleep until you've bathed, husband. You smell like an old shed."

"Probably true," he conceded. He pushed himself upright and stretched wearily. "A bath first, and then a quick snack before bed. I've never needed a bed more in my life."

A few moments later they were sprawled in the hot water. Calesh soaped himself listlessly and then leaned back against the side with his eyes closed, too tired even to watch her through half-closed lids as he usually did. Almost at once his breathing slowed. Farajalla pulled herself over beside him. Her muscles loosened and eased in the water, but her concern didn't recede.

He was a hard man, this husband of hers. The scars he bore were testament to that. There was a broad white mark on his left forearm, where a badly made shield ring had chafed again and again before he could repair it. A thick thread of warped skin ran over one collarbone, and there was a star-shaped white mark on his left bicep where a knife had gone through the flesh. A myriad of other nicks and scrapes were scattered across his body, too small to be worth comment but easy enough to notice in bed, or in the bath with him. And there was the ugly gnarl just above his right knee, of course, where the assassin's crossbow bolt had poked its nose out after tearing through the flesh. Such things were the marks of fighting men, and part of the life they all lived. But most of Calesh's hardness was inside, in the heart and courage he carried. She knew well that nothing daunted him, or made him turn aside even if it did. Her father had seen it too, immediately, with the precise perception that was so much part of him.

"What manner of man can drive himself so?," Sevrey had asked, watching Calesh change horses and prepare to ride straight back out again, dusty and blood-smeared as he was. His tabard hung in tatters on one side. "Does he never sleep? Or rest at all?"

He did, of course, but not until what needed to be done, had been done. He made a judgement in his own mind and acted on it, without regard for the favour of his peers or the dangers that might come from the choice. Exactly the kind of man the stories said a woman was always meant to marry, and who they very seldom did, because such men were not easy to find. Farajalla sometimes half-believed that he could write a treatise on the art of command while battling three hostile soldiers with his other hand.

So why was he overcome by weariness now, when she and the other two men were not? All of them had been on the road for several days, but while that was arduous, it wasn't killingly tough. During the hurried departure from Tura d'Madai she and Calesh had faced hardships just as strenuous. He'd come through those tired but unbowed, so why now this torpor, at the first mention of a warm bath and a warmer bed?

"Calesh," she said. He didn't stir, so she put a hand on his shoulder and shook him gently. "Husband."

He lifted heavy eyelids. "What?"

"Go to bed." She wanted to breathe on his throat, stroke the inside of his thigh with her fingertips, the way he liked her to touch him. For days she'd been looking forward to the chance to rumple the bed linen; ever since they left *Kissing the Moon*, in fact. Frustration settled in a sour ball behind her heart. "You're not in any condition to do anything, even eat. Get some rest."

He pushed himself higher in the water with a sigh. "Maybe you're right." There was no sparkle in his eyes: he might have been asleep already. "I must be more tired than I thought. The stress of coming home, probably, and seeing my friends again."

She hid her concern behind a nod. "Whatever it is, you need to sleep. Dry yourself off and go to bed."

He nodded and hauled himself out of the bath. He didn't even kiss her, which was more than merely unusual. Farajalla watched him towel his hair, then pad noiselessly back into the receiving room. The door opened and closed again, and there was silence.

She rested her back against the side of the bath with a frown. Something was wrong here, beyond her ability to identify. Calesh had always spoken of the Hidden House as a haven, the spiritual home of his people and his own soul, but Farajalla couldn't rid herself of a sense of unease.

Eight

Custodian

"What do you think?" Raigal asked.

"About what?"

"Calesh," Raigal said, and then added, "Both of them." He paused for a moment, thinking. "All of it. The army by the Rielle, and being here at the Hidden House again. Everything."

"There hasn't been much time for thinking," Baruch said. His back was to Raigal, so his friend's expression showed only when he caught a glimpse in the mirror above the sink. Baruch laid his razor down and surveyed his chin critically. "I swear my beard's getting thicker, and coarser too. How can that be, when my hairline is receding every year?"

"Sunlight," Raigal said. When Baruch turned to face him he shrugged. "Sunlight falls on the top of your head, right? Not so much on your chin. Sunshine makes you go bald."

"That doesn't make any sense."

Another shrug. "It's what my dad told me."

"But then women would go bald as well," Baruch said. "And horses and dogs too, for that matter."

"I only told you what my dad said. Back home we rub squirrel droppings in our hair to make it grow back."

Baruch made a face. "That's disgusting."

"Well," Raigal said, "we're still half barbarian, remember? We worship God the same as you do, but we also rub bear grease in our skin to keep out the cold. And in Sarténe you can't even *buy* bear grease. Now stop changing the subject. What do you think?"

"I think we can talk about this over a bottle of wine," Baruch said. "Let's go make ourselves comfortable."

Presently the two men were seated in the receiving room, Baruch in a chair and Raigal sprawled hugely over the whole of the divan. The big man piled a plate with cold cuts of meat and fruit, and used the wine to wash down great bites without seeming to chew. He always ate as though afraid tomorrow would bring a famine. The way he went at food, it probably would.

Baruch drained half his glass, a good dry white wine from the vineyards east of Parrien, and leaned forward to refill it. "Ah, that's better. I ache in places I'd forgotten I had muscles."

"Mmph," Raigal said around a mouthful of beef.

"I'll tell you what I think," Baruch said. He reached down to adjust the cushion and then relaxed into his chair. "I think we're in the middle of something very ugly indeed. I think that army by the Rielle is going to come at us as soon as the spring rains are over, which they pretty much already are. And I think the All-Church will know everything we do as soon as we do it. I could name you two dozen of the Basilica's informants in Mayence alone, and for each one I know of you can bet I missed three. If something important happens here they know it in less than two days."

"Calesh hasn't been near Mayence," Raigal said.

"Parrien was enough, believe me. How often were our patrols ambushed in Tura d'Madai? Sometimes it seemed every bush hid a shepherd ready to run tell the warriors where we were – and that was if the bush didn't hide an assassin with a slingshot or a bow. Any time we went more than ten miles from the barracks we were in trouble."

"That's true," the big man agreed. "We used to ride hell for leather from one fort to another, or else find fifty bowmen shooting at us from the rocks. Always annoyed me no end."

It had more than annoyed Baruch. The Madai didn't fight the way soldiers and knights did in Gallene or Rheven. Here, two armies manoeuvred their way towards each other, found a flattish area, and went at it until one side or the other broke and ran away. Only cowards fled in the face of a charge, or hid behind makeshift barricades when the numbers were close to even.

The desert warriors wouldn't fight like that unless they were certain they were going to win. Faced with a bigger force, or better trained soldiers, they melted into the sand and rock and waited for another day. They never came to battle at all without preparing an escape route first, into rocky hills or the sand-blown deserts where only they knew the trails. Between times they popped up sporadically to rain arrows down on unprepared men and then scatter. That was dishonourable behaviour, according to the Crusade's commanders. Decent men ought to stand and fight, shoulder to shoulder and facing the foe.

It had been Luthien, inevitably, who pointed out the flaw in that claim. What was honourable behaviour to the Crusaders was plain foolishness to the Madai. They had their own ways, born out of their own culture and way of life, of which their style of warfare was only one facet. This was the open desert, not the rain-drenched fields of Gallene or Rheven, where room to manoeuvre was limited and tactics had evolved differently. The All-Church army couldn't expect their enemies to change those tactics for their convenience. To win, it was the Crusade which would have to change.

Slowly, the commanders came to agree. It took time, and there were still some who refused to adapt, but since those men tended not to live very long their stubbornness hardly mattered. Soon patrols began to take with them a contingent of mounted archers, ready to cover a retreat or answer a sudden volley of fire. Infantry abandoned their steel armour and replaced it with toughened leather, which allowed them to move more quickly away from an exposed position. Foot and horse troops alike learned to move in looser formations, offering a dispersed target to bowmen while still being close enough to support one another. It was a strange way to fight, but when the old approach no longer worked, the only way to survive was to develop a new one.

The changes had helped, but probably not enough, in the long run. Even today, if Baruch could believe what he heard, the Crusade army was restricted to the captured cities and a handful of forts, and a few miles of land around them. Go outside those areas and you were not very likely to come back, unless you went in numbers. Or could run very fast. Perhaps a goatherd would catch sight of the patrol, or a passing merchant would smile and nod as he passed and then hurry to tell the nearest warrior that the hated invaders had emerged again. The nearest warrior was never very far away. And the devil of it was that while the soldiers never knew *who* was an informer, or a warrior, they could be almost certain that someone nearby would be.

The army by the Rielle had been intended to change things, enable the All-Church's soldiers to push out from its bases for the first time in years. Instead it would come west, into Sarténe, and the mere rumour of that had brought Calesh home with all the Hand of the Lord, perhaps a tithe of the total strength of the Crusade in Tura d'Madai. Baruch didn't like to think of how the men who remained must be struggling now.

"The Basilica will know Calesh is here very soon," he said, shaking the thought away. "They'll also know he left Tura d'Madai with all five thousand men of the Hand who were still there. The other Orders will have sent messages while our men were still loading cargo at the docks. And since there's only one reason for them all to have come home, my large and extremely hungry friend, the All-Church won't need long to find them here."

"What do you think they'll do? Send assassins?"

"Almost certainly. As a first move." He chewed his lip. "I can't help wondering about that priest who was murdered three months ago. Rabast, his name was. He was sent to gather information on what the Basilica calls heresy. The Dualism, Raigal. Everywhere you look in Sarténe there are round temples and Elite in dark green robes. Most of the churches are empty, and so are the collection plates. All this has happened right under the nose of the Margrave, and dear old Riyand hasn't done a thing to stop it, which is bad enough. But then the killer, whoever he was, made the crassly stupid decision to name the Margrave to his victim, and was overheard. So now the All-Church has an excuse to bring Riyand to book."

"What's your point?" Raigal asked. He took another slice of beef.

"I met Rabast when he came to Mayence," Baruch said. "I was on duty when he spoke with the Margrave one time, and a more arrogant and supercilious priest would be very hard to find. So my point is: why send him, of all people? Why pick the most unsuitable emissary imaginable to conduct the most delicate negotiation the Basilica has faced in years?"

The big northerner stared at him. "You think they did it deliberately? They provoked Riyand into murder?"

"I think it's possible. God knows Riyand is easily fool enough to fall for it." Baruch pushed his plate away with a sigh. "I wish his father had lived. There was a man with guile."

"His brother was all right too," Raigal put in. "Bohend. He wasn't the match of his father, but still, he was no idiot."

"I can't think of many men," Baruch said, "who were the match of the old Margrave. Not many at all."

"All right," Raigal said, after a brief silence. "We're in trouble, then. We've been in trouble before."

"So we have. But you asked what I think, my friend, and I'm telling you." Baruch poured himself another glass of wine. "I think we need every one of those men Calesh brought back, and as many again, and it will still probably not be enough."

"Ah," Raigal said around a mouthful of turnip, "but you and I are here, and Calesh too. We showed the Madai how to fight, didn't we?"

"We did. And won a few acres of dust for our trouble, only to lose most of it again the moment we turned our backs." He stared morosely into his glass. "We could really use Luthien's help."

Raigal smiled. "What do you think? That he'll abandon the oath he swore when the need is great enough?"

"No," Baruch admitted heavily. "No, I don't."

"But you and I will stay with Calesh no matter what," Raigal said. "For friendship. For the first time we were here, in the Hidden House, and for everything that's happened since."

"And by God, a lot has happened," Baruch said. "You know, I envy you. You've a wife, and a business of your own, and a son to pass it to when you die. I've never seemed to find the time for that."

"You still have time. You're only thirty."

"I'm married to the Hand," he said, and then suddenly he was too weary to argue it. "Oh, maybe you're right. Perhaps in five years I'll be dandling children on my knee."

"I'm damned sure I will be," the big man said. "Though I'd have preferred never to go into battle to defend my boy. I did my fighting so I could gather enough plunder to start my inn. When I came home I thought I was done with it, except for telling my stories by the fire." He settled back on the divan with a grunt. "You're right about Luthien, you know. We could really use his help. Can you believe he took the Consolation?"

Baruch could, actually. Luthien had been a scholarly, devout man even before the Crusade left for Tura d'Madai, always eager to bury his nose in some barely comprehensible treatise on apologetics, and prone when he did so to forget about basic things like dinner. The difficult thing was always to reconcile that bookish man with the Luthien they lived and laughed with, a wine glass in one hand and a thick cut of mutton in the other. It was the latter who became a cold-eyed killer on the battlefield, the most brilliant swordsman Baruch had ever seen. He was surprised when someone told him Luthien was Elite, but only for a moment. Once he thought about it, he found it made perfect sense.

The strange thing was that none of the other three had really changed. Oh, Calesh and Raigal were married men now, and Raigal was a father, but they were still the same inside. It was as though what happened here at the Hidden House eleven years ago had marked them for life. *Entangled us*, he thought with a wry smile. All Luthien had done was find a way out of that net, and good luck to him. It was what he wanted. There was even a chance the All-Church would let him alone, as long as he didn't fight.

It was, Baruch thought, only a small chance. Calesh said he expected the All-Church to smash its way across Sarténe and burn what it left behind, and that seemed likely. There were a lot of men in the army by the Rielle who had fought alongside the Hand of the Lord, or else had expected to. In order to bring them to fight *against* it they would need to be made to see the Hand as monsters, revealed to them now by the mother church as heretics whose existence put souls at risk and made angels weep in Heaven.

The Elite would not escape. Perhaps if they recanted, threw aside their green robes and accepted forgiveness from the All-Church, they might be spared. But those who refused to back down would be killed, probably crucified or burned alive… and Luthien would not back down. Not ever, any more than he would abandon his oaths to take up a sword again. Which meant the All-Church would never give up hunting him, and men like him, until the last of them was dead.

"It will be a cleansing," he said into his wine glass, "when they come. And I'm afraid, my friend, because they will leave nothing behind but bones."

*

Calesh was still asleep. It wasn't like him to slumber for so long, right through the evening and into the weary hours before dawn, but Farajalla was content to let him rest. He would need it, in the days to come. He and his friends talked of *if the army comes*, but the truth was starker; the army *would* come, now. The All-Church had gone too far to pull back, whatever the Margrave might say in attempted mitigation. The negotiations Ando Gliss had spoken of, back in *Kissing the Moon,* were futile, a flailing of the air, in the lull before the storm broke and wolves came padding through the rain.

She slept herself for a few hours, and then lay awake with her head on Calesh's chest and listened to him breathe. His skin was still tanned from his years in Tura d'Madai, even after two months on board ship as they travelled from port to port on their way to Sarténe. Farajalla liked the contrast of her skin against his, caramel laid on bronze; she liked to feel him against her, as well, even while he slept. He was hers alone, at such times. No friend of long ago, no cause or memory could take a part of him away from her.

She finally rose when the case clock by one wall chimed softly to mark the third hour past midnight. It was still dark, but a lamp in the receiving room threw pallid beams through the bedroom doorway. Farajalla pulled the door almost shut as she padded through, and drew shutters across the lamp so it wouldn't disturb her husband. Then she poured a cup of fruit juice and settled in an armchair to read a book, Madai myths built around the quest of the hero Lim-Galen to find the island of eternal life. The seneschal at her father's court had been quite certain the island existed. He wasn't so sure about immortality though.

"The tale is an allegory," Anvuda told her one day, sitting on the steps of the summer garden with the river flowing beneath, cool and silent in the moonlight. Farajalla thought she must have been about fourteen. "Lim-Galen never does find the island, but he finds love, and when his son is born he turns for home at last, with his wife beside him. So you see, he does find immortality after all, in the way we all do: through our children."

"If it's an allegory," she said, thinking it through, "why are you so convinced the island is real?"

"All myths have some truth in them," he said, laughing.

Perhaps they did. Farajalla knew enough of legends to believe that most held seeds of truth at their heart, hidden behind scarcely credible tales of strange lands and quests, and stranger creatures. She'd read the tale of Lim-Galen many times, trying to find whatever hidden truth Anvuda had seen. Tonight, though, the wanderer's long quest couldn't hold her attention. She put the book down and went to check on Calesh again, to find him still sleeping.

For a moment she stood in the doorway and watched him. *The wanderer's long quest*, she thought; and then, *Is that his destiny, and mine? To roam in search of a chimera, and never find it? With no home waiting at the end, and no child to ease our loss?*

It would not be, while there was a path for Farajalla to take or a choice before her. She would not allow it to be so. When she looked at her husband something hot and fiery blazed in her breast, a flaming seraph that never cooled and yet never burned her. She would do anything to keep him safe. If men died screaming for his cause and in his name then so be it, as long as he lived.

    She thought about that for a moment. Then she went back to the receiving room to change. She always slept in one of Calesh's shirts, which she stripped off and bundled into a corner, and after a little searching through her bags she found a cream shirt and skirts divided for riding. They had been well packed, but two months in storage had left several faint creases, which made her purse her lips. She couldn't do anything about them though, and it didn't really matter. If she was found wandering the Hidden House she would appear no threat, but merely a lady walking restlessly in the dark before dawn.

    She pinned her braids back with a silver comb and went to the door. Halfway there she came back, rooted around until she found a pen and parchment, and wrote two lines to tell Calesh not to worry. Surely he'd wake before she returned. With that she slipped out of their rooms and into the darkness of the garden, with no clear idea of where she would go. Sometimes she was restless, that was all, and walking was better than lying abed and counting cracks in the ceiling. So she told herself, and if there was a small whisper in her mind that said she was hunting the secrets of the Hidden House, she didn't listen to it.

    The garden was silent. It had been hard enough to see past the first foliage even in daytime, and now it was impossible. Two lanterns on the wall behind Farajalla spun pools of yellow light out to the nearest shrubs, and cast everything beyond in still deeper blackness. Trees loomed up like dark sentinels, seeming to crowd her against the wall. It was hard to believe this was an enclosed atrium, just eighty yards across. It felt too wild for that. Farajalla had an immediate sense of alertness, as though the house itself was watching her, and waiting to see what she would do.

    She almost turned and went back inside right then, except that her eye was caught by a faint spark between the leaves, the glow of a lamp somewhere in the garden. At three in the morning. And she had her pride, of course, learned in her father's courtyards, where everyone knew she was his daughter and would not admit to it. Farajalla had never backed down, never retreated from a fight or allowed an acid-dipped sneer to pass, no matter what her mother said about turning the other cheek. She hesitated.

"I might find an answer here as easily as anywhere else," she muttered after a moment. She reached up to unhook one of the lanterns from the wall and set off into the arboretum.

Fronds began to pull her clothes at once, and after mere yards the gravel path branched into three. Farajalla went right, towards where she'd seen that flickering firefly light, but almost at once the path divided again. She discounted the one that led back towards her rooms, and picked the leftmost of the other two. It led over a hump that might have been a fallen tree, and then the path twisted to avoid a pool of clear, rippling water. She followed it around, gravel crunching under her feet, and felt the sleeve of her blouse tear as it caught on something with thorns. It was very hard not to curse.

A few minutes later she *did* curse, when the path she was following brought her back beside the pool from the other direction, and her lantern showed a tiny strip of cream material hanging from a thorn. The light she'd seen was away to her right, leading her on yet always out of reach. How that could be so in an enclosed garden eighty yards wide was beyond her. She considered calling out to whoever was there, but just then her gaze fell on a narrow strip of gravel on the far side of the pool. She hadn't seen it before, when it was hidden by the hanging curtain of an offspring tree, the tips of its branches almost touching the ground. They had been trimmed to leave them suspended in the air, she saw. Offspring trees kept their seeds at the ends of their branches, and where they touched, a new tree began to grow. Left to run wild, the trees soon exterminated every other plant, and formed a carpet of domed branches heavy with thin, sharp-edged leaves. Farajalla had seen it many times in the land around Harenc.

She decided to take it as a good omen and stepped forward, and almost at once emerged into a small arbour.

The Lady of the Hidden House sat on a plain wooden bench, facing a small pool backed with fitted stones. Herbs and shrubs grew between the rocks, filling the little glade with scents. The water vanished under a spray of greenery near where Farajalla stood, then merged with the pond she had twice stumbled past. A lantern had been hung on a branch to one side, its light rippling on the pool, and near it stood Gaudin in his pure white robes.

There was no doubt that this was the Lady. She was old, seventy at least if Farajalla was any judge, a small bony woman with white hair and papery skin that crinkled around her eyes and mouth. Her blue gaze was clear though, and it fastened on Farajalla at once.

"Sit with me," the Lady said. She patted the bench beside her. "I am Ailiss. You may leave, Gaudin. I'm sure Farajalla and I will manage."

The servant hesitated before he gave a bow and slipped away. Farajalla didn't think he would go far; the glance he bestowed on the Lady as he left held something very close to love. Probably he'd stay close enough to overhear. She would have to bear that in mind.

"Thank you," she said aloud. She perched on the edge of the bench, too wary yet to relax. It was one thing to set out to explore the secrets of the Hidden House, quite another to find the key to them sitting outside your door. "You've been waiting for me. How did you know I was awake?"

"I have some small abilities," the Lady answered. "Especially here, in my own place. Glamours and weavings learned by the loremasters in the deserts of Magan, long ago. Most of them are rather minor, to be honest. Party tricks and flashes of light, and suchlike."

That was either disarmingly honest, or Farajalla was being made fun of. "Really?"

"Really. Your husband has seen a few of them." Ailiss studied her critically. "I would have expected him to tell you. Calesh is the kind of man who either gives his heart or not; there are no half measures in him, no compromises where love is concerned."

"That's true," she said, surprised.

"Of course it is. Did you think I wouldn't know him?" Ailiss sounded amused. "I have made a point of understanding Calesh for eleven years, ever since I met him for the first time. There was something compelling about him even when he was still learning how to be a man, and what sort of man he would be. The other three knew it as well, though I don't think they realised it then. That first day, when they came into my hall, they all stood half turned towards him, as though waiting for him to move or speak, before they decided what to do."

"I'm afraid I don't know what you mean," Farajalla said. "Calesh has told me next to nothing of what happened here."

"Nothing?" Ailiss repeated. "Well, that surprises me, but it's sensible of him. Speaking of me is one thing: speaking of what I asked, and what they did, is another. I made sure all four of them knew not to speak too freely, right from the beginning, but I always expected them to talk at least a little."

Ailiss reached down beside the bench and produced a pair of small cups, and after them a teapot. She handed Farajalla a cup and poured for both of them, some sort of blueberry tea to judge by the scent. "There was a time I would have brought wine, you know, but I find it's not warm enough any more. Not even mulled. I wonder sometimes why God gave us bodies that fall to pieces as we grow older. To teach us humility before we go to Him, perhaps."

Farajalla cradled the cup in her hands, and the old woman was right: it *was* warmer. She didn't reply though. She didn't have any clear idea of what to say.

"Sometimes I am granted glimpses of events before they happen," Ailiss said after a sip of her tea. "It sounds wonderful, doesn't it? But in fact it's more maddening than useful. A vision without understanding is a frustrating thing. Still, eleven years ago I was wondering how to fetch the Book of Breathing from burial in Elorium, before some inquisitive All-Church sniffer began to root around in those tunnels and found it. I had no idea how it could be done, and then the faces of four young men came into my mind, with their names whispering in my ear."

"The All-Church would burn you, and all your household besides, simply for that," Farajalla said quietly.

"Yes, they would. They'd call it witchcraft, or some such silliness. In truth it's just ancient arts though, things forgotten by the wise men of today." She snorted disdain. "The old men in the Basilica believe that nothing is of value unless it was mastered in a church, by a churchman, and in the name of the church. Art is not art if it was created by an outsider. Science must be false if discovered by a heathen. If something comes from beyond the All-Church, or before it, they say it must be blasphemous, and they burn it when they can."

"Ah," said Farajalla. She thought she was beginning to understand. "There was something in the Book of Breathing, wasn't there?"

Ailiss sipped from her cup. "It's a very ancient book, that one. It was written in the time of Adjai, who in All-Church doctrine is the son of God. Or perhaps it was written very soon after his death. It contains many of his teachings, and several phrases which are claimed as direct quotes, the exact words he spoke. The scribe was a man named Muret. You know of him?"

"One of Adjai's apostles," Farajalla said.

Ailiss nodded. "Every child raised in the All-Church knows the name. One of the first converts to the Faithful, as the Basilica tells it today. Muret begins the Book with a plain statement: *These are the words which the living Adjai spoke, and I recorded.*" Her blue eyes locked with Farajalla's. "In one passage, Adjai says that God is one, unique and indivisible, and denies the claim made even then by some among his followers, that he is God's son."

Farajalla winced.

That made it all clear. The priests of the All-Church could not discredit Muret, or claim he was an apostate and his writings heretical: he was too important in their canon of blessed men. Name as heretic a man who had walked with the God-Son, and shared his travails? Indeed not. If the priests learned of that book they wouldn't hesitate to destroy it, or suppress it by any means they could find. That certainly included killing anyone who knew what was in those pages before they could speak of it: the Basilica had done such things before. It was still doing them, most likely, using Justified highbinders or its own secret killers to silence dissenting voices with knives in the dark.

Ailiss was right. Anything which contravened the doctrine of the All-Church, or challenged its view of the world and of God and his Son, it believed to be self-evidently false, and therefore fit only for burning. Anything that *might* do so was burned. There had been great bonfires once, in the dying days of the old empire, when books and scrolls were gathered from libraries across the continent until they made great piles in the streets, which were then set alight under the gleeful eyes of the clergy. Universities had been accused of fostering paganism, and endangering men's souls, so they were closed and their remaining books used for kindling. Only writings sanctioned by the Church could be allowed. All others were hunted, and destroyed.

Nothing like those bonfires had been seen for hundreds of years. But then, the All-Church had long ago burned any book it deemed heretical, in the lands where its priests held sway. Now their soldiers had conquered parts of Tura d'Madai, and Elorium itself, lost books might be found again.

And they might prove the All-Church wrong.

"Also," Ailiss said, her voice quiet, "Adjai says, in the Book of Breathing, that only the spirits and souls of men are divine, and made by God. The world of matter, of flesh, was created by Belial, the Adversary. As the Dualism teaches."

"That's why they will come down on you," Farajalla realised. "With that book you challenge their vision of God, in the words of their own saviour."

The Lady nodded. "Precisely. I worked to avoid that, and succeeded. We concealed the book. In another thirty years, perhaps less, the Dualism would have grown so strong that not even the All-Church could destroy it. Already Elite have gone north to Rheven, to establish new branches there. Raigal Tai comes from one such clique. More teachers have gone to Alinaur, and wherever they appear they find converts, because the priests of the All-Church are more interested in money than salvation, and because they are *wrong*."

"And now my plans are ruined." Ailiss paused to take another sip of blueberry tea. "Wrecked by the utter, irredeemable idiocy of the Margrave and the fool, whoever he was, who killed that priest by the river. It no longer matters what I do, or even whether the tales told in the Book of Breathing are true or false. The All-Church will come down on us."

"How did you know the book was in Elorium?"

"I always knew it," Ailiss said. "It was in Elorium when the Madai captured the city, seven hundred years ago. The last king hid it in the tunnels beneath the city just before the invaders broke through the walls, near the Valley Gate. People had been dumping their garbage in those catacombs for years, and they did so after the Madai conquered Elorium, too. And so the book passed out of history. As far as I could discover, nobody had seen or heard of it since. And someone would have heard if it had been found, or sold. Such a treasure would be noticed. So I thought, even after so long, that it might still be there."

The old woman sipped her tea, and without thinking Farajalla did the same. It was very good. Her suspicions of the Lady had faded somewhat now. Ailiss was obviously shrewd, and as wily as a fox, but Farajalla detected no deception in her. She did wonder about one more thing, even so.

"Why are you telling me this?" she asked. "This house is a secret place. Not many come here, and of those, I think few learn anything very much. So why are you here, waiting for me in the small of the night so you can unburden your heart of all its cares?"

"It would take some time to unburden it all," Ailiss laughed. "But why? Because I am old, and it is time I chose an heir."

The bluntness of the reply caught Farajalla off guard. She stared for a moment in voiceless silence, and then finally managed, "Me?"

"Yours is the face I have seen," Ailiss said placidly. "I will teach you the things you must know, before my time is done."

"But the All-Church is about to fall on us," Farajalla said. "I've seen them at work, Lady, and I don't think they'll leave much standing when they're done. Certainly not the Hidden House."

Ailiss studied her with those brilliant blue eyes. "Sometimes a flower must die to cast its seeds in the air. If things had been otherwise this would not have been necessary, but now it is, and we must deal with the world as we find it. Not as we might wish it to be."

She thought the struggle here was as good as lost, then. A sudden wave of sorrow washed over Farajalla, both for the home she had lost and the new one she had hoped to make here, if the god was kind. She remembered a cobbler named Vadalin, who had owned a shop under the Moon Balustrade in Harenc, near the silver dome of the High Temple. He'd inherited the shop from his father, and he from his father, and it seemed the sons of that family were born into the world with tacks between their lips and small hammers in their hands. Sevrey himself had always bought his boots there, and tinpot dukedom or not, it was still quite something for a cobbler to shoe a lord. The boots and shoes Farajalla had brought from Harenc had all been made by Vadalin.

But the shop was gone, together with the rest of Harenc. Vadalin's sons would never grow up to the *tap-tap* tune of craftsmanship in the shop their fathers had built. It was a little grief in the midst of greater ones, yet to that family it was everything. If any of them had survived. Farajalla tried not to think of such things, but sometimes the loss rose up her throat and demanded to be felt, and then it was difficult to breathe.

"You want to send me out into the world, custodian of the treasures you hold here," she said. "But there's a land yet to be saved yet."

Ailiss cocked her head to one side. "Do you think it can be? I already know Calesh will want me to leave the Hidden House, and go to a fortress in the Aiguille. Adour, probably. And he'll want my support in taking control of the Hand, no doubt."

"My husband will ask what he asks," Farajalla said. "But I think we act as though Sarténe can be saved. Why else did Calesh and the army come back?"

"And if we fail?"

"Then we fail," she said. "Nothing in the world we know is forever. Grief awaits us every day, until our souls go home."

"Very true," Ailiss said thoughtfully. "And you grieve for the child you can't give your husband, do you not?"

Farajalla spilled her tea. She caught the falling cup with an instinctive dart of her hand and turned back to the Lady, unsure what to say. Again Ailiss's bluntness had caught her by surprise. She schooled her features to stillness and waited, refusing to pick up the gambit.

"Sometimes," Ailiss said, "when a woman cannot conceive, there is nothing wrong with her at all."

Farajalla opened her mouth, and then closed it as the impact of the Lady's words hit home. She felt her eyes widen. Something cold coiled around her heart.

"Calesh?" she whispered.

Ailiss nodded. "It need not stop you. Most things can be overcome, with the knowledge of the lore."

"How?"

"Go to him," the Lady of the Hidden House said. "I have already worked a glamour. A simple enough thing." She made a dismissive gesture. "You wondered, I'm certain, why he was so tired when the rest of you were not. It only remains for you to use what I have done. If you wish to."

"Now?"

Ailiss nodded. "He will still be sleeping when you reach him. Wake him, but don't let him speak. Not a single word until it is done, but you must not tell him why. This is my gift to you, in the hope of trust between us."

Farajalla rose and started for the door, but halfway there she stopped and turned. The Lady's blue eyes were on her.

"For this," she said, "you will have my thanks forever. I swear it."

"Forever is a long time for a promise," Ailiss said softly. "Come tomorrow, and we will talk again."

Farajalla hesitated, but there were no words that would mean anything now. She turned and went from the arbour, to find Gaudin waiting just around the closest trees with his hands hidden in his sleeves. She felt his eyes on her as she went past him, but she never gave him a glance. He didn't matter now. Nothing mattered except reaching Calesh before he woke.

It had never occurred to her, in all the months of increasing worry, that her failure to conceive might be through a fault in Calesh. *Not a fault*, she thought with a flash of anger: *he is not to blame, any more than I would have been, were the lack in me.* But the truth was that she would have blamed herself, even knowing it was unjust, for the simple truth of failure in something that mattered so much. To him, deep in the secret recesses of his heart where he could not keep his memories quiet, and to her as well. She could admit that now. It mattered to her, just as much as it did to Calesh.

She struggled to make herself walk calmly, when she wanted to run. Her hands were clammy and her throat as dry as desert stone. She crunched over the gravel path to the door of her chambers, and for a moment she stopped there in sudden uncertainty, but then her jaw firmed. Ailiss had not deceived her. A lie in this would destroy any chance of trust between the two women, and the Lady surely knew it. She had told the truth. She must have told the truth.

Farajalla went inside.

*

He was dreaming, standing beside Farajalla on a ship in a wide sunlit ocean, with dolphins breasting the waves as they raced alongside. She laughed in delight and he smiled, content simply to watch her, but then she put a hand on his arm and he woke to find her there beside the bed, myriad black braids hanging over one side of her face.

Sleep left him all in a moment. He began to push himself up on his elbows, wide awake and rested, and she placed quick fingers against his lips. She didn't speak, but he read a strange mix of hope and urgent fear in her dark eyes, and he stopped moving and waited for her to explain.

"Not a word," she whispered. "Oh, my love, not a word. You must trust me."

He nodded slowly, not understanding. She took her fingers from his lips then, and sitting on the edge of the bed she reached up to her cream shirt and fumbled with the buttons. She was clumsy enough to pull one off, and then another, which he'd never known her do before. He opened his mouth and her fingers shot to his lips again, pushing them back against his teeth. He hesitated but was silent, wondering, as she slipped out of her clothes with her gaze on his face all the while. His eyes followed her movements, helpless as sand in the wind, and his breath caught. In an instant her hand covered his mouth again, though this time he hadn't meant to speak. He saw her realise that, and then she stood and slid the divided skirts past her hips and into a ragged heap on the floor.

She stretched herself out half on top of him, smooth as falling water, and ran a hand down his bare chest.

"You are all my world," she said, her voice trembling. He could not remember ever hearing that tone from her before. "And if I am yours, my love, then you will not make a sound."

He still didn't understand, but she was much more than just the world, and he smiled.

Nine

They are Coming

A traveller approaching Mayence from the north or east found the road climbing ever more steeply, until at last it levelled out and emerged from the jumbled hills into a small plain. Fields clustered on either side then, their appearance as sudden as sunlight through a broken window, with little farmhouses piled together here and there from seemingly random materials, and roofed with whatever came to hand. After almost a mile of that the road went over a broad stone bridge with the river Kair rushing beneath, still white and cold after its descent from the Raima Mountains. Sometimes in summer great blocks of ice were moored at the quays, floated down from the heights to adorn the city's famous iced wine but melting gently in the heat.

Up from the far bank of the river sloped the side of the plateau on which Mayence itself sat, high above the river behind a tall wall set regularly with towers. A little distance from the centre was a shallow mound, the highest point within the city, and there the Margraves had built their seat.

The citizens called it the Manse. To visitors, come to gape at the splendours of the jewel of a city nestled at the feet of the mountains, it was simply a palace. Many kings owned no house so large or fine. It was public confirmation of the wealth of Mayence, and so of its Margraves, and impossible not to notice. It rose above the city, just as the city rose above the plain. Deeper within the Aiguille there were more precipitous crags, some with fortresses perched on them like great stone eagles, but nothing anywhere near as big.

The view from the Manse's eastern balcony was reputed to be one of the finest in the world. The city spread out below, a crowding mass of buildings kept apart by the four wide avenues which ran to a central plaza just in front of the Manse. Smaller squares were dotted here and there, some crammed with the striped awnings of traders' stalls. There were chapels of the All-Church, and tulip-domed towers atop temples to Anu of the Madai, who some said was just God in another suit of clothes. In amongst them were two types of shrine to the Jaidi star god, one for those on each side of the schism of a century ago, and who could fathom the intricacies of that? Even the minarets looked the same. The desert people said that the star god was Anu too, at least in origins, but the faiths were so surrounded by different rituals that it was hard to know. Religion was never far away in Mayence. It was enough to make a man's head ache.

Every chapel tower was matched by a carved minaret, every flat roof by an onion dome. There was even one of those perched atop the Hall of Voices where the city fathers met to discuss the city's complex affairs, brilliant crimson in the spring sunshine. Mayence had no difficulty embracing different ways. It had done so first to survive, and now did so because it had made them its own.

There were ordinary homes as well, of course, though recently money had been set aside to redevelop some areas where crowding had become especially severe, or where the sewers had broken down completely. That had led to the innovation of building many homes in a single large block, each storey smaller than the one below to allow residents to enjoy little rooftop gardens, or useful vegetable plots. Space was at a premium in Mayence, hemmed in as it was by vital fields on one side and the rocky sprawl of the Aiguille on the other. The tenements had provided a solution, at least for a time. One day, if Mayence kept growing, there would simply be no more room, and the homeless and dispossessed would cluster in ragtag temporary shelters outside the walls, however often the Guard cleared them away. One of the lessons of the city's growth was that ambitious provincials would always want to come to the capital. Even Parrien was not usually good enough. It had not, after all, been good enough for Ando Gliss.

He had advised Riyand to spend some time each summer in the harbour town, perhaps even to build a summer residence there. That might encourage more growth there, instead of allowing it all to focus on Mayence. So far the Margrave hadn't done so, and Ando was reluctant to raise the matter again. Riyand had enough people nagging at him to do this or that, behave in such and such a way: he didn't need the same from Ando.

Beyond the river Kair lay farms, and then to the east the scattered buildings of the monastery an earlier Margrave had ordered built, almost a hundred years ago in the midst of a sprawling orchard. Apparently the All-Church had wanted the site because it helped achieve tranquillity. Only two structures rose above the leaves; the tower of the main dormitory building, and the spire of the chapel itself. It had been prudent to build such a large and imposing structure for the All-Church priests, to allay the suspicions which grew like mushrooms in their minds. Margraves had even gone to worship there from time to time.

Further away yet the land rose in a broad vista of half-barren hills with olive groves and vineyards trying to clamber up their sides. At the very limit of vision it was possible, on a clear day, to see a distant gleam that was sunlight on the windows of Parrien, and espy the thin blue strip of the sea. Today there was a light haze, spring pollen hovering in the air, so the hills faded into a blur of brown and green. That didn't really matter to Ando, as long as Riyand was near.

He knew people talked, of course. He would have to be a complete fool not to. Tongues wagged all the time, spreading tales of the dissolute Margrave and his lover, while a wife sat forgotten in her chambers and busied herself with embroidery or tapestry, or whatever it was such women were expected to do. Certainly the servants chattered, as they did all over the world. There was no way to stop it. So everyone seemed to know Riyand of Mayence preferred to share his bed with men – well, with *one* man, anyway – and in this world of warlike lords and pinch-lipped priests, that could be dangerous.

So while Riyand stood at the balcony rail and looked out over his city, a wine glass in one hand, Ando stayed back and out of sight, and all that well-known view was denied him. No need to give the rumour-mongers fresh gossip to feed on. From far below they would look up at their lord, a well-made man with coiffed black hair and a narrow beard that followed the line of his jaw, and while they might wonder if Ando was there they would not know for certain. It was better so, and Ando was content enough.

He knew Riyand hated the talk of the commons. One that particularly annoyed him was the claim that his wife, Ilenia, was still a virgin even after ten years of marriage. Ando doubted it, though he had never asked: it was simply that on occasion Riyand went to his wife's chambers late in the evening, usually after a fair amount of wine, and it didn't take much imagination to understand why. But there was still no sign of a child, and no sign that Ilenia would take a lover to give her one. Ando had considered finding a nameless youth on the streets, some thug or other with more muscles than brains, to sire a child on her. But he had shied away from it because of those wagging tongues; someone would be bound to see, or to hear, and the talk would begin. Or the thug himself would boast about it one night, deep in his cups. It would be easier for Ando to do it himself, if it could be arranged, though his mind flinched at the thought. He had no more interest in women than Riyand did.

Something had to be done, though. Riyand's brother Bohend had died young, victim of the plague that had swept through Sarténe twenty years ago and filled the graveyards with a carrion stink. Riyand was the younger, surplus to requirements, and probably destined for the clergy of the All-Church – not that his father held any love for the Basilica or its priests, but it was another way to turn suspicion aside. Nobody had bothered to teach Riyand how to hold a sword, or handle the intricate politics that permeated every land on God's earth. There was no point. The clergy would teach him what he needed to know.

And then suddenly Riyand was heir to Mayence, thirteen years old and almost completely untutored. His time had always been his own and he spent it as he chose: painting, for which he had a rare talent, or walking in the woods before an evening shared with whichever poets and singers happened to be nearby. All that changed in the space of one grim autumn. After the plague Riyand's days were crammed with lessons on statecraft and decorum, rhetoric and the classics, and any time left over was spent in the tiltyard behind the barracks, getting bruised and cut as he struggled to learn the sword.

For which, Ando had to admit, his lover definitely did *not* have a talent, rare or otherwise. He wasn't even a very good rider. It might have been different if Riyand had first begun to practice the sword when he was eight, as his brother had done, though personally Ando doubted it. Some men picked up a sword for the first time as adults, and yet quickly became fighters to be feared. Others started as young boys and never learned the knack; in battle they were liabilities, kept alive only by the efforts of men dedicated to the purpose. Riyand held the sword as though afraid it would bite him. He might conceivably be able to kill another man, but probably not because he was trying to.

That thought turned Ando's mind to Calesh Saissan, and events at the pissant little inn at the harbour five days ago. There was a man born to fight. In many ways Calesh was exactly as Ando had imagined him, tall, with shoulders like a roof beam, and wearing command as though trained to it from the cradle. Perhaps he should have been the Margrave's son, and Riyand a farmer's boy; at least then Riyand could have become a musician or painter, which was so clearly where his talents lay. One of God's jokes, that.

Yet Calesh was different too, harder and more direct, with little patience for the fripperies and distractions of everyday life. Ando had put the words of a speech in the man's mouth in *The Lay of Gidren Field*, and the words now seemed clumsy and inappropriate;

> *Be not afraid, though others quail*
> *Come with me and shape a tale*
> *Of glorious gallantry.*
> *We stand today with God's good grace*
> *To shelter us, and in this place*
> *Pride will humbled be!*
> *Put fear aside*
> *We've turned the tide*
> *Now rise, and follow me.*

Ando suspected that Calesh would not have said anything like that, if he made a speech at all. Certainly he would not have referred to glorious gallantry. *Stick by me, lads* was about as eloquent as he was likely to get, in the moments when his soldiers prepared for a charge: what they called a dragonnade. He was all competence and no romance – which was no bad thing for a soldier, perhaps, but extremely frustrating for a poet.

You could improve those lyrics with an axe, he'd said, back in Parrien. The worst thing was that now, having met the man, Ando almost agreed.

"If the message is what I think it will be," Riyand said from by the rail, "I'm afraid I might have led Sarténe to disaster." His voice was light, a man's tone but gently so, more the voice of a baritone than a tenor. "My father would have been so much better able than me to face this. Or my brother."

"I doubt it of your brother," Ando said, jolted from his thoughts. "Unless he needed nothing more than to oil his biceps and strike heroic poses. At the first call for intelligence he would have been lost."

The Margrave glanced back over his shoulder, amusement playing around his lips. "You shouldn't speak ill of the dead, you know."

"I do know," Ando said. "It's terribly bad luck. No doubt my next opus will be roundly detested by all, and my name will fade back into obscurity before the end of the year."

"I will still listen," Riyand said, and grinned suddenly. "Even if that opus is as detestable as the last one."

Ando burst out laughing, surprised by the quip. He took a sip of his own wine, which on this hot spring day was pleasantly chilled. It was relatively easy to fetch ice from the Raima in summer, when the nearest snow-clad peaks were less than twenty miles away. A team of workers stayed in the mountains all year around, cutting ice into blocks to be floated down the Kair on rafts. Summer wine in Mayence was unique because of that. In his regular travels to other lands, even to Rheven in the north where mist clung to the forests and houses were dug into the earth itself, Ando had never encountered anything like it.

"I wish," Riyand said quietly, his mirth fading, "that the priest hadn't been killed. The one by the Rielle," he added, as though Ando might not know which murdered clergyman he meant. "Everything happening today can be traced back to the idiot who staved his head in."

Ando knew that was true, though he didn't recall Rabast with anything even close to affection. The priest had been the All-Church's worst sort of fool, arrogant and overbearing, and always rude. He had referred to Riyand's sexual tastes, barely bothering to be oblique, as *foul abominations in the sight of God*, and had then repeated the comment at a public dinner. The first was appalling manners, but the second was a blatant insult.

Ando was saved the need to say any of that when a discreet knock sounded at the inner door, the one that led back into the Manse. He and Riyand turned together, and Ando saw that his lover had turned suddenly pale, the whiteness vivid in the afternoon sunshine.

"Enter," Riyand called, his soft voice steady.

Two men emerged onto the balcony. The first was short and nearly bald, and so thin that his clothes hung loosely about him, which made him look like a scarecrow dressed inexplicably in silks. Not that Cavel had ever cared about such things. He simply served the Margraves, with absolute loyalty and dedication, and given long enough life he would likely still be serving them when God brought an end to the world.

The second man was taller and bigger built, as all these soldiers seemed to be, though perhaps not as broad-chested as Calesh Saissan. Reis commanded the Guard, and did so ably as far as Ando could judge. Even so, he didn't trust the soldier the way he trusted Cavel. He had overheard Reis talking once, and the memory had never left him.

"I served his father, and promised the old wolf I would serve the cub as well," Reis had said, *"but Riyand is a weakling and a fool, quite apart from his... predilections."* His voice thickened with loathing. *"And for those he will suffer torments, if there is any grace in God at all."*

It was not the kind of thing a man could forget, Ando thought, even as he offered both men a neutral smile. They knew Riyand asked for his advice, and often heeded it. He knew they resented that. None of them ever spoke of it.

"Well?" Riyand asked.

"I have received word from the river," Cavel said. "From two sources, my lord, within minutes of one another. The first is an agent of my own, who reports that the army beyond the Rielle has begun to cross the river on rafts and boats, and anything else they can find that will float."

It's come, Ando thought with a swooping in his stomach. They had all expected it, but the news still hit him like a punch to the belly. Riyand was already pale, but more colour drained from him as Ando watched, and the Margrave steadied himself with a hand on the back of a chair.

"The second source?" he asked.

"The All-Church, my lord." Cavel handed him a sealed letter. "I thought it wise to bring Commander Reis with me, in case this note contains information he ought to know."

Riyand's hand trembled as he took the letter, and he needed two attempts to slice it open with a fingernail. He read, then handed it to Ando, which he had never done before. They were always careful to observe protocol, aware of the men who disliked the life they lived. Riyand had forgotten in his shock, and Ando disregarded it as well and read. He skimmed past his lover's titles, and over the opening paragraph of greeting, to the meat of the missive below.

Not only has the rule of Church law been continually flouted in your lands, but you have ignored efforts at rapprochement. We are reliably informed that children are stolen for use in vile ceremonies, at which worshippers spit upon the Cross and deny the divinity of Our Lord, Adjai, the Son of God. Yet you have done nothing to prevent this heresy, and have even encouraged it. We are therefore resolved to tolerate this insult to Heaven no longer.

The Hierarch declares you expelled from the auspices of the All-Church, and calls Crusade upon your land and your person, that the world may be rid of the obscenity you have fostered. We shall not stop until the last trace of it has been burned from the pages of history.

The Hierarch calls upon you to repent and make your peace with God, lest your soul be damned forever.

He passed the letter back to Cavel, who accepted it with a miniscule nod. Ando's heart was beating very fast.

"Nobody sacrifices babies." Riyand's voice was a stunned whisper. "Where do they hear these things? Who says them?"

"It doesn't matter who says them," Ando said quietly. "Or if anyone does. They're horrible things to accuse us of, that's all. A way to make the soldiers in their army see us as devils."

"That is correct," Reis said. "Such accusations are always made when the All-Church has an enemy to defame. It makes their soldiers eager for the fray. They say the same of the Madai and the Jaidi, even today." He had the letter now, and scowled down at it as though it had insulted him personally. "Well, they are coming, then. What are your orders, my lord?"

"What are your suggestions?" Riyand asked at once. "Cavel?"

"I have no suggestions," the seneschal answered. "You asked me to try to negotiate a settlement, my lord, after Rabast was murdered by the river some months ago. I have indeed tried, as you know, but evidently I have failed." He pursed his lips regretfully. "I could not even find allies among the kings and nobles. We are alone, my lord, I'm sorry to say."

The Margrave gripped the back of the chair. "Reis?"

"Militarily we cannot face that army," the general said flatly. This was his moment and he knew it, quite clearly; the time when diplomacy made way for warfare. "Not in the open. They have many times as many men as we can raise, and in a fair fight they will smash us."

"Mercenaries?"

"If the city's finances will support them," Reis said.

"Perhaps a company or two," Cavel said in his dry voice.

"Not enough to make a difference, I'm afraid. We have spent a great deal of money on civic projects. There is little left."

"We have to do something!" Riyand shouted.

Reis looked at him. "And we will, my lord. But that doesn't mean we should throw away the lives of our soldiers in a futile and doomed attempt to gain a victory we cannot achieve. I suggest," he raised his voice as Riyand tried to interrupt, "I suggest, my lord, that we send the treasury and our families to a safe place in the mountains, while I gather every soldier I can find. Then we shall defend the Aiguille, if we can, but *without* offering a fair fight. We know the land, which they do not, and a large army will find it difficult to operate in these hills."

Riyand stared at him, breathing hard.

"That means abandoning the plains and the coast," Ando said. He was surprised at how calm he sounded.

"It does," Reis said.

"Including Parrien."

The general's smile was grim. "I'm aware of where the coast is, Master Gliss. I can send riders to warn the people of the danger, but no more than that. I will not risk the men."

"Then do so," Riyand said. "Do it your way, commander."

Ando had to turn away, so he didn't have to look at the expression on his lover's face. He was afraid he was going to be sick and swallowed hard, forcing the nausea back down. He heard Reis and Cavel murmur their respects to Riyand, and then their footfalls moved across the balcony and the door closed behind them, but still he didn't look up.

"Sometimes I wish I had been born a farmer," Riyand said contemplatively from the railing. "A poor farmer with a simple life to lead, untroubled by all these affairs."

Ando sighed and made himself turn towards his friend. "You would still be troubled by them, Riyand. The All-Church isn't coming here for you alone, or merely for the great and the good of Sarténe. They're coming for all of us, and they will kill all of us. Farmers as well as lords."

"And musicians?" the Margrave asked with a quizzical smile.

"Musicians too," he said. "I'm afraid that the only songs left to us after this will be songs of sorrow, my dear."

"Most of them are anyway. Dreadful dirges of lost love, or pining for things we can never have." The attempt at levity fell flat, and faded into a familiar introspective expression. "And me, Ando? Would you still love me, if I were no more than a poor, unconcerned farmer?"

"I would still love you," Ando said.

Riyand smiled and held out his arms, and Ando went into them.

*

So they will come, thought the Lady of the Hidden House, sitting neatly on a chair in her rooms. A square of folded paper lay open on her lap. It bore the same message that had been delivered to Riyand less than an hour before, if in a different hand, and though she wasn't aware of the precise timing, Ailiss would not have been surprised.

It was useful to have an agent in the Basilica. Ailiss always knew what those malignant monsters were thinking, what they were likely to do in a given situation. It was that, as much as incantations and glimpses of how the future might be, which had allowed Sarténe to hold its own in the endless diplomatic skirmishing of the past decades. Her word was listened to in this land. Why not? It was she who kept the sacred books. The trust had been hers, and that of the women before her, for more years than she cared to recall.

It was a trust she had failed, it seemed. Not through her own fault, perhaps, but she had been aware of Riyand's shortcomings from the start. She didn't mean his preference for male lovers: who a man brought to his own bed was his own business, as far as she could see, as long as both partners were willing. But the lad had never been destined for the High Seat in Sarténe, and never been fit for it either. His father and grandfather had both been remarkable men, clever and guileful, able to feint and dance with the All-Church while throughout Sarténe the Elite multiplied like greenfly on leaves. Riyand's elder brother had shown signs that he might be the same, before the plague seized him.

Such a small change, Ailiss thought, still sitting in her chair beside the fireplace. Such a small change, for Riyand to be taken instead of Bohend. There was always grief for a death, and perhaps she should not be so willing to trade lives, as though it was she who sat in the highest seat of all and passed judgement on souls. But it was hard, so hard not to sometimes. Bohend would not have blundered in dealing with the emissary the All-Church had sent, Ailiss was sure. And he wouldn't have ordered the man killed by the river either, as she was almost certain Riyand had done. Either thing could have been used by the Basilica as an excuse for war: an excuse, really, was all they had been looking for. The game had been to deny them that, to profess shock at this alleged heresy, and then smile and say *but really, it can't be that bad, can it?* Promise to look into the claims. Waste time sending messages to and fro, to and fro, checking some insignificant point of detail or other without ever actually doing anything.

All ruined by the Margrave's stupidity, and by the even greater idiocy of the murderer by the river, who had not only killed a priest but had allowed a witness to see it all, and not noticed him.

People will die for it, she thought bleakly, and was glad when a soft knock preceded Gaudin into the room.

His expression was sombre, and with reason. Behind him came the four visitors, Calesh and his wife at the front, with Baruch and Raigal Tai looming behind them like sentinels. She felt her heart lift a little as they approached. What her vision – call it that – had shown her all those years ago had been true. These three men had found the Book of Breathing exactly where she had said it would be, and had brought it back to her across the sea. She had allowed herself a moment of exultation when Baruch put it in her hands. It was a fine thing done, and for all the fame that had come to Calesh for his courage and skill in open fields, Ailiss knew which deed was the greater.

It had been these three, and one other. Luthien Bourrel was missing now, gone to answer a higher calling, and there was no blame in that. Still, Ailiss believed there might be a part left for him to play, before all was over and the wind played idly among broken stones. There were always four corners to a square, four points to a compass, four elements in the world. Earth, air, fire, water. A motif that recurred in stories told across the world was *giant, wise man, soldier, king*. Here were three, the giant and the soldier, and the king who led them. But they needed their wise man, if they were to rediscover their strange alchemy and be complete again.

They would need to be complete. She drew a breath and faced them, and they came to a halt before her chair.

"They are coming," she said simply.

Gaudin looked at her with compassion in his dark eyes, but Ailiss was watching the others, and they behaved just as the four had when she first called them, eleven years before. None of them shifted, exactly, but there was an air of turning half towards Calesh, waiting for him to respond. *You are the king my dreams chose,* she thought as she studied him. *Be that king. We need you to be, if anything is to survive.*

"Lady," he said finally. He came forward a step. "Will you give me your support, in taking control of the Hand of the Lord?"

"I will," she said. "This is your war, Calesh. You must fight it."

"And the Margrave?"

"Rules Sarténe," she answered. "I don't see why that should interfere with your generalship, do you?"

He nodded, satisfied with his business but not pleased by it. That was as it should be, and he'd never been a prideful man. He hesitated and then came forward again to drop to his knees before her. "I've dreamed so long of what I would say if ever I saw you again, Lady, all the questions I would ask. And now there's no time. Will you bless me before I go?"

She stood up, and put her hand slowly into his hair. "You have had my blessing, such as it is, since I first met you. This is your time. May you walk in sunlight through it, and may Heaven guide your steps. You deserve it." She smiled at the surprised look in his eyes at that last. "You have suffered me to speak, and this shall be your consolation. Go in love."

He rose, and taking her hands he kissed the palms. "Thank you, Lady. We'll leave you now. You will go to the fortress at Adour, in the Aiguille?"

"I'll go," she said. She looked at Farajalla, standing with the others a little behind Calesh. "And you, my dear? Do you ride with your husband, or with me?"

The woman's eyes went to Calesh, and for a moment their fingers brushed together.

"With you," Farajalla said. "Until my husband comes for me."

Calesh looked as though he wanted to kiss her, but something of the mood in the air must have reached him, for he squeezed her hand instead and strode away. Baruch and Raigal followed after him: neither of them had spoken a word since they entered the room, though Ailiss's blessing had been as much for them as for Calesh alone. She thought they understood that. If not they would have knelt themselves, but these men had always stood together, since that first day. What was given to one was given to all.

Perhaps even to the one who was missing. Ailiss couldn't see the end of that thread. Her days were drawing short now, and more was hidden from her eyes than had been, when she was young.

She turned to Gaudin, standing solemn and silent by the door, and he felt the weight of her gaze and looked up at her.

"Well, old friend?" she asked quietly. "Will you help me pack, and come with me to Adour?"

"I will come," he answered, limpid-eyed.

"Thank you," she said. Her throat felt tight and she pushed the feeling away: it was a weakness, and she had no time for it now. "We had some good times here, Gaudin, didn't we?"

He nodded mutely.

"When we leave we'll burn it," Ailiss said. "Burn all of it, so those murdering beasts cannot walk through these rooms of ours, and make stories of what we did there."

There was shock in Gaudin's eyes, but Ailiss ignored it and turned towards the door. There were tears in her own. Tears, for the first time in half a lifetime, and she did not want him to see.

Book Two

Wise as Serpents

... be ye therefore wise as serpents, and harmless as doves.

Matthew 10: 16

Ten

Highbinder

Once, this had been the city of emperors.

Marks of that time remained, even after centuries. A visitor might pause to admire the triple tiers of arches that carried an aqueduct over a steep, wooded valley just outside the walls, though the aqueduct was broken now and carried no water. He might set aside a day to visit the ruins of the great arena, where captive slaves had once fought and died for the amusement of their masters. Almost certainly he would stop and gape when he came in view of the old walls, around the feet of which houses clustered like a child's discarded toys. They were among the most massive defences ever built in the world. Every street had its relics, every plaza its memories. In Coristos the past loomed large, always.

Not everything had survived, of course. Massive the old walls might be, but they had been breached once, when the clan army of the Vothar broke into the city. Nobody was sure how, even today. They didn't leave enough behind them to allow certainty: just rubble, and ashes that smoked through all that autumn, thin grey fingers reaching out of the ruin. Most of the city's houses had been lost in that fire, and much of its street plan as well. Only the monumental structures remained, echoes of an ancient glory.

The All-Church began to build on the site before the smoke stopped rising. Making a new glory, people said now. An early Hierarch had claimed the Vothar were God's means, and fire His tool, for the cleansing that would make the site pure enough for the Houses of the Lord.

None of the statues of the emperors had survived. All had been taken away and smashed into dust and rubble, their features lost forever. Once the emperors had claimed to be living gods. Now they were merely dead men with forgotten names, in the city of the One God, who admitted no rival.

Today, the Old City was the preserve of the All-Church. Inside those gigantic walls lay cloisters and monasteries, quiet gardens and arbours, tabernacles, cathedrals and minsters. At the heart of it all, somewhere deep in the network of avenues and boulevards shaded with cypress trees, was the Basilica. Its spires reached higher than any in the city, by force of law, but not so high that they could be seen from outside the walls. Only those judged worthy might look upon the sacred House of the Lord. It was unusual for an outsider, one unconsecrated to the clergy, to be permitted to enter the Old City at all.

Elizur was aware of the honour. He was the first soldier in living memory to walk these streets.

He had to leave his weapons at the Gate, of course. Elizur had expected that – no one could go armed into the city of the Lord, naturally – but it was a surprise to be told he must leave his clothes as well. He didn't like leaving his surcoat behind. He even wore the crimson cross insignia of the Servants of the Justification when out of uniform, so every man knew to whom he belonged. But the acolytes were quite insistent, and the four men of the Order of the Basilica fixed him with hard eyes when he hesitated. They didn't frighten him, not a mere quartet of soldiers, but in the end Elizur folded his clothes into a neat pile on his sword. After a moment's thought he gave the soldiers a significant look and took a pair of bone-backed black gloves from his pack, to lay them atop it all. Two of the men went pale when he did that, and the older of the priests turned his face away.

The clergymen gave him a robe of simple brown wool, belted with a cord, and a pair of sandals. The first itched and the second chafed. They were not what he was used to at all.

"Don't even dream of touching anything," he said to the captain of the Order soldiers. "Don't unsheathe the sword: I'll know if you do. And I counted the coins I have in my purse."

The officer's face darkened, and he smoothed his white and gold tabard with one hand as though to remind Elizur who he was. "The Knights of the Church do not steal, captain."

Elizur gave the man a thin smile. All-Church soldiers might not steal, but they certainly borrowed, and they rarely remembered what they owed. The Shavelings had changed little since the days when they were made up of thieves and cutthroats, offered the choice of salvation through holy war or death for their crimes. Some of them still *were* slipfingers, he had little doubt about that. Still, he had only brought a few coppers with him today, enough to buy half a loaf of bread and some butter and honey on his way back. It wasn't worth the risk for a soldier to *borrow* from him. And they knew who he was, of course; Elizur's name had been ticked off in a ledger when he presented himself at the Gate. If nothing else dissuaded them, the sight of those bone-backed gloves certainly ought to. They must know what he would do to a *borrower*.

"Come," the oldest acolyte said. He actually tugged on Elizur's sleeve. "We must not be late."

"Why not?" he asked lightly. "Will the Lord strike me down for impudence on the spot?"

The second would-be priest blanched at that. Elizur thought he might pass for fifteen, in poor light. The first was closer to twenty, and his lips twitched as though he was trying not to smile. "Perhaps he will, captain. I'd be more concerned about the Arch-Prelate, myself."

"He is not here," Elizur said pleasantly. "I am, however. If you lay a hand on me again, boy, I will tear off one of your fingers and force you to eat it knuckle by knuckle, do you understand? Do it a third time and I'll lay you open from throat to groin and leave you thrashing in the gutter. I hope that is clear to you."

The acolyte went white, and his lower lip trembled as though his papa had just refused to take him to the circus. If he'd ever known his papa. Elizur sometimes believed that priests hatched their acolytes in some secret place in the Old City, and had them raised as boys by bloodless men who never smiled. At any rate, the boy's voice was paper thin. "It is, sir."

"Excellent!" Elizur put on a wide smile. "Shall we go?"

They led him into the Old City.

At first glance it was a disappointment, not much different from the streets outside, save for their emptiness. No people, no mangy dogs slinking close to the walls, no horse dung or waste water that might foul his shoes. Elizur had half-thought there would be angels on every corner and a divine light shining above, though really he knew that was nonsense. Only children really thought of Coristos that way. Still, it was a holy place. Surely *something* should have changed.

As he walked, he began to realise something had. The avenues were very wide, shaded on both sides by cypresses and date trees, and every building was fronted by an immaculately manicured lawn. It created a sense of space, more like a town park than the heart of a city. But there was more to it than that. Nothing seemed to move here; or if it did, it moved silently, as though fearing to disturb the Lord's well-earned rest. There was no creak of wagons, no shouting of exasperated drivers or chatter of the multitudes; none of the bustle and noise of a city, in other words. He couldn't even hear sounds from the New City, outside those ancient walls. It was eerie, more like a dream than the real world.

An occasional priest or acolyte passed by, and they did so noiselessly, except for soft-murmured chanting and the patter of sandals. They seemed not even to see the three men walking towards the centre.

No, that wasn't it either, though it made Elizur's city-bred fingers twitch. There was… something else.

Elizur wasn't sure what it might be, but he felt it in his flesh and bones, and in his soul. Sanctity reached into every corner here, suffused the air, drifted into a man's spirit as he breathed. Over long ages it had seeped into the stones themselves, which now leaked it back into the world at large. It was indefinable… but it was there. Here Heaven drew close to the world, and God was watching. To carry a sword here, or to wear everyday clothes, would be almost heretical.

He thought about asking the acolytes whether they might stop to pray, which the Arch-Prelate who had summoned him surely would not object to. In the end he decided not to. Anything he might say would be meaningless in the face of this. He was only a soldier, after all: an extremely good one, and as watchful a warden of the Lord's word as he could find it in himself to be, but still just a soldier. Later he could visit a chapel outside the walls and spend an hour in prayer, offering thanks for the gift of this experience, but not now.

There were no inns and taverns, no shops or dwellings, though sense told him the clergy had to sleep and eat somewhere. After a while Elizur began to think he was passing the same stretch of road he'd walked before, though that couldn't be, since he had turned neither right nor left since leaving the Gate. It was just that one minster looked very like another when you'd already seen a hundred today, or felt as though you had. He wondered if there might be something faintly blasphemous in that thought.

We have turned neither right nor left. That raised an interesting possibility, and Elizur raised an eyebrow at the older of the acolytes. "Am I to go to the Basilica itself, then?"

"Maker's Mercy, no!" The lad made a circle with thumb and forefinger, an ancient invocation of the God. "My instructions are to take you to the Tabernacle of the Redemption. It almost faces the Basilica."

"You will be permitted to look upon the Basilica," the younger priest said in a squeaky voice. Trying to sound authoritative, Elizur thought, but he was too callow to carry it off.

Elizur put on his best smile, with lots of teeth. "Don't be frightened, little man. I won't eat you."

The youth nodded and kept his head down. Wise of him.

They knew who he was, of course. Half of God's world knew of Elizur Mandain. Infidels quaked at the mere name. The higher clerics probably put their noses in the air and sniffed when they heard it though, so Elizur thought these two boys might have done something wrong and been given the duty of escorting him as punishment. Or maybe not: some among the acolytes would admire Elizur's deeds, and might have tried to wheedle their way into meeting him. A number of these men were the leftover sons of nobility, after all, prodded into the priesthood by their fathers when they would much rather have chosen life as a mercenary or Crusader.

He doubted these two were that sort though. Neither appeared comfortable with him, or excited, or even the least bit interested. Maybe both boys had entered the clergy through a true sense of faith. Such things did happen, though not as often as the All-Church liked to claim. If so, then their interests lay in prayer and ritual, the unchanging daily routine of serving God. For such men that meant the comfort of a haven from the real world. They would have little interest in the soldiers who fought to preserve their tranquillity.

Elizur hoped the Gate guards weren't fiddling with his gear. If they did he'd know as soon as he laid hands on his gloves, and they would pay for it, somehow. Especially if they touched his sword. It wasn't done to simply murder a Church soldier, but a way could always be found.

Presently the acolytes turned towards a wide path of dressed stone, leading up to a building of reddish granite. Flying buttresses flanked a high doorway, above which a carved man stood bathed in light, one hand raised in benediction to an unseen throng.

"You told me I would see the Basilica," Elizur said.

The older acolyte stopped and pointed. "There. Just to the left of the date tree on the corner."

Elizur could just make out the edge of a building, made of the same red stone as the Tabernacle before him. He grunted to himself. *Almost faces the Basilica*, indeed. These boys had been playing a game with him, like shysters at a travelling fair when a country lout strolls up to their pavilion. His cheek twitched. Perhaps a way could be found for them as well.

"Show me to this Arch-Prelate," he said.

The two youths blinked at him with identical expressions of distress. They must have expected him to fall on his knees and give thanks for the honour of laying eyes on the great Basilica, even one meagre corner of it. Elizur had to push the younger of them before they moved on up the path.

As they reached the steps someone emerged from the doors above, dressed in the white robes of a priest.

"You are late, my son," he said in forbidding tones. He was old, surely nearing seventy, with scrawny grey hair that clung around his head like weak grass on the side of a cliff. But his voice… that was what the squeaky young acolyte wanted to sound like, one day. The man boomed, even in the open air. He would intimidate most men with one word, Elizur thought.

He shrugged, showing he was not most men. "I didn't know my way. I could only come as fast as these boys could guide me."

The basilisk glare turned to the acolytes. "You have been lax, have you? Very well. You will go to the Chapel of Penance and tell the Master what you have done. You will go now."

The boys murmured assent as they bowed, and departed. Neither so much as looked at Elizur. He started to climb the steps.

"I am Arch-Prelate Sarul," the priest said as Elizur reached the top. "And you are Elizur Mandain, of the Justified, or you had better be." He looked the soldier up and down with what might have been a faint sneer. "Somehow I thought you would be bigger."

"I am as big as I need to be," he said stiffly. He didn't like the diminutive name for his order, *Justified*, always spoken with a faintly supercilious undertone. He *really* didn't like to be reminded of his height. "A lot of men expected me to be taller, or broader in the shoulders. Most of them are dead."

"Most are," Sarul said indifferently. "Not all."

Elizur's cheek twitched. "There is time, yet."

"Then we should not waste it," Sarul said. He beckoned Elizur with one hand as he turned back towards the Tabernacle.

Inside it was large and extravagantly ornate. A lone, eight-armed candelabrum lit the far end of the large chamber, and Elizur was glad that was all. Any more light and he would have been blinded in the presence of so much silver and gold. Even the backs of the pews bore gold leaf, traced with intricate patterns. This temple was never meant to be used, he realised. Elizur had seen certain wealthy nobles carry swords with ivory handles and scroll-worked blades, toys meant for show and not for battle. This tabernacle was the same, a visible ornament, and a reminder of the wealth and power of the All-Church. As though anyone who came here would need reminding of that. It was ostentation, pure and simple, and Elizur tried not to let his lip curl.

Two men waited by the candelabrum, seated in large armchairs that nearly concealed them. Elizur could see they wore the same white robes as Sarul, though. Arch-Prelates, then, and whatever brought three of them together to meet a soldier inside the Old City itself, it was sure to be important. Elizur smiled. He liked to feel important.

He went to meet them with a joyful heart.

*

Irrian made sure his face remained expressionless as the two men approached. It wouldn't do to reveal his inner thoughts too clearly. Beside him Karch also wore a bland look, his true feelings hidden deep inside. Sometimes Irrian thought the denizens of the Old City could conceal any evil behind their masks, like plotters in a puppet play, and probably did.

"This is Captain Elizur Mandain," Sarul said as he reached the circle of light thrown by the candelabrum. "Captain, meet Arch-Prelates Irrian and Karch, both members of the Hierocracy."

"An honour," the soldier said with a smooth bow.

"The honour is ours, of course." Irrian studied him from behind steepled fingers. Elizur was muscular and looked awesomely fit, and like many of the best soldiers he moved on cat's feet, always poised and balanced. The soldier looked back flatly. "Hmm. I thought you would be bigger."

Elizur's cheek twitched, and anger flashed hot in his eyes before he could cover it. "I am as big as I need to be, Arch-Prelate."

So. The reports Irrian had read suggested the man was sensitive about his stature, which was evidently the case. And that a tic showed in his cheek under stress. If that much was correct then it was likely that the rest was too. Irrian lidded his eyes and watched as Sarul pointed the soldier to an armchair and then sat himself, arranging the folds of his robes.

This is a dangerous man, he thought inwardly, behind the studied mask of his face. Any fighting man was dangerous, but with Elizur there was more to it. Under his outward litheness ran a thick thread of tension, something hot and tight and barely restrained. It showed in the sharp snaps of his movements: that revealed his grace as a learned skill, not nature's gift. Irrian thought he would not like to be nearby when that rage broke loose.

He laughed suddenly at himself. Elizur might be dangerous, in his way, but that was not unusual in the Old City. Sarul's desire to be the next Hierarch ate the man alive every day of his life: *there* was a genuine inner heat, and it would scorch and scald anyone who tried to baulk him. Karch could not dream of such rank – he knew his colleagues saw him as a fussy little stick of a man, and would never elevate him further – but his frustration at that emerged in envy and petty jealousy. There were dangers everywhere in Coristos, some of one kind and some of another, but any might be deadly to a careless man.

"What we are about to discuss," Sarul said in that magnificent voice of his, "must not be spoken of outside these walls. Understand that, Master Elizur. Mother Church commands it."

The soldier nodded once.

"Karch," Sarul said.

The bony man was quick to take up proceedings. "This morning the Crusade army on the river Rielle received new orders. I don't doubt you've heard the rumours?" He raised his eyebrows but didn't wait for a response. Irrian knew why: Karch had learned long ago that if he paused for breath someone else would begin to speak, and the little man would be forgotten. "They are true. The All-Church has called Crusade against the heretics of the Duality, in Sarténe, and will erase their foulness before the summer is ended."

"I am certain all God-fearing children of our Mother Church will be delighted at the news," Elizur said.

"Of course they will be," Sarul said dryly. "Our beloved children are always so *very* eager to accede to our interventions, after all."

Irrian swallowed a great gust of laughter, though the effort made him break out in a sudden fit of coughing. He fished a handkerchief from inside his robe and wiped at his nose, peering over it at the others. "A touch of hay fever, I'm afraid. Don't concern yourselves."

"You suffer hay fever?" Karch asked dubiously.

"I'm a martyr to it," Irrian assured him solemnly. "A perfect martyr. It grieves me that the beauty of summer is so marred for me, but no doubt the Lord has his reasons."

"No doubt," Sarul said, his tone now frosty. "Is it vaguely possible we might move on, do you think? Thank you *so* much."

"There is a difficulty we had not anticipated," Karch said, hurrying over his words with a quick glance at the other Arch-Prelate that almost made Irrian laugh again. The little man was like a child trying to please a grumpy uncle. "Somehow, the Hand of the Lord in Tura d'Madai learned of our intentions some time ago, and has returned to Sarténe already."

Elizur blinked, visibly discomfited for the first time. "All of it? That will leave our forces in Elorium short. Especially if the reinforcements are sent to Sarténe and not Tura d'Madai."

"You need not concern yourself with that," Sarul intoned from the depths of his chair. "Would you direct the armies of the Lord now, my son? Have you sat in our solemn convocations, and prayed for the guidance of the Lord God under the White Dome of the Basilica? I thought not." He flicked long fingers in dismissal. "Leave the decisions of high leadership to those accustomed to their burdens, and go where you are bid."

"Of course, Your Grace," Elizur said, and his smile was so sudden and bright that Irrian couldn't keep a flicker of surprise from his own expression. Nobody's mood changed that fast, except for a madman's. He hooded his eyes again and let himself sink deeper into his own chair, watching the soldier surreptitiously from the concealing shadows.

"The problem," Karch went on doggedly, "concerns the men we expect to lead the Hand in the fight to come. Baruch Caraman, Luthien Bourrel, Raigal Tai… and Calesh Saissan."

By the time the fourth name was spoken Elizur had gone rigid in his chair, his hands tight on his thighs as though only a great effort kept them there. He closed his eyes briefly and took several deep breaths, clearly calming himself. His cheek twitched twice.

"Do you remember the names?" Irrian asked idly.

Karch snorted. "He'd better, or this is all for nothing."

He did, Irrian was certain. The Hierocracy had known that before the man was brought to the Old City, which of course was why they had chosen him for the task they wanted performed. They had taken some care to be sure they had the right man. An experienced killer, superbly talented with the sword, and with a personal grudge against those four men. Especially Calesh. Elizur's reaction was enough to tell Irrian the choice was a good one.

"I remember," Elizur said. His knuckles were white, but no strain showed in his voice. "They are together again?"

"Either that, or they soon will be," Sarul said.

"Then the All-Church has a problem," Elizur told them.

Sarul leaned forward in his chair. "Our army is perhaps four times as large as anything the heretics can raise against us. Our forces are rested and supplied, while Sarténe's are still scattered and unprepared. I fail to see, captain, why it is we who have a problem."

"Nevertheless you do," Elizur said. His cheek twitched again. "Those four men are very good. No, I take that back. These four men are *magnificent.* Alone, they're talented soldiers, each one of them. Men to reckon with. But together they become something remarkable. And Calesh Saissan," he shivered when he spoke the name, as though caressing it, "has the most precious gift any commander can possess, better than any possible knowledge of an enemy or a battlefield. He makes men want to fight for him, yearn to fight for him, and because of that they always fight better. Any one of his men would gladly die for him."

"You sound as though you admire him," Irrian said smoothly. He'd known that Elizur hated the Sarténi, but not that the hatred ran so deep. All the soldier's previous aplomb had vanished now.

Elizur frowned, perhaps sensing a threat. "I admire his skill. As to the rest, a good soldier always knows his enemy."

"And you are a very good soldier," Sarul said, interceding now they had come to the point. He leaned forward in his chair. "You spent five years in Alinaur fighting against the Jaidi, and never suffered a wound of any importance. After that the Justified attached you to their Highbinders, the elite group of assassins and other specialist killers, and you were sent to Tura d'Madai. To date –"

"There's no such group among the Servants of the Justification of God," Elizur broke in.

Sarul's eyes narrowed. "And the bone-handled gloves you left at the Gate? What of them?"

"An affectation," Elizur said, with the air of a man admitting an embarrassing truth. "Sometimes it helps for people to believe I'm more than I am."

"More than you are," Sarul repeated softly. "Tell me, Captain Mandein, do you really think we would allow an Order of knights, founded in the name of the All-Church, to form such a highly-trained elite – and not know about it? Captain, do not take us for fools. Or shall I offer more details to persuade you that I do indeed know?" He grinned, a shark's hungry smile. "The head of your sect is Aravan Gleve, though officially he is only a middle-ranking official in the requisitions department. To date you have received twenty-three assignments, under both Gleve and his predecessor, in various regions from here to Tura d'Madai. Each has been successfully completed. You have been twice decorated, once with the Six-Pointed Star, in silver." He paused, then gave a thin smile. "And of course, three years ago you won the sword tournament at Caileve, against more than two hundred men from all over the known world. I believe you actually killed your opponent in the semi-final."

"He was Madai," Elizur shrugged. "How do you know these things about my Order? Our group is highly secret."

"All the Orders are formed in the name of the All-Church, and exist only with our blessing," Karch said prissily. "Do you really think we would not concern ourselves with the things they do?"

That came close to admitting there were spies among the Justified, and to judge from Elizur's slitted eyes he took it as such. Irrian didn't like the soldier's behaviour: it was too intense, from the jumping cheek muscle to his white-knuckled hands. He watched and kept silent, waiting to learn more. *The hardest thing about patience is the waiting*, he'd joked as an acolyte, long ago. The jest hadn't been funny then. Now it was bitter indeed.

"Why do you tell me this?" Elizur asked after a thoughtful pause. "You must realise I'll tell my commanders, and we'll find your agent among us if we can."

"We admit to the existence of no agents," Karch said, far too quickly, and then wilted under Sarul's burning stare.

"We know perfectly well what you will do," the older clergyman said. Every word he spoke seemed intoned, as though he was reciting the most holy rituals of the Church under the White Dome of the Basilica itself. "We judge it worth the risk, in view of the prize we aim at. The Hierocracy wishes you to undertake a mission for the All-Church, Master Mandein."

"What mission?" the soldier demanded.

"We want you to go to Sarténe," Sarul said. "You may requisition anything you need, any weapon and whatever supplies you believe you will need. Once there you are to kill Calesh Saissan, his three friends, their families, and anyone else you find with them. Any measure you deem necessary will be supported, and the rewards will be great."

Elizur's reward would be to find himself abandoned the moment disaster struck, if Irrian had learned anything about how the Church worked, and all knowledge of his actions denied. By the Hierarch himself, if necessary. Even if he succeeded, the soldier was likely to find himself bound and stuffed in a sack, then tossed in a river to drown. That way the Hierocracy could be sure their actions would always remain secret.

Another mask, Irrian thought, another cruelty done in the name of God, and then hidden behind a smiling clergy which spoke of forgiveness and love.

  Elizur didn't appear to register any of that. His lips had curved into a tight smile. "I can kill Saissan."

  "Yes," Sarul said. "And his friends."

  Irrian doubted that the other three mattered very much to Elizur. It was Calesh he wanted above all, because despite Sarul's earlier words the highbinder had *not* succeeded in all his assignments. He had failed in one, a twenty-fourth mission whose existence was denied by the Justified – even those few Irrian had found who admitted the Highbinders existed at all. That mission had been in Tura d'Madai, against the enemy captain whose brilliance threatened to destroy everything the All-Church armies had achieved, and drive them back into the sea. Against Cammar a Amalik.

  As far as Irrian could discover, it had been Elizur's third assignment in Tura d'Madai, and it had come because he was in the right place at the right time. That was often the way: whoever was closest was given the task, if possible. One highbinder was as expendable as the next. Only the very best, the most brilliant of the expert killers recruited into that select group, could choose their missions. There might be two men so favoured, three at the most, and killing Amalik would take Elizur to the very top. He would join the elect, doing the Lord's work from the shadows, much as Sarul was doing now. Atrocities excused by necessity, and later denied.

  All he had needed to do was kill one man. There was no way to creep up on Amalik, surrounded as he always was by dark-skinned Madai. So Elizur had delayed until the next battle, in a valley known as Gidren Field, and placed himself with a unit of Justified in the centre of the Crusade line, where Amalik liked to strike. Then he waited for Cammar a Amalik to come to him.

  He would have done, except that the soldiers around Elizur gave back, the unit rippling with incipient panic, and the assassin had to retreat with them. It might not have mattered… but then someone raised a shout, a unit of the Hand of the Lord came rushing in, and everything changed.

  Elizur had been heard to say, with contempt, that Calesh had been lucky. That he'd made a mistake, abandoned his position in the line because he panicked, or had no regard for orders, or some other character flaw. *Fortune favours fools* was the phrase he used, *but not forever.*

  All the Justified were equally dismissive. What couldn't be denied was that the death of Amalik had turned the battle, perhaps even the war, and it was Calesh who had killed him. The soldiers knew that, those who had been there, and neither the Glorified nor the Order of the Basilica had reason to lie. Calesh's fame spread. Honours were proposed for him, one after the other, and the Justified blocked them when they could while Calesh himself never seemed to notice, or to care. In the meantime Elizur Mandein stood to one side and nursed his own bitterness, while his commanders showed with sidelong looks and veiled hints that they blamed him for all of it.

He wanted Calesh dead, on his own blade, to expunge that shame from his memory, and made no secret of it. That was why the Hierocracy had picked him for the task. Elizur would do it, so single-mindedly that he wouldn't stop to think of anything else until it was done. And by then, of course, the trap would be closing around him in its turn.

Irrian watched from the recesses of his chair, and wondered whether Calesh would be a match for this man.

Eleven

Shrouded

"We were never going to be able to stop it," Irrian said. He stood with his back to the room, gazing out over the cloisters and spires of the Old City. Evening sunlight gleamed from windows and domes. Quarter of a mile away the Basilica was a red-gold flame. Irrian spent as much time as he could here, in the apartments which were the only place in the entire Old City where he felt truly at peace, and safe. There were traps everywhere in Elorium. One slip, one misplaced word at the wrong time, and you would never be forgiven.

"Truth to tell," he went on," I don't think we've had a chance since the priest was murdered by the river. Perhaps since he was sent to Sarténe in the first place. Sarul must have *known* what an offensive dolt that man was."

"Of course he did," Jayan said. He was taking clothes from a large basket by the wardrobe and folding them into neat piles, to be ironed later. He didn't look over to the window. "Everyone's known it for years. I take it you'll still speak against the policy in the Convocation?"

"Of course I will. For all the good it will do." Irrian rubbed at tired eyes. "I might actually be able to persuade a handful of Arch-Prelates that an invasion of Sarténe is a gross over-reaction. Even an act of crude barbarism against fellow believers. And to what purpose?"

"None at all," Jayan admitted morosely. He shook his head and smoothed out the sleeve of a white shirt. "A Crusade aimed against people of the Faith. I can hardly believe it."

Irrian looked at his servant with a wry smile. "They aren't really people of the Faith, my friend. You know that."

"Close enough," the other man muttered. "They worship the same god, and use some of the same canons."

"And many different, as well."

Jayan nodded. "I know. And yet, I've heard you say the Madai god is the same as ours before now, and the Jaidi one as well, but we share no canons with those faiths at all."

"True enough," Irrian admitted. He made a flicking gesture with his fingers to dismiss the subject and threw himself into an armchair, scowling. "The Dualists haven't helped their own cause, you know. They used to conceal their beliefs, and at least give lip service to the All-Church, but that's changed. I wish I knew why. If I could only go there and *see...*" He trailed off, then shook his head. "Well, no use wishing for what can't be. At any rate, now the Dualists flaunt their beliefs, and never give a thought to what the Basilica might do."

"Then why do you think it's wrong to attack them?"

"For many reasons," Irrian said. "Because I've never believed faith can be spread with the sword, for one thing. You can force people to their knees, but you can't force them to believe. All you achieve is to create resentment, and that will explode in your face, in the end."

"And why else?" Jayan asked. He was still folding clothes.

"You know as well as I," Irrian growled. "The All-Church soldiers already in Tura d'Madai need help, or they'll be overwhelmed. Especially now Calesh Saissan has withdrawn the Hand of the Lord. Five and a half thousand men gone from the lines, just like that! Our army should be sent there, while our best evangelical preachers go into Sarténe, to woo people back to the Faith with words. They work better than swords, in the long run."

"Sarul doesn't believe that."

Irrian's mouth twisted. "Sarul is a fool."

He was worse than simply a fool, in fact. Sarul always saw what he wanted to see, and persuaded himself it was true – except where the endless, labyrinthine politics of the Old City were concerned. When it came to matters of personal advancement Sarul possessed a mind like a polished jewel: clear and bright, with a hundred facets, but utterly cold. A fool would not have been such a danger as this ambitious man whose diamond mind saw only what he wanted it to see. Irrian had hated him for a long time, taking care to hide it behind lazy smiles and hooded, watchful eyes. Masks again, he thought; the endless game of deception. He was sure Sarul didn't know how he felt; if he had, Irrian would have been banished from Coristos on some false charge, or killed, long ago.

"Sarul," he said, "will join the army himself, as Hierarchal Legate. He will advise the generals."

"Sarul doesn't *advise* anyone," the servant answered. "He tells them. Or shouts. Or threatens."

"And he will be the new Hierarch when old Antanus finally dies," Irrian said. He could taste bitterness in his throat.

This time Jayan did stop folding clothes, and glanced across at the chair with concern clear on his square face. "I was afraid of that."

"I almost dread to think what Sarul will do when he wears the mitre," Irrian said. He rubbed his eyes again. "Anyone who wants something that badly shouldn't be trusted with it. And Sarul doesn't even want to be Hierarch *for* anything. There will be no new revelations, no reinterpretations of the faith or edicts of forgiveness. No fresh insights or understandings. Missionaries won't be sent out to bring new converts into the Faith. Corruption won't be addressed; and that *needs* to be addressed, Jayan. If the priests hadn't been charging for services which ought to be free, the Dualism might never have taken hold in Sarténe."

"Masses and confessions," Jayan agreed, nodding. "Even for funerals, if the rumours are right."

Irrian scowled. "The rumours are right. But Sarul hasn't thought about any of that, and wouldn't have an idea even if he had. He's not interested in the future of the Faith, just in his own future, how much he can achieve. It's enough for him to *want*, and to him, taking the mitre will mean he's won another struggle, and proved himself the best."

"I could deal with him for you," Jayan said after a moment, his voice a bare whisper.

Irrian sighed wearily. It was a suggestion Jayan had made before, and one Irrian knew he could fulfil. "No, my friend. I won't condone the Faithful killing each other if it can be avoided."

"Ah," Jayan smiled. "I knew that was why you oppose sending the army into Sarténe."

Well, perhaps it was. The Dualists had changed many of the God-Son's teachings, even to the point where they denied his divinity. They taught the soul was created by God, but flesh by the Devil, and life was a constant struggle between the two. That was why their Elite forswore all pleasures of the flesh, from wine to sexual congress, in order to purify their souls. All-Church priests were supposed to do the same, though they rarely did. Irrian himself had a weakness for a glass of wine with his supper. Flesh was weak, whoever had created it.

But the Dualists' belief that flesh was tainted by evil meant the God-Son could not have been divine, clothed in flesh as he was. In turn, that meant he could not have risen from the grave, and the redemption he offered was thus false. One of the Elite had even gone so far as to claim Adjai must have been an agent of the Devil, sent to lead men from the true path. Irrian couldn't imagine anything more likely to rouse the Basilica to fury, unless it was the speed with which the heresy was spreading. A generation ago nobody had heard of Dualism. Today it had all but pushed the All-Church out of Sarténe, and crossed the Raima Mountains to establish itself in the north of Alinaur. Other fingers had stretched into Rheven and Caileve, and even beyond. Pockets of the new religion sprang up as though out of the earth itself, spawning open air services and green-robed Elite, and leaving Church pews half deserted and the collection plates empty.

In another twenty years it might have gone too far to be stopped. That was the nightmare which haunted Sarul, and which he played on to frighten others into action. It was that fear which had led to Rabast's mission to Sarténe, and then to his murder by the banks of the river.

Still, even with all that, the Dualists worshipped the same God, and taught lessons from the older books of prophets, the ones which predated the ministry of Adjai. They remained among the Faithful as far as Irrian was concerned, for all that they denied so much that the All-Church taught. What mattered was the search for God, the willingness to accept Him into your life, not the manner of the hunt itself. What did it matter where you prayed, or what words you used? Sending an army against them to enforce a certain method of worship was unjustified. Doing more would be abhorrent.

"Are we right?" he murmured, asking the question of himself more than Jayan. "I wish I could be certain. Is what we do right, or do we sin against God, without even knowing it?"

Jayan shrugged. "We follow our conscience as best we're able. That's all God asks of any man. And it's a little late, Irrian, to start thinking we've done the wrong thing all these years."

"Yes. Yes, I suppose it is." He rose and went restlessly back to the window, wincing slightly as he did so. Arthritis had invaded his left hip some years before, at the early age of forty, since when sitting down or standing up had caused increasing pain. It was unfair that he should suffer twice for one ailment, he thought. "And you, Jayan? Do you ever doubt?"

"Never," he said quietly. "Not for a second. I saw what the All-Church called salvation when I was a boy."

So had Irrian, of course. Both of them had grown up in Sarténe, both close to the borders, though here in the Basilica they never mentioned that. Irrian thought it likely that nobody remembered it now. Sarul, if he knew, would use half-spoken insinuations to create a cloud of suspicion around them, something he did easily, except this time he wouldn't be the only one. But Irrian and Jayan had witnessed the priests who gave masses only for those worshippers who could pay, and ignored the pleas of poor folk who feared their souls would be lost. They'd heard priests claim poverty as a virtue and then line their pockets with silver sesters, and eat roasted meats washed down with vintage wine while their parishioners went hungry. It was such abuses which had weakened the grip of the All-Church in Sarténe, and allowed the Dualism to work its roots into the ground.

Irrian still believed that priests – good ones, honest men serving God – were a surer way to end the heresy than violence. But the Hierocracy of the Basilica had set its face against any alternative to its teachings long ago, and it was one thing that would never change, no matter who wore the Hierarch's mitre. Worshippers could not be allowed to believe the All-Church's doctrine might be false, or even open to question. The sacred texts were the words of God, divine and infallible. The smallest deviation from them would place souls in peril: it was the All-Church's *duty,* its obligation, to save men from such an insidious danger.

Irrian had said before that the All-Church needed to remember that it stood for the worship of God, not for the worship of writings which priests said were holy. A subtle difference, but like most such it was important. But he was swimming against the tide: it was Sarul, and the brand of cast-iron certainty he championed, that was in the ascendancy now. It had been for some time, in truth. Whole treatises of apologetics had been written to justify every word of the Canons, and apocryphal theories were simply not allowed.

"Doubt cracks the façade of faith," Sarul had said, in a memorable phrase some years ago, *"and apostasy slinks through the gaps."*

Sarul might as well be Hierarch already. A third of the Arch-Prelates were already in his camp. Another third, perhaps more, would support him in Convocation because they could smell the changes in the wind, and hoped to share a little in the blessings they brought. It was a majority for anything Sarul might propose short of slaughtering infants, and even that might be approved for babies born outside the

Faith. Usually the Old City was a welter of factions arguing for this and that, their alliances shifting from day to day and one Convocation to the next. Sarul's implacable rise had put an end to that, at least until he wore the mitre. Then it would start again, the Arch-Prelates manoeuvring in the race to succeed him, to achieve power for themselves. It had always been the same. It probably always would be.

It was, Irrian thought ruefully, the worst possible time for all this to have happened. If the priest had not been murdered there might have been a delay, a year at least while the Hierocracy debated what to do, or looked for a plausible excuse to invade. Since old Antanus began to fade there had been an air of inertia about the Old City, while Arch-Prelates and priests waited for him to die and power to pass to new hands, offering a new direction. Even the Convocations were limp things, lacking their usual fire. Left to itself the Hierocracy would have done nothing, and by the time it did the army by the Rielle would have been in Tura d'Madai. It was even possible that when Antanus died, and Sarul had his posterior seated firmly upon the Eternal Throne, he would no longer feel such an urgent need for a great cause to champion. Things might have been different then.

But it was all ifs and buts, because Rabast *had* been murdered beside the river, by a man with unshaven cheeks and rundown heels. All that was known about the killer were his parting words, overheard by a fisherman down by the water's edge: *the Margrave of Mayence sends his regards.* Words so rash and ill-advised that it was tempting to believe they were a lie, concocted by some young zealot in order to advance his career in the Hierocracy. Irrian didn't believe so, in fact. Such zealots existed, but they weren't nearly as numerous as common people of utter, stupefying, irredeemable stupidity.

So, events were in motion. They had been for some time. The inertia in Coristos had slowed them though, because Antanus had still not died. He was bedridden now, hardly able to eat even when food was pushed into his mouth, but he lived and he was still God's advocate upon the earth. The Convocation could discuss and vote all it liked, but until Antanus approved their plans on one of his increasingly rare lucid days, nothing happened. That near-paralysis had granted Calesh Saissan more than two months to bring the Hand of the Lord back from Tura d'Madai. It was more time than Irrian had thought he would have. Perhaps he ought to have had more faith.

But his faith had cracked long ago. He supposed Sarul would say that apostasy had slunk through the gaps.

He sighed and looked back at Jayan. He felt very tired. "Repeat the message back to me before you go."

His old friend linked his hands together and began to recite, like a schoolboy who has learned a poem by rote. "An assassin is on his way to kill Calesh Saissan and his friends. He's a Justified highbinder named Elizur Mandain. He plans to blend into a mercenary company and enter Sarténe with them, using a false name and probably a more extensive disguise as well. Meanwhile, Sarul will accompany the army, as Hierarchal Legate advising General Amaury."

"Good," Irrian said. *Sarul as Legate. God in Heaven, it just gets worse and worse.* "Go now, Jayan. Pass the message to the Lady of the Hidden House. Tell our friends what is coming."

He waited until the door closed before he went back to the chair. These days the constant ache in his hip meant he found it easier to rest sitting up than in bed. He leaned his head back and closed his eyes, and as he drifted towards sleep memories played across his eyelids.

*

For Irrian it had started thirty years before, when he was a young acolyte still learning the ways of the Old City.

There had never been any doubt he would be a priest. He was the third son of a minor baron in the south of Gallene, just inside Sarténe. An unneeded sprig of nobility, in a family barely able to afford him. The eldest brother was trained as heir, in knighthood and administration. The second joined a mercenary company, learning similar skills at greater risk, and most importantly at someone else's expense. He was the spare, needed only if something fatal befell his elder brother. And the third? It was a choice between the clergy and the life of an itinerant, and really that was no choice at all. At fifteen he entered his name in the rolls of the cathedral at Rosiem, and was accepted as an unsworn acolyte.

He had thought sometimes, in the years since, that he might have done better to become a musician. Sarténi troubadours were spreading across the world now, playing to nobles in Caileve and Alinaur, even going north to Rheven to perform in great dank castles with the forest all around. There was an endless stream of rumours about singers who had found their way to the beds of the noble ladies who hired them, then slipped away before the husband could return from hunting. There must be young nobles in six countries who had been fathered by musicians, children growing up in nests once visited by a cuckoo.

Several players had retired to small villas by the sea, with servants of their own and much younger wives. It wasn't a bad life, Irrian supposed, but it had never really been for him, despite the occasional regrets. He liked warm beds too much to spend his life walking the road.

Besides, he had wanted to serve God. It was easy, after all these years of suffering and forbearance, to forget that fact. *The hardest thing about patience is the waiting*, he thought again. It still wasn't funny.

Among the unwanted and unloved who made up the unsworn acolytes, many boys were obviously not suited for the clergy. Those who preferred fighting to study, for the most part, bullies who scowled in ferocious puzzlement over simple sums and sweated when told to sign their names. They were winnowed out soon enough, the worst of them to be sent home, but most recruited instead by the Order of the Basilica to swell their gold and white ranks. They might not live long, but they could serve God and perhaps, just possibly, they might win a smattering of glory. Promotion to captain of a company in Tura d'Madai was better than going home in shame, even if it meant you never went home at all. Not alive.

Those who remained were the clever ones. Sometimes uneducated, as Irrian was, for his family had never wasted a tutor on him. All he knew were scraps gleaned from his brothers, when they deigned to notice him at all. But Irrian had found, somewhat to his surprise, that he was able to learn. He was even more surprised to find he wanted to.

By the time he was sixteen, Irrian had read all the books and scrolls in the cathedral. Fourteen of them, all told, including the Canons. One day when the bishop lectured the boys on the proper performance of devotions, Irrian stayed back afterwards to ask some questions. He had enough sense not to raise them in front of the class. The bishop blinked a little at first, then frowned, and finally peered at Irrian from under heavy brows, eyes glittering in calculation.

A month later Irrian was sent to study at the burgeoning Academy in Parrien, and his true journey began.

The All-Church had never really trusted any educational establishment it didn't control itself, fearful of what might be taught without suitable guidance. Still, the days of book bonfires were over, and if you wanted the best education you went to the Academy. In those days there had been no talk of heresy. Or at least, it was whispered talk, spoken in corners to trusted friends, and not to an unknown youth in an acolyte's robe. Certainly the rumours didn't reach high in the ranks of the All-Church: if they had, Irrian would never have been sent to such a nest of unbelievers. But sent he was, and bit by slow bit he began to learn, everything from history to theology and apologetics. And bit by bit he began to hear the whispers, until his quick mind understood what was happening around him.

His reaction was one of interest, rather than shock. Perhaps his new-found education lay behind that: he thought of God now as an abstract, a concept, rather than a physical being. No less real for that, of course, and no less important to the lives of men either. He started to listen in earnest, if carefully, and to dig out scrolls and books from dusty library shelves. Sometimes he asked a question, when he could mask his true interest behind a screen of theological orthodoxy. Even then he was wary, careful not to ask *too* much, or of the wrong person. If people realised what he was doing they might start to question him, an All-Church acolyte nosing into things better left undisturbed. But he was sure this new form of worship couldn't have sprung fully-formed from nothing, like a pagan goddess from the head of her father. There had to be a point of origin; more, there must be a reason why people found it attractive. All those whispers concealed a secret, and even at eighteen he knew people would kill to protect secrets.

He was struggling to translate a cartouche from an ancient desert tongue, very late at night, when a sound made him look up.

"The word you need is *shrouded*," the woman before his tiny desk said. "Though that's a literal translation, and rather misses the true meaning. The symbols within a cartouche should be taken together, you know. Perhaps *hidden from prying eyes* would be better."

He stared at her in astonishment. "How did you –"

"Know which word you were puzzling over? Ah, now. That is a secret you shall not learn yet, I'm afraid." She moved a little more into the light, and Irrian realised his midnight visitor was a beautiful woman indeed. He put her age at about forty, but there was no grey in her dark hair, and her skin bore few lines. Startling blue eyes studied him serenely. "You have been looking for me."

"Looking for you?"

"Oh, yes," she said. "Although you may not have realised it. That happens a lot, in fact. Still, you will know me, I think." She sat gracefully down on a rickety stool, unconcerned by the dust that stirred around her fine green gown. "I am the Lady of the Hidden House."

Irrian was aware he was staring. He knew that name, of course. It lay at the bottom of the mystery he tracked, and *hidden from prying eyes* described it perfectly. He'd ploughed through a dozen books without finding more than a mention of it, and even that oblique. Until now he had learned almost nothing of the Hidden House except that it existed. He might never have learned more, except that its mistress had come knocking in the night.

"I'm honoured," he said.

That made her smile. "I hoped you were as clever as you seem. My weavings told me you would be, but I prefer to see for myself, if I can."

"Weavings?" he asked, bewildered again.

She told him what she meant. Then she told him more: about himself, about her, about the world he had walked through in ignorance. It was one thing to realise, intellectually, that you knew nothing. It was quite another to be shown it in sharp, undeniable clarity. Being told so by a beautiful woman in a musty library as midnight passed away was something else again.

By the time she rose he was convinced. He was half in love with her too, though he wouldn't realise that until he found her in his dreams, night after night in the months to come.

"I must go," she said. "Talk to the history lecturer, a man named Cerain. He knows me, and can teach you."

"Will I see you again?" he blurted.

"Undoubtedly," she said. She moved away from his desk, out of the light of his lantern, and Irrian stumbled to his feet in a clatter of quills and fallen papers. By the time the rattling stopped he was two paces from the desk, and he could no longer hear the Lady's footfalls on the flagstone floor.

He saw her again two months later, and a third time not long before he left Parrien for good. It would not be safe for him to return. His future lay among the cloisters and monasteries of Coristos, behind the towering wall of the Old City, where – she told him with calm certainty – he would be counted among the great one day. And where, thirty years later, he still remembered the beauty of the woman who had come to him in that dusty room, and dreamed of what might have been if he had dared to kiss her in the light of the lamp.

*

Irrian dozed for a time, but full sleep wouldn't quite come to him. Memories churned through his mind, mixed with images of countless soldiers swarming through Sarténe with flaming brands in their fists, and in the end he woke. At some point Jayan must have come back, because a blanket had been placed around Irrian and tucked in at the sides. That made him smile. He might live to be ninety, and still Jayan would think he needed to be cared for like a child.

When he stirred went back to the window, wincing once more at a stab of pain in his troublesome hip. None of the chiropractors could tell him why arthritis had struck at one joint and left the others alone, even a decade later, but he supposed he should be glad of the mercy. Antanus the Hierarch was crippled in both hands and knees, so that every day he was martyred by his suffering from the moment he woke. Irrian could at least still hold a quill. His lips quirked in an ironic smile. Perhaps God was telling him he had chosen the right path.

Outside night was falling. Irrian watched it and let his mind run on a familiar track, calculating risks and possible gains. He wished it was Sarul who suffered crippling pains in his hands, or else Elizur Mandain. Someone who deserved them. It was unkind of him, but Irrian hoped both men would be struck down by agonies before they could join the Crusade. He didn't really expect they would be, though. It was strange that the cruel and self-serving always seemed to escape while the pious went through torment.

But Irrian had done what he could. Jayan would pass his message to a Notary in the outer city, if he hadn't already. The coin-counter would encrypt it in a secret cipher and send it by pigeon to someone in Mayence: Irrian had never known who. From there it would rapidly reach the Hidden House, and the Lady. Irrian had been sending her messages that way for thirty years.

Three months ago he'd sent a message to someone else for the very first time, a hastily-scrawled missive meant for Calesh Saissan, far away in the deserts of Tura d'Madai. Everything that followed now would be partly because of him: the lives lost, the lives saved, all the joys and griefs. When he thought too much about that it brought a chill to his skin.

The Lady of the Hidden House must be well into her seventies by now. Twenty years older than he was. He supposed if she could bear her burdens, he could shoulder his own.

He hoped he might be allowed to see her again, before it ended.

Twelve

Departures

A frayed-looking man with sawdust in his hair balanced a wooden board over a broad window, trying to hold it in place with his knees while he twisted to hammer in nails. Half a dozen stuck out at unruly angles, and he hadn't fixed the board when he struck his own thumb so hard that blood spattered in bright, sparkling drops. He yowled and dropped the board.

Strong hands caught it before it moved more than an inch.

"Hasty hands make for sloppy work, friend," Luthien said. "Calm yourself. Your life is not in peril today."

The grounds keeper saw his green Elite's robe, and broke off in the midst of another ripe curse. His face went red.

"Er," he managed.

Luthien looked over his shoulder, to where Academy students were streaming past along the gravel path, heading for the manor house. "I'd appreciate a little help, if someone could spare a moment."

It was gratifying, really, to see the number of youths who detached themselves from the tide and moved towards him. Most saw that others were ahead of them and veered back to the path, but three came over and lifted the far end of the board into position. He didn't know any of them. Presumably they came out of respect for the green robe.

"Perhaps you could hammer those nails straight now," he said to the grounds keeper. "And don't worry about your swearing. Really, I heard far worse oaths in the Hand of the Lord."

He wished he had the words back as soon as he spoke them. Luthien could actually *see* the man wondering whether to ask when he was going to fetch his weapons and prepare for the coming battles. Several of the students glanced over too, though they hastily looked away again if they thought he might notice them. One or two of the more percipient flicked eyes from the path to the window and back, visibly calculating the distance Luthien must have moved to catch the board as it began to slide. Which wasn't the point, of course. Nobody would have had the time to cover the five yards or so from where

Luthien had been, walking calmly in the gravel, to where he needed to be.

The trick was in knowing where you had to be before you needed to be there. He'd always found it rather simple.

"The nails?" Luthien said after a moment. The grounds keeper gave a start and picked up his hammer, pausing to suck blood off his wounded thumb before he began to work.

It was only a clumsy hammer stroke, but Luthien had seen other signs of panic already. Students loading bags onto a hired donkey until the animal's back was bent under the weight, then adding more. People at the quayside in Parrien trying to buy passage on a ship heading out, heading anywhere, at extortionate prices that only got worse as the day wore on. Other townsfolk had formed impromptu caravans and trudged away westward, towards Mayence. So far the exodus was slow, the roads uncrowded, but behaviour like that was contagious, just as fear was.

Word that the All-Church army was crossing the Rielle had spread through Parrien during the morning. It had reached the Academy too, passing through the halls in a ripple of whispers, like a pagan god flying on winged feet. Parrien could at least shelter behind its walls and ramparts, poorly maintained though they were, but the Academy was exposed, a rambling sprawl of buildings set in woodland and orchards. It would last only for as long as it took horsemen to ride through and toss burning brands inside the doors. Parrien wasn't much better: anyone still there when the army came would likely be trapped until the fighting was done, and no matter if his father was a Duke in Boromil or a Baron in Rheven. Sieges were ugly things, drawn-out torments in which the innocent starved right alongside the guilty, and died with them as well. The realisation of that truth was in every one of the passing faces of the students. They were heading for the main hall – if they could all still fit inside – to hear the Dean tell them what the faculty intended to do.

Luthien would quite like to know that, as well.

"You know," he said in a low voice to the grounds keeper, "a sheet of wood won't keep soldiers out of the lecture halls."

With nails held in his mouth, the hammerer shifted them deftly to one side of his lips before he answered. "Might slow them down."

Not much, it wouldn't.

The man was dreaming, but at least he hadn't already begun to throw belongings into bags and flee for the hills. Plenty of people had done so the moment they heard the army was coming. Luthien supposed he couldn't blame them: the size of that force appalled him too. It was one thing to see tens of thousands of men unleashed on infidels in a faraway land, but the likes of Gallene and Rheven hadn't seen an army like that since the days of the Empire, half a millennium ago. Not even the wealthiest kings could afford to pay for it. But the All-Church could, and it went where they ordered.

And the soldiers? Some would fight for money: there were always enough like that to keep wars raging until God made an end of the world, or else the last human lay dying with a spear in his belly. Others would believe whatever the All-Church priests told them, however horrible or unlikely, about the Dualism. There were always plenty of those men too, willing to accept the vilest slanders as truth if the speaker wore the cassock of a man of God. Still more would harbour doubts but follow orders, held to the purpose by bonds of brotherhood and trust, forged in battle and almost impossible to break. Luthien knew a little about such ties, and he couldn't blame people for them either.

A few might defy the priests. Not enough, Luthien thought; a thousand would not be enough. Only a very small number of men had the clearness of mind to recognise a lie through several disguises, and the moral courage to act upon the knowledge. And there would be lies, he was sure. The All-Church would make outrageous claims of their enemies; that they defiled the Cross, murdered children for use of their blood in unspeakable rites, and practised bizarre sexual acts upon each other. The same sort of things that had been said of the Madai before the first Crusade was launched, and of the Jaidi before then, when the Basilica was gathering men to retake Alinaur from the desert folk. It was outright mendacity and Churchmen ought to be above such things, but it worked, and it didn't help that the Margrave of Mayence so patently preferred men in his bed. That was the well-known fleck of truth which would gild the lies, and make them seem true.

The army would go where the All-Church aimed it. That was obvious, but it would need days to cross the Rielle, and perhaps another week to reach Parrien. Still, many of the townsfolk had decided not to wait. There was no such thing as leaving too early, but a person could certainly leave it too late, though too much haste might lead to mistakes. One knot of refugees had actually fled *east*, straight down the road the All-Church army would shortly march up. The soldiers would steal the food they brought and take the women for their own amusement, most likely. The thought made Luthien grimace.

He should not be thinking about armies anyway. That part of his life was over. He turned his attention back to the grounds keeper, and lowered his voice still further. "If you have family, it might not be a bad time to pay them a visit. Especially if they live outside Sarténe."

Nails moved back across the man's mouth. "All my people are here." He shrugged. "All my life is."

He was not a garrulous man, it seemed. Luthien didn't press him further. With the board nailed up he stepped away and nodded thanks to the three students who had helped. The boys rejoined the stream of youths heading for the manor, which was thinner now that most had already gone by. Luthien dusted his hands, pleased with a job well done, and that was when he noticed five men in uniform watching him from twenty feet away.

They were Hand of the Lord, he saw immediately, their black and white coats dusty from travel. Soldiers of the Hand always kept their uniforms clean and mended, which meant these men hadn't had time for such niceties. That made them newcomers to Mayence, and *that* meant they almost certainly belonged to the companies Calesh had brought back from Tura d'Madai. It was simple logic – simple, but even that much was usually beyond most people, which always frustrated Luthien. He knew he shouldn't pity those who were less clever than he was, but it was a weakness he couldn't seem to shake.

The men weren't wearing armour, so Luthien didn't think they meant trouble. Still, the cadaverous-looking man at the front was gazing quite openly at him. Luthien walked over and raised an eyebrow.

"My name is Amand," the gaunt man said, not at all perturbed. His uniform bore the remnants of well-ironed creases, underneath the dust. "I'm here on the orders of Commander Saissan, and you're Luthien Bourrel, of course."

*

It was the glasses which gave Luthien away, he knew. They were still virtually unheard-of in Sarténe, though one of the Jaidi professors at the Academy wore a pair that perched on the end of his nose as though always on the point of slipping off. Like Luthien, he had acquired his glasses in the desert, where there were craftsmen with the skill to make such things. Perhaps they would be able to manufacture them in Sarténe, one day. Until then Luthien had to treat them as carefully as the souls of little children.

He was the only Elite who wore them. He knew they made him distinctive, especially taken together with the sandy hair that curled over his ears and the nape of his neck. People noticed Elite anyway. That went double for one with strange lenses before his eyes.

"I am," he said to the gaunt man. When caught by surprise he often took refuge in irony, and he let his eyebrow climb a little higher. "Does Calesh expect five men of the Hand to save Mayence, then? I know you're very good, but his opinion is considerably higher than mine, it seems."

"Hardly," Amand said. He really was incredibly thin, as though he had been boiled until all the moisture was gone from his flesh and only leathery skin remained. His face was all planes and angles, with no softening features at all. He looked to Luthien like a strip of old leather, and just as tough. "We're not here to fight. We came to inform the Dean that the Hand believes it will not be possible to defend these buildings."

"Calesh doesn't waste any time," Luthien muttered. Something heavy had lodged in his stomach with the soldier's words. *The Hand believes it will not be possible* sounded bland enough, but Luthien knew the meaning of that phrase well enough: the Hand would make no effort to save the Academy, come what may. "But you've had a wasted trip. I think the Dean knows already."

Amand brushed at the dust on his coat, making the dust into streaks. "Will he abandon the Academy?"

Students were still passing on the path, craning their heads to look at the soldiers as they passed. Luthien thought rapidly. "I suspect he will allow the students to return to their homes, on a temporary basis. You can stay to confirm that, if you like. But abandon the Academy?" He shook his head. "You don't know Cerain. He'll already be planning to come back."

"I hope he has the chance," Amand said. "But that's his choice. My orders were only to warn the Dean, not to order him to one path or another."

"Orders from Calesh?" Luthien asked shrewdly. Amand nodded. "He's acting as though he's in command of the Hand here."

The gaunt man's gaze flickered. "The Marshal Commander is a drunk, Elite Bourrel. What would you prefer?"

"I'd prefer that none of this was happening at all," he answered, a little tartly. That was somewhat impolite but he let it pass without chastising himself, instead stepping closer to the soldiers so he could lower his voice. "What does Calesh plan to do?"

"Fight," Amand said laconically. "But not here, or anywhere else too exposed. He plans to withdraw to the Aiguille and fight in the hills. Hit the All-Church and run, over and again."

Luthien stared at him as realisation struck. "That would mean abandoning Parrien."

"We can't defend it," Amand said. He too kept his voice low, so the last students straggling past them could not overhear. "The wall here isn't high enough or well enough maintained. You were a soldier, you know that's the truth. We don't have the men, or the time to find them."

"May God shelter us all," Luthien breathed. "Because the Hand obviously won't. You'll be running for the hills while Parrien burns, and its people are butchered behind you."

"A strange thing for you to say," the soldier noted. "Given that you will leave your sword in its scabbard while people die, though you know you could save them if you chose."

"You bastard," Luthien ground out. "You bastard. How can you throw that accusation in my face?"

"Why not? You threw it at me." Amand glanced back at his four men. "I have to go, Elite Bourrel. I only stopped because I recognised you, and wanted at least to meet the man behind the name. I almost wish I had not, now." He began to turn away. "I wonder, will you still stand with your hands at your sides when women are killed in front of you? Or children?"

It took an effort to keep from hitting the man. Luthien had never been so close to violence since he had sworn the Consolation, three years before. Maybe it was just a question of time. He had never sworn either until Japh had made him curse in the manor house last week, and now here he was cussing again. He sucked in a needful breath. "I will keep my oath to God."

"Then I hope he forgives you," Amand said, "for loving that oath more than you love the hurt and the dying."

He turned away, gesturing to the men to follow him. They had started along the gravel path before Luthien could find his voice; he was so choked with fury that he thought he might burst. But it was helpless rage; he was Consoled, and forbidden from violence. His fists clenched.

"I swore an oath!" he shouted after the soldiers. "Is that fact too much for your thick-skulled brain to grasp? *I swore an oath!*"

None of the soldiers acknowledged him, though several passing townsfolk gave Luthien surprised looks. It wasn't often that an enraged Elite yelled insults in the street, and certainly not to soldiers. Their glances chilled his anger into a fragile calm. Underneath rage still roiled in him, but at least he could think, once he got past the terrible urge to give someone a ding upside the ear. Sometimes he almost thought God *wanted* him to break his oath. He made himself put that aside, breathing deeply until the tightness in his chest passed.

The Hand of the Lord was abandoning Parrien. He had to concede that it was a sound strategic decision, though thousands would die as a result of it. More interesting was that Calesh had given the order; not Darien, the leader of the Hand, and not Baruch either as the second-in-command in Sarténe. That Darien was a drunkard was common knowledge, but it was still surprising that he had surrendered his position so easily. If he had. It was possible that Calesh had simply taken authority on himself. He was capable of that sort of direct, decisive action, and Luthien could easily imagine the soldiers following him.

He wondered suddenly if Calesh had gone to the Hidden House, and Ailiss. If he was seizing authority here in Sarténe it would be the logical thing to do, to give his orders some legitimacy, but it would require time Calesh probably didn't have. Luthien hesitated, wondering about that, but there was no way he could know. He certainly wasn't about to run after Amand and ask.

So Parrien was to be thrown to the wolves. If the Hand was abandoning the town then Luthien was almost certain the Margrave's Guard would do the same, probably so both forces could make a stand later, in the Aiguille. It was a way to trade space in return for time – time to build supplies for a siege, to recruit and train more men and build defences for them to stand behind – but it doomed Parrien. A couple of thousand decent soldiers might, just possibly, have been able to hold the walls against the All-Church army. Artisans, traders and watchmen would not, at least not for more than a few days. Anyone who had fled Parrien already had been right, whether they had left by merchant caravan or ship, or simply by walking with their lives packed into sacks on their backs.

The five soldiers were out of sight now. Luthien knew where they would be, at the small compound the Hand maintained in the Academy, ostensibly for recruitment purposes. Not many students joined though, especially from outside Sarténe. Mostly the compound was there so the All-Church would know that it was, and to make fathers feel their sons were safe in the lecture halls. Luthien would achieve nothing by going there. Instead he turned the other way, towards the manor house and the assembly he had been heading for when he stopped to help a grounds keeper with a makeshift shutter.

He was calmer when he reached the entrance hall. Walking always cleared his mind, however angry he might be, and today he was glad of it. He found the hall bustling with activity. Lines of students snaked from the doors to an assortment of carts or ponies, boxes in their arms, or small scrips thrown across their shoulders. Sometimes books poked their corners into sight, or balanced atop the boxes and tried to slide away whenever the owner's arm joggled or his attention wandered. A couple of laden donkeys were already being drawn away on leading lines. Many of the students kept their eyes on the ground rather than meet anyone's gaze. Obviously not everyone was waiting for the Dean's announcement. Luthien found himself the focus of attention as he moved walked up to the doors.

"Tutor Luthien, do you know –"

"Can you tell us –"

"Is there news -?"

"I've heard nothing," he answered quickly, without slowing down. He had to repeat the phrase over and again, and only realised it was a lie when he was through the throng and walking up the gravel path towards the offices in the old manor house. He said such things so as not to pre-empt one of the Dean's decisions, and evidently it had become habit. He'd heard the Hand was abandoning Parrien, of course, and would not defend the Academy when the army came. The students would learn about that soon enough; morning at the latest, Luthien thought, if rumour sped as it usually did. There would be a surge of panic then. The few students who had already left, boxes in their arms or mules at their heels, would seem as wise as serpents when that happened.

"Luthien!"

Cerain hurried across the hall towards him. "Where have you been? We have word of the Hand."

"I know," he said, his voice dull. "They're leaving Parrien."

"How do you know that? Never mind." Cerain waved away his own question, words tumbling as he hurried to get them all out. He caught Luthien's sleeve and drew him into the shelter of a doorway. "I'm going to send the students home. I'll tell them we plan to reopen next spring, but for now it will be safer for them to leave Sarténe, if they can."

"Reopen in the spring," Luthien repeated. He couldn't help a snort of laughter. "Cerain, my friend, by the spring there will be nothing here. The All-Church army will destroy this place completely."

The Dean stared at him. "Why would they do that?"

"Because they hate it," Luthien said, "and fear it, too. The Academy, I mean. We teach things no priest would approve of. Some of our tutors openly debate the indivisibility of God, when the Basilica insists there is no debate. We have Cailevi philosophers, and theologians from among the Jaidi. We have been trying to light a candle here, a spark of knowledge, and the All-Church hates knowledge it doesn't control. You know they do. In God's name, Cerain, the all-Church hates *mathematics.* They will smash this place flat, believe me."

"But nobody will be here."

"That doesn't matter." He felt suddenly tired. All he had tried to do here, all that the tutors and scholars had attempted to achieve, would be lost. It had been for nothing. "They're coming to Sarténe to burn, Cerain, to smash and destroy everything they can reach. When they get here they'll set fire to the buildings and piss on the rubble. It's the symbol they will wreck. Tell me, did you truly believe there were no book-burners in the clergy any more?"

Cerain stared at him, jaw working, and said nothing. There was such an expression of loss in his eyes that Luthien felt like crying. The old man had given his life to the Academy, from when he'd been a boy hired to help clean the stables on the far side of the pear orchards. From there he had enrolled, winning one of the few scholarships made available by the Margrave's money. He had studied for six years, graduated in mathematics, and become a tutor soon afterwards. Everything he knew, or had known for decades, was within this campus. He *was* the Academy, and Luthien's soul wept for him.

"I'm sorry," Luthien said. He rubbed his eyes. "Go talk to the students, Cerain. Send them home."

"I will," the older man said in a husky voice. He cleared his throat. "And then I'll speak to the faculty. We have to decide what to do."

"Do?" Luthien stared at him. "Weren't you listening? There's nothing we can *do*. The Academy can't be defended. Maybe we should have built it like a castle, and run a moat all the way around with angled spikes in the water."

"So the Academy can't be saved," Cerain said. "All right. I accept that. But the books can be. We've spent almost a hundred years building up our library, and I am *not* about to let a mob of savages burn it all to ash." The Dean's thin face was grim. "The Muses have not been silenced yet, my friend."

Luthien frowned at him. Cerain was a lugubrious man most of the time, but just then his face bore an expression of stern determination. It was hard not to be intrigued. "There are over eleven thousand original works in the library. How can you hope to get them all out?"

"That's better," Cerain said. "Don't tell me what can't be done, Luthien: tell me how to *do*. I need you thinking clearly, not letting yourself sink into despair. How? Wagons."

Luthien thought about that. Losing the buildings of the Academy was bad, but not fatal: it was the books that really mattered. With them everything could be remade. But if they were lost... they were the product of decades of work in lecture halls and libraries, by discussion groups and students and scriveners, and copies made word by laborious word. Perhaps, in time, all that could be rebuilt. And perhaps not. Luthien wouldn't wager on it, himself.

But the idea of transporting it all away was unthinkable. All the wagons would have to be covered, and preferably with rigid oiled fabric against which books could be piled, tied together in tall stacks. It would have to be waterproof, in case of another heavy storm like the one a few nights past. And it would have to be escorted, by enough men to keep the cargo safe even on roads thronged with refugees, half of them turning to banditry, and all of them desperate for transport and willing to throw out some old papers to acquire it.

"You're a lunatic," he said.

"There's no other way," Cerain told him. "We'll never be able to arrange for a ship in time, and even if we could the rush would mean there were unsecured items, which would certainly be ruined by ocean spray. So we have to go by road. We don't have a choice."

"They'll never make it," Luthien insisted. "Someone will hijack the wagons before they've covered ten miles. Desperate people who can't walk fast enough, or whose children need somewhere to sit. Your books will be thrown on the road before they even reach Mayence."

"Ah, but I have a way to stop that," Cerain said. "Two ways, in fact."

Luthien looked at him. "If one of those ways is me, old friend, you had better put it out of your mind. I am Elite."

"You're a soldier," the Dean said. "You always have been."

"I'm beginning to get tired of people telling me what I am," Luthien said in a strained voice. "You all seem to think my oath is a trivial thing, to be tossed aside when it becomes inconvenient. But the Consolation is holy, it's sacred, and I will not abandon it when the world fills with trials. I am Elite." He looked up at the thin man through his glasses. "If you think I'll use violence to defend your books, you are making a mistake."

Cerain shrugged. "Well, if that's so, I still have the second part of my plan."

"Which is?"

"The students," the Dean said. "They're leaving anyway, and a lot will head west on their way home. And many of them are the sons of nobles or wealthy merchants, and have at least a little ability with a sword. I'm not saying they're a fighting force, Luthien, but they ought to be able to protect our manuscripts on a journey through the Raima Mountains."

"*Through* the mountains?"

"Into Alinaur, yes. I have a friend in Samanta, on the coast, who might be willing to store them for us."

He would have to be a wealthy friend, with perhaps a country villa he didn't happen to be using at the moment. A suspicion began to grow in Luthien's mind. "Cerain, exactly how often have you met this friend?"

"Well, never, in point of fact," the Dean said apologetically. "But we have conversed by letter quite often."

Luthien stared at him. "He's a pen pal."

"He's a scholar," Cerain corrected. "A man who would hate to see books put to the torch."

"You want to take eleven thousand books and scrolls across the mountains with an escort of students, and then store them with a pen pal," Luthien said. It didn't sound any saner this time either. "You're out of your mind."

He wasn't really thinking of that, though. There was an unspoken part of Cerain's plan, one which Luthien had seen at once: he himself was the logical choice to go with the wagons. Of all the faculty only he had fought, and the students knew that. Having the famous Luthien Bourrel along would do wonders for their confidence. More, it would take Luthien neatly out of Sarténe before the fighting began, thus saving him from the question of breaking his oath. Except that a wagon train of untried students would be *bound* to find trouble in the Raima: Luthien could think of nobody more likely than students to find trouble anywhere, let alone in those wilds. It might seem that the wagons protected his oath, but in truth, he thought it probably placed it at greater risk than ever.

But it was impossible to turn down. If Luthien tried he would only make himself look foolish, because he really *was* the best choice for the task. Besides, why would he refuse? So he could stay and watch Mayence burn, and the Academy, while his oath forced him to stand aside? And in any case, Cerain needed hope, or he would have nothing.

"We'll have to be quick," Luthien said finally.

Cerain nodded. "I know."

"No, I don't think you do," Luthien disagreed. "The All-Church will send cavalry units out to scout the land, and to spread fire and fear among the people. Some might be here very soon. Perhaps within two or three days."

"That's hardly any time at all," Cerain said.

"It means a long night for everyone on the faculty." Luthien sighed. "Oh, all right. I'll go along with this mad plan. Tell your students to go home, Cerain, and not to return until they're sure it's safe. The tutors from Alinaur or Temujin, as well. The All-Church won't show them any mercy. You have to warn them in time to get away."

"I know," Cerain said sombrely. "I've been trying to put that off, but you're right. I'll do it right after I speak to the students. If you're willing to begin hunting down some wagons, and preparing to load the books."

"Of course I am," Luthien said.

He would not take his armour though, or his weapons. Japh had asked why he kept them, if he truly never meant to use them again, and Luthien had not had an answer for him. He did now. He had kept them to remind himself of what he had left behind, and why he must never go back to that life. Luthien's armour would stay in his rooms, to be found by the All-Church soldiers when they arrived, or perhaps to be used by one of the defenders. It didn't concern him any more.

Thirteen

The Highland City

    The sun was shining and already the day had begun to grow warm, though it was still only mid morning. Little puffs of dust rose about the horses' hooves. The storm a week ago had laid down enough water to settle most of it, something Calesh was glad of. Riding in armour was unpleasant enough without having to breathe dirt as well.
    The men of the Hand of the Lord stretched out in a long column along the road, winding in and out of rocks that dotted the top of the ridge. On their right groves of oranges and olives covered a south-facing slope with patches of green, while on the left the ridge's northerly face was marked by plough furrows, through which the shoots of early barley had yet to peek. Every mile or two the riders passed a village, clustered down in the valley to the south where a small river splashed between jutting stones. The farm folk came to the edge of the houses, or stood in the fields and shaded their eyes, to watch the soldiers ride by. Village life was dull enough to make any diversion worth a moment, and the passage of nearly two thousand armoured men was not just any diversion.
    Calesh wondered whether these people knew yet what was coming. Before much time had passed there would likely be a good deal more than two thousand soldiers in these high valleys, and they would do more than ride peacefully past. Armies on the march did unpleasant things, he knew: he'd seen some of them. Livestock and crops seized, houses burned, men murdered and women raped. Some of the villagers would escape in time, and find a cave or high crag to hide in among the stones, but they would have to abandon their goods. In any case, temporary shelter was one thing and safety something quite different. Even those who survived would creep back to the valleys to find their goods and homes taken or destroyed, and smoke still drifting from blackened walls. The winter would seem a long and bleak prospect then.
    He remembered a day in Elorium, not long after the Crusade had taken the city, when a drayman's horse had run amok and careered through the narrow streets dragging a cart behind it. Barrels tumbled from the cart and smashed on the cobbles. People who didn't

fling themselves aside in time, or who didn't have room, were flung aside nonetheless. And alone in the middle of the street, her mother God knew where, was a little girl of perhaps two years old, her feet frozen to the street with fear.

Raigal had hurled himself in front of the cart and rolled, catching the girl as he did so and cushioning her against his ample chest. As he came back to his feet he uncurled like a blossoming flower and the girl sprang out of his arms, and now *there* was the mother, actually whimpering in fright. Not of the dray horse, though. Her terrified eyes had darted one glance at Raigal Tai before she hurried the girl away, retreating to the safety of a crowd's anonymity before the evil foreigner could torment her child. It didn't matter that he'd saved the girl. Mother had heard too many stories of the savage invaders, and their crimes, to delay long enough even to thank him. That was the fear that invaders brought, whoever they were, however pure their goals.

But Calesh couldn't change what would happen here. He had to protect what he could, and try not to hear the cries of those he could not. It was always the same, for any commander. There was a price for every decision, and it was paid in the lives of soldiers and the blood of innocents. This time the bill would fall due first in Parrien, abandoned to the advancing wolves of the All-Church, because Calesh had ordered it so.

He made an effort to put that out of his mind and enjoy the sunshine of early summer. He kept catching momentary smells he had almost forgotten existed; damp earth drying in the sun, the tang of orange blossom, rosemary bushes straggling among the rocks, and a hundred other things. It was as though the air itself wanted to remind him that he was home, back in Sarténe after more than a decade away. In all honesty, he had never thought it would happen. He still half wished it had not. He'd been *happy* in Tura d'Madai, despite constant battle and danger. Happier than he'd ever been.

Whatever happened in this war, it had already brought him back, after he had stayed in Tura d'Madai when his three great friends returned home. There had been nothing for Calesh in Sarténe then. His mother had died when he was very small, and then the plague had taken Tavi and turned Calesh's father into such a grim, unsmiling man that it had almost been a relief when he died as well, six years later. By the end of that summer Calesh had sold the farm, shedding it along with the griefs it carried. He used the money to buy a battered mailshirt with a hole under one arm, and a sword so notched and chipped that it broke in half barely a month later. The only purchase he got right was the horse, a bay for which he paid half its true value; he'd learned from his father how to judge horseflesh.

He didn't even need the new gear, as it turned out. The Hand of the Lord provided its own weapons and armour, most of it bought from the master blacksmiths down in Samanta, in Alinaur. Calesh's purchases were taken from him, to be melted down for scrap or else repaired and sold on. He hadn't really minded. What mattered was that the Hand had accepted him.

There was nothing for him in Sarténe. Very well, then, he would not make his future there. A young man with talents might forge a respectable career in Alinaur or Tura d'Madai, fighting against the heathen Jaidi and Madai, and when the fighting was done there would be new lands to farm and wealth to enjoy. That the war was fought for a Church in which Calesh placed no faith didn't matter. He was going for himself, not for God. For anyone's God.

He had achieved more than he had ever really dreamed he might, except in those foolish boys' fantasies played out with his brother among the orange trees when they were both so young. At the end of the five years of service the All-Church required as a minimum, Calesh had been famous throughout Tura d'Madai, and a captain. Soldiers he had never met stood up to salute when he rode past. The Madai began to call him *the Sand Scorpion*, and when the Church soldiers learned of the name they adopted it with enthusiasm. They would cheer his name and rattle spears against their shields, while Madai women snatched their children off the street with quick warding signs against evil, and hid until he was gone.

And then his friends had left, all three of them, when their five years were up. He could not understand it.

"We have other things we want to do," Baruch said when he asked. "I love the Hand, Calesh. It's my life, but I miss Sarténe. I want to see it again, and not wonder every morning if I'll have to fight that day."

"And I want to see the fog on the forests of Rheven," Raigal Tai rumbled. "I miss fog."

It was Luthien, sitting in a corner with a book propped on his lap and a wine glass in one hand, who found the words Calesh remembered best. Of course it was. Who else would it be?

"We all want to make a future for ourselves," he said, and turned a page with one careful finger so as not to stain the paper. "You never have, Calesh. All you want is to forget the past."

They had found the Lady's book long before. It had taken a good deal of careful scurrying about, and some surreptitious digging through the catacombs beneath Elorium, all the while trying to make sure none of the Glorified or Justified noticed what they were doing. It was hard, to fit the search around their work of patrolling streets and chasing down raiders, but the Lady had told them not to trust anyone else, so they had to make the best of it. Sometimes when they had to ride out it meant nothing was done in the tunnels for a month at a time.

But they had stuck at it, and finally their efforts paid off. Baruch had emerged from a cloud of aeons-old dust with a cloth over his mouth, coughing like an ancient beggar and his eyes streaming, with a thick tome clutched in one hand and scraps of cobweb billowing around his shoulders. The book, when Raigal Tai seized it excitedly, turned out to be brass-bound and leather-backed, exactly as the Lady had told them it would be. But they could not read the inscription lettered in silver on the cover. They needed Luthien for that.

"It's a dialect of the Madai language," their resident scholar said when he blew the dust off the book and studied it with grave eyes. "Quite obscure. Kamandas of Temujin wrote a version of his histories in that tongue, so I've encountered it before. I'll need time to translate it fully, and the style is new to me." He ran his fingertips across the faded gold glyphs. "It's rather distinctive, don't you think?"

There was a moment of silence.

"By the blood of the God," Raigal growled, "that's the greatest lot of words I ever heard that didn't say a damn thing. Stop flapping your tongue and tell us; is it the Book of Breathing or not?"

"Yes," Luthien said simply.

They could not simply send the Book of Breathing back to Sarténe, of course. They kept it with them, nestled at the bottom of Luthien's saddlebags, because nobody would think it unusual for him to have a book even if they saw the shape of it. Nobody would dare challenge him about it if they did, come to that. Luthien's reputation was growing. Once he accepted a challenge from three men of the Order of the Basilica, furious that he'd spilled wine on their gold and white coats. It was cowardly of them to set on him while he was drunk, of course, but that proved not to matter. After less than a minute all three men were down, each of them groaning as he clutched wrist or thigh or elbow, and Luthien was raising a refilled glass of blood-red wine to them in elaborate, mocking salute.

So the book stayed until the three of them returned to Sarténe, when it travelled wrapped in a scraggy old piece of linen in the bottom of Luthien's clothes chest. Luthien had sent Calesh a carefully-worded letter to let him know they had arrived safely, and that the book had been delivered to the Lady of the Hidden House. Their task was done.

Luthien wrote twice more, and Baruch once. Calesh replied to them all, but he had little to say except to relate the endless, brutal struggle that was life in Tura d'Madai. To tell them of things they had chosen to leave behind, in other words. The letters felt desultory, and somehow pointless. He wasn't going back to Sarténe. They would never see each other again.

The Lady's task might be done, but Calesh passed through life without touching it. He bought no land, owned no home, and had no family. He moved from day to day unchanging, as constant as the desert itself. He fought when he had to and merely marked the days otherwise, counting them off one by one, and never mourned their passing. In the end the letters tailed off. It was not so much that they had nothing to say to each other, but that there was no need for them to say it. Not yet. Looking back Calesh thought they had been waiting, a held breath not yet ready to exhale.

Then he had gone to Harenc.

Everyone knew of the town, of course, but few westerners cared to go there. It was too small and too far away from Elorium, and such scant pleasures as this austere land offered. But anyone crossing the eastern peaks came by one of three passes, and Harenc sat astride the lowest and best, in a smallish valley watered by several little springs. A patch of greenery amid endless arid stones. Its wealth, such as it was, came from tolls levied on passing traders. It was a nothing town, notable only for its strategic importance astride that pass. In seven years Calesh had barely thought of it.

But slowly the Madai were recovering their strength, after the terrible blows they had suffered when the Crusade arrived. They were recovering their courage too. That was the way of the war in the desert: the military Orders would bring new forces and drive the Madai out for a time, only for their soldiers to return home and allow the Madai to rebuild. Now the ships were sailing away, taking soldiers a handful at a time and leaving Elorium and its environs weakened. Around the edges of the conquered lands raiders began to appear, striking deeper and deeper as their confidence grew, and one of their targets was Harenc. Calesh led a company of the Hand to root them out.

Ten days later he rode into the courtyard at Harenc, swung out of the saddle, and turned to find a tall woman with her hair in a hundred braids staring at him from the steps.

That was where his journey home had begun, long before the letter from a sympathiser inside the Basilica. He missed her now, though they had only been apart for two days. He liked to be able to turn and see her eyes already on him. She always seemed to know when he was thinking of her, or about to glance her way. Now, without her near, he found his thoughts kept wandering, whenever he turned and she was not there.

You are all my world, she had said, a finger pressed to his lips to keep him from speaking. *And if I am yours, my love, then you will not make a sound.*

She explained later, as they lay tangled in bed sheets and drowsy again with each other's warmth. Farajalla told him everything, including the Lady's implication that their failure to have a child was due to something in him, and not her. He suspected that might have hurt her as badly as if it had been the other way around: hurt her for his sake, and for the pain of hearing it. Strangely, he didn't very much mind, especially if they had conceived a child now after all. It would be worth it, ten times over, if it stopped Farajalla worrying he might leave her for a woman who could bear him sons.

Leave her? Not in this world, and under this sun.

Raigal Tai rode where Farajalla normally would, with Baruch a little way behind talking with one of the other soldiers. Baruch had taken over Amand's duties, since Amand himself had gone ahead to Mayence to check the situation there. As for Raigal, he was happy now he knew Kendra and Segarn were on their way to the fortress at Adour, where they would meet the Lady of the Hidden House. Twice already that morning he had broken into one of the long, mournful ballads of his homeland in Rheven, telling the tale of a love struck warrior whose passion led him to tragedy and death. He only chuckled when Baruch told him to shut up.

The world was nearly right again, Calesh thought as he followed the road down the ridge and into the southernmost valley. Raigal Tai was with him, and Baruch was trying to make the northerner be quiet. All they needed now was Luthien, and what did it matter that he was Elite? It would be enough for him to be there, trying to read a book in the saddle while his horse wandered all over the road, and likely at any moment to say something so abstract that the rest of them would shrug their shoulders, not even bothering to exchange puzzled frowns. *The greatest lot of words I ever heard that didn't say a damn thing,* Raigal had said all those years ago. That was Luthien all over. But he was part of them, one of the group, and however irrational it might be Calesh didn't believe anything could stop them if they were all together. He would stand before the wrath of God himself on the strength of that feeling.

The road rounded a shoulder of rock, and suddenly Mayence was spread out ahead, slightly above the column of soldiers and little more than a mile away. Fields and orchards filled the space between, bright and fresh after the bare stones around the road. In the Aiguille a traveller could come on places suddenly and without warning, almost stumbling into them before he knew they were there. Calesh reined in and reached for his water flask, glancing back to make sure none of his men had fallen behind. They were all in their places. He hadn't really expected anything else.

"I'd forgotten how pretty it is," Raigal Tai said.

Calesh nodded. He'd forgotten as well. Mayence glittered in front of them, seeming all spires and domes and minarets, and windows that flashed in the sun. In eleven years it seemed only to have grown more glorious, and his heart tugged at the thought of what was to come.

"I'd be happier if it was a bit uglier," Baruch muttered. "Where are the crews working to reinforce the wall? Why isn't anyone digging trenches beside the road, or across it? Riyand must be asleep, or lolling on cushions while his favourite bards pluck their lutes for him."

"So must Darien," Raigal agreed.

Calesh nodded again. He'd hoped as well, though without very much expectation. Everything he had heard of the Margrave portrayed him as a dilettante, wasting half his days and bungling the rest of the time. Still, that was a problem for another day, if all went well. One thing at a time.

"Our business isn't with Riyand," Calesh said. "Not today." He flicked the reins and started across the fields.

*

The men put on their helms as they approached the Gate of Angels, in Mayence's east wall, and they wore their shields slung across their backs with the black and white colours turned outwards. Only Calesh left his head bare. It made him stand out, in the age-greened copper armour Sevrey had given him at Harenc, when Calesh married Farajalla. That was as close as the duke could come to admitting she was his daughter. It was an excellent gift, but it did make Calesh an easy target. On the other hand, it made him recognisable to his own men too, able to raise morale just by riding past. Like so many things it was a trade: you gave with one hand, and took back with the other.

On the arched gateway winged figures watched the road with stone eyes: in Mayence even the city defences were embellished with sculpture, as though that might somehow conceal their true purpose. Beneath them ten members of the Margrave's Guard stood sentry, taking it in turns to check wagons and walkers into the city. Their livery of red and yellow stood out brightly in the throng. Several of them pointed at the approaching riders and presently one spoke an order, sending a younger man scampering into Mayence, almost certainly to take word of their arrival to the Manse. The officer didn't bother to close the gate though, which in a time of war with soldiers drawing near was more than merely sloppy. Calesh saw Baruch's mouth tighten.

Merchants waiting to take their wagons into the city pulled to the side of the road when they saw the column coming. Farmers manoeuvred their carts out of the way. Travellers on foot stood and watched the soldiers ride by, prudently waiting until the armed men were gone before they resumed the jostle trying to get into Mayence. Their eyes followed Calesh, the only bareheaded man in the company, clad in his strange armour. Only the nine gate guards remained in the road in their uniform coats: blood and gold, they called the colours, perhaps thinking that made them seem braver. They stood in a single line as though to block the way, but their wide eyes and pale faces gave them away. Deer sometimes looked that way, when they saw the hunter only in the instant before the arrow was loosed.

Calesh led his men onto the bridge before the gate, over the rushing river Kair. The crowd behind him had fallen silent, watching.

"Halt and declare yourselves," the captain of the gate guard said. His men shuffled their feet as the column came to a stop.

"Do it," Calesh ordered.

"My name is Baruch Caraman," he said. He didn't remove his helmet, and his voice echoed metallically from the cheek guards that came over his jaw. "I am a Commander of the Hand of the Lord, whose soldiers these are. This is Calesh Saissan, the Marshal Commander of the East, whose name you may have heard." He raised his voice slightly at the last, letting it carry. Murmurs rippled back through the throng.

The officer only nodded. "You may enter with no more than ten men. The rest must go –"

"We are going to the Preceptory of the Hand of the Lord," Baruch said in that reverberant voice. He kneed his horse forward, letting it dance until it was sideways on to the officer. He and Calesh had talked about this, working out how best to make both a dramatic entrance and a statement, but without harming anyone or making needless enemies. "Under Sarténi law we have that right. You may not impede us. Stand aside."

"All of you won't fit in the Preceptory," the man pointed out, not unreasonably. He was hopelessly outnumbered, and the law was against him too, but he'd still retained the ability to think clearly. Calesh rather admired him, and made a mental note to find out the man's name. He might be useful in the days ahead.

"That is not your concern," Baruch said. "If we men of the Hand choose to sleep standing on one another's shoulders, it is our affair and none of yours. Stand aside." The horse danced forward again, crowding close to the officer. "Or I will ride clean over you."

The officer stood aside. He had no choice really, with just nine men on foot against so many horsemen. If he'd had the gate closed before the Hand arrived it might have been different, but it was too late now. The first company of soldiers rode under the arch, into a wide avenue flanked with cypress trees and filled with suddenly staring citizens. A troubadour standing on an upturned crate stopped reciting and let his lute trail away, a last few forlorn notes hanging in the air before they faded.

"Some welcome," Raigal Tai complained. His voice, always loud, was magnified by the helmet into a giant's boom. "If the Gate of

Angels leads into Heaven, I think we had the right to expect cheering crowds and flowers tossed in the street."

Calesh snorted. "It's not the same Gate of Angels, I'm happy to say. If it was, we'd already be dead."

"Wait a month and we might be," Baruch put in grimly.

They advanced down the avenue, a wide thoroughfare known as Waggoner's Way, along which much of the trade of Mayence flowed. By now it was late morning, past the time when most of the morning carts had been brought in and unloaded, but before evening's second spate of deliveries. A few vendors had set up stalls along the road, by the raised walkways on either side, and city folk moved to and fro between them in the shade of cypresses. But the crowds weren't heavy, so there was plenty of room for shoppers to move aside as the cavalry paraded between the trees. They did so willingly enough, and a hush fell. Whispers ran through the onlookers, trailing a respectful silence broken only by the clop of iron-shod hooves.

"God bless the Hand!" someone shouted suddenly. There was a cheer, ragged and spontaneous, and all at once the whole avenue was filled with shouting men and women, some waving their arms in the air and others capering like fools at a country dance. Several soldiers in the lead company shifted hands towards their sword hilts, but began to relax again even before Baruch could speak to them. There was no threat here, among their own people. One or two of the riders exchanged grins.

"There's your welcome," Calesh said to Raigal Tai, over his shoulder. "Are you happy now?"

Down the street the throng grew thicker, as word spread and the citizens of Mayence rushed to see for themselves. People hung out of windows and waved their arms, or threw hats into the air in delight. They must have heard the All-Church army was coming, and in the appearance of so many of the Hand they thought they saw salvation. Well, perhaps they did, though more fighting men would be needed to turn the tide.

"They need to hear you speak," Baruch said.

He grimaced. "I'm not much for speeches."

"It's too late for you to say that," his friend said. His voice was very soft, and wouldn't carry far. "It was too late the moment you decided to lay claim to command. You've put your feet on this path, and Raigal and I are with you, but some things you have to do."

He was right, as he usually was. Calesh had won the fame, Luthien was the best swordsman and Raigal simply terrifying in battle, but it was Baruch who spoke sense when it was needed and kept the others from going too far. *We need to be together,* Calesh thought again.

He wondered how it was for Baruch. Calesh had found Farajalla, though he'd never looked for love. Raigal had his wife and son, and Luthien his love for God, but Baruch had never had anyone. *I am married to the Hand,* he said, but what would be left to him if the Hand was lost in this war? As it seemed likely that it *would* be lost, shattered by the very All-Church in whose name it had fought for so long. Soldiers in black and white surcoats lay in graves from Alinaur's hills to the sands of Tura d'Madai, but their sacrifice counted for nothing any longer.

A pair of Elite watched the column from the entrance to one of their temples, a small round building of white stone that shone in the sun. One was grizzled and grey, perhaps a veteran of those half-forgotten battles of the Hand, and the other a young woman with straw blonde hair and eyes of a blue bright even at this distance. Calesh thought he recognised her from the camp outside Parrien, when she had given a sermon to his men in the dark. She wore an expression of surprise, for some reason. He was seized by a sudden wild urge to rush over and scream at her; *why couldn't you be careful? Did you have to flaunt your unbelief in the All-Church's face, until they were so enraged that they came for you?*

"We were none of us careful," he said quietly to himself. The words barely trembled on his lips, a mere breath in the air, yet Baruch half turned in his saddle and gave a thin smile, sad and terrible.

There was a church on their left a little further on, its narrow windows boarded over and the doors barred shut. Near the stone floor they had a charred look, evidence of an arsonist's interest in the abandoned chapel. Mayence would not be a safe place for the clergy of the All-Church just now. Calesh wondered where the priest was: hiding in a cellar perhaps, or fleeing eastwards in the dark and cowering under hedges by day. The thought cheered him, bizarrely. He hadn't thought he was so vindictive.

The vanguard passed into Musicians' Square, though nobody played or recited just now. People stood dozens deep all around the plaza, squeezing the would-be artists from the provinces up against the walls and leaving only a narrow way clear. They began to cheer and applaud as the Hand of the Lord rode through, and then sent up a roar when the lead riders reined their horses in. Calesh took a deep breath and swung down from his saddle, then jumped from the stone coping to the statue of the lute player in the middle of the pool. He was able to wrap his hand around the figure's neck and stand with one foot on a stone knee, lifting himself up above the crowd. Baruch was right: people needed to hear from him. He raised a hand for quiet.

It came slowly. Baruch looked uneasy, and when he spoke rapidly to the man beside him several soldiers turned to scan the crowd, looking for any threat. But the crowd continued to clap and cheer, and Calesh shifted his foot on the statue's leg. He looked over at Baruch and Raigal and made a helpless movement with his free hand. Laughter ran through the throng, and in its wake the cheers died to murmurs, and then to silence.

"Thank you, people," Calesh said. He didn't have a clear idea what to say. "Uh, I know we in the Hand are mostly your own family, your own sons, but we're certainly glad of the welcome anyway."

At that the crowd went crazy again, whooping and stamping their feet in delight. Farajalla had suggested he mention that, back at the Hidden House, to remind the citizens that the men of the Hand were their own flesh and blood. She constantly surprised him with her cleverness, this exotic outland wife he had found. Calesh raised a hand for quiet once more, and this time it came more quickly.

"You know what we face," he said. Words began to come to him, more easily, now he'd begun. "The All-Church has called Crusade against us. Their army has already begun to cross the river Rielle, and there's no way we can raise a force anything like as strong."

Silence. From outside the square came a murmur, as of a throng restless with impatience.

"I know war," Calesh said. "I know how hard it is to win against an army so much bigger than your own. Every one of us will have to do whatever he can, all that he can, if we are not to be lost." He let his gaze rove across the crowd. "You will be asked to make sacrifices. Remember, when you do, that the Hand of the Lord will be sacrificing as much as any."

"The All-Church tells its people simply to believe. To accept, and not to question. Our faith tells us to find God in our own hearts, and not in the crooked words of misled men." Calesh paused. "I prefer ours, and by my heart and eyes, I'm going to fight for it."

The roar came all at once, even from some of the soldiers of the Hand themselves. Raigal Tai steadied Calesh's horse as he leaped back across the pool and swung back into his saddle; he even got a shout of approval for that, as though mounting a horse was a virtue. He raised a hand in acknowledgement, redoubling the roar.

"Nice speech," Raigal said. "It's a good thing Ando Gliss couldn't hear you speak. He'd have fainting fits through sheer excitement."

"Words have never won a battle," Calesh said. He motioned for the vanguard company to start moving again.

"Wrong," Baruch said quietly. "Words sometimes make men believe the battles can be won."

There was truth in that. Soldiers were a strange lot, tough and cynical, yet they could also be superstitious and moody. A word of comfort here, or a son's name remembered there, could make all the difference to them. They didn't need pretty oration, and indeed held it in contempt, but they did want to feel valued by a leader who fought and bled alongside them, and knew what battle was. Calesh had done so, and they knew it. Two words from him were worth a whole song from a troubadour back home.

But words to civilians hardly mattered at all. Maybe they would encourage a few young men to join up, but not enough to make any difference. There wasn't time to train them anyway. But they could repair crumbling walls, or dig cavalry ditches across roads, or any of a hundred other things. And in the end, perhaps they could man those walls with pitchforks and wood axes in their hands. It might mean enough to count.

A small voice whispered that they would die in droves. Calesh ignored it; he knew that anyway. The question was whether they would achieve anything by their deaths, and whether that fate was any worse for them than the one the All-Church brought.

The streets were still lined with crowds when the Hand of the Lord arrived at the broad granite block of the Preceptory. There were Chapter Houses all over Sarténe, and more in Alinaur and Tura d'Madai, but this was the heart of the Order where the big decisions were made. The first company rode past the steps and fanned out to form a double line, behind which the rest of the army drew up. Ahead of them the road ran over a bridge lined with bronze horses, and then past the Hall of Voices with its crimson dome and fluttering flags. Their course had brought them back to the river, lined on both banks here by groves of orange trees. Calesh could smell blossom on those branches.

He swung down from his saddle when the others did. They all moved at once to gather around him.

"All right," Calesh said. He paused, hesitant for the first time, and looked up at the square bulk of the Chapter House. A figure emerged and began to walk down, and he saw it was Amand.

You are strong enough for this, Farajalla murmured in his memory. Baruch was watching him. Calesh stood straighter.

"It's arranged," Amand said as he reached the riders. His gaunt face twisted in distaste. "I can see the need, but nothing in my career has made me feel as dirty as this."

"I know," Calesh said. He gripped the other man's shoulder briefly. "But it must be done."

Amand nodded. His uniform was perfectly ironed, the creases sharp enough to cut. "The Quartermaster is in Alinaur on a fact-finding mission, but his deputy is here and will support us. The Chief Elite is here, and he backs us too. His name's Alcalde."

"I remember Alcalde," Calesh said. "A tall man, bearded. Or he was when I last saw him."

"He still is," Amand confirmed.

"We have a quorum of the senior men, then," Calesh said. He took a mental breath, careful not to let it show. "You've done well, Amand. Thank you. Let's take care of business."

They had barely started up the steps up when a knot of men emerged from the front doors. Most were Hand armsmen, hastily cramming helmets over heads or pulling on gauntlets as they hurried to form two lines of welcome. Such haste indicated carelessness to Calesh, because they should have known the moment armed men entered the city, and been ready for their arrival. He suspected that the cause of the laxness was the white-haired man who emerged at the head of the steps, staring down at the armoured men climbing towards him. The ends of his thick white eyebrows twitched as they approached. Beside him stood Alcalde, his beard and hair as dark now as they had been eleven years ago. The Elite broke into a bright smile when their eyes met.

"Commander Saissan," Darien intoned. The new arrivals came to a halt in front of him. His sharp-eyed gaze flicked over them:

he must not have been drinking this morning. From what Baruch said, that was unusual. "I must commend you on your swift return to Sarténe."

"Thank you," Calesh said. "We need to talk."

Darien's eyebrows jerked again. He would have noticed the lack of a title or a salute, and also that Calesh hadn't *asked* to talk. His eyes narrowed. "I know you have been away a long time, Marshal Commander, and you have been the ranking officer among the Hand in Tura d'Madai for a long time. But still, I must insist on the basic courtesies, I'm afraid."

"And I must insist that we talk," Calesh said.

"Perhaps when you have rested," Darien answered. He smiled tolerantly. "Men are not at their best after a long journey. Perhaps your behaviour is merely due to weariness."

"I'm not tired." Calesh let his gaze slip beyond the old Lord. "Good morning, Alcalde. It's good to see you again."

"And you, Commander," he answered with another bright smile. "I trust you are well?"

"Very well," he said, and turned back to the old commander. "Baruch and I must speak with you. At once."

"When you have rested," Darien said again. His smile stayed in place, but there was a terrible understanding in his eyes. He knew, Calesh realised: the presence there of Alcalde made it hard for him not to. He knew what was coming, but an old soldier's pride made it impossible for him to accept, or even admit. And Darien Serran had been a fine soldier once, leading the Hand of the Lord for fifteen years in its struggle to drive the Jaidi out of Alinaur. He'd earned his scars, and his rank, many times over.

But some old soldiers never grew used to life away from the battlefield. Many couldn't shake off the nightmares that plagued them, and became hollow-eyed shells of who they used to be. Others never found something to fill the space where the old excitement had been: a sick excitement, to be sure, made as much of terror as anything else, but still addictive. Darien had filled that empty space with brandy. Whatever he had been, he was no longer, and for all the sadness in that he had to move aside.

"I didn't want it this way," Calesh said quietly. "For the past twenty years you've led the Hand well, Darien. But the Hand needs decisive leadership now, and I think I can best provide it."

"Ah," Darien said. "Are you so familiar with current affairs in Sarténe, then? Only a week after your return? It seems your talents are more impressive than I was led to believe."

"I will have advice from people who *are* familiar with those affairs," Calesh answered. Beside him Baruch stepped forward.

"I agree with him," the stocky man said clearly. "Command in Sarténe has been a post suited to a decent administrator for a long time, Darien, but not any more. We need energy and action now, the best battle leader we can find. That man is Calesh Saissan."

"I am Lord Marshal of the Hand of the Lord," Darien began. He cut off when Alcalde cleared his throat.

"I believe Commander Baruch is correct," he said. Alcalde smiled often and genuinely, but there was no hint of softness in his iron tone. "As Chief Elite, I no longer have confidence in you as Lord Marshal, and I must insist you step aside, Darien."

It stopped the old man, but only for a moment. "I am entitled to a full hearing. And the Quartermaster is not here."

"The Quartermaster is a clerk," Calesh said, "responsible for nothing more than requisitioning, and signing the accounts at the end of each month. His department will support me, but under the laws, you're right, Darien. Are you really going to insist on a full hearing?"

"I am," the old man said. "And until that time I remain in my position, of course."

"Of course," Calesh repeated. "Tell me, Darien. Do you think the officers don't know you're a drunk?"

Darien froze. His expression never changed, but somehow what lay beneath it became brittle, so fragile that a breath might shatter it. He swallowed, and still did not speak.

"I'm sorry," Calesh said, more gently. "Truly I am. But understand me: I won't let you lead in this war, Darien, or even pretend to. So far you've done nothing at all that I can see. Those men down there follow me because I fight beside them, and usually I win for them. I keep them alive. That matters more than familiarity with what passes for politics in the Manse these days."

"We'll let you keep your rank," Baruch said, "but only if you accept that Calesh has effective command of all soldiers in the Hand of the Lord. Write that out for all the company officers and there'll be no need for a hearing, Darien." He flinched at the look in the old man's eyes. "I'm sorry too, old friend. But it must be this way."

"Must it?" Darien shook his head. "I used to think you were such a fine man, Baruch. Now I wonder if you will not regret this in Heaven. If you even go to Heaven." His gaze went back to Calesh. "And as for you, Marshal Saissan. I might have been happier if you had stayed in the desert after all, but it seems I have no choice."

"No," he said. "None at all."

"Perhaps it doesn't matter," the old man said. "Perhaps a battle leader really is what we need, as Baruch says, but I doubt that even your skills will make a difference to what is to come. We will die in the end, won't we? A glorious end is the best we can hope for now."

"I won't accept that," Calesh said tightly. "And hearing you speak I'm glad, for the first time, that we've removed you from command. We will do what we can, and trust that it is enough."

He turned to Baruch. "Send soldiers to all the posts to inform them of the change in authority. I want every senior officer to attend a briefing in the Vaulted Hall at the dusk bell tonight. And send a man to the Manse, as well. Tell the Margrave I will attend him there at his earliest convenience." He looked around the circle of his friends. "Now it begins."

"Or ends," Raigal rumbled. There didn't seem a great deal to say to that.

Fourteen

Close to Heaven

A page trotted up to the group under the trees, bending to whisper in Cavel's ear. The bony seneschal sat rather awkwardly in a chair shaded by a sycamore tree, flanked on both sides by youths clad in the red and green of the palace servants. Officially the colours were blood and lime, though the green was like no lime Cavel had ever seen. Beads of sweat stood out on the servants' heads.

Cavel was damp under the arms too, even in the shade. A little to one side Riyand sprawled on a divan, propped on one languid elbow as he listened benignly to a young troubadour sing his newest ballad with the gentle voice of the stream for accompaniment. Across the arbour a young blonde woman in an Elite's green robes sat with her back against an acacia tree and picked at a bowl of fruit, seeming not to listen.

Closer, yet hardly noticed, the Margrave's wife was seated in a cushioned chair, head bent over needlework or embroidery. Ando could never quite remember the difference, or see how it mattered. There was not much for Ilenia to do except sew, and perhaps enjoy long soothing baths. Certainly Riyand rarely troubled her. He supposed Ilenia was pretty enough, in a quiet sort of way, big-eyed and with shining brown hair. She could have had a litter of children by now if Fate had brought her a different husband.

Ando wondered whether she minded. She might be glad Riyand was so rarely in her bed, or she might hate Ando for taking the Margrave to his. She might even have lovers of her own. Perhaps he ought to find out, if he could. But he never knew what to say to Elenia, or she to him it seemed. They orbited each other in silence save for polite inconsequentialities, neither of them willing to be the first to speak of her husband.

This was the first time the weather had allowed them to enjoy the palace gardens since winter passed. It would likely be the last time events allowed them to. Scouts reported that the All-Church army had completed its crossing of the river Rielle and was edging closer to Parrien, its progress slow but inexorable. Some of those scouts had already been lost, to fast-moving advance forces that ran ahead of the main army. Sarténi forces had begun to gather in response, in the valleys of the Aiguille around Mayence. War was coming. There would not be many slow, idle afternoons left.

And given a choice, Ando would not have chosen to spend this one listening to a second-rate singer perform his third-rate songs.

The laughter of friends, the stars above,
Praise freely given for art performed,
And a woman's breathing beside me at night.

Such comforts fail when the wind is cold,
Doors are barred, and I am far from home,
In a place where God is little loved.

The troubadours had been part of life in Sarténe for almost a century now, yet many of the singers still couldn't get beyond the old, weary phrases and images. They made Ando think of an ancient carpet on the floor of a poor man's home, frayed and worn thin by too much use. What this excuse for a singer did wasn't art, to Ando's mind, any more than digging out old drainage ditches was art, or slopping whitewash on a weather-faded wall. He was just revisiting what had been done before, and by better artists. Ando was glad when the song ended, on an entirely unnecessary flourish of plucked notes, and the troubadour bowed over his instrument as though expecting applause.

He didn't receive any.

"I do wonder," Riyand drawled idly, ignoring the player, "what news was so important that a page brought it to you here, Cavel."

Looking back at the seneschal, Ando saw that the messenger had already departed again, and one of the two who'd flanked Cavel before was missing as well. He sat up on his divan. These days the merest hint of trouble caused hearts to beat somewhat harder.

"A disturbance at the entrance," the seneschal said smoothly. For all his outward poise he still sat stiffly on his chair. Cavel was more at home pushing papers than listening to singers in the sunshine, but when the Margrave wanted to sit and relax, then the court sat and relaxed. "I don't think you need concern yourself, my lord."

"The entrance to the Manse? Of course I should concern myself," Riyand said. He didn't stir from his propped elbow though. "Who was it? Our dear All-Church clerics, again?"

"Not this time," Cavel replied. "The Hand of the Lord."

Ando swung his feet to the grass and set down his wine, but he was given no chance to speak.

"I sent a message that I would see Commander Saissan tomorrow," Riyand said petulantly.

"Commander Saissan?" the blonde Elite said from her place by the tree. "Is that who's at the entrance?"

"You know him?" Riyand asked in a surprised voice.

"I was in Parrien when he and his men came ashore," she said. "I held a brief service at their camp that night. Some of those men hadn't received proper rites since they left for the desert."

"You were there?" Cavel's eyes were narrow. "That seems rather a large coincidence."

"Really, Cavel," the Margrave said with a laugh, "you must not be so suspicious. We can trust Elisande. I'm sure she had a perfectly good reason to be in Parrien."

Perhaps she had. She could have had a good reason and some foreknowledge too, Ando thought. He'd only been in Parrien himself because he already knew the Hand was coming home, and the harbour seemed an obvious place to wait for it. How Elisande might have known was a mystery. Perhaps Riyand thought so too, which was why his laughter sounded forced to Ando. Nobody else seemed to notice though. Perhaps he had imagined it. Either that, or he knew his lover's moods more intimately than he had believed.

Elisande tossed her golden hair. "I was travelling the coast, holding services in the towns and villages I passed through. It's hardly an uncommon thing for an Elite to do. I didn't expect to be questioned about it."

"Such are the times we live in," Ando shrugged. "It's unfortunate, but trust is a precious thing these days."

He frowned as he heard his own words. There might be a song in that concept, something about how distrust grows like a weed in the dark. Or rancour in a poor man's soul. He almost laughed at himself: here he was comparing the poor troubadour before them to a worn carpet, and yet his own ideas were just as old and tired. That reminded him that the singer was still there, standing a few yards away with his lute clutched in both hands. Ando picked his wine up again and nodded to the man.

"You'd best leave us," he said. "If you want somewhere to play tonight, go and see the barkeep at *Spring Blessings,* on Three Lords' Street. The pay is all right, and they throw in a good supper too."

The troubadour bowed and hurried away, almost breaking into a run as he hastened across the gardens. Ando watched him go and wondered why he'd made that last offer. The man wasn't really good enough to make a living from his own songs; Heaven only knew how he'd managed to finagle an invitation to play for the Margrave, however briefly. His voice wasn't great either, but perhaps he could scrape along singing other people's work. Some few of the troubadours allowed that, more from vanity than for any other reason. It showed how grand they were, or so they believed.

"What did you think of Commander Saissan?" Cavel asked behind Ando. "Did you speak with him?"

"No," Elisande said. "I only saw him briefly. At Parrien, and again today, on Waggoner's Way."

"Coincidence upon coincidence," Cavel murmured. Elisande raised a manicured eyebrow at him.

Riyand's voice drifted over theirs, lazy and bored. "I do not wish to talk of Commander Saissan, or any other soldier. This afternoon is for relaxation. I will return to business later."

"I don't think you have a choice," Ando said.

He had been watching the singer retreat across the lawn, so it was Ando who first saw uniformed servants erupt from a side door of the Manse like a cloud of disturbed fruit flies. Several of them seemed to be trying to block the entrance, but to no avail: into their midst pushed several large men who flashed silver as their armour caught the sun. Ando could pick out black and white surcoats, the Hand's colours. More men shoved through, scattering the palace staff across the paths and into a flowerbed. One of the servants actually ran in a circle with his hands flapping, like a witless chicken.

Cavel shot to his feet. "This is intolerable! Where is the Guard? My lord, you must be taken to safety. I will –"

"Safety?" Riyand snorted. "If I'm not safe in the Manse I'm not safe anywhere. Be still, seneschal. I doubt the Hand means me harm."

A knot of the Guard came running around the corner of the building, saw the emerging men of the Hand, and quickly formed tight ranks. They paused then, and with reason; already thirty of the Hand had poured into view, and more were coming. With a clear advantage of numbers the men in blood and gold might have risked a confrontation, but even that wasn't certain. The Hand of the Lord had a formidable reputation as fighting men, and besides, when the All-Church army came these men would fight side by side. It would not be a good idea for them to smash one another's bones now.

"That's him," Ando said as he caught sight of a familiar figure. It was too far for him to see more than the man's height, and his nondescript brown hair, but there was something in the way he carried himself that caught the eye. He remembered that from *Kissing the Moon*. "Calesh Saissan, I think."

Cavel shaded his eyes to look, and Elisande stood up so she could see. The soldiers formed a rough group and began to advance steadily across the lawns, not reacting even when the little knot of Guardsmen rushed along a gravel pathway to try to intercept them. It was too late. The Hand battalion drew closer, all the men armoured but none wearing a helmet or carrying a shield, until they came beneath the shade of the trees and halted.

Except one. Calesh stepped forward alone, limping very slightly as though tired. He was the only man of them not wearing armour, just a light coat in the colours of the Hand. His expression was carefully blank, but Ando was experienced at reading what people tried to hide. A songwriter needed to see what others missed, and in Calesh he thought he saw barely-restrained anger in the tautness around his eyes. In fact Calesh looked furious, ready to spit nails, and Ando shot a sudden uneasy glance at his lover.

"Commander Saissan," Riyand said. His voice was cool and cultured, the tone of a lord in his element, controlling the scene. "I've heard a great deal about you, and I'm delighted you could pay us this surprise visit. Please, sit and join us in a cup of wine."

"Elite Elisande," Calesh said. He offered the golden-haired woman a slight bow, ignoring Riyand completely. "I thought it was you I saw on the street this morning. It's a pleasure to meet you properly at last. My men were grateful for the service you gave them that night in Parrien. Perhaps you'd consider speaking for us again?"

"Of course," Elisande said. "I offer the rites wherever they are needed, Commander."

"And Master Gliss." Calesh nodded to him. "I hope you've forgiven me my harsh words concerning your lyrics."

He had forgotten them, in fact, but Ando didn't reply. Riyand, rudely ignored in his own grounds, had turned pink in the face, and it was to him that Ando owed loyalty. The Margrave forced a smile.

"It's always pleasant to meet old friends once more," he said, and this time the thread of tightness in his voice was too obvious to be missed. "Join us, Commander. Sit and drink."

Calesh turned to him then. All at once the veneer of politeness he had shown to Elisande and Ando was gone, replaced by a hardness that was very nearly cruel. Anger flashed across his face. Across the arbour Ilenia paused in her work and watched them, her hazel eyes keen.

"I am not at leisure to dawdle the day away until my wits are sodden with wine," he said coldly. "Your land is under attack, Margrave. Had you forgotten? Or do you not care?"

Heart suddenly thumping, Ando watched his lover rise to his feet. Riyand's wine glass fell to the grass, unheeded.

"I do not permit anyone to speak to me that way in my own house," the Margrave said. "Not even close friends. And you, Commander, are neither a friend nor likely to become one. I will accept an apology, if you offer it."

"I will not," Calesh said. "I have crossed half the world to defend my home, and I think I could fairly expect that you would want to defend it too. Instead when I request an audience your page claims you are too busy, and then I find you taking the sun and enjoying fine wine in your gardens, surrounded by singers and sycophants. Tell me, Margrave, where is your army now? How do its provisions stand? How far have additional defences progressed? You will forgive me," he added caustically, "if I do not expect you to know the answers. I doubt you've spent any time at all trying to find out."

"Command of the army is given to general Reis," Riyand said. He sounded rattled now. "Such questions should be directed at him."

"Not true," Calesh shot back. "Do you really believe you can lounge in your gardens and leave the work of defence to others? You are the *Margrave!* My hands and heart and eyes, do you take responsibility for nothing? Will you idle away your days with fripperies and a string of lovers, and never give a care for what happens outside your walls?"

"That isn't fair!" Ando snapped. Part of his brain told him it was that casual mention of *a string of lovers* which had angered him, but he plunged on anyway. "We have been working, but we need some rest. You have no right to make such accusations."

"Don't I?" Calesh snapped at him. "I have to decide when and where to commit the Hand of the Lord to battle. Men will die because of the choices I make in the days ahead, singer. And it's hard to ask those soldiers to fight for me, to risk death for this land, while its lord fans himself in the sun *and does nothing!*" His voice cracked on the last, making Ando jump. "The days when he could sample the city's arts and culture at his leisure are *over*, do you understand? Perhaps you, balladeer, and others in this city feed him milk and honey and never expect anything from him. I will not be part of that."

"You don't under –"

"This is war," Calesh said, riding right over Ando. Ilenia was watching him closely, her needlework forgotten in her lap. "War is not a forgiving mistress, Master Gliss. It is hard and cruel, and there will never be enough time to do half the things that need doing no matter how hard we work. Men will die for the things I can't find time to do, as well, but I will not let a single one die because I couldn't be bothered to make the effort!"

"He does! He works –"

"Excuse me," Cavel said, and his dry tone cut through Ando's rising voice. "You said you would decide when to commit the Hand, Commander Saissan. Is Darien no longer Lord Marshal, then?"

"Darien remains ranking officer of the Hand," Calesh said curtly. "Command in battle will be mine, however, until this crisis is over."

"I see," Cavel said slowly. Ando could almost see the aged seneschal's mind working. He knew what Calesh's words meant as well, however carefully couched they were: Darien had been ousted from power within the Hand of the Lord, and Calesh had replaced him.

"What do you suggest we do now?" Cavel asked. He was trying to take them away from their anger, Ando realised, losing the talk in detail until all the passion faded away.

"The first thing is to abandon Parrien," Calesh said at once. "It might have been possible to defend the town if you'd begun making preparations two months ago, when word reached me in Tura d'Madai that the All-Church would be coming here. But you've missed the chance. All of Sarténe up to the Aiguille will be lost to the fire because of that."

"I was trying to negotiate!" Riyand shouted. Calesh only flicked his eyes at the Margrave and then dismissed him, not bothering to hide his contempt. Riyand began to go red again. He picked up his glass, poured it full of wine and drained it in one long swallow.

"Whatever we should have done two months ago," Cavel murmured, "we can't do it now. What is past can't be changed, Commander. Perhaps you might advise us on matters we can still affect. General Reis," he added, "has already advised us to abandon Parrien, in fact."

He was the smallest man there, bony and bald, but it was Cavel who seemed able to deal best with the big soldier. Calesh knew it too, evidently. He answered the seneschal when he had ignored the Margrave. "At least someone is thinking clearly. With Parrien and the lowlands abandoned, we can withdraw to the Aiguille. It might be possible to defend Mayence; certainly we can try. But we have to start working *now*, immediately, and keep on until we drop with exhaustion and sleep where we fall. And then wake, to work again. For one thing, we need to send out parties of cavalry to clear the farms of livestock and crops, anything we can eat, and bring it here."

"No," Riyand said.

"If we do this, we might be able to hold out until summer is over," Calesh went on. Again it was as though Riyand hadn't spoken. He aimed his words at the seneschal – and Cavel was listening, Ando saw with dismay. He wasn't simply trying to defuse a tense situation after all. He was reacting to a shift in the balance of power, riding the changing tide, as a good diplomat must. "If the All-Church army is still sitting outside the walls of Mayence when the autumn rains come, the Basilica will find it to keep it supplied and almost impossible to stop dysentery breaking out in the camps. Time may do our work for us."

"No," Riyand repeated.

"There are other things," Calesh went on, ignoring him once more. A hundred of them. We have to repair the wall, cut ditches across the roads, and dredge shallow places in the river if we can. The bridges must be broken to make the gates more secure. I'll want every goose feather we can find used for fletchings, and all the carpenters in the city set to making arrows and spear shafts. All available warehouse space must be set aside for siege preparations, principally the storage of food and other essentials. Reliable men must be formed into a corps to stand guard on them, and enforce rationing. Most of all, seneschal, we must start at once. We're abandoning Parrien in return for time, so we need to use every moment of it before the All-Church comes."

"No," Riyand said for a third time. He stood up, facing Calesh across the little glade. "I agreed to abandon Parrien because I had to, but I will not abandon this valley as well. Certainly I won't send out men to pick the countryside clean, like some horde of scavengers. If we do that people in the villages will starve in their thousands come the winter."

"If so, it's because you failed to do your duty before now," Calesh said. "It's disingenuous of you, Margrave, to complain the roof is falling in when it was your task to repair the tiles." He held up a hand to forestall Riyand's irate retort. "Spare me, please. I know not every man is a gifted leader, or wishes to be, but I do at least expect an effort. You have said and done nothing that might suggest you even accept responsibility for your shortcomings, and I'm not in the mood to listen to another feeble excuse. By God, boy, you're as useless as a whelp that can't bark and won't bite."

Riyand's red face began to shade towards purple. Ando could see past his lover to Ilenia, and he thought he saw a tiny smile touch the corners of her mouth before she concealed it. She did resent the emptiness of her life, then. "You show me no respect, captain."

"You do nothing to earn it," Calesh shot back.

"Earn it?" Riyand shouted. "I am the Margrave of Mayence!"

"Does that make you harder to kill?" Calesh demanded. "My heart and eyes, rank doesn't mean a thing in wartime. I've seen nobles freeze in terror and die blubbering like children, while farmers and cutpurses fight like badgers in a sack. In the East you live or die according to what you do, not who your father was. Your noble blood, *Margrave*, won't stop a blade, and it won't get you one step closer to Heaven either."

"I wonder," Cavel said in his dry voice, "whether you think this bitter argument between two of our leaders is a good thing, Commander Saissan. How many nations have fallen because they were split inside?"

"Many," Calesh answered, not in the least abashed. "And many have fallen because their leader was a fool, and the men around him too weak to act on that knowledge."

"Fool!" Riyand almost screamed. Ando recognised the signs of real fury building and moved quickly to his lover's side to put a hand on his arm, which Riyand shook off at once. The Margrave actually took a step towards Calesh, his fists bunching. "Guards!"

"Don't be an idiot," Calesh said wearily. "Look, I'll go find this general Reis, and he and I will work out a plan between us. But I won't let my decisions be influenced by you, Margrave, or by your unwillingness to work. I came home to save this land, and I'll do that if

I can, no matter what obstacles I have to deal with and who I might annoy."

He turned and started away. Riyand was actually shaking with rage; he tried to shout after Calesh but was too angry to manage anything more than a stutter. Ando stayed close beside him but didn't speak. He didn't really know what he could say. Calesh had twisted everything, made Riyand seem so much worse than he was, but his views were speckled with truth. They had all known for months that the army would almost certainly be sent across the river Rielle, and they had done nothing but talk, and hope for the best.

"An intriguing man," Elisande said quietly. She had been silent so long that Ando had almost forgotten she was there. "If he is as good as he thinks he is, we might have a chance."

Riyand glared at her, but it was Cavel who answered, pursing his lips. "Intriguing? Yes, but more than that. Calesh is what every noble ought to fear; a base-born man brought by events to a position of power, and with the talents to use it. He was right, you know."

"About what?" Ando asked, baffled. "Right about what?"

The seneschal looked at him in surprise. "About noble blood, of course. It doesn't stop a blade or get someone a single step closer to Heaven. The times when common people remember that are the times when kings fall."

"Very true," Ilenia said quietly, making them all jump. "My father used to say the same thing."

"Shut up!" Riyand shouted. "I don't want to hear what your father said, so just shut up!"

She met his hot gaze with a cool one of her own, then turned her attention back to her needlework. Ando frowned at her, then turned to watch Calesh Saissan vanish into the side door of the Manse, his men following like smoke sucked into a hearth. He'd never considered the friction between nobles and common-born men before, but an earlier thought came back to him, of Cavel riding the tide of power when he felt it change beneath him. The old seneschal was loyal, Ando knew that, but he could still notice when sands shifted under his feet.

As if to reinforce that point, Elisande rose and dusted off her green robe. "I believe I will accept the offer to hold rites for the Hand of the Lord again, with your permission. My thanks for a pleasant afternoon, Margrave."

Riyand waved a feeble hand in acknowledgement, but he didn't speak. As she turned away Elisande's gaze caught Ando's, and he thought he saw the shine of compassion there. He felt a surge of anger in response. Elisande thought power had changed hands here today as well then, and she felt sorry for him because of it. It would be easier to bear if he didn't think she was right.

*

"I heard," Reis said in his gravelly voice, "that you were extremely rude to the Margrave. As good as told him he's a dissolute wastrel who'd rather drink and play with his boyfriend than do any work."

"That's more or less true," Calesh admitted. He allowed himself a little smile. "I rode straight here after I left the Manse, general. Quite how that piece of news outran me I don't know, but my compliments to whoever's job it is to keep you informed."

'Here' was a pavilion two miles east of Mayence, in a narrow-throated valley just off the main road that ran down out of the Aiguille towards Parrien. Tents filled the dell in neat rows, enough for maybe two thousand men, though about half of them were mismatched and some were little more than sheets stretched between poles. Close to the stream rough wooden shelters had been built, large enough for thirty or forty men to sleep at a time under their shingle roofs: another two were taking shape from a welter of chopped logs. Horses stood in picket lines downstream of the cook fires, and further down still branches had been woven into screens for the latrine pits. It was a good camp, sited and laid out by men who knew their work. Calesh was glad to see it.

The Guard had begun to gather. Some of the men looked no more than fifteen, recruits whose training was barely begun, while others had too little hair and too few teeth, veterans gathering to the banner when they ought to be warming their bones by a fire. There was nothing to be done about that: every sword was needed. The Hand would be the same.

The pavilion itself was large and well fitted, with a folding bed behind a screen, and a desk and chair by one canvas wall. But it was plainly a working man's place: the two other seats were a beanbag and half a barrel turned upside down, and two broad planks laid over beer kegs made the table. Just outside, where the folded-out wall of the tent became a roof for shelter from rainstorms, a pair of junior officers worked their steady way through thick sheaves of reports. In short, Reis's command centre was everything Riyand's should be, and so patently was not. That was more than a relief. Calesh had begun to worry that Sarténe would muddle its way to oblivion before it truly understood the need to act.

"I like to stay up to date," Reis said. He was a large man, nearly as tall as Calesh and twenty years older, somewhere near his fiftieth birthday. Grey flecked his brown hair. A lifetime spent out of doors had left his skin tough and weather-beaten, but his brown eyes gleamed with shrewd alertness. "If you're half the man rumour makes you, you'll know why."

"I'm only just starting to realise rumour has made me anything at all," Calesh said wryly. "Time will tell what sort of man I am."

"Don't you listen to gossip?"

Calesh let himself smile again. The question was a trap, and he wasn't about to plunge into it. "Of course I do. It helps me stay up to date. If I can tell the truth from the lies."

"Hmph." Reis went to the table and pulled two small plaster cups from under a pile of jumbled papers. "You're clever, at least. Half the young officers in the Guard these days have trouble reading their own name. All the educated fellows seem to end up at that Academy in Parrien, learning how to argue that up is down in three different languages."

"I have a friend who would hate to hear you say that," Calesh said. "He tells me education is the only way to improve lives."

"Hasn't improved mine much," Reis grumped. He handed Calesh one of the cups. "Is it too early in the day for brandy, do you think?"

"Not for a small one," Calesh said. He savoured the mild aroma that rose from the cup; he hadn't tasted good Sarténi brandy for years. "And I believe he means the life to be improved is the student's, in fact."

"Now, that makes more sense." Reis sat on the upturned barrel and propped one boot on top of the other. "Tell me, then. What was it really like, between you and Amalik?"

"There never was any *me and Amalik*," Calesh answered. "Our units met each other on the battlefield. I killed him before he could kill me. That's the start and finish of it."

"Hmm." Reis surveyed his guest critically. "I like what I hear about you, Marshal, and I like what I see too. I'm not in the habit of delaying my judgement of men, and we don't have time for that sort of thing anyway. So here's what I suggest. You and I will work out how to fight this war together, and tell young Riyand what we've decided after it's agreed. That way we'll lure the All-Church into our clutches, catch them a good smack when they're not looking, and all be home in time for harvest."

Calesh laughed. "Sounds good to me."

"Sounds damn unlikely to *me*," Reis said. "Just one thing, my new friend. Riyand is the Margrave, and you have to treat him as such."

His smile slid away. "Riyand is a wastrel and a fool, exactly as I described him. He isn't fit to run a grain store, let alone all Sarténe."

"He's been a decent enough leader these past few years," Reis disagreed. "Most of the time lording is just waving at the crowds and not falling on your face, while the clerks and clerics do all the work. Riyand knows that, and he has sense enough to stay out of the way and let Cavel run the country. But things are different in war, and that's what's shown Riyand to be a fool." He swirled his brandy thoughtfully. "His father was a fine man, Calesh. A fine man. You don't often get two like him. Riyand is half the man he thinks he is and only quarter the man his father was… but he *is* the Margrave."

Calesh hesitated. "You're sure we can keep him out of things?"

"Certain sure," Reis said. "I've been doing it for years. I promised his father I'd stick with Riyand, you see. I've done the best I could."

"If Riyand has made a decent fist of leadership until now, I'd say you've done pretty well," Calesh said. "All right. I'll bow my head and smile when he talks, just as meek as you like."

Reis guffawed, snorting through his nose. "The day you're meek, I'll eat my boots with pig turds for seasoning." He reached out and clinked his cup against Calesh's. "Deal, then?"

"Deal," Calesh said. They swigged the brandy back in simultaneous swallows, which was when Calesh discovered the stuff was about three times as potent as the scent had led him to believe. He held it for a moment and then coughed, unable to help himself. Reis chortled once more and slapped him on the back, heedless of Calesh's armour.

"My own vintage," he said, "from my estate by the coast. You wouldn't believe how many people have been fooled by that gentle aroma." His expression grew mournful. "I can't spare the men or the time to fetch my stock out before the All-Church gets there. Shame to think of fine brandy wasted on a bunch of thugs like that."

"Vines can be replanted," Calesh said, his voice slightly hoarse. "Let's just make sure there are people to do the planting."

There was a rap on the officer's table just outside the entrance, and a moment later a young soldier put his head in. Evidently Reis didn't stand much on ceremony when in the field. Calesh liked that too. "There's a band of armed men coming up the east road, sir, with six wagons. I'd say about eighty or ninety of them. They're not ours."

Reis stood up. "Did the scouts get a good look at them?"

"I did myself," the lad answered. "They're not flying colours, and they don't look professional to me, general. Some sort of militia, I'd guess. Maybe coming to join us."

"Interesting," Reis said. "Are you expecting reinforcements from Parrien, Calesh?"

"I pulled nearly all the Hand's men out when I came through there last week," he said. "But I don't like those wagons. There could be two dozen armed men in each one, all ready to jump us."

"My thought exactly," Reis said with a grin that was all teeth. "You know, I think it might be time to see how fast my light cavalry can scramble to a bugle. Shall we find out?"

Ten minutes later they rode out of the narrow throat of the valley and turned left along the road, with the westering sun directly behind them. Fifty of the Hand accompanied him, together with a hundred of Reis's light cavalry, who had turned out to scramble pretty fast. It was enough to deal with eighty-odd men if things turned violent. Even if there were more soldiers in the wagons, the cavalry could cover a retreat with showers of arrows while the party withdrew to the main army. One result of fighting in Tura d'Madai was that almost all the Hand's men could shoot a bow at least competently. Still, Calesh unbuckled his shield from his pack pony before he left and rode with it hitched to the side of his saddle, covering his leg and hip. Reis saw it and nodded to himself, no doubt thinking just what Calesh was: soldiers don't get to grow old by being careless.

"There," the young soldier said as the road ran around the shoulder of a rocky hill. "Just by that stand of trees."

Reis shaded his eyes and squinted. "Damn, but I wish my eyes were young again. I can't see any – what's that thing?"

The last was aimed at Calesh, who had taken a small brass tube from his saddlebag. He twisted the middle and held it to his eye, sweeping the lens sideways until he found the approaching wagons.

They were still two miles away, but with the spyglass he could see them easily. "Just something I picked up in the desert. Here, you try it."

Reis peered doubtfully at the tube, but held it to his eye and gave a soft gasp of delight. "My heart and eyes! I can see everything!"

"A useful attribute for a general in the field," Calesh noted. "That's my best spyglass, but I have another one back with my men. I'll let you have it. If you want it, that is."

"Of course I want it," Reis said. "And thank you. I'll give you a couple of bottles of my brandy in exchange, if I ever see them again." He handed the glass back and raised his voice. "There's a bridge half a mile further on. We'll wait there for our visitors. I want twenty men to stay back with bows ready in case we have to retreat. Let's get to it."

The bridge was simply built, stout wood with a shoulder-high rail on either side, and broad enough for two carts to pass side by side. The span was flat, not arched, which offered no protection to soldiers advancing on entrenched positions, and the wooden rail gave little cover either. Below it all was a V-shaped trench with a trickle of water at the bottom, deep enough to shelter a man from arrows but too steep-sided to let him climb out quickly. Calesh nodded in appreciation. Reis knew his ground well.

"Are your men willing to block the road?" Reis asked. "They're the best troops we have here."

"Best in the world," Calesh said automatically. He nodded for Amand to see to it. "We'll block it. And I'll be with them."

He lifted the eyeglass again, studying the approaching men. At this distance he could pick out faces, but he didn't recognise any of them. All of them seemed rather young though, twenty summers at most, which seemed unlikely for a mercenary company or a raiding party. The wagons were buttoned down tight and told him nothing at all. He stowed the eyeglass in his saddlebag and walked forward to join his soldiers close to the near end of the bridge. Amand had dismounted them and sent the horses back, out of the way of any stray arrows. For a few moments nobody spoke as men checked their weapons and armour, the practised routine of experienced men, and then they paused and waited for their captain.

"If those men out there are enemies," Calesh said, "it falls to us to fight the first battle of this war. Remember it, and give the troubadours something to sing about." He looked up and down the line of them. "Right. Set for standard defence. Do it."

They assembled around him in three rows, with Calesh front and centre. The first rank locked their kite-shaped shields together and gripped their swords, while behind them the second hefted spears, ready to thrust through gaps or leap to replace fallen comrades. The third held their shields high and angled, as cover against arrows dropping from their long arcs. Calesh breathed deeply, filling his lungs, and drew his sword. His heartbeat slowed, waiting.

Mounted men came around a slight bend in the road, some two hundred yards away. They wore what seemed to be normal clothes, though perhaps more suited to a town than a country road. The nearest pointed to the soldiers arrayed across the bridge and they stopped immediately, waiting while first one wagon and then another lurched into sight behind them. More riders cantered up to join the vanguard, and the wagons came to a halt.

One of the drivers leaned forward as though pulled by the nose. It was hard to make him out, shaded as he was by the canvas bulk behind him, but something about him drew Calesh's eyes. He couldn't think what it was. And then the driver leaned further forward yet, so the light fell on tousled sandy hair and glinted oddly in front of his eyes, and Calesh knew.

He laughed out loud. Taking a step forward, he thrust his sword into his scabbard and turned to shout over his men. "These are friends, Reis! You can stand down. They're friends!"

He turned again, and walked across the bridge alone. At first, anyway; he had managed only four paces when Amand snapped something and the squad hurried to catch up. That didn't matter. He lengthened his stride, grinning like a fool. A couple of the wagons' escorts kneed their horses forwards and then stopped, and the wagon driver sprang down from the riding board and strolled up the road. His green robe was heavy with the dust of travel. Those clothes were different; but the easy grace of his movements, the questioning tilt of the head, were the same, just as Calesh remembered them.

They stopped only a few feet apart. Calesh reached out to brush the green linen with the back of his hand.

"I'd heard you took the Consolation," he said. "I'm glad for you, truly. Is it all you hoped it would be?"

"Much more than that," Luthien Bourrel said. His green eyes crackled with intelligence, just as they always had. It was easy to forget how bright they were, and how they danced. "And what do you think of your home, my friend? Is it all you remembered?"

"Much less than that," Calesh said. "And it will be less still, if we lose this war the All-Church brings down on us."

Luthien's lips quirked. "You never were one for small talk."

"It wastes time," Calesh said. He stepped forward and caught his old friend in a hug, pounding him on the back; it was hard not to cry. "My heart and hands and eyes, my *blood*, it's good to see you, Luthien!"

The smaller man pounded him in return, and for a moment didn't speak. Amand rode up with the bridge guards, now returned to their saddles. At a gesture from Luthien the wagons creaked back into motion, and he drew Calesh to one side before they could be run over. They went to the verge and exchanged another long look, and slowly their expressions became sombre.

"First things first," Luthien said. "Congratulations on your marriage. I hope she knows what a man she's won."

"You'll have to ask her," Calesh said. "All I know is what a woman I've won. That's enough."

"Good," Luthien said, and then, "I am Consoled, and as close to Heaven as I can come in this world. I will not fight, Calesh, not for you or anyone else. Not ever again. It's over."

"I know," he said. He reached out to touch the green robe once more. "It makes sense, you wearing this. I think part of me always knew you'd end up Consoled. I won't ask you to fight, Luthien."

The other man stared at him, then pushed his glasses up his nose. "Do you know, I was certain you'd say that? Everyone else keeps trying to persuade me to take up a sword again, but not you."

"I know what it means to you," he said. "And I know what oaths mean to you, as well."

"I'd forgotten how perceptive you are," Luthien said after a moment. "You always did see deeper than others."

"Save your praise," Calesh advised. He found himself embarrassed by the words, which was ridiculous. "I do have a favour to ask. I want the four of us together through this war, so I want you to minister to the Hand until it's over, Luthien."

"Gladly," the other man said at once.

Calesh had thought he might refuse, or at least try to demur. He ought to have known better. Luthien knew exactly how hard it would be for him to stand beside a battlefield, or in its midst, and resist the urge to take part. That made no difference; his friends needed him, and he would be there, even if he could not raise a weapon. There was a courage in that which Calesh found humbling. He had to clear his throat to speak.

"I need to talk with Reis," he said. "But Baruch and Raigal are at the Preceptory in Mayence. They'll be as glad to see you as I was, Luthien. I'll join you later if I can."

"Two minutes after we meet again, and already you're moving on to the next thing," Luthien said quietly. "You've always been like that, as well, either immersed in something or not involved at all. You're right in the heart of the dance; and you know the steps so well, Calesh, from the first trumpet sound to the last blood spilled. Did you ever wonder when it will end?"

"When I die," Calesh said.

Fifteen

The Zigzag Stairs

This was where bandit chiefs used to hold sway.

Three hundred years ago, before the Jaidi came boiling out of their southern deserts to conquer most of Alinaur, the foothills of the Raima Mountains were a borderland that no nation ruled. Maps might show they were claimed by this king or that Margrave, but the truth was that none of them sent soldiers there, or tried to dislodge the tinpot lordlings and outright brigands who ruled from their precipitous crags. The local strongmen were free to loot and despoil, and to charge outrageous tolls on the caravans and travellers who wanted to walk the passes. It was said there were bandit families in the Raima who could trace their lineage back further than most monarchs.

They even survived the Jaidi conquest, though in much diminished fashion. The desert folk might not be able to conquer the fortresses lodged in their mountain eyries, but they could slaughter the men who ventured out from them, if they went too far. Many did. Some of the outlaw bands simply dwindled away, starved of the bounty they needed to survive. But most clung on, living hand to mouth in the harsh high valleys as best they could.

Then the All-Church called Crusade against the Jaidi. It might not have been possible if the desert's proud sons had remained united, but by then they had broken into a melange of bickering states they called the *Taifa*, and they were vulnerable. The Hierarch in the Basilica had his own problems, too many landless sons fighting for land in Gallene and Rheven and elsewhere, men whose energy needed to be harnessed for something better – at least as the All-Church saw it. The military Orders were formed. Soldiers poured into Sarténe from a dozen countries, and none of them were willing to pay transit fares to a collection of bone-chewing thugs in the hills. The Faithful, too, had more experience of sieges than the Jaidi, and one by one the outlaw towers were taken, until finally the Knights of the Glorification of Heaven came searching up the higher valleys of the Aiguille, and there on a crag they found Adour.

A summer later they went away again, defeated by the thick walls, while the outlaws jeered and hooted and threw offal at their banners.

Some time afterwards the Hand of the Lord came. They didn't try to capture the castle, but instead sat down outside and waited. And waited. It was almost three years before the bandit chieftain asked to negotiate. The Hand might not be able to take the fortress, but they could stop the brigands from raiding, and apparently they meant to. The end of it was that those outlaws who wanted to leave could do so. The rest, Dualists to a man, were invited to join the Hand. Nine did. The others departed, and the Hand of the Lord took the bastion.

Studying it as she climbed up the only trail, Farajalla could see why it had beaten the Glorified. It was only a small redoubt, but she had to tip her head back to see it from the track, its walls looming thick and high atop the shoulders of the steep-sided hill above her. The slope was strewn with stones scattered over uneven, tilting rock. A river splashed down to the hill and divided to run around it in twin streams of foam. Beyond that the sides of the narrow valley clambered steeply up in a welter of small cliffs and treacherous scree in which almost nothing grew but lichen. A besieger would have no room to place catapults or trebuchets, and even if he cut space into the rock, the valley's shape was such that the stones flung at Adour would overshoot it. There was no weakness, no place an attacker might probe or from where he could try to draw the defence, before launching a sudden strike. There was only the wall, smooth and sheer, and a single gate flanked by square-cut towers.

From the far wall something climbed even higher, but the angle was such that Farajalla couldn't see what it was. She decided not to ask. All her breath was needed for the climb.

Twenty soldiers held the fortress for the Hand of the Lord. It was enough: there was no lord for miles around with the strength to take it by force. Some of the men must have seen the little party approaching, for slowly and with much screeching of anguished metal the main gates began to swing open. They were halfway back when one of them stuck. Two figures emerged to scowl and scratch their heads. One of them gave the door a kick.

"Rest for a moment," Gaudin said. He and the soldiers from the Hidden House were leading the horses, and the pack ponies with their belongings. The brass-bound chest was among them, tied to a girth strap with a canvas sack on top. It had struck Farajalla as foolishness to enter the pass with so few, but nobody had appeared to threaten them. They hadn't even seen another human for two days. "You can sit on that rock, Lady."

Ailiss glared at him, and then the rock he indicated too. "I don't need to rest. I'm perfectly able to finish this climb."

Farajalla, who wasn't convinced she could make it herself, didn't speak.

"I'm sure you are," Gaudin said equably. "But the air here is just thin enough to fool you. Better to sit and rest now, than press on and spend tomorrow abed with a throbbing head."

"You nurse me like an old maid," Ailiss grumbled.

"Someone should," Gaudin answered. "Please, Lady?"

She muttered something and went over to the makeshift chair, arranging her skirts as though she was in a lord's mansion preparing for a dance. Farajalla found a perch not far away and leaned her hands on her knees. It had been a long climb from the pass through the mountains, following the river up an ever-narrowing valley from which vegetation gradually disappeared. At times the track was faint and rough: at others it vanished completely under loose stones and stubborn, spiny plants. There were not many travellers up here. Farajalla couldn't imagine why. Her thighs ached and her calves were fire. She would be happy to make camp here and sleep, and leave the last three hundred yards until tomorrow.

"Will that satisfy you?" Ailiss asked Gaudin, after what seemed like half a minute. He only gave her a smile, utterly unfazed by her manner. The old woman rose, and with a groan Farajalla pushed herself to her feet.

They resumed climbing. Farajalla went slowly because that was all she could do, and also because she wanted to make sure her foot was planted securely before she put weight on it. Sometimes footing that looked solid slid away when she shifted fully onto it, once so quickly that she'd had to grab hold of a rock to avoid being dumped down the slope that ran down to the white-foamed river. One of the six soldiers hadn't been as lucky, weighted down as he was with armour and weapons. He held onto the harness of a pack pony as he walked now and still limped, favouring the ankle he had twisted learning to be wary.

The track swung sharply left to skirt a huge boulder, ran obliquely up the angle of the slope, and then abruptly switched back again. Farajalla's knees popped. A hand took her elbow and she looked around to find Gaudin smiling encouragingly down at her. It was a surprise; usually he strayed no more than ten feet from Ailiss, however she grumped at him and flapped her hands. The climb didn't seem to have affected him at all.

Yours is the face I have seen, Ailiss had told her at the Hidden House. *I will teach you the things you must know, before my time is done.*

They had been travelling since, and there had been neither the time nor the energy for teaching. But Farajalla had seen the books, the three great tomes that lay at the centre of the Dualism, and the lore of which the Lady was the keeper. *The Unfurling of Spirit,* a foot tall and three inches thick, patterned all over with gold leaf. *The Opening of the Ways,* smaller and more slender, criss-crossed with delicate filigrees in silver and gold. And the *Book of Breathing,* brass-bound leather so old it seemed to cling to a touching finger as though thirsting for the moisture of skin. The book her husband had been set to find.

She wished Calesh were here. His work had always taken him away from her at need, and she had long been reconciled to that if not exactly happy with it. But this was different. It was the first time she hadn't known when he would be back, even if all went well, and that was an uncomfortable feeling. Even worse was the knowledge that Calesh was involved in a war of annihilation, with nowhere to flee to if he failed and no haven that might take them in. Because the danger was greater, the risks he was likely to take grew too. That was just how he was: he would do what he needed to do to win, just as he'd done when leading the counter-charge against Cammar a Amalik and the Nazir. On the face of it that had been a mad gamble, laughing in the face of the odds, but Calesh had calculated in that instinctive way he had that it offered the best chance of victory. So he had done it, and it had paid off. There was no guarantee that the next risk would work as well.

She couldn't bear to lose him now.

Sometimes she would realise she had laid a hand on the flat of her belly, unconsciously trying to feel the life that Ailiss assured her was quickening there. Farajalla couldn't feel it, though old crones in Harenc had told her that a woman always knew. She wouldn't quite believe it was true until she did, until the babe kicked perhaps, or there was some other incontrovertible sign. Except that part of her *did* believe it, and Calesh didn't know it yet, and so she could not bear to lose him now.

At last the track ran into the shadow cast by those monolithic walls, and then of a sudden they were at the gates. The one on the right was still stubbornly stuck halfway open, but the two men worrying at the lower hinge with a can of grease abandoned the effort and turned to the new arrivals with smiles.

"Welcome to Adour," the nearest said. He was stocky and thick around the middle, with a fringe of iron-grey hair that clung around his ears and ran away into wisps at the back. "I hope it was worth the climb. We always say that," he confided. He dry-washed his hands as he looked at Ailiss, nervousness and joy warring across his lined face, and then his expression cleared and he smiled. "Welcome, Lady. Oh, be welcome to Adour, truly."

"The greeting makes it worth the climb," Ailiss said graciously. "But you forgot to give us your name."

"I'm Rissaun, Lady. And this," he jerked a thumb at the second man, "this is Seran. He doesn't talk very much."

"Rissaun is one of God's chatterers," the other man put in. His voice was reedy, probably because of the squashed blob that had once been his nose. Farajalla dreaded to think how often it must have been broken to become like that. "Everyone else, as a consequence, has to be content with listening."

"I'm sure I'll be delighted to hear you talk," Ailiss told the stocky man. His uncertain grin showed he didn't quite know how to take that. "I will introduce my companions inside, if I may. That was a long climb, worth it or not, and we could all use some hot tea and a bite to eat."

Rissaun was instantly all solicitation, ushering them through the unlit tunnel that ran to a second gate twenty feet away, this one standing open. It wasn't usually closed, he told them, simply because there was no need. They did oil it every spring though, just to be sure it wouldn't stick. He was still talking as they emerged into the courtyard, forty yards across and almost all in shadow, and Farajalla saw what it was that climbed higher than the far wall.

There was a thumb of rock there, jutting almost sheer-sided out of the crag on which Adour was built. A pinnacle atop a peak, Farajalla thought as she craned her head back to see. Stairs zigzagged up the vertiginous flank, most of them tilting crazily one way or the other, as though a giant had picked them up and let them tumble down any old how. At the top stood a narrow temple, little more than a round tower with tiny windows, from which a needle-thin spire poked a few yards towards the sky. The main walls of Adour ran into the butte, using it to make a corner for the fortress. The sides of the spire were at least as sheer as the walls, smooth granite that looked to have been polished until it shone. Not even a spider would be able to climb up, except by the canted stairs.

"I don't believe that people actually worship in there," she said.

"Yes, we do," Rissaun said brightly. "Twice a week. We don't often have an Elite here, so most of the time we take turns to give the sermon. Until last summer we used to race each other to the top in pairs, though we had to stop that when Othaer slipped and broke his leg. He tumbled most of the way down before we could reach him."

They all looked at him, and after a moment Rissaun shifted his feet. "It can get boring if you're here too long."

"I don't doubt it," Farajalla said dryly.

Around them other soldiers had begun to emerge from side doors set into the thick walls. They stopped just within view, eager to see the Lady of the Hidden House but too nervous to approach her yet. None wore armour or uniform. Several had obviously been working, and now wiped their hands on rags or leaned on pitchforks as they watched. All of them looked to be over forty, and most were the wrong side of fifty. She thought this was a place where ageing soldiers were sent when they were too old for fighting, but had been in the Hand of the Lord so long that any other life was unthinkable.

It made sense, but Farajalla found it somewhat unsettling. Baruch might have ended here, if he had remained in the Hand as he so obviously meant to do. Or worse, Calesh could have come, if he hadn't chanced to lead the patrol that rode into Harenc that summer's day.

"Lady," Rissaun began, and broke off. Farajalla already had some idea of how rare it was for him to hesitate, and even now it only lasted a moment. "Lady, would you lead us in prayer, before you go?"

"I would be glad to," Ailiss said. "But for now, what I want is hot tea. And something to eat. Off you go now."

Farajalla thought he would never have gone, if Ailiss hadn't told him directly. He did though, calling something to one of the other men as he went. The little group from the Hidden House stood in a cluster in the middle of the courtyard and looked around themselves. There were doors on all sides, no doubt leading to sleeping chambers and kitchens, store rooms and a barracks, all of them set into the wall itself. A long opening in the north wall was clearly a stable, though it seemed empty at the moment. Most impressively there was a well, a steady trickle of water that fed a stone basin two feet across, what in Tura d'Madai would have been called a tank. The defenders of Adour would not go thirsty.

Farajalla thought of the walls, twenty feet thick and standing atop a steep hill strewn with rocks.

"You could hold this place against an army until the world grows old," she said at last. "Until the All-Church falls, and its name is forgotten."

"Perhaps not quite so long as that," Gaudin said, unsmiling.

"No," Ailiss agreed. She went to a stone bench and sat down, pushing her feet out in front of her. "Perhaps not so long. But we could try."

*

Ailiss began teaching Farajalla the next morning.

The *Book of Breathing* was made up of ancient writings by a man who had known Adjai, the God-Son of the All-Church, when he was alive. Or who had claimed to. Ailiss admitted there was a degree of uncertainty, and some of the texts might have been amended later, perhaps by as much as a generation. It was hard to be sure. The book had been lost for many centuries, and in that great span of time much more had been forgotten.

But the bulk of it was genuine. Ailiss was certain of that. It formed the first part of the *Unfurling of Spirit,* the tome which lay at the centre of Dualism. It was there that God and the Adversary battled, there that God created the souls of men in purity and light, only for Belial to cloak them in sinful flesh and so corrupt them. The words of all the holy men were written on those pages, words spoken in strange tongues from forgotten lands and yet which echoed across as much as three thousand years since. Farajalla read parts of them, just to gain some idea of what they contained, and they made little impression on her. She had been raised by Madai servant women, in a court dominated by soldier men of the All-Church faith, and she found it hard to think of the tales as anything more than just another myth system, no more or less likely than either of those she had grown up with.

The *Opening of the Ways* was different.

This was a collection of ancient texts from all over the world, often from cultures Farajalla had never heard of in lands she could not place. Some she did know, such as Magan, the ancient desert civilisation that survived today only in a few blasted ruins in the sand, and in legend. Others were new to her, like the Long Barrow Men, who wrote in angular glyphs she couldn't understand; or the Gesantes, whose script was narrow and flowing and just as unfamiliar. The texts covered a wide range of subjects, many on the art of geomancy, more on the gift of second sight, which the writers claimed could be learned as easily as language by those who knew how. The Long Barrow Men spoke of stone circles and the forces they harnessed, and of earthlights and the powers which drove them. The Gesantes' writings were full of references to theurgy and scrying, divination and even alchemy, unlikely as that seemed. It was almost all gibberish to Farajalla. Even when Ailiss translated a page for her, the words taken together made very little sense.

Back in Harenc, the old servant women would have called the book a grimoire, and made quick warding signs against evil with gnarled fingers. But evil or otherwise, known or unknown, all the writers traced the beginnings of their knowledge, the originators of the Lore, back to the same source. To the long-ago navigators who had sailed the world on currents nobody else knew, bringing learning and wisdom in their foaming wake, and who were known by a hundred names in as many lands. They were the Oarsmen to one people, the Seafarers to another, simply the Watermen in Magan. The Long Barrow Men called them by a complicated curly glyph that Ailiss said meant *Windjammers*. But it was all the same people, and Farajalla knew them without any need for Ailiss to explain.

The Gondoliers.

"All that we know comes from them," Ailiss said. She and Farajalla were seated facing each other in a cell in the north wall, with tallow candles burning to increase the light that crept in through the high window. "All the Lore, every trick and art and deception. All the raptures I know. Some of them have come through other peoples, by such twisted routes that their origins were forgotten by the writers, but still they come from the Gondoliers."

"Who were they?"

"Oh, such a question," Ailiss chuckled. "Who were the Gondoliers? They were the first to build, the first to carve, the first to write. The first to remember. Before them, men were half-clever creatures who ate wild berries and gathered in tribes for protection, and quivered with terror when the thunder boomed. The Gondoliers took that skin-clad savage and showed him what he could be, if he freed the spirit inside him."

Farajalla frowned, thinking the answer over. "That doesn't actually tell me anything at all."

"In the Dualism we believe that men and women are born in sin," the old woman said. "How could it be different, when we're clothed in flesh, like a cage built around us by the Adversary? But inside shines our spirit, our soul, which was given to us by God. With that we can become whatever we choose to be. Pure, honourable, forgiving: anything at all. The Elite say that if we bring forth what is inside us, it will save us. The Gondoliers taught the same."

"I don't understand."

"Then learn," Ailiss said, as she always did when Farajalla pressed her too directly. "Learn, and the answers will be yours. Only learn."

It was halfway through the third day, and Farajalla was no further forward than she had been on the first, when Gaudin tapped on the door to tell them visitors were coming.

Rissaun was at the gates when Ailiss and Farajalla reached them. He had opened the postern gate set into the wall to one side, but left the main doors shut. He shrugged when Farajalla gave him a questioning glance.

"We opened the big gates for the Lady," he said. "Or we would have done, if one of them hadn't jammed. Whoever these new people are, they're not important enough for that."

Or perhaps, Farajalla thought, the main gate was still jammed.

The new people were still half a mile down the trail, and advancing slowly and with frequent pauses. There were only five of them, all leading their horses. Most wore the livery of the Hand of the Lord, and Farajalla searched eagerly for the age-green armour of her husband before she admitted to herself that he wasn't there. One person she knew was though, a small woman walking in the middle of the group with a baby in a sling across her chest.

"That's Kendra," she said, realising. "That's Raigal's wife and child. He must have sent them here for safety."

"Very wise," Ailiss said.

"I'd hoped it would be Calesh, or Luthien," the old soldier complained. "I haven't seen them since they left for Tura d'Madai."

"You know them?" Farajalla asked, surprised.

"Know them? I taught them," Rissaun said. "I was in charge of training their group, when they first joined the Hand. You could see straight away that Luthien had a rare ability. As quick as lightning, he was, and he never made the same mistake twice. Or once, usually. I've never seen a more naturally talented boy, and I doubt I ever will. Raigal Tai could make him work, though. It was hard for Luthien to get inside the sweep of that great axe."

"And Calesh?" she asked, when she had the chance.

"Clumsy as a three-legged cow at first," Rissaun told her cheerfully. "He had a mailshirt with holes in it and a sword that would have broken with the first blow, and it was obvious he'd never used either. But he learned fast. He could never get near Luthien, but then, nobody could. Still, he was a decent swordsman by the time he sailed. He knew enough to stay alive, anyway."

"He's the one that matters," Ailiss murmured, breaking into the flow of the old soldier's words. Rissaun sometimes seemed he could talk forever if he wasn't interrupted. "The other three are important – giant, wise man, soldier – but it's the king that makes them special."

Rissaun looked at her in evident confusion, but Farajalla knew enough now to understand. A little, anyway. Certain motifs recurred in myths and beliefs, just as certain numbers did: forty-nine was significant for some reason, as was seventy-two, though she hadn't yet learned why. The combination of giant, wise man, soldier and king appeared in Sarténi legends, among others around the world, and was always thought to stand at the centre of great events. Sometimes it even influenced them. Most of all, though, the quartet was said to bring luck. Farajalla hoped it did this time. They were going to need it.

My husband, a king, she thought, and had to stifle a bubble of wild laughter. She would have taken him if he'd been a common soldier, or the pig farmer his father had once been. She would prefer him to be either now, and safe, than riding into danger, king or no.

Kendra and her escort of soldiers reached the shadow of the wall, turned to follow it, and came to the gate a moment later. Raigal's wife looked very tired. Dark circles lurked under her eyes and she was waxy pale. In his sling across her chest little Segarn slept, oblivious to it all. His cap of blond hair looked to have thickened even in the few days since Farajalla saw him last.

"They told me you would be here," Kendra said to her. Weariness laced her voice with heavy threads. "You landed yourself in some adventure when you married your man, didn't you?"

"It looks that way," Farajalla said with a wry smile. "You too, with Raigal Tai. And I'll bet you don't regret it."

"Not for a moment," Kendra admitted. "How could I, with this little one still nursing?" She indicated Segarn, then turned to Ailiss. "You must be the Lady of the Hidden House. I'm pleased to meet you at last, but the truth is I'm too tired to greet you properly. I need to rest. These men were kind enough to see me safely here, and they need to rest too."

The foremost of the soldiers shook his head. "No thank you, mistress Kendra. We have to get back to Mayence as quickly as we can."

"You should rest," Ailiss put in. "Even if only for long enough to eat. The heights can drain you before you're aware of it."

"Even so, Lady." The soldier offered her a bow, but he shook his head. "We all must take risks. We'll head straight back."

They would take Calesh's orders ahead of the Lady's, Farajalla thought. She doubted there were many men who had denied Ailiss, since she took up residence in the Hidden House. Well, the older woman had wanted a king, so she could hardly complain when he acted like one. "Is my husband well?"

"Well, and driving himself and the whole city hard. More than hard. Riyand spends half his time cursing the Commander's name, and the other half sulking." The soldier's lips cracked in a grin. "I'll hardly be surprised if he steals from his own treasury and slips away to the Jaidi kingdoms one night, to while away his days with no thoughts of battle in his mind."

"Calesh would hunt him down and kill him," Farajalla said, "If it took ten years, he would."

"I know, Lady," the soldier said, "and so does Riyand. That's why he won't do it, in truth. With your permission?"

She nodded, and he turned the party around and set off back down the trail, leaving Kendra's bags standing in the road. Rissaun beckoned someone to come and fetch them, while Farajalla struggled with the urge to fetch her horse and ride after the soldiers, back to her husband so she could aid him when he so clearly needed her. Driving himself hard, indeed: she knew Calesh, and suspected that if other soldiers said *hard,* she would say *savagely.*

But he was alive, and not in immediate danger by the sound of it. Besides, she had promised to come to Adour with Ailiss, and learn what she could of the Lore in such time as they were given. She made herself turn back into the fortress. Half an hour later she was settling back down in that gloomy cell, the *Opening of the Ways* in front of her and the Lady of the Hidden House seated across the table with a pot of tea at her elbow.

"Perhaps it would be best," Ailiss said as she handed Farajalla a cup, "if you first learned to scry, and could watch your husband from afar."

Farajalla stared at her. That had never occurred to her, even while she was trying to push worries over Calesh out of her mind for long enough to concentrate on the text. It still wasn't as good as being there with him, but to see his face and know he was well would ease her heart considerably. Even if the ability came and went unreliably, as Ailiss said most of them did, it would help. She could hardly believe she hadn't thought of it herself.

"Then let's get started," she suggested, and bent over the book.

Sixteen

No Room for Strays

Parrien was always busy in late afternoon, shoppers flocking to the markets looking for the bargains that always came just before the vendors packed up for the day. Empty wagons should have been making their way out of the town, or been parked idle in side streets while their drivers laid the day's dust with a tankard or two of well-earned ale. Everything ran at its own pace, humming but not hurrying, and there was rarely any great rush.

Today Parrien was almost bursting.

Japh and Athar could see it from the ridge, two miles west of the town where the road emerged from the hills. The gates in the west and north walls were half hidden by heaving, sweating swarms of people, huge numbers of them jostling and shoving as they tried to enter all at once. Most of the men carried boxes and balanced bags, or had burlap sacks slung over their shoulders, or all three at once, filled with every possession they could carry when they fled their homes. The women usually carried infants and held older children by the hand, trying not to lose them in the crush. Many of the younger children were crying in fear and dismay, clinging tight to their mothers. Japh saw several goats amidst the press, and once a cow. Squawking chickens scattered from a pile of splintered wood that had once been a cage as a fight broke out in the wreckage. The noise was incredible, and the smell worse. Japh wanted to wince just looking at it all.

"The whole countryside has come here," he said, awed. "We're never going to get through all that."

Athar shifted his shoulders, settling his black and white shield more squarely on his back. "We're going to try."

It was a struggle from the start, but their big horses gave them an advantage. They tried to ease their way along, pushing gently into gaps as they opened and not forcing people aside, but it was useless. The crowd shoved and shouted and swore, everyone sure his need was more urgent than the next man's, eager get inside the town quickly so there would still be lodgings to rent and food to buy when they made it. Japh doubted there would be any of either. The first wave of this swarm would have filled all the inns already, filled them to bursting; innkeepers had probably sold pallets in their parlours and piles of straw in the stables, and there was no more room. But there were more refugees, still trying to cram themselves into the town before the All-Church came.

The gate guards must have lost control, or simply stood aside and let the tide of people flow past them. Japh couldn't see the gate house clearly enough to tell whether any were still at their posts. He swore as someone seized his foot, but the hand was torn away before he could see who it belonged to.

"This isn't working!" he shouted to Athar. "We'll still be here at nightfall if we don't go faster!"

Ahead, the other man cupped a hand around his ear and shrugged, unable to hear him in the din.

Easing along was no good though. They would make their way a few yards forward, then find themselves pushed to the side before going back a pace or two. Athar began to curse repeatedly, the oaths given form only by the shape of his lips: Japh couldn't hear a word of them. And Athar had it better than Japh, because he wore the surcoat and shield of the Hand and that made people marginally more willing to move out of his way, when they retained the sense to notice it. Japh wore neither. The recruiting sergeant had said he hadn't grown the muscle to support a coat of mail all day yet, and there weren't enough shields or surcoats either, so here's a sword and good luck. Japh was wearing a boiled leather vest over his old stable clothes, and trying not to be annoyed about it. It wasn't how he'd thought soldiering would be. He leaned forward to whisper reassuringly in his gelding's ear, feeling its growing tension just a moment before it gave a snort and stamped angrily. But he was good with horses and it responded to his voice, at least to the extent that it didn't kick someone. It would soon, whatever he did.

"Easy now, boy," he soothed. The gelding had once been a stallion, after all, and if he still was he would have laid about him with his steel-shod hooves by now. "This isn't how I thought it would be either, so be easy and we'll get through together, what do you say?"

He had actually thought that being in the Hand of the Lord would be fun. Adventure could wait a while, perhaps until he went to Tura d'Madai or Alinaur, and had a chance to make his name. But still, in the last fleet years before he reached adolescence he'd wanted to be Calesh Saissan, or at least be with him, riding to battle on a great black warhorse to thrash the wretched Madai yet again. Calesh was the greatest soldier alive – or so the lads of Parrien assured each other, their voices awed to whispers – laughing at death, and sharpening his blade on the rays of the rising sun. Everyone wanted to grow up to be Calesh, except the girls, who just wanted to grow up to marry him.

Sitting an increasingly fractious horse amid a screaming throng was *not* what he'd expected when he joined.

"The hell with this," Athar bellowed. The crush had driven him back until he was more beside Japh than ahead of him. "Are you willing to shove through? We'll still be here at midnight if we don't get a move on."

About time you realised that, Japh thought, but he was still stroking his mount's neck and whispering soothing words, and he wasn't sure they were working. He spared the other man a nod.

"Right," Athar said, and shortened his reins. "Here we go." He drove forward into the throng.

Before his dreams of heroism in the desert, Japh had wanted to be Abhara the Sailor, exploring the wide seas with his brave crew, all dressed in flaring trousers and colourful shirts with cutlasses at their belts. He would fight pirates and sea monsters, battle evil sorcerers, and sail home with a hold full of ancient treasure to spend on women and wine, until it was time to sail out again. Because the point of the journeys wasn't the gold, or the women. It was the journey itself, the thrill of sailing unexplored waters to the mysteries that lay beyond them. Japh would sit on the thatched roof of the stable in the evening, his work done, and looking out over the mast-crowded harbour he would dream of the day when he and his crew of likely lads would steal a ship and go adventuring at last.

If he was honest, a little of that longing had still been alive inside him on the day the horizon sprouted a field of sails and the Hand of the Lord returned from Tura d'Madai. The dreaming remnant of that boy had been breathless with excitement when Calesh Saissan himself – *Calesh Saissan!* – walked along the quay to speak with him. And there was hardly any romance at all. Calesh simply asked to be taken to Raigal Tai, while all around him hard-faced soldiers worked efficiently to unload crates and horses from the ships. Japh hadn't even realised the owner of the tavern next door *knew* Calesh. Much less that Raigal Tai was his friend, and a hero himself besides.

"Mind where you're going!" a large man with a bulging bag in each hand snarled. Japh's gelding had just sent him stumbling out of the way: the man was big, but no match for a horse. "Or I'll pull you out of that saddle and ram your head down your neck, you hear?"

"Important business," Athar called, leaning across. He pulled his cloak around so the man couldn't miss the black-and-white circle emblazoned on the chest. "Hand of the Lord. Shut up and clear the way."

The man scowled, which he surely wouldn't have done a week ago, but he did step aside. Japh wished he had a cloak in the Order's colours, at least. He was going to get stomped on because of the lack of one at this rate. A fine start to his life as a soldier that would be.

Calesh had turned out to be ordinary, but a greater shock still had been the sight of Farajalla, and the realisation that she was Calesh's wife. So much for the doe-eyed dreams of all Parrien's girls; the man whose face they imagined in the night was already married, and to a Madai besides. It was then that Japh had begun to realise, perhaps belatedly, that his childhood imaginings were wrong in almost every way possible. Using his horse to shove helpless refugees aside in the road, he could hardly doubt it any longer.

They were within twenty feet of the gates before the guards saw them. They were still at their posts after all, a thin line of blood and gold livery strung across the open gates. One pointed them out and yelled something, and though the words were lost in the cacophony two men emerged from the gatehouse and dashed up to the line. With shouts and blows from their cudgels they drove the throng back, just for a moment, but that was all the horsemen needed. Athar urged his horse into the gap and Japh followed, so close that his gelding could have taken a bite out of Athar's saddle. The crowd roared angrily and surged forward again, pressing in from all around the gate.

"You have to close it!" Athar screamed at the nearest soldier. "Close the gates, and just let people in through the portal door. If you don't they'll trample right over you in the end!"

The guard shrugged. He had a livid bruise on one temple, and the hint of blood under his dark hair. "Mayor wants the gates kept open!"

"But the All-Church army –"

"If it was up to me I'd send the whole lot of them back to the farms." The guard jerked a thumb at the throng to show who he meant. "But it isn't my choice. Now get moving friend, you're blocking the way."

Athar hesitated, his head turning as he searched along the line of guards. Looking for the officer, no doubt. Japh reined closer to him. "It isn't our problem, Athar. We've more important work to do."

For a moment Athar didn't move, but then his lips twisted in a grimace and he pulled his horse around. The animal huffed through its nose, but once it was heading away from the heaving mayhem outside the gate it calmed considerably. Japh rode up alongside, glad to be in the relative calm and shade of the passage under the wall, but it was only a few steps until they emerged back into sunlight, and the crowded town streets.

They weren't as busy as the road outside, but this was Japh's home, and he'd never seen Parrien so full. People were everywhere, standing thick as wheat along the pavements, leaning out of windows, huddling in doorways or in clusters down narrow, dank alleys. Most buildings had their windows boarded up, but a good many of those boards had been broken down and the windows used as makeshift entrances, the shops as temporary shelter. Japh wondered how many families would be sleeping twelve to a room tonight, on a floor that wasn't theirs. Then he looked at the pallid faces of the people on the pavement and wondered how many would sleep in the open, each resting his head on his neighbour's shoulder.

"How will they eat?" he asked aloud, horrified. "When the army comes, I mean. Parrien can't hold enough food for so many."

Athar's mouth twisted again, and he heeled his horse forward without replying. The two men rode down the middle of the street, followed all the way by turning heads and wide, fearful eyes. Behind them still more refugees made their way through the gate tunnel and into the town, those the guards had thought deserved a place or who had the money to pay a bribe. Probably the latter, Japh thought sourly: the guards at least would be doing very well out of this, like crows feasting on the dead. But he felt little better than them, riding past all this misery as though it didn't concern him. It did, it turned his stomach, and he wasn't sure that duty was enough of an excuse to keep riding.

The avenue gave suddenly into a square, and the silent crowd thinned. After the tight press outside it seemed like open countryside, though refugees still stood here and there in ragged clumps. From here on progress should be easier though. Japh prayed it would be. He didn't even want to think about feeling those hungry eyes on him again.

"Thank God for that," Athar said. "Right, then. You grew up here. What's the fastest way to the dovecote?"

For a moment Japh couldn't remember. Part of it was just the shock of all those fugitives, but the rest was surprise at being asked. Athar hadn't shown much interest in his opinions before. He was only a few years older than Japh was, twenty perhaps, but he was a full member of the Hand of the Lord, even if he hadn't seen battle yet. Until now he'd behaved as though that gave him the right to make all the decisions without bothering to ask what his companion thought. Japh supposed it did at that, and he'd tried not to be annoyed. But Athar was a Mayencer, born and bred in the city in the hills, so of course he didn't know his way around Parrien very well. At least he wasn't too proud to ask when the need was there. Japh looked around and tried to think.

"Come on," Athar prompted impatiently. "Make your mind up before that mob gets through the gate, will you?"

Japh took a moment longer to check he was right, then nodded to himself. "Down that street on the left, and then we hang a right just before the Theatre. The Hand's dovecote is just inland from the harbour. Not too far from where I used to work, in fact."

"I didn't ask for a geography lesson," Athar grumbled. He turned his horse with clicks of his tongue and set off, leaving Japh to scowl at his back and hurry to make up the distance.

Athar rode straight past the turning by the Theatre, which gave Japh the satisfaction of shouting at him to come back. He asked innocently if the other man would benefit from a geography lesson. Athar muttered something indistinct and then broke into a reluctant grin. Sometimes, when he forgot to be serious, he really did seem no more than twenty.

They clattered down a cobbled street, beyond the end of which a paltry few masts bobbed against the shining sea. Japh supposed most ship owners must have left already, heading for ports a long, safe distance away. Just before they would have reached the quayside road they turned left again, and drew rein in front of a wide doorway set in the base of a white-plastered tower. A bearded man was looking out of a window above the door, his face tight. The noise of the crowd was a murmur here, but it turned the air febrile, and when the man noticed two riders dismounting below his expression turned to suspicion in an instant.

"I've no room for strays," he began, and broke off when his eyes caught the black and white of Athar's cloak.

"Yes," the soldier said. "We're Hand men, and if nobody's found a uniform yet for Japh here, you can blame that on a whole lot of hurry and not on him. Now open the door. We're here to check for messages."

"Right," the man said. He vanished from view and the window banged down. Japh stroked his gelding's broad nose and led it towards the door. He had to wait what seemed a long time before a bolt rattled and a key turned, and the door swung open to reveal a straw-floored room the same size as the tower. It was divided into half a dozen horse stalls, only one of them occupied. The bearded soldier ushered them inside and locked the door again. He looked about forty to Japh. When he moved he dragged his right leg behind him.

"The horses need water, and oats if you've got them," Athar said briskly as he handed over his reins. "We'll take some fruit and cheese, and a bit of bread. Are there any messages?"

"Only one," the man said. "It came in two mornings ago."

"And you didn't send it on?"

The bearded man looked at him. "Send it on? Usually there's three men at this post, but when Commander Saissan rode out he took the other two. Every single one of my birds had been sent out by then. So tell me, son, how was I supposed to send the message on, eh?"

"All right," Athar muttered. "Sorry, then. Now where's the message?"

"Slots by the door of the loft," the older man told him sourly. "By God, son, you can make an apology sound like a complaint. Is that the best manners the sergeants teach you these days?"

"I said I'm sorry," Athar snapped back.

Japh left them bickering and went to the far door, then up the wooden steps that ran around the walls of the tower. After the second flight he passed another door on his left, through which he caught a glimpse of a table and simple chairs beside a window – where the bearded man had been sitting when they arrived, he assumed. A hearth was set in the far wall, with a tin chimney flue above it. That was all he had time to register before he went on, his boots clattering as he took the steps two at a time. A second door gave into a bedroom with six narrow cots and small lockers. Japh went on climbing, and finally he turned left and stepped onto a platform with a wide window sill on one side and a long, high pigeon cote on the other. The solitary bird perched within fluttered its wings and cooed, its head bobbing back and forth as it tried to focus on him.

Beside the cote half a dozen slots had been cut into the wall. Japh hunted along them until his fingers closed on a tiny roll of paper, sealed with a shapeless blob of green wax. He turned to go back down, hesitated, and then went over to the window and looked out over Parrien.

He wasn't high enough to see the streets unless the angle was such that he looked directly along them. But all of those were lined with ranks of refugees, the plazas were thronged, and even the flatter rooftops were crowded. The noise was incredible. People fleeing from the farms and villages were still crowding into Parrien, pouring into the city in their thousands, and it seemed the guards on the west gate were doing a better job of keeping them out than some. Most of the people who could leave had already gone, so there were empty houses all over the town, but Japh thought every one of them would be home to five families before night fell. All the boarding houses would be full, all the inns bursting with patrons sleeping pressed together on the floor or on benches, propped against each other for support. People would pay high prices for a place on a stable floor, or leaning against the stove in a kitchen. And still there would be people on the streets, huddled in doorways or against the walls of fountains, clustered under trees, laid head to toe across the parks like some vast breathing carpet. He wondered if Parrien could actually hold them all, or if it would burst, breaking open under the strain like a ripe tomato.

He raised his eyes and froze.

Outside Parrien, over the low wall to the east, was what the refugees had fled from. The afternoon sunlight gleamed off breastplates and pikes, helmets and the points of spears. It was too far for Japh to make out details, but the orderliness of the groups of men, and those tell-tale glints, were enough: the All-Church was here. Japh would not have thought it possible for them to arrive so soon. His appalled gaze followed the army around, from the east to the north and further yet. Cavalry were hurrying west to encircle the town. His breath stopped dead. He and Athar were very nearly cut off.

He turned and flung himself down the stairs, clattering madly as he slipped and skidded from one landing to the next. One shoulder banged hard off the wall and he grunted, but he didn't stop. Once he dropped the tight-rolled paper and had to go back for it, cursing at the wasted time. Every moment might count now. Finally he bounced off the wall and shot into the stable like an arrow from a bow, panting as much with excitement as exertion. Athar and the bearded man were still glowering at once another, but both broke off their staring match and turned to Japh in surprise as he burst in.

"What –?" Athar began.

"Army," Japh broke in, still gasping. "Already halfway round the town. We have to go!"

Athar stared at him. "Are you sure?"

"I saw it!" He leaned a hand against the wall for support. The bearded man pushed past him with a snort and vanished up the stairs. "I saw it, Athar, and those idiots at the gates will never get them shut in time. If we don't ride now, we'll never get out."

"All right," Athar said slowly. "What was the message?"

Japh gaped at him for a moment before he remembered. He slit the wax seal with one fingernail and unrolled the scroll, and as he read it he felt the blood leave his face. Athar plucked it from his hands and read quickly. When he looked up his eyes were wide.

"No time to eat," he said. "We have to get this out right away, even if it kills the horses. Are you fit for another ride?"

Japh was already going to his gelding. He hoped the animal's flared nostrils meant he could draw in more air, because he was likely to need it before the day was done. One of them, he or Athar, had to get through. The message, written on paper headed with the lion-flanked cross of the Basilica, was proof enough of that.

A Justified Highbinder has been sent to kill Calesh Saissan. He is posing as a mercenary from Alinaur, come north to offer his services, and may have accomplices.. His name is Elizur Mandain. Be wary.

Japh had heard the name. Elizur Mandain, said to be the finest swordsman in the world. If he reached Calesh undetected, Japh was very much afraid the Commander would die before he knew he was in danger.

*

"How did they do it?" Calesh muttered to himself. He was sitting in his saddle on a ridge of rock overlooking Parrien from the west, spyglass to his eye and trained on the town. "How did they get here so soon?"

Raigal Tai frowned at him. "But you wanted to come here to see. You must have known they'd get here this soon."

"I wanted to be here when they arrived," Calesh said, not taking his eye from the glass. "And I got here early because I don't like unpleasant surprises. But I didn't expect this."

He had prepared for the worst, in other words, without expecting it to happen. It was one of the things a good captain did, Luthien knew. Another hallmark of skill in a commander was the ability to move troops quickly, to reach an unexpected place at an unexpected time, and the man in charge of the All-Church army certainly seemed to have that gift. Calesh had done the same, but all he had here was three hundred Hand cavalry. They had come to watch, not to interfere. Ahead of them a wooden bridge ran over a deep, rocky ravine, carrying the road into the farms around Parrien. Calesh wouldn't let them cross.

The town wasn't going to hold for long. The walls were too low, and hadn't been properly maintained for years. What was the need? There hadn't been any real danger of fighting here since the Jaidi threat was at its height, two hundred years ago. Since then all Sarténe's wars had been fought on other men's land. So the walls were weak, and so was the will of whoever was in authority. A strong leader would have shut the gates against that horde of refugees, trapping them outside where their only hope was the doubtful mercy of the All-Church army. Inside they would need food and water, straining the resources of the fence past breaking point: outside, they would just get in the way of the besiegers. It was cruel, and condemning men to such suffering might well doom a man to an eternity of torment when he died, but that was war. Luthien could consider practicalities with a clear mind and ice in his veins, and still have room in his heart for the compassion of his God.

If Riyand had done his job properly the walls might have been strengthened by now, the gates buttressed with wooden beams and weapons stocked in towers and on rooftops. None of that had been done, Luthien knew, and there was no point now in wishing it had.

"The Glorified are at the back again," Calesh said. His tone was almost absent, as he told the others what he saw while his mind judged and calculated and assessed. "Afraid to get blood on their nice grey cloaks, I suppose. I can't see many Justified. There are a lot of regiments from outside the Orders, but most of the men at the front are Shavelings."

"Perhaps their commander is too," Amand suggested.

"Very likely," Calesh said. The spyglass panned across the field as he spoke. "For a Crusade called against good church folk, the Basilica will have wanted one of its own men in charge. Someone it could rely on. But most Shavelings couldn't move an army this fast. You know what they're like."

"Spend too much time praying and not enough organising," Amand said.

Calesh snorted. "Praying, and wasting time polishing armour and ironing cloaks when they should be drilling. But this man must be different. I wish I knew who he was."

The Order of the Basilica was to lead the crusade, then. Luthien supposed Calesh was right: they should have expected that. This was a war aimed at destroying what the All-Church called heresy, and they would want their own men at the forefront, white and gold uniforms bright under the God's sun. The Shavelings were not as well trained as men of the other Orders, and certainly they were less well equipped, but they were fanatical in their devotion. Luthien suspected that their leaders believed an excess of zeal made up for imperfect methods and chipped swords. The trouble was they were often right.

Abruptly Calesh leaned over to pass Luthien the spyglass. "You have a look. See if you can spot something I've missed."

He took the glass, but for a moment Luthien didn't put it to his eye. He nodded towards Calesh's belt. "My memory might be playing a trick on me, but I think I've seen that horn before."

"Your memory isn't playing tricks," Calesh said. His fingers went to the horn, narrow-necked ivory banded with greening copper that matched his armour almost perfectly. "You've seen it."

Raigal Tai craned around, trying to see past Calesh's saddle. Luthien ignored him. "It's the battle horn of Cammar ah Amalik."

"That's right," Calesh said, as Raigal chuckled. "I thought it deserved blowing, one more time. It won't be today, though."

"Amalik was an enemy," Luthien said mildly.

"Amalik," Calesh said, equally soft, "was a better leader, and a finer man, than anyone likely to be swaggering around under those banners across the field. Are you going to look or not?"

Luthien took off his spectacles and put the spyglass into the socket of his eye, peering at the sprawling All-Church army. His mind was elsewhere though, drifting through memories while his eye was left to scan the field unattended. He was surprised by how little Calesh had changed. Oh, much was different about him in some ways, but here at the edge of battle he was just the same, exactly the man Luthien remembered from the past.

In Tura d'Madai he had been called the Sand Scorpion. Both armies used the name, as did the common people caught up in the endless maelstrom of the war. By the time you saw the barb coming it was already too late to dodge, they said. Part of that was because he was in the Hand of the Lord, the only one of the military Orders to concentrate exclusively on battle. The Shavelings were preachers and tax-gatherers as well as fighting men. The Glorified were sailors and marines, and the Justified had their oft-denied corps of assassins and their endless, single-minded pursuit of political power. But all the Hand's soldiers were trained simply to *be* soldiers, equipped with the best steel from the forges in Samanta, and drilled until their muscles were like corded rope. It was said that a fighting man of the Hand was expected to be able to march for two days and nights without a break, and then fight a battle at the end. Many of them could. Many of them had.

But there was another reason why Calesh was such a good leader, and that was simply him. He understood war, was suited to it in a way that few men were, and all of them – ironically – seemed to view it as an ugly necessity, rather than finding any glory in it. They saw the moonshine for what it was. Cammar ah Amalik had been like that, if the stories were even partly true. He had borne the adulation of his men and the common folk of Tura d'Madai, but he'd borne it as a burden, not something to be treasured or embraced. Calesh was the same way, immune to the siren song that promised fame and renown, and he was capable of a ferocious work rate besides. Added to which he possessed the intangible ability to encourage other men, to inspire them, and he had luck. Every general needed luck. Without it, energy and talent meant very little.

Luthien pushed such thoughts away and concentrated on the view through the eyeglass. The nearest cavalry units of the All-

Church army were sweeping around Parrien now, closing the road that ran out to the west, and to where the three friends sat in their saddles and watched. The three hundred men behind them seemed scant protection against the mass ahead. Nobody seemed to have spotted the Hand yet, but that wouldn't last.

Further away, serried ranks of Shavelings were parading across the fields. North and east of Parrien the plain spread perfectly flat, but the farms now were lifeless, almost barren. Every field was bare, every chicken coop empty. No pigs snuffled and snorted their way through orchards. The land had been stripped, except here and there where hands had not been available to clear a field before the army came. Warehouses within Parrien would be bulging with grain sacks and barrels of salted pork. Nothing that could be moved had been left behind. And it wouldn't matter at all if the wall could not be held.

Baruch could have helped here, Luthien thought as he turned the spyglass towards the town itself. He was the most dependable of the four old friends, solid and thorough, and he had a flair for organisation that was just as much a gift as Calesh's ability to inspire, or Raigal's indomitable good spirits. But such a talent could only be used in one place at a time, and the key to this whole war was, Calesh believed, the defence of Mayence. If the city held then Sarténe held. Luthien agreed, in fact, which meant Baruch was needed more there than here. Parrien would have to manage as best it could alone.

They all knew what that meant, though nobody spoke of it. Parrien was being thrown to the wolves, abandoned because it could not, in truth, be defended. There were not enough men, and not enough time to rebuild the wall now Riyand had thrown two months away with his dawdling. That was the hard reality, and so Calesh was trading space in exchange for time. Let the All-Church have Parrien, if it cost them a week to capture the town and then to prepare for their next move. Use those dearly bought days to assemble more soldiers from the outlying areas, and perhaps to hire mercenaries from Alinaur or give the Hand soldiers there time to come north. Use it to train merchants and labourers well enough that they could take their places in the line. And then dig in, and let the All-Church either throw its men onto carefully planned defences, or lay a siege and see which army began to starve first, the one outside the walls or the one within.

Luthien scanned the walls, tracked the spyglass down to the harbour… and then swung back, squinting. It only took a second to be certain.

He lowered the glass and handed it back to Calesh. "Check the north gate. I think the All-Church has broken in already."

His best friend stared at him in shock. It was a moment before Calesh seemed to remember the spyglass and put it back to his eye, peering across the plain to the walls of Parrien. He was silent for a long time, and then spat out an oath of such bitter ferocity that Luthien actually flinched. He hadn't heard language that foul since he left Tura d'Madai.

"Some dumb son of a bitch must have been asleep at his post," Calesh snarled between his teeth. "What kind of fool doesn't pay attention at the *start* of a siege? He can't have dozed off with all this going on."

"Might be a traitor," Raigal Tai rumbled. "Or more than one. Not everyone in Sarténe is a Dualist."

That was true. Men shifted uncomfortably in their saddles behind the three friends, but it was true. Half a dozen men might have been enough to seize a gate tower and hold it for long enough for the army to reach them, if they were well organised and they timed it right. Such things had happened before. But still, someone in command was careless not to have the towers buttoned down tight early, or else a captain on the spot was lax, or perhaps both. It only needed one weak link for a chain to snap.

"The same thing could happen in Mayence," Calesh said thoughtfully. "I'll have to consider that."

"You can't throw people out of their homes for fear of something they might not do," Luthien said quietly. He put his glasses back on and pushed them higher up his nose with one finger. "You can't, Calesh. Not if you want any part of your soul to remain untarnished."

"You're the one who chose to polish his soul," Calesh answered. "Mine never did gleam all that much."

Luthien smiled. "Yes, it did."

His friend raised his eyebrows but didn't reply. Ahead, a squadron of Justified cavalry peeled away from the main body and rode towards the bridge, pennants flying from their uniformly slanted spears. It seemed the watchers on their ridge had been noticed.

Saddles creaked behind Luthien again as the soldiers checked weapons and armour.

"Commander?" Amand said, not far away.

Calesh didn't turn his head. "Wait. They're no threat."

Fifty Justified horsemen were indeed no threat to six times as many Hand of the Lord. The approaching riders apparently reached the same conclusion as soon as they came close enough to recognise the black and white armour of the men on the ridge. They reined in, and one man went galloping back to the main host with dust flying from his horse's hooves. All-Church soldiers were still pouring across the fields to encircle Parrien, a tide of them that stretched all the way back to the horizon. It wouldn't be possible for the Hand to remain on this ridge for much longer.

"I think the north gate has fallen," Calesh said. He was still peering through the glass. "The All-Church got there very fast. Looked planned to me, so maybe there really was a turncoat inside. My heart and eyes, I hoped the town would hold for longer than this."

Luthien couldn't see, without the eyeglass to help his vision, but he didn't really need to. Once fighting had begun at the gate towers the end was almost inevitable, unless the defenders could overwhelm their antagonists and shut the portcullis again. That wasn't likely, and evidently it hadn't happened, at least not in time. Parrien had fallen in less than an hour. It would be an unpleasant place to be a Dualist in the days to come.

A second contingent of Justified cavalry was approaching the bridge, this one much larger than the first. Luthien put their numbers at about five hundred, including the earlier squadron, which fell in as the newcomers reached it. It was too many for the Hand to face, he knew. They might win, given their superior quality, but the cost would be too high when they needed to conserve their numbers for the campaign ahead. Luthien had always been able to observe and calculate such things at speed, and though it was a battlefield gift he would have been happy to lose, it seemed it remained with him.

"They're not going to talk," he said to Calesh. "They'll cut us down if they can. We ought to leave."

"Not yet," his friend replied. Raigal Tai pulled that great axe from its loop and hefted it in one hand.

"Commander?" Amand said, for the second time.

This time Calesh nodded. "Yes, I think so. Give the order."

"Helmets on!" Amand bellowed. He was a natural field sergeant, efficient and tough and very, very loud. "Make sure your sword is loose and your prayers are spoken. Archers, stand by for my word."

"Archers?" Luthien said.

Calesh nodded. "Something we learned in the desert. Almost all our men can handle a bow now."

The Justified came closer. Their lines rippled as they changed formation, moving from long rows to a narrow column six men abreast, able to cross the bridge in good order. They did it flawlessly, a difficult manoeuvre accomplished with drill yard precision. Their pace began to pick up. Luthien felt his heart jump with remembered excitement, and hated himself for it.

Hooves hit the bridge. The Justified were charging now, pounding over the boards at a full gallop, and the first of them came back onto solid earth in moments. The Hand of the Lord tightened ranks and waited for orders.

"Now," Calesh said.

Seventeen

True Belief

"We're inside the walls," Amaury said, as though Sarul couldn't see as much perfectly well for himself. "It was the Order of the Basilica which broke in first. Driven on by zeal, no doubt."

Sarul was careful not to react to that last, laconic comment. It was sometimes difficult to be sure when Amaury was being sardonic, and when what might be sarcasm was actually no more than the Rheven general's flat farmer's vowels. Uncertainty was not a thing to which Sarul was accustomed. He didn't care for it very much, but he did know it was important to make the other man unsure of him, too. So he kept his expression blank and his eyes on the town, and waited for Amaury to speak again.

The two men were standing at the open front flap of the command pavilion, which had been hastily set up by a crew of servants as soon as it was safe. Sarul thought it had been safe from the start, actually, but if Amaury wanted to be cautious that could be allowed, for the moment. Let the general make some decisions now: that would make it easier to overrule him when it mattered. From the pavilion they could look over the wide fields that stretched the mile to Parrien's walls. The Sarténi had swept the fields bare, leaving nothing for the All-Church army but useless stalks and empty chicken coops. That might be a problem in time, but not now. If the food ran out men could always be ordered to fast, to purify their souls for the scourging to come. It would even be good for them.

Sarul didn't think Amaury would object. The squat general might have an unfortunate tendency towards sarcasm, and he wore a square black beard that would be more suited to the eastern churches with their bizarre concepts of the image of God, but he knew his task here. Marshal the army and do what the All-Church Legate, which was to say Sarul, told him to do. Even a thick-witted soldier ought to be able to manage that.

And if he could, then here was where this obscene Dualism would begin to die. There had been long years when Sarul had wondered whether it was God's plan to allow the heresy to fester like a pus-filled boil, or a plague sore that turned slowly black with gorged blood. After all, God had allowed it to fester for years before the

Basilica even became aware of it, growing like a malign tumour under the All-Church's skin. Sarul had tried not to let himself think that way, had prayed daily for the strength to continue his struggle to bring these misguided people back into the embrace of the mother Church, but sometimes treacherous thoughts had whispered in his head despite all he could do. He had doubted, that was the heart of it: oh, sweet Heaven, he had doubted. As time went by he prayed more and more often, gaining a reputation among the clergy of the Old City for extreme piety. That image was enhanced by the ferocity of his constant, untiring exhortations against heresy, and the need to cleanse the stain.

Those things had brought him to the position of Hierarch, to be taken when old Antanus died at last. He could be sure of that now. And they had brought him here, to this pavilion overlooking Parrien, where the cleansing would begin. He thought now that God had kept Antanus alive for so long, little more than a husk through which breath whispered ever more faintly, to give Sarul time to wipe away the heresy before he took up his destiny as the Lord's regent on earth. Already men would be setting flames to that God-cursed Academy, where so many false beliefs had been taught as though they were pure fact. He was pleased: in that nest of evil they had taught only the wisdom of serpents.

It was very hard not to laugh with joy in fact, though Sarul was not a man much given to laughter. But a hot, savage delight thrummed in his chest, in his very soul where only God could see it. He felt as though his body was lit from within by a holy flame.

A messenger dashed up and handed Amaury a folded sheet of paper. The general opened it and read, while Sarul pretended not to notice. Let the man imagine he was in charge here: there would be opportunities to disabuse him, in time. It would all be the same in the end.

"My captains say the streets of Parrien are so thronged they can't tell who is who," Amaury said in his flat country vowels. "With your permission, I'll order all civilians to be held until we can ascertain which of them are Faithful and which are not. When the town is secure we can –"

"No," Sarul said.

He had wondered if God meant for the heresy to flourish. He would wonder no more. He was here, the army was here, and it was time to end it. Those people in the town were heretics and shelterers of heretics, collaborators in blasphemy and apostasy. They would claim to be faithful, loyal sons of the All-Church, all of them, to a man. The truth was that they were all guilty. Those who had stood aside and done nothing while evil flourished in their midst were no more to be forgiven that the apostates themselves.

  The avengers had come. Sinners would not be forgiven.

  "My lord?" Amaury asked.

  "Kill them all," Sarul said. He heard the surety enter his voice, that rich and sonorous tool that God, in his wisdom, had bestowed upon him. "Kill them all. God will know his own."

*

  The crowd roared up ahead, a sound made half of rage and half of fear. Suddenly people were fighting to get back past Japh and Athar, turning the street into a mass of heaving flesh. A smallish man just to Japh's side stumbled, flailed a hand to snatch at his stirrup, and when he missed fell headlong on the cobbles. The throng trampled right over him. Japh doubted their wild eyes even saw him before he was crushed.

  "This is hopeless!" Athar bellowed over the din. He had moved his shield from its place by his saddle so it rode on his back, and couldn't catch in the struggling mass all around. "We're never going to get out this way!"

  "Got to try!" Japh yelled back. They could have reached out and touched fingers, but still the two men could barely hear each other's shouts. "The Commander has to be told!"

  Athar grimaced. That was the nub of it, all right: if Calesh wasn't warned, then Elizur Mandein might be able to walk right up and slide a knife into his ribs before the Commander knew there was a threat. The Justified always denied they employed assassins, but everyone knew they did, and that they were good. Mandein was unusual in that his name was known, mostly because he'd won the sword tournament in Caileve a few years ago. You had to be brilliant even to be allowed to *enter* that contest, and winning it made Mandein more than merely good. He was a genius, and if he got close to Calesh he would certainly kill him.

  Japh wondered who had sent the letter from the Basilica. Obviously someone had a spy there, or at least a sympathiser, and an active one at that: this wasn't even the first time a warning had been sent. Calesh Saissan had brought the Hand home in response to another. Japh had no idea who it might be, and he didn't suppose it was important. A cleaner could overhear plans being laid as easily as an Arch-Prelate could lay them. What mattered was that the warning had been sent: the thing to do now was make use of it.

Easier said than done.

"By my heart and eyes!" Athar swore. He pulled his belt knife and cracked the hilt down on the head of the man trying to drag him from the saddle. The man staggered and let go, hands going to where blood already darkened his hair, and then he went down in the crush. Japh thought he heard the beginnings of a shriek. He swallowed and looked away.

"Turn around!" Athar shouted to him. "For God's sake, Japh, we have to find another way out. We'll be lucky to stay in our saddles here, and if we do, we'll only find ourselves facing whatever it is this lot are running from. And we both know what that is."

Japh hesitated, then gave a reluctant nod. The crowd was fleeing from All-Church soldiers, of course. Smoke already rose from buildings close to the northern and eastern walls, evidence that some of the Crusading force had broken through the walls and was inside the town. There was no escape from Parrien that way. Japh looked over his shoulder, towards the west gate, and wondered if the All-Church had reached that far yet.

"The harbour!" Athar called. "It's our only chance now."

"I really hope you can handle a boat," Japh retorted. He'd never reefed a sail in his life, and wasn't even sure what it meant for that matter, but he knew the other man was right. The gates were all blocked now, and would lead only into the All-Church army anyway. The sea was the only way out. If the wind stayed down they might even manage to take it.

Athar pulled at the reins and his horse reared on its hind legs, front hooves flailing as the crowd scattered in renewed fear. That gave him room to turn the animal in a circle barely larger than its own length. As a gap opened on his right Japh turned too, though his gelding was clumsier than Athar's mare and needed more space. Athar had already spurred forward and Japh fell in behind him, trying to stay close so the throng couldn't press in and separate them. They forced their way down the middle of the street, towards a small plaza where the crush would be less, at least for a time. Someone grabbed for Japh's stirrup and he lashed out with one foot, landing a blow to the man's head that sent him crashing to the street.

"He was trying not to fall!" a woman cried, right beside the gelding. "He was just trying not to fall!"

Japh grimaced and looked away, sick at himself, and so he saw the man who seemed to spring out of the crowd and drive a wickedly curved dagger into the throat of Athar's horse.

The mare screamed and reared on her hind legs again, fighting the air with her hooves. Athar kicked his feet free and sprang back out of the saddle. His sword flashed as he drew it. Japh was still staring, frozen with disbelief, as Athar landed and swung his blade.

The blow spun the dagger-man around in a fountain of blood, an ugly red gash laid under the line of his beard. It was only then that Japh saw his coat: white with a cross of gold, the colours of the Order of the Basilica. The invaders had come this far already then, slipping into the town amid the chaos at the gates. Probably they'd concealed their uniforms until they were inside, but Athar hadn't done so and they'd known the black and white of the Hand for what it was. Japh grappled for his sword but his gelding danced back from the dying horse, snorting in fear at the blood, and he was forced to grab the reins again to control it.

Athar rammed one shoulder into the dying Shaveling and sent him flying into a second white-coated soldier, and then whirled his sword in a wide circle around himself. Both Church troops fell. A third Church soldier jumped to avoid his falling comrades and took Athar's sword in his shoulder, staining his snowy tabard with a splash of crimson.

The crowd scrambled away from them all, tumbling over each other in their haste to get away, and somewhere glass shattered. Beyond the fight some people had started to clamber up the side of a building to escape the killing crush below. Athar's mare gave a final kick and then lay still.

"Go!" Athar shouted to Japh. Three more Shavelings were emerging from the press of bodies, and more pushed up behind them. Athar swung his kite-shaped shield onto his arm and went into a battle crouch, feet apart and knees bent. "Get the message through!"

"I can't leave you!" Japh drew his sword: it felt heavy and awkward in his shaking hand. "Get up behind me, and we'll leave together!"

"Just move!" Athar bellowed. He parried a thrust from a Shaveling and took a second on his shield. The next man darted in from the right, forcing Athar to jump back. He struck as he leapt though, slashing a neat line in the man's surcoat. "In the name of God, Japh, *go!*"

Men in white and gold were pouring into the street, and Japh went. The crowd around him roared, trying to squeeze itself into alleys and doorways that couldn't possibly take their numbers. It opened a gap into which Japh sent his gelding at the run, ramming his sword back into the scabbard. He flung a glance over his shoulder and saw Athar barrel into his assailants and throw them back, but more were coming up to encircle him now. Japh swallowed and turned his eyes forward again. He didn't want to see Athar die.

His headlong progress lasted until he reached a narrower street, packed from side to side with townsfolk. Looking over them from his saddle Japh could see at least three fights going on, one of them between a woman and two much bigger men. She was keeping them back with snarling spitfire bravery, but they would overwhelm her in the end, and there was absolutely nothing Japh could do to help her. She was too far away, with too many heaving bodies in the way. And he had more important matters to attend to, much as it stabbed his conscience to admit it. Calesh had to be warned, or more than one woman would die.

He'd been going the wrong way, he realised, fleeing without thought of his direction. He looked quickly around and then wheeled the gelding towards the harbour - and stopped dead when he saw a regiment of Justified pouring into the street to his left, the white crosses on their shields vivid against the crimson background.

Japh wasn't wearing the colours of the Hand, but he was an armed man on a horse, and the All-Church men sent up a jubilant shout as they spotted him. Most had swords already drawn, and blood had splashed in intricate spatters on the metal and their surcoats. The All-Church had not hesitated to start the killing. Japh didn't wait to see more. He leaned low over his horse's neck and clapped his heels into its flanks, going to a dead gallop in three strides and back out into the wide avenue, where he might be able to slip away.

He had covered less than fifty yards when an arrow slashed through the air above his head. It wasn't really close but he did hear the hiss as it passed, and tried to lie still lower over the plunging horse. A moment later the gelding gave a queer snort and simply collapsed, sprawling belly-down on the cobbles with its legs flung out like compass points. Japh had an instant of warning from that grunt, and remembering what Athar had done earlier he pulled his feet clear and leapt instinctively out of the saddle.

He misjudged the jump, and came down half atop the skidding horse. His ankle buckled with a sickening snap and Japh cried out as he fell over on his back, sliding away from the animal. He fetched up against stone coping with a thump that rattled his teeth, driving his scabbard into his knees. The impact didn't hurt him any worse though. He hauled himself upright, trying to stand mostly on one foot, and looked back down the street.

The gelding was still trying to get up, but there were two red-fletched arrows in its neck, as close as a pair of fingers. Beyond it the Justified soldiers had fanned out across the street and were trotting towards Japh, not hurrying any more now they were sure their prey couldn't escape. They were right, too. Japh's ankle throbbed, and when he put weight on it his vision swam. He drew his sword clumsily. One of the soldiers laughed.

Looking around desperately for a way out, Japh realised that the coping he'd hit was actually a step. A moment later he raised his eyes and saw he was at the foot of the steps to the Cathedral. It was one of the largest and finest All-Church buildings outside Coristos, or so people said. A thousand people at a time could worship under the corbelled vaults of its roof. Barely a quarter as many came these days, at least for services, but today citizens swarmed around the walls and heavy doors with their hands raised in supplication, pleading for entry. Some held infants up, or pounded on the thick stone walls, but the doors were closed and they stayed that way. Japh wondered how many people had already sought sanctuary inside. He wondered if any of them would find it.

Not there, he thought. *Not in a place of the All-Church, because their faith is flawed, and the Saviour they worship as an aspect of God himself was just a man, as mortal and imperfect as any of us.*

He sighed and turned back to the approaching Justified. With some shuffling of his feet he managed to gain something close to the stance Amand had shown him a week ago, though with the weight off his bad foot. One of the soldiers laughed a second time.

"Boy," a heavily bearded man near the centre of the line said, "you might stab yourself with that pig-sticker, but you won't stab me. Why don't you put it down and come with us?"

"Why don't you eat my shit?" Japh said. His sweaty hands slipped on the hilt. There was no time to wipe them.

The bearded man scowled. He came forward in a rush, easily ducking under Japh's first swing and thrusting his blade straight ahead. It was an easy move, the first one Japh had been taught, and by then he was no longer there. He twisted away from the thrust and slashed downwards, trying to take the man's arm off at the shoulder. Bones ground together in his ankle and he cried out, his blow skidding off the man's bicep and away. The soldier stepped back with an oath. Two more men joined him and he gestured them back.

"I'll give you to the priests, boy," he growled. Blood welled gently through the gash in his shirt, where Japh had cut him. "When they get their pincers and irons hot you'll beg to be allowed to confess to whatever they ask. But first," he hefted the sword, "I'm going to cut slivers off you until you shriek like a woman. I don't reckon it'll take long."

He started forward. While he spoke Japh had kept his weight on his good foot, easing the bad ankle as best he could, but it wasn't going to be enough. *I should never have joined the Hand of the Lord,* he thought, and then grinned despite himself. It was crazy, but he didn't regret it. There were heroes in the Hand, just as there was salvation in true belief. Some things you just had to do. He tightened his grip on the sword hilt.

When the man came Japh didn't even try to dodge. He couldn't anyway; his ankle had swollen now to twice its proper size. He hop-stepped forward, ignoring the blade that swung for his middle, and drove his sword straight ahead without even an attempt at defence. The bearded man realised what he was doing and started to cry out, but then the sword went into his chest, right over the heart. At the same time pain flashed white-hot in Japh's side and he fell, the sword tumbling from nerveless fingers. It hurt so much he couldn't even cry out. His vision went grey. He heard a thump beside him and knew the bearded man had fallen too.

There was a hollow boom, far away but clear over the noise of the crowd. Japh tried to raise his head to see what it was, but then something slid into him from behind, and everything fled away.

*

"*Now,*" Calesh said, and Amand bellowed an order.

Arrows flew from the brush behind them, trailing tendrils of smoke from the burning rags wrapped around the points. Half fell short or flew long, or else dropped harmlessly into the ravine. The rest struck the bridge.

Flames blew skywards in great gouts as the oil on the wood caught. Boards were flung up as well, or blasted through the fire in a storm of burning splinters. Men and horses screamed. Luthien could see shapes blundering through the inferno, blind and shrieking. Several walked right off the edge of the bridge. Many more fell straight through, to be dashed against the rocks forty feet below. One of them went on screaming even after he hit.

Roughly fifty of the Justified had crossed before the fire erupted. Some were flung out of their saddles by the blast behind them, or by horses that reared and threw them off in panic. Most managed to stay aboard though: they were good horsemen, whatever their other faults. They hesitated, suddenly aware that they were outnumbered now. Half of their comrades were stranded across the gully, and the rest were shrieking or still. Even Justified could count. They drew together, waiting for the charge.

Luthien swallowed. Men were burning, in the gully and above it, their flesh crackling like pork in a fire. He'd seen nothing as horrible as this since he came home, six years before. And now, God help him, now he would see the dragonnade, the charge of the Hand of the Lord with which he'd once been so intimately familiar. He had thought it left far behind him once.

"Amand," Calesh said.

His voice was perfectly calm. A commander's had to be, to impress confidence upon the men he led, and though Luthien knew how his old friend hated death he still found it hard to believe, at that moment. Calesh wore a slight smile, showing a glint of teeth. Luthien could not have done so. He had seen his share of death in Tura d'Madai, had dealt a fair amount of it himself, but he was a different man now. Killing was a sin he had no part of any more.

Amand urged his stallion forward, flanked by large soldiers who held their shields ready in case the Justified had an archer in their ranks. None of the All-Church men moved though. Amand went forward ten yards and then stopped, raising his stentorian voice above the crackle of flames.

"Stay here and we will not harm you," he called to the Justified. "Follow us, and we will kill you all. Make no mistake about that. But if you stay, take this message to the general of your army: Sarténe is not yours to despoil. You will not be allowed to pillage and slaughter your way across our land. Go back while you can. Only death waits for you here."

None of the cavalry answered. It seemed there would be no dragonnade after all though, for which Luthien was profoundly grateful. He wasn't sure he could have dealt with that, on top of the burning. After a moment Amand turned his horse and rode back to rejoin the Hand of the Lord. Raigal Tai rolled the handle of his axe nonchalantly over his fingers, but Luthien thought he actually looked disappointed. That was insane. What kind of man would actually *regret* being denied a chance to die?

A voice inside him murmured that Luthien too had once felt that way, in those strange febrile moments when battle is close but not yet decided on. He ignored it, as he had grown adept at ignoring whispers in his mind and heart. No man was perfect in every corner of his soul, but that was all right. It was mastering those dark shadows that counted.

Calesh stayed on the ridge as Amand began to order their men to withdraw. He put the spyglass back to his eye and studied Parrien, from which smoke now rose in black lines through the still air. A large mass of soldiers had crowded together just outside the north gate, and their shouts drifted across the burned fields, louder than the noise of panicked citizens inside the walls. Over it all came a faint crackle, like pots banging in a distant kitchen. Luthien knew what that was. He had hoped never to hear it again.

"Oh, Japh," Calesh said softly.

Luthien and Raigal exchanged glances behind their friend's back. Neither spoke. Calesh was not such a fool as to go charging into Parrien in an attempt to rescue the youth, however badly he might feel at having sent him there in the first place. That he *would* feel badly was a given. It was just as certain that he wouldn't let it affect him.

After a moment Calesh snapped the glass closed and stuffed it into a side pocket of his saddlebag. He glowered at the silent knot of Justified, as though hoping for an excuse to order his men to ride in and cut them all to pieces. They did nothing except look back at him, their expressions hard to read under their helmets. Raigal twirled his great axe again.

"Sometimes you have to roll the dice and pray," Luthien said quietly. He pushed his glasses back up his nose. "And sometimes you take what you have and walk away from the table. I think this is one of those times."

"I think so too," Calesh said. From his tone you would never guess he had just been spoiling for a fight. "What about you, Raigal? Shall we head back to the Preceptory, and a mug of beer?"

"Might as well," the huge man rumbled. "Since those bastards will drink all of mine."

Kissing the Moon was by Parrien's docks, of course. Luthien had stayed there a few times, though he had less in common with Raigal Tai than with either of the other two men. He liked the big northerner well enough, but Raigal was too loud where Luthien was soft-spoken, too impetuous where he was measured. It had made things difficult, in the years since they came back from Tura d'Madai. With Calesh missing, there had sometimes seemed little to share with Raigal.

It was different now, because Calesh *was* back. Luthien turned his horse and rode away with his friends, and tried to decide if he believed it would make any difference.

*

"That was Saissan," Sarul said.

He was sure of it. From the moment that fire-rose had blossomed away to the west, even before the boom had rolled across the fields, he had known. The common soldiers had stopped to look, and two regiments of Glorified not yet committed to the assault on Parrien had hastily begun to turn to meet any possible new threat. None had come. But that didn't matter: it *would* come, when Calesh Saissan decided he was ready.

Already Sarul had his agents in the Basilica hunting for the spy who had sent a warning to the Hand of the Lord, in Tura d'Madai. Maids and servants would be questioned about that, and if their answers were unsatisfactory then they would pay for it. If not for that cursed message Saissan would still be baking in the desert with the lizards, and orders could have been sent to the Justified and Glorified there to arrest all the Hand in a simultaneous strike. Meanwhile command in Sarténe would be between a known drunkard and the foppish, indolent Margrave with all his filthy ways. Instead the Sand Scorpion was here, and deny it as they would, the men of the other Orders were a little in awe of him.

But the matter was in hand. Sarul had set plans in motion long before he travelled north to join the Crusade army. Elizur Mandein was on his way to Saissan now, and he would kill him. After which, of course, Mandein himself would have to be dealt with. Really, the All-Church could hardly be seen to tolerate assassins, however useful they might be at times. It helped that Mandein was a thoroughly unpleasant man. When he was found floating in a sack in the harbour, it might be that nobody wanted to fish him out.

But first, he could deal with Saissan. Sarul's hands clenched into fists at his sides and he kept staring west, even when the fire at the bridge had died away and Parrien began to burn behind him.

Made in the USA
Charleston, SC
21 March 2014